TWIN
TIDES

TWIN TIDES

HIEN NGUYEN

DELACORTE PRESS

Delacorte Press
An imprint of Random House Children's Books
A division of Penguin Random House LLC
1745 Broadway, New York, NY 10019
penguinrandomhouse.com
GetUnderlined.com

Editor: Bria Ragin
Cover designers: Trisha Previte and Tatiana Guel
Interior designer: Ken Crossland
Production editor: Colleen Fellingham
Managing editor: Tamar Schwartz
Production manager: Tracy Heydweiller

Library of Congress Cataloging-in-Publication Data is available upon request.
ISBN 979-8-217-02393-6 (trade) — ISBN 979-8-217-02395-0 (lib. bdg.) —
ISBN 979-8-217-02396-7 (ebook)

The text of this book is set in 12-pt Garamond Premier Pro.

Manufactured in the United States of America
1st Printing

The authorized representative in the EU for product safety and compliance is
Penguin Random House Ireland, Morrison Chambers, 32 Nassau Street,
Dublin D02 YH68, Ireland, https://eu-contact.penguin.ie.

To motherless daughters:
May you never feel shame
for your grief or your ferocity.

PROLOGUE

The Ghoul

I lie in the bottom of the riverbed. My eyes are shut as I pretend to sleep, but my skin, punctured and tattered, feels everything. The wake of fish zipping above. Tiny, microscopic beings. In the bowels of the river, the bed load layer is full of heavy grit and gravel too coarse to float. The sharpness grates along my skin. Here, the velocity of the water is slow, so whatever makes its way to the bed load is in for a lifetime of languid rotting.

I know this water well. It is my home.

A jolt shoots through me, and my mind finds a sudden clarity, like a voice speaking to me after years of silence. Irritation stirs in my chest.

The voice tells me that this "home" is another place. Home is another body of water.

I haven't always been here.

I belong elsewhere.

And yet, I can't remember the place.

I've forgotten what it was like to hope as I've trailed this river. I once imagined a life beyond the water and its stillness of decay. I hoped for the next stage of death and imagined unloosing whatever tether held me here. I hoped for a future.

There is no future. There is only my now, which stretches both forward and backward endlessly.

My body aches, and I sit up, the sediment that settled on my torso scattering into the water. Thick bands of caliginous algae and death coat my tongue. My throat. My eyes. Only the lost remain in this area of the river—the corpses of moths and birds and weeds. They've become a part of me, entwining with my body until I feel almost whole again.

What does it even mean to be whole?

My body that is not quite a body slips into deeper water. I blink, the mud sliding off my eyes and streaking my face like tearstains. I am relieved that everything in the river belongs to itself. Dirt dissolves into more dirt. Leaves decompose and give way to seedlings. Everything in the water is reborn and given a chance to start a new life, one unencumbered by its last.

Except for me.

I recall a story uttered when I was small and lived elsewhere.

Back then, I was told first by my sister, then many others, that the water deserved respect. It deserved fear. The drowned. The dead. They—the local storytellers—called the spirits who haunt the waters Ma Da. Drowned ghosts. Bloated with weeds and white as bone, Ma Da were cursed to waste away in purgatory, unable to leave this life and move on to their next.

That is, unless they drowned a *new* victim so that another person could take their place. The lore said evil lurked in the depths, waiting to ensnare children and drag them under the tide.

If warnings went unheeded, they'd become trapped. I once believed it was merely a tall tale to frighten and keep children safe.

I laugh, the gargle pulling in a thread of larvae and decay.

Safe.

I dismissed the tales of ghouls in the water as fallacy, and now I've become one.

I swim upstream, where the cliffs above jut out and the water clears. Something will be there to satisfy the hunger in my belly. More death awaits me, but so do the fat walleyes and pikes that nourish me, no matter how insufficiently.

Above the surface, I hear whispers of me. The living are afraid of the perverse and special type of power I wield.

A ghost that punishes naughty children.

The ghoul that ensnares the foolhardy and unwise.

A reaper of the rivers and lakes.

I am untouchable. And I punish them, the ones who bear their sins openly. I take pleasure in luring them into the water and digging my fetid fingers into the soft concave of their throats. My favorites die slowest.

One. He came to the river to wash off his wife's blood, unaware that he was releasing the acrid scent of his crime into my domain. It clung to the roof of my mouth, dissipating only once his body stopped moving and I replaced his scent with mine.

Two. An old and decrepit fool, his sins long faded but still wafting from his skin. I counted multiple victims . . . all girls.

Three. She carried her son in a bag and threw him into the water, so freshly murdered that the boy still smelled of baby powder.

There have been six in total . . . and the scent of their immorality is etched on me. It's been many months since my last kill.

And every time one dies, I remember they can take my place. I could leave. I can leave. Pass on to begin anew.

But I couldn't possibly do that. *I have a talent for killing.*

Here, they do not call me Ma Da.

Here, I have no one name. The story from my childhood . . . the cursed fable . . . is the only thing I still remember. It acts as a guide.

My life was taken from me; thus, I will take life in turn. That is my nature. And all I have left is my vengeance.

The current comes to an end as the murkiness shifts. It is then that the disturbance in the water reaches me, waves so violent, they remind me of the man throwing my body against rock. Something is in the water, and it doesn't belong here.

Tentatively, I swim toward the origin of the quake. The vibrations intensify, rippling through my skin even more. I swim as fast as I can manage.

I approach the shore, the water's surface darkening because of dense cypress branches reaching down to the earth. This place . . . is familiar to me, but I can't remember why. Anticipation fills in my chest as the water shallows and stills in the slough.

It's then that I see her: a girl caught in a tangle of cattails and bur reed. I notice when she suddenly stops. The water is taking her, and she begins to drown.

I stagger, clawing through the slippery mud toward her.

My skin is aflame in the faint sunlight, melting as I finally reach for the child's still body.

Something about her small face—closed eyes and gaping mouth—both terrifies me and triggers a strange heaviness inside me. My fingers graze the threads of her dress.

4

Save her.

Protect her.

Please.

I push the girl's body toward the shore. She sinks a few feet deep.

"Oh my god, there she is!" a foreign voice says. In it, there's panic. Fear. A tremor that conveys an all-consuming love. That of a mother.

As the girl stirs in my hands, a face above the water makes eye contact with me. I've forgotten to hide. I ready myself to retreat, but the woman's eyes move past me, widening in shock.

She is silent before she screams, a note both bloodcurdling and shrill. I don't have much time to think before the tiny girl is snatched from me. My arms freed, I turn to look at what is behind me, and a swollen face catches the sunlight. I realize that this is the cause of the mother's continued screams: a body buoying to the surface.

The body undulates and drifts closer to the shore. It's a woman with long black hair and a vibrant red sweater with pearl buttons. Her face is serene.

It is *my* face.

My new body weakens, sinking back into the water's depths. The wailing from the mother does not stop. Images of my death return to me, as does the sensation of my body dying. It is the same pain from moments ago—a sting slashing through me.

I picture his face and remember how his hands gripped my throat.

His pale skin wrinkled as his face contorted from the effort of squeezing. As I died, I considered that the folds of his neck formed a perfect divot for my fingers to puncture a hole and fill him with maggots. Once I was reborn . . . I became *this*.

Ghost. Daughter. Monster. Mother. Ghoul. Wife. I remember his laugh, a grotesque and jagged sound as I receded into the river. The echo of his laugh tears through me with such violence that a hole cracks at my core.

For all these years, I've wandered the water. I've forgotten my humanity. I was on the hunt, but I've long forgotten what I was hunting.

Seeing my face and my body returned to water awakens me, as does a thirst revived. The scent of the man's blood lingers on my tongue, and I tremble. There is no longer a heart beating in my chest, but I feel its phantom: a frenetic and agitated pulse. It flutters, then ruptures . . .

like bombs
like shrapnel
like persistent memories
In my memory, there are gaps that were once full—
of words written
of words spoken
of words sung
of my history
I lost them all when I became trapped in this water. My life before I became stuck here . . . what was it like?

The man who killed me knows. And I will find him.

CHAPTER ONE

Aria

"Hello, miss. This is Officer Gordon Badiou calling from the Les Eaux Police Department. I would like to discuss information regarding the disappearance of Xuan Giang Nguyen. Please call me back at your earliest convenience. It's okay if it's after hours— I understand you are busy. This number should forward any new messages to me directly."

The officer's voice plays in Aria's mind, and she shakes off the gnawing anxiety caused by ignoring his voicemail. It's the kind of call Aria's been waiting and praying into existence for the past fourteen years. But when she heard his voice, Aria could process the information only matter-of-factly, like she was learning about some politician on TV or a stranger she'd read about online.

In this moment, Aria wants to pretend the news this officer has is innocuous, like he's somehow found the ID card she lost in middle school. She tells herself all she needs to do is survive the day. So she hasn't called Officer Badiou back. Instead, she continues her walk toward Kim's Laundry and Dry Cleaning in disbelief that it's already *that* time of year again.

Every year, around December especially, a bone-deep yearning returns. It's a missing that no words can explain. It usually crushes Aria, but she can't afford to let that happen anymore. Between school, taking care of Aunt Thu, and *barely* holding it together, there isn't time to wallow. Inside the organized box in Aria's head, she tucks away Officer Badiou's message into the *missing mom* folder. Aria becomes fully numb, as she always does on the anniversary of her mother's disappearance.

"Hey, Ari. Your dress is ready," a voice calls from beyond the drying machines. Aria's sitting on an orange plastic chair in a neat laundromat, looking toward the back hallway that snakes behind the stacked white coin dryers. The room is monochromatic, with white laminate floors and white painted walls. Mrs. Kim says it's easier to keep everything clean when she can see every spot. But with the sun shining through the plastic blinds and reflecting off the colorless surfaces, everything is too bright, too pure, and too clean. Aria's eyes hurt today.

She stands, letting her backpack fall into the plastic chair's seat with a thud before following the voice coming from the back room. She rubs her eyes, the gritty sensation of two-day-old eyeliner smearing under her fingertips, as she turns the hallway's corner. On the other side of the ajar red door to Mrs. Kim's office, Philip stands with a wry smile on his face and a garment on a hanger draped over his skinny arms. He's uncharacteristically dressed-up, wearing black slacks with a waffle-knit white button-up.

"What's the occasion?" Aria asks, moving to take the sheathed dress hanging from his arms and lightly jabbing him with her elbow. "Do you have another blind date to go on?"

Philip smiles, the edges of his lips curling. He pauses for a second, clinging to the dress before letting it go.

"You think I'd go on a date looking like I sell insurance?"

Aria chokes out a laugh, the tension of the day and the un-answered voicemail dissolving the tiniest bit. Philip's face finally breaks into a genuine smile, his front teeth fully exposed in the goofy way Aria adores. He leans back onto Mrs. Kim's desk and crosses his arms.

Philip is about a head taller than Aria, making him both taller than the average Korean kid and short enough that Aria knows he still lies on his dating-app profiles. His black hair is lightly styled, ear length and falling away from his face to expose a tanned fore-head. Staring at his pouting lips and hooded dark brown eyes, Aria can't help thinking of the girls in high school who'd squeal about how much he looked like their favorite drama actor. Suddenly it dawns on her that all the ramen bags in her house have this specific actor's face on them, and the realization makes her cheeks heat up. Is she subconsciously surrounding herself with different iterations of Philip?

"No? Then dare I inquire if you have a job interview? Or a college interview?" Aria says, averting her eyes and pretending to scan the length of the dress in her arms.

"Aria, stop with that," Philip says.

"Stop what? Encouraging my *terribly* talented but devastat-ingly unambitious best friend to quit being afraid of success?"

Aria silently applauds herself for diverting Philip's attention away from her blushing face. The second allows her to get her bearings, and she sneaks a glance back up at him. His gaze is fixed at a spot on the wall, his eyes downcast and lips held taut.

"I mean it, Philip. I don't get it." Seriously. Aria doesn't get it, but she has a suspicion of where he's coming from.

Philip's dad abandoned his family when Philip was barely standing on two wobbly legs. On occasion, Aria catches Philip searching for news about Gabriel Kim's latest Silicon Valley successes (she does her part by pretending not to notice).

Aria knows that Mrs. Kim keeps her brother—Philip's father—abreast of Philip's life through sporadic voicemails. As far as Aria knows, Philip's father has never returned a call.

She wondered what Mr. Kim would think if he heard that Philip and his childhood best friend both got into Georgetown. Though Aria had been the only one at first-year orientation because Philip declined his hard-earned spot, claiming he had to keep handling things for his aunt Mrs. Kim (the business of the laundromat *and* the business of keeping her company). Philip had told his aunt he didn't get accepted and begged Aria to maintain the lie.

A lifetime of friendship, and Aria has never been able to say no to his pleading face.

"I know you're not talking. I thought you said *you* were going to stop your little side hustle," Philip says, his tone clipped. His voice drops to a whisper as he gestures at the dress in Aria's hands. "I shouldn't be enabling this. You're going to get caught, Ari."

"I'm not," Aria says, unsure if she's mustered enough confidence to convince Philip she's right. She glances down at the garment in her arms. The clear plastic bag encases a silky asymmetrical cocktail dress, pastel blue with a slit edging precariously high. There is a gold pin near the collar—a delicate enamel tulip.

It's a dress that costs more than a three-credit class at George-town and all the required textbooks. A knot of jealousy mixed with awe grinds inside Aria, so she shoos it away.

"What does the tulip mean?" Philip asks, pointing to the pin on the dress. It's an abrupt question that catches Aria off guard. "Fortune. Notoriety, even. You know, you don't have to ask me that every time you see a flower."

"But I enjoy asking you about flowers." Philip smiles at her. She doesn't know when his goofy grin changed, but now it makes her feel twenty emotions at once.

"I know you don't care about flowers . . . You're lulling me into a false sense of security so you can lecture me some more," Aria says, pretending she's unaffected, before returning her attention to the dress. It has deep pockets, discreetly sewn so as not to interrupt the structure of the dress, and in one is an envelope. Aria pulls it out, the thick weight of the cash in her fingers triggering a slight thrill. She counts to make sure everything is there—exactly eight hundred bucks and a brief note. On it are the initials F.M. and the scribbled words *Thanks, you're a lifesaver. See you next semester.*

"Thanks, bud," Aria says, slipping the envelope back into the pocket.

Felicity Mackey, a girl who lives a few doors down in Harbin Hall, needed someone to take her Principles of Microeconomics final. Felicity claimed to have the flu last minute, allowing Aria to take the exam via the remote portal. Somehow Aria pulled it off. It's not like Aria didn't have her own tests to pass, but the bill for Aunt Thu's last hospitalization had come in, and there was an extra digit they weren't expecting. Aria already needed to pivot, anyway. She used to be able to sustain her business on essays and term papers, but then AI arrived on the scene. While Aria is un-detectable, AI is cheaper.

Turning Philip and Mrs. Kim's business into the unsuspecting front for a fraudulent academic consulting gig wasn't originally Aria's intent. Heck, she didn't even intend to be part of this scheme herself.

It happened by accident, when, earlier this fall semester, Aria's roommate begged for Aria to help her. Aria's insides had screamed *no*, but she couldn't ignore how upset Stephanie was.

Too soft for your own good.

That's what Aunt Thu always says.

Aunt Thu's health had been declining since Aria was in middle school, and her aunt had used the rest of her savings to pay for the part of tuition that Aria's scholarship didn't cover. Aria day-dreamed about ways to rescue herself and Aunt Thu from their financial black hole, with most scenarios involving Aunt Thu's sudden recovery or discovering a suitcase brimming with cash. Of course, Aria was asking for too much. After Aunt Thu had given up everything for her, Aria felt it was only fair to return the favor.

It was just one paper, and her roommate's offer was for more money than Aria had ever seen in her life at one time. Aria's knee-jerk reaction was to use the laundromat as a safe liaison point. It was a reaction probably borne from nerves. Philip's favorite theory was that the side of Aria's brain responsible for academic work had stolen all the wrinkles from the other parts of her brain.

Before he'd become a curmudgeon over it, being a part of the scheme had thrilled Philip, back when it was still new, and all Aria had to do was write a single short paper on Locke or log into someone's student portal so they wouldn't get dinged for an absence. It was quite a seamless system. Students in the know would message Aria via an encrypted app and ask her for a dry cleaner recommendation. Then all communications and money exchanges would happen far from campus, through Kim's Laundry and Dry Cleaning.

The truth is, operating out of the laundromat protects Aria's pride on campus. She is her honest self in class, in front of her professors . . . or at least, she can pretend she is her honest self—a minor victory in the grand scheme of things. Her totally-normal-college-freshman cosplay. There, she is simply any old college student and not this distorted version of herself.

Philip follows Aria as she walks back to the main room of the laundromat, dress and ego barely in tow.

"Thanks again. I'll . . ." Aria says, flustered by Philip's presence behind her. It's been happening more often lately. His closeness, that is. And Aria's annoyed by the thought of Philip treating her the same way he did when they were ten years old, like he's a big brother who needs to protect her. Is she the only one whose feelings are changing?

"Not so fast," Philip says, grabbing Aria's free arm and swinging her around to face him. "That tree is still blocking your mailbox, so the mail guy dropped it all off here."

"I'll grab the mail later—" Aria starts, but she's already too late: Philip has darted off. Damn his long legs.

Instead of leaving as she planned, Aria drapes the dress over a chair. The row of drying machines rattles in front of her, hunched and vibrating against the stark white backsplash of the laundromat and a wall of meticulously arranged celebrity photos. Well, "celebrity" might be generous. Aria kicks her feet against the laminate floor and sinks into the plastic chair, letting her eyes glaze over as she scans the images. They are cursed relics, a literal time capsule pulling Aria back to a place she's doing her best to avoid.

Mrs. Kim is a diminutive Korean woman with a photo collection of notable men—old senators, C-list Hollywood actors, and important journalists with wiry hair. Some of the more recent photos include selfies of actual celebrities: a K-pop boy group who came to see her after a show at EagleBank Arena during their US tour.

The images of Mrs. Kim aren't from the laundromat, though. Her dry cleaning skills haven't earned her great renown or anything. But the old Chinese restaurant she ran with her late husband in Chevy Chase, Maryland, before she was forced to shut down? Aria heard it was amazing. So the relics of her glory are preserved here, in a small corner of a laundromat situated south of an adult entertainment store and a vape shop.

Nestled in the lowest row of pasty senators and unshaven actors is one out-of-place picture. It's partially torn, but the left side is carefully preserved. The image is of a woman wearing a vibrant red sweater with pearl buttons. She's standing nearly a foot taller than Mrs. Kim. She has long, braided black hair that falls neatly to her waist. There's a quiet fierceness in her expression, a severity that penetrates through the faded photograph's matte finish. Peeking out from the billowing silk of her pants and clinging to her knee is Aria in a ruffled gingham outfit.

An Aria from a different life.

Aria doesn't remember this toddler version of herself, doesn't remember the restaurant in its early days or why she looks so damn scared.

Aria sees the contours of her own face in her mom's. A wide forehead and inner epicanthic folds sharpening almond-shaped brown eyes. Full lips and a subdued Cupid's bow. It's the reason Aria always chops her hair off at the shoulder; Aunt Thu would never say it, but Aria with long hair bears too much of a resemblance to her missing sister.

Aria's mom has freckles on her face where Aria does not. Her mother's skin is golden, with even more freckles dappling her arms from the sun. Aria doesn't go outside much. She stares down at her pale arms now, wondering if she and her mother would resemble each other more in wintertime. This sole picture helps Aria to remember what her mom looks like. Or *looked* like, considering she'd have aged.

Xuân, or "spring." The season of flower blooms and vibrancy. Aria knows her mother's name but barely remembers who she is. There are remnants, hints of memory Aria thinks she might resurrect if only she could get over her trauma and focus. Details of the past are blurry, hanging around in the periphery of her head.

She recalls plum blossoms and lemongrass. The sound of Xuân's voice, low, gravelly, and rich despite her slight frame. When Aria strains, she can feel the exhaustion in her mother's reprimand and the panicked love as Xuân holds Aria's small wrists in her own.

With a blink, the mental image of Aria's mother disappears. She wonders if the memories are even real or if they are merely an invention of her desperate mind.

"Here you go, milady," Philip says, materializing in front of Aria with one hand behind his back and the other holding out a stack of mail. His appearance dissolves the weight in her chest a bit, and Aria takes the stack with a reluctant smile.

"Thank you, good sir. I am eternally grateful."

"There's a weird one in there, by the way. It doesn't have a return address, but it's made from some fancy paper."

Aria freezes, her hand hovering over the stack of letters as she's about to look through them. *The letters.* Aria's letters. Her secret.

"Probably some spam from the school. Like recruitment for a club or something . . ." The mention of the letter makes Aria's heart race, and she hopes Philip doesn't notice. She hasn't received one since she started at Georgetown a few months ago. Gulping down the anxiety, Aria forces herself to calm and stand as nonchalantly as possible. She'd have to make time to read the letter, alone, later.

"I gotta go. Thanks for this," Aria says, shaking the dress with an awkward flap of her arms. "I'll give you your cut shortly in the form of baked goods and pizza."

"Hey, wait."

"What? Is there something wrong?" Aria asks but is interrupted by Philip patting down her hair and smoothing it behind her left ear.

"When was the last time you showered? You look like that Yorkie I walk on Tuesdays."

"Excuse me?" Aria is startled by the statement but tries to suppress a smile. "Are you comparing me to a dog?"

"You should be honored. Sir Barkley van Floof is very cute but terrible at taking care of himself. I'm saying the semester looks like it swallowed you whole."

"You're not wrong," Aria replies. There is a weighty lull after she speaks, and a grating feeling claws its way up Aria's throat.

"Are you feeling—" Philip begins before Aria cuts him off.

"I'm fine." Aria avoids Philip's probing stare and does her best impression of being emotionally totally okay. "I promise."

There's a good reason they're friends. Two children living with stern aunts and not their moms. Left to their own devices, Philip and Aria ran around a corner laundromat as their guardians were busy, wreaking havoc on unsuspecting customers by swapping laundry baskets and playing hockey with Tide Pods and brooms. They bonded over the weight of absence. Philip's mother died, and Aria's disappeared.

He knows what today's date is. He remembers every year, even when Aria tries to forget.

But it doesn't make Aria feel any better; it makes her feel lonelier. Every year, Philip remembers his mother's birthday and celebrates it with Aria. Despite his selflessness and good intentions, it reminds Aria that her mother isn't around to celebrate.

"When are you gonna be done? I can grab a birthday cake from Wegmans."

"Don't get a cake."

"Come on. You look like some cake will do you good," Philip says, his joking voice belies his sympathetic expression.

Aria's first instinct is to push Philip away, but she pauses, staring into his earnest eyes. Her thoughts turn to the voicemail waiting on her phone.

"Actually, can you come over to help me with something after I get back to the house?"

"Sure. What do you need?"

"I need help opening something. I'll text you once I get home." Whatever is writhing around inside the *missing mom* mental box has to be unleashed, no matter how much Aria might want to avoid it.

Philip nods despite his obvious confusion and doesn't stop Aria as she makes for the door, her feet echoing against the floor.

Once she winds out of the building and past the parking lot, blaring horns and the steady noise of the Virginia streets greet her. The service road leading to the laundromat is alarmingly close, with only a thin strip of snow-dappled grass and paltry juvenile trees acting as a barrier between the row of businesses and the roaring street.

As a child, she'd enjoyed all the sounds. The chaos was a reprieve from the disquiet Aria felt in her chest—a persistent melancholy haunting her.

The bus bay appears ahead, the shattered plexiglass of the canopy duct-taped with a blue tarp and pieces of plexiglass swept haphazardly beneath the bench. Before sitting, Aria pulls her phone out of her pocket and glances at the broken screen. Her breath coats the cracked screen protector. When the fog clears, she's hit with another dose of reality.

Notifications from Bank of America that a minimum balance is due. An overdue-payment alert for the water bill. Flicking the notifications away, Aria settles on a nearby bench, a loose metal screw burrowing into the tender spot between her shoulder blades. She slips in her earphones, picks a discordant EDM-and-string-orchestra medley from her hyperpop playlist, and turns up the volume.

Alas, the aching comes back. Even after all this time without her mother, the heaviness she hoped would fade holds steadfast.

Today is her mother's birthday.

And fourteen years ago, when Aria was four, on this very date, she disappeared.

Vanished.

And oftentimes, on this day in particular, Aria wishes most urgently that she could vanish, too.

CHAPTER TWO

Caliste

Contrary to public opinion and her own social media feed, Caliste Hà does not like these bitches. But today is a day when she wants to get completely wasted and dance to synthpop remixes of the same thirty songs on repeat. And the best company for nights like this are the girls who talk about her behind her back. (Integrity isn't a prerequisite for having a good time.)

Caliste sits amid a gaggle of Instagram models dressed in bedazzled crop tops with bags slung over their shoulders that either wealthy parents or sponsorships paid for.

The bass speakers make the U-shaped leather couch under Caliste shake. Combined with her fourth zero-calorie peach-flavored spiked seltzer of the night, the vibrations lull Caliste into a comfortable numbness. The table Winslet booked sits in a corner, cordoned off by black velvet ropes and sheer tulle curtains, promising exclusivity and privacy.

Caliste didn't particularly want to end up here tonight, but beggars can't be choosers. Winslet's a royal kiss-ass, so of course she insisted on going to Beverly's favorite club. Rufus Ambrose, the owner of HAUS (yes, the club's name is simply pronounced "house") and Beverly's uncle, was notorious for his decades-younger arm candy. He usually left Beverly's friends alone but recently mixed up Caliste with another Asian girl and earned a slap to the face for it. Bev sent a bouquet to Caliste as a symbolic apology the next morning because she secretly knows exactly who her uncle is.

In the corner, Melina and her latest love interest are locking lips. Caliste considers for a second that he looks like the love child of a 2010s-era Abercrombie model and a pool noodle. It's Melina's usual type.

Meanwhile, Winslet is chatting up the DJ. Her impeccably flat-ironed, sleek copper hair blows behind her thanks to a monstrous fan.

Melina Martinez. Winslet Abara. Caliste Hà.

The trio closest to Beverly "Bev" Ambrose, the daughter of a revered California senator. Beautiful, kind, and gracious—a girl *Mayflower* descended and Portola Valley raised. At least, that's the image Bev portrays. Caliste has been exposed to her . . . less-savory qualities. Beverly can be vindictive and moody but values loyalty above all else. Being in the inner circle of a powerful clique doesn't guarantee happiness, but it does guarantee immunity in a world where who you know reigns supreme.

The queen herself is late to the party, which is a little out of the ordinary. Caliste's mind wanders to her first encounter with Bev in ninth grade and her first real introduction to *true* American old money. Caliste's dad had sent her to Lockshire Academy, a prestigious boarding school tucked away in Sonoma County's hills, hoping she'd rub elbows with the elite, a world he desperately wanted to be part of. Caliste was angry with her dad, and then angry at the invisible wall between her and the other students. She was jealous of how easily everyone else found their place within the social fabric of Lockshire and especially jealous of Beverly, who controlled what that social fabric looked like.

Outside of boys with questionable dating preferences, no one had touched Caliste socially. Apparently, she was new money, and she'd been told multiple times that she might have a better time at one of "those international schools." Did generational wealth come with some weird nose to sniff out impostors? There had even been an absurd rumor going around the halls that her father's company, Ha Foods Corporate, was some front for Vietnamese gangsters. It was a joke meant to invalidate Paul Hà's hard work.

It had been near the end of a terrible first fall semester at school when Beverly found Caliste eating lunch solo—a daily occurrence—under a Judas tree. She'd plucked a sprig of baby's breath from the grass and tucked it behind Caliste's ear.

You're gorgeous. You know that, right? Caliste had kept that flower, pressing its delicate white petals between two sheets of wax paper in her chemistry textbook.

When Caliste returned to Lockshire after winter break that year, it was as if she had always been a part of Beverly's little crew. Caliste was absorbed seamlessly into Bev's inner circle, and the rumors stopped. That was all it took to launch their friendship. The past stirs apathetically inside of Caliste now, causing her to grimace.

To wash away any thoughts of high school, Caliste pours back her drink. The sweetness makes her teeth ache more than her heart. The tips of her black stiletto nails dig into her palm and leave behind small crescent welts. The DJ switches to a song that has everyone screaming.

"Honey, you look *awful*."

Caliste's head snaps up, and standing in front of her, wearing head-to-toe Valentino (a lavender minidress and matching silk pumps) and with a martini in hand, is Beverly Ambrose. She's tall, which is convenient for staring down her enemies. Her honey-blond hair cascades until it ends in rounded curls at her waist.

Caliste's vision becomes hazy, like someone turned the brightness up to one hundred, and her heart races. There's a rise of uncomfortable heat in her chest that threatens to suffocate her, an all-too-familiar sensation. She rises unsteadily, the edges of her blurred vision shifting as she focuses on the pathway out of here. *Crap. Crap. Crap.*

"I'm sorry. I need some air," Caliste says, standing on wobbly feet. She hears an indignant laugh as she stalks past Beverly.

It's too loud.

It's too intense.

And there are too many damn people, and there's too little air.

"Babe! Where are you going? You need to take a shot with me!"

Caliste hears a voice, moist and uneven, close to her ear, and an arm wraps around her waist. When she turns, she identifies one of Beverly's henchmen, Bobby or Connor or something. He has a mop of unkempt chestnut hair. Caliste vaguely recognizes him as one of the guys Winslet used as a rebound last year.

Caliste plasters on the smile she's used to wearing. It's joyful without being extra. A smile equally vacant and relaxed. Easy. Chill. A simple-enough front—one that's slipping with every passing second.

"I'm going outside. I'm feeling a little sick," Caliste says, fluttering her hand in the air as she untangles herself from his sweaty grip. "But I will be taking this . . ." With a wink, she snatches the tumbler from his other hand.

She's so sick of these bitches. Sick of the men lusting after said bitches.

Sick of feeling suffocated and alone at the same time.

The VIP area has an entrance that snakes through the back to a private lot, where Rufus parks his vintage Carrera. Caliste's heels *click-clack* on the dark polished floor, the sound echoing unevenly as she stumbles. The bouncer acknowledges her with a polite nod, letting her pass through the heavy matte-black door. Caliste finally gulps down some cool air like a suffocating fish.

"Shit," Caliste says into the silence. She takes a drink of the whiskey and spits an ice cube into her hand, rolling it between her fingers. The cold sensation bites at the tender skin rubbed raw during her last manicure (she usually tells the nail tech to keep scrubbing until instructed to stop) while her heartbeat slows. She starts counting her breaths—four seconds in and eight seconds out, like her therapist taught her. In the middle of the third breath, her phone buzzes.

Caliste squats, butt to heels, leaning against the brick wall of the club for support. Squatting too low, she feels the wall's jagged texture digging into her shoulder blades. Caliste plops her crimson Bottega vanity bag on the ground and digs out her phone, the screen lit up with a notification. Some semblance of relief bubbles inside her when she recognizes the name and the avatar of an illustrated sloth. She's never seen his face, but Caliste likes to imagine that the human behind the avatar is equally sleepy.

Artemis8072 sent you a private message

Artemis8072: hey. How's the party? Kill anybody yet?

Sitting upright, Caliste drops the melting ice cube onto the concrete and rapidly taps on her phone.

not-cali: hey, can u talk?

Artemis8072: all right, love. Give me a min

The churning in her stomach settles slightly, and Caliste smiles. It's cringy . . . but somehow Art's cheesiness is endearing. With half her life online polished and curated to perfection, joining a gaming chat room full of angry dudes was a social reprieve. She'd met Art four years ago during a *League of Legends* tournament, and they got close. Amid all the testosterone raging around her, Art was different.

If Bev is one of her few real-life friends, Art is her only virtual one. Their meeting was initially confusing for Caliste. Artemis was a goddess and not a god, and Caliste *typically* expected a male name from the average chronically online teenage boy. When she'd asked him about his username—Art told her Artemis was his grandmother's name. It was sweet, and Caliste had yearned for more sweetness.

Caliste guards Art from her real life. No one else knows of his existence—not that anybody would care. Art knows her hopes and fears, has unfettered access to the real her—not Cali the daughter; Cal, Bev's right hand; or the online persona Caliste cultivates. He knows the parts of her that scream over the microphone and get pinkie finger cramps, have father issues, and are perpetually afraid a panic attack will hit at the absolute worst moment. He knows about her fear of water and her competitive side. Art's never seen her face; she's never seen his. (Although she suspects Art's looked up her social media accounts by now). That fact provides her with an odd sense of peace.

25

She knows Art has a bit of a temper but is patient, specifically with Caliste. He has a sickly father and few friends he hangs with, too. He both knows her and does not.

When Caliste's phone lights up again, she doesn't even let the first ring finish before tapping the green answer button.

"Why the hell are you still awake?" Caliste says. Art goes to school somewhere on the East Coast, where it's almost three a.m. She misses when he used to call from his hometown and she could hear his grandfather clock chiming in the background. The chimes were evenly spaced but unevenly shrill, and Caliste would tease Art about having the tastes of an old man.

"I was worried about you. Are you holding up all right? Today is . . ."

"Stop," Caliste shouts, tensing at the question. It's a knee-jerk reaction, and she's immediately regretful. She's startled that Art remembers what today is. Her dad hasn't even uttered a word yet. "I'm sorry. Just . . . Can we talk about something else?"

"Of course . . . What are you looking at right now?" Art asks, his modulated voice tempering Caliste's nerves. He uses the same voice mod on calls as he does for their live games: a low-pitched male voice with an English accent (Art is decidedly American). She's a little disappointed that he hasn't let her hear his true voice, but she's never pushed. He respects her boundaries, and the least Caliste can do is return the favor.

"That creep club owner's puke-colored car."

There's a silence before he laughs. It's a humorless one, which means Art is annoyed.

"Has he tried anything since last time?"

"God, no. But . . . now that I think about, it's weird I haven't seen him at all tonight."

"What's weird is that your friend still hosts parties there," Art says, the thinly veiled disdain leaking out of his voice.

"She apologized," Caliste lies.

Beverly isn't someone who has your best interests at heart. Be careful, okay? I can't help but think she's just using you. Art's warning drifts to the front of Caliste's mind. He isn't wrong, but it doesn't matter to Caliste. She's paraded around at company events when her dad needs to cosplay a good father, so she's used to being an accessory.

"I'm sure she did," Art says. "Why is she your friend, again? From the way you talk about her, you don't seem to like her."

"Maybe not. But I like you," Caliste rebuffs, putting her phone on speaker and nestling her chin between her knees.

"You're drunk."

"Ding ding ding! Please claim your prize. What's your wish?"

"For you to stop drinking and grab a safe ride back home."

"No can do," Caliste says, throwing back the rest of the watered-down whiskey and ignoring the growing nausea in her stomach.

Art sighs, which means he's admitting defeat.

"Are you going to tell me how you're feeling?"

"I'm fine," she says, the last syllable heavy on her tongue. "Can you stay on the phone with me?"

Art says nothing else but stays on the line. Caliste is grateful for the silence. With her free hand, she picks at the dried skin on her lips, the red from her lipstick caking under her nail. Looking up, she stares at the black and starless sky and pictures the sun rising on its path over the Atlantic Ocean.

When she was younger, Caliste used to wait every year until the Earth and the sun returned to the same spot they were in when her mom disappeared, hoping that cosmic positionality might return her mom to her. Eventually, she realized that wasn't possible. Her notions of the universe were merely fantasies.

Caliste stands, suddenly restless, and walks toward the vintage green Carrera. It's polished within an inch of its life, and both her face and the security light behind her reflect off the passenger-side window.

"You know, my dad always complains that I look like her."

"Do you?"

"I . . . I don't know," Caliste replies, her voice slurring. Before she can stop herself, Caliste is hiccupping, and tears are rolling down her cheeks. She doesn't *think* she resembles her mother all that much. But it doesn't matter. It's enough of a resemblance to torment Paul Ha.

She serves as a daily reminder of the day his wife disappeared without a trace.

"God, you sound wasted. I'm gonna call a car to take you home," Art says. "Where are you?"

"No need. Thanks for staying on the line. Bye, loser," Caliste says before hanging up, barely able to keep her voice level. Once the call ends, sobbing overtakes her.

Caliste imagines how her mom might've aged. If they stood side by side now, how similar would the two look? Caliste traces her features in the Porsche's window and looks for the connection, but she can't find it. On the day her mom disappeared, Caliste was four years old. It was also the exact same day as her mom's birthday: December twelfth. Caliste used to celebrate her mom's birthday . . . wondering how her mother's face may have changed year after year. Eventually she forgot the celebration and remembered only the mourning.

She stares at her reflection. Taut and tanned skin with a sunken face. (Her friends often compliment her cheekbones, and Caliste politely accepts without telling them that grief is the secret to having a sculpted face.) Waist-length reddish-brown hair extensions that match her dyed locks. A wide forehead, eyebrows artificially arched higher by the best microblading tech in LA, and lips in the shape of a perfect heart. Primped, polished, and exfoliated. A face and body altered enough to soften the similarities between her and her mom. Caliste pictures her mom's face; then it fades. It always does.

"I hate you," Caliste says, clumsily swinging her arm back to punch her reflection, which has reappeared in the window's surface. The momentum stirs the nausea bubbling in her stomach, and she feels a sudden acidic rush up her throat.

"Dammit!"

She vomits, and now the Porsche is *actually* a puke green.

♊

Caliste's memory from last night is hazy. After throwing up on Rufus's car, she vaguely recalls stumbling into the back of an SUV before waking up in Beverly's room. Her head is currently *pounding*, and every nearby vibration feels like needles stabbing Caliste behind the eyes.

Winslet, Melina, Beverly, and Caliste were all chauffeured from Bev's house to the shoot location for Bella Vera, an all-natural beauty brand (a company helmed by someone in the Ambrose social circle, who apparently hired staff based on "astral alignment" and vibes, and Beverly invested in). Now Caliste sits in a marigold Dolce & Gabbana sports-bra-and-leggings set, with her hair styled into one long cascading braid. The focus of today's shoot is a line of products geared toward fitness, which is on-brand for the kind of content Caliste creates as a full-time fitness influencer. The products they will be touting for this shoot include dry shampoo (made with lemongrass, lavender, and vanilla musk), an all-natural deodorant Caliste's prepared to sweat straight through, and a sunscreen stick.

"Hey!"

Caliste jumps in her seat before registering that Winslet's whispering. Winslet leans from her chair toward Caliste, her shimmering champagne nails clutching the vanity in front of them.

"A little birdie told me you got that commercial shoot with Adidas? That's huge!"

"Ahh . . . thanks," Caliste says. "It's not *really* a big deal. It's a commercial for their pop-up event for Valentine's . . ." Her voice trails, and she lets Winslet prattle on in excitement.

Beverly and Caliste were the final two in consideration for the Adidas commercial shoot. The casting director allegedly wanted a more "all-American" girl-next-door type, and Caliste was surprised when she ended up being the final pick. Beverly was congratulatory, but Caliste has been bracing herself for petty backlash.

"Hey, babes. Test photo time!" Beverly yells, her voice lilting upward. There's a note of authority hidden behind the facade of cheer. If it weren't for the staff here, Beverly's tone wouldn't be half as pleasant.

Caliste walks mindlessly as she's ushered toward a pastel pink wall. Soundlessly, she sinks into her designated seat closest to Bev. From the corner of her eye, Caliste sees Melina giving her the stink eye. Caliste once coveted the spot next to Bev—it was a sign of their friendship. She realized too late that, in actuality, it's a sign of who is most willing to fall in line. But she's not that girl anymore, the one in high school who was too weak to stand up for herself and too naive to think anybody else would stand up for her.

Despite the main shoot not having started, Caliste is already tired. The interior of the studio reminds her of every hotel lobby in West Hollywood. It's minimalist without much character—filled to the brim with white marble, gold accents, and various shades of pale pink. Even the furniture—natural wood tones and a lot of wicker—emulates a sterile beige version of luxury. The air is coated with the scent of Diptyque's Tuberose, intensifying Caliste's headache.

"Cal, arch your left foot a bit more. Lemme see those quads pop," a photographer yells from behind his camera, waving playfully behind the lens like he's commanding a perky little dog.

Caliste obliges, extending her leg farther into the foreground (but still behind Beverly). There's a series of shots peppered with instructions for the girls to adjust themselves, all of which have the same goal: to make them appear as thin and cheerful as possible. Caliste can't decide if this is better or worse than last week, when she had to pose for shots while pretending to eat a salad.

"All right, ladies. You all look great. Let's take a few minutes and start?" the photographer says, the question clearly targeted at Beverly.

Bev looks like she's walked straight out of a Ralph Lauren ad, wearing a blush-colored tennis skirt set that makes her seem sweet and harmless. Caliste stifles a laugh.

"Thank you in advance for your hard work!" Beverly says with a nod. She turns toward Melina, Winslet, and Caliste, clapping her hands.

"Champagne?"

"Do you even have to ask?" Winslet says, accepting a gold-rimmed plastic flute from the staff member who pops up right next to them.

Caliste shakes her head as the platter is offered to her.

"I'm hungover from last night. I'll pass."

"Ah. Are you sure? I think it will be good for you to loosen up," Beverly says with a smile. Her eyes are focused on Caliste, her lips pursed in amusement.

There's a silence in the studio, with only the shuffle of staff moving things around in the background. Caliste swallows, the ringing in her head rising an octave higher.

"Sure. I'll take one," Caliste says, teeth gritted. Choosing battles is necessary for her tenuous existence within this group. The problem is, Beverly is the one waging *all* the battles, no matter how small.

Beverly lifts her glass for a toast, and Melina, Winslet, and Caliste follow suit. Caliste downs her glass until the rosé coats her throat and the saccharine layer cancels everything else out. Like a machine, another staff person materializes to take the flutes away from the girls so the shoot can officially begin.

"Okay, we're taking the slow-motion video. Start moving in three . . . two . . . one . . ." the woman says.

Caliste suppresses a wince as a confetti cannon goes off. Above them, a shower of gold and periwinkle tissue flakes bursts and falls, the scratchy pieces scraping down Caliste's arms. She grins wide, throwing her hair back. The mood today is supposed to be light, confident, and happy. That alone makes Caliste laugh.

Beverly is at the center, chin upturned and an effortless smile on her face. If there is anyone who personifies main character energy, it's Bev. Caliste isn't resentful, though. No, she's glad to be in the background.

Main characters want to lead quests and fulfill everyone's expectations. But background characters? They can disappear, and no one cares. Sometimes Caliste imagines disappearing.

"Listen up, ladies! The first photos will focus on the lemongrass-scented dry shampoo."

Scent.

Caliste often replays a memory on nights when she's unable to fall asleep. In it, she lies in bed between her mother and her father. Her mother's hair falls between their bodies, its length reaching Caliste's toes. Notes of plum blossom and lemongrass coat Caliste's nostrils softly. They linger, and Caliste nestles into the carefully woven blanket of familiarity.

Mom leaves for the kitchen to brew coffee, and Caliste groggily climbs out of bed. Her mom returns with a clean outfit for Caliste and dresses her for school, patiently coercing clumsy limbs into the right place. Mixed with the fresh smell of laundry is the sweet grassy fragrance her mom wears.

This memory isn't sad. Caliste doesn't feel alone. At peace, a younger version of herself hugs a big doll in her outstretched arms.

"Give your hair a flip, Caliste!" the photographer yells, ending the memory.

They then cycle through the two other scents for the dry shampoo, and after so many repeated sprays into the air, Caliste's head is foggy from sensory overload. Modeling the sunscreen and the deodorant is a blur.

Everything is finally wrapped up after a few hours, and the glittering decor starts to come down.

Caliste brings her wrist to her nose and inhales her own fragrance, Chanel Chance Eau Fraîche. The jasmine-and-citrus perfume is the closest she's found that mimics the memory of her mother's essence, but it's still not quite right. It's fading from her skin, fusing with the salt of her sweat. Nonetheless, the fragrance grounds her.

"Cheers, loves! Thank you all again for today. You did ah-maz-ing!" Beverly exclaims and settles next to Caliste, who feels the soft waves of her friend's hair brush her arm. Marching behind her are two frighteningly efficient staff offering tall glasses of fruity drinks. Caliste chooses one that's fizzy, neon green, and has a tiny umbrella. It tastes disgusting.

"What are you talking about? It was all you, Bev," Caliste says.

"Anyway, I appreciate your support today, and I'm glad we resolved that little mistake," Beverly says, leaning away from Caliste to look purposefully at her. There is an emphasis on the word *mistake.*

Caliste inhales sharply, her fingertips gripping the condensation-covered bottom of her glass.

"What do you mean, 'mistake'?"

"Oh. That thing with Uncle Rufus. He didn't mean it, so I'm glad you saw it that way, too."

Mistake is not the word Caliste would use to describe the events that transpired with Beverly's uncle.

Don't make a fuss, Cal.

Don't make a fuss. Don't make noise. Be pretty and quiet and help me. *Even though my uncle is a creep.* That was one test of this *friendship*, among a slew of others:

- Caliste and Melina scoping out Beverly's competition for senior class president and planting some carefully engineered rumors.
- Everybody icing out Bev's ex-boyfriend's *new* girlfriend until she left Lockshire entirely.
- Winslet "accidentally" tripping the English teacher on the way to her car, conveniently causing an entire stack of tests to fall into a puddle. (Beverly got an A+ after being allowed to retake the test.)

Within the halls at school, serving as Beverly's henchman provided ironclad social protection and the authority to look down on everyone else.

In some ways, it's been an exhilarating experience . . . a give-and-take that Caliste can wrap her head around.

But, staring at Bev now, Caliste can't help but think it's always been more *give* than take.

Beverly tosses her hair over her shoulder and swirls her glass like a cartoon villain, the tiny umbrella bobbing to align with her movement. "Cheer up, babe. You aren't going to be the all-American girl Adidas wants looking like that," Bev says. Her tone is teasing, but Caliste knows she's not.

Beverly's fickle friendship and vast connections gave Caliste something she desperately wanted: an identity not associated with her absentee dad. It gave her an influential circle of friends, no matter how superficial. It gave her the illusion of control over this fragile life of hers.

Caliste, with her missing mom and a dad who could be bothered only to have an assistant take her out to birthday dinners.

Caliste, who was forced to attend a boarding school miles away, regardless of how she felt. Caliste . . . drifting at the whim of the universe and adults making *very* important decisions without her. All Caliste ever wanted was to feel in control of *something*, and her social life and curated online identity were it.

Caliste shook her head. "We don't see things the same way, Bev."

"Oof. You're testy today," Beverly snaps back, her signature smirk pulling at her peony-pink lips.

"I'm gonna go," Caliste says.

"If you're sure."

"I'm positive."

"Well, we have a campaign for the New Year. Don't forget to diet, 'kay? It's going to be too late to alter the pickleball dresses we ordered."

It's not a question but a warning. *Be a good sidekick. Don't mess with our image.* Beverly is smiling as if she weren't being a grade-A bitch. The other girls sit with their glasses in hand, eyes boring into the wall. Beverly is frightening when she's mad. Triggering her brought Caliste a small amount of petty joy. This version of Bev is familiar, and a new memory provokes a gag.

That never happened.

Caliste was back in the halls of Lockshire, before that fated meeting with Beverly under the Judas tree. A hand held Caliste's hair in a tight grip, the points of long, gel-coated nails digging viciously into the tender place between Caliste's scalp and neck.

God. Who would call you pretty? You're lucky Asian girls are trending right now.

Caliste felt the cool edge of the toilet bowl on her forehead right before her hair was yanked back by the hand of Lauren

Harwell, the junior class president, whose ire Caliste had somehow drawn. With the taste of her own blood in her mouth, she counted to ten, imagining herself transforming into a snake and escaping under the bathroom door. The counting didn't help, and her entire body was drenched in nervous sweat.

Caliste thought she was going to die.

She doesn't remember how long it took, but Lauren, chief of the Caliste tormentors, finally got bored. Caliste used her cardigan to wipe away as much blood from her face as possible and staggered through the bathroom doorway, unimpeded by the onlookers, who had stepped aside. As Caliste stumbled toward an exit in shame, she swore she spotted a pair of blue eyes and a curtain of blond hair in the periphery of her vision.

In a nanosecond, the shadow she thought was Beverly disappeared into the flock of spectating teen girls.

Once they became "friends" Caliste had mustered up the courage to ask her: *Were you there? Did you stand by and watch me get tormented?*

That never happened, Beverly had claimed.

Caliste accepted the lie because their delicate friendship wouldn't last otherwise. But she no longer needs protection from bullies.

"I only have your best interest at heart, Cal," Beverly says to Caliste now, a smirk on her face.

"Screw you, Bev." An audible gasp comes from Melina, and Caliste does a pageant wave before turning her back.

"I made you, Cal. Don't forget that."

Caliste doesn't look back at Beverly's final warning but flips her off instead.

God, that feels good.

CHAPTER THREE

Aria

Aunt Thu has been to Georgetown's campus only once, during the week in late summer when Aria moved into her dorm. Aria recalls walking with her from the Starbucks near the hospital to the building's entrance, Aunt Thu's wiry hand gripping Aria's tight.

It was a relatively silent walk, but Aria could see the warmth in her aunt's serene expression and feel it through her hold. Aunt Thu pointed out the squirrels on campus for being too chubby and asked random questions about interesting structures (to which Aria's most frequent response was a shrug and "con không biết," because she really had no clue).

Aunt Thu's favorite parts of campus were the greenery down by the library and the ever-impressive Healy Hall with its Gothic tower jutting into the sky. Aunt Thu settled on a bench under the shade of a tree on the lawn and stared for a good fifteen minutes at the tower before Aria was able to wrangle her home to rest.

This campus, with its beautiful architecture and manicured lawn, is a sight that makes Aunt Thu feel joy. In contrast, Aria feels like she's suffocating here.

Aria stares at the bench now as she pauses on the path from the library to the building where the Department of Government's offices are. Aunt Thu was so proud when Aria chose to be a political economy major. Would she still be proud if she knew what Aria was doing? Aunt Thu's boasting about Aria's grades and intelligence—would it all stop if the truth came out? *Of course it would, you cheater.*

A surge of cool air brings Aria back to reality, and she shakes off the thought, turning away from the bench and continuing her trudge to Professor Tzu's office. She is careful, stepping in her worn hiking boots over the dying wet grass, afraid of slipping. It isn't cold enough yet for the snow to stick, for which Aria is grateful. Philip calls her his favorite klutz, and she hates that he's right. Wintertime is usually a dangerous time for her to be walking around.

Breaking a bone would truly be the cherry on top of this hellish semester. She's studied and worked hard in school. Aria follows the immigrant-kid Monopoly board, but she's merely a game piece mindlessly circling it. She can pass Go, but can move no farther. She's miserable here—stressed out and exhausted—and Aunt Thu's health will never get better. All her hard work feels so fucking pointless in the grand scheme of things. Good grades can't cure sickness.

Something wet trickles down her face, and Aria realizes she's crying. Sniffing in a trickle of snot, Aria arrives at the large wooden doors of the hall and reaches toward the brass handle.

The door suddenly swings open, the heavy edge slamming into her shoulder. She yelps, jumping backward to avoid a collision with whoever pushed it open.

Christ, is someone mad about their last final this morning?

A pale white boy appears with a stack of books in his hands. There is something imperious about his gaze and the way he carries himself, as if Aria is invading his space and not the other way around. His dark honey hair is pushed back, and Aria notices his face is tinged pink underneath a smattering of light freckles. For a nanosecond, Aria freezes at his expression. He seems so familiar, but she can't place him.

"Are you okay?" Aria asks, knowing a beat too late that he probably should be apologizing to her.

"You."

Aria steps back, the word rattling her.

"Do you know me?" she asks, staring at the stranger's pursed lips. He's not a classmate and definitely isn't someone who took advantage of her services. "Who are you?"

"Everything you're not," the boy snaps, his voice dripping with a disdain that startles her.

She recalls her aunt's instruction for encountering hateful people and takes a deep breath. She walks past, avoiding the boy's tense gaze, and the door swings shut with a pathetic whistle of air. Before it does, she can hear the boy utter one last phrase.

"You better enjoy your time here while it lasts."

Whirling around, Aria pushes back through the door, prepared to give him a piece of her mind, but he's already disappeared down the path. Screw it. She doesn't have time for spoiled brats. He isn't the first she's come across, and he certainly won't be the last.

♊

When Aria peeks her head into the doorway of Professor Tzu's office, it looks as it has all semester: a chaotic whirlwind of books and papers alongside a collection of Asian snacks in a wicker basket on the desk that Aria herself eats half of throughout any given day.

"Hi, Professor Tzu," Aria says as she taps on the door with her knuckles.

"Aria!" Her advisor's voice rises from behind her desk, her back turned toward the door as she faces her computer. "Take a seat. I'm finishing up some emails."

"I'm only dropping off the book I borrowed," Aria says, placing the book on a stack sitting precariously on Professor Tzu's bookshelf. She eyes the copy of Rey Chow's *Writing Diaspora*, making sure it won't disrupt the Jenga of books and make the tower topple over.

"I'd like to chat with you for a moment. Is that okay?" Professor Tzu says, and Aria can tell she doesn't really have a choice. Aria can't help but feel like she's being addressed by an auntie and not a professor.

"Take your time. Should I shut the door?"

A nod from Professor Tzu prompts Aria to close the office door. She lets her book bag drop onto the worn red carpet of the office floor and sinks into a plush chair across from Professor Tzu. "By the way, do you know a skinny blond-haired kid in this department?"

"You must be more specific, Aria. There are many skinny blond-haired students in the department."

"He has a mean-looking face," Aria says, trying to picture the boy again. "Thin. Freckles. Was wearing a navy peacoat and a tan scarf today."

"Emory Hane? He was in Professor Carson's office next door a minute ago. Why?" Professor Tzu grimaces as she says this. "I've heard his name far more times this past month than I'd care for."

"No reason . . . I ran into him on my way in," Aria says, her voice drifting off as she considers this information. Emory. The name doesn't ring any bells. "Wait . . . Why have you heard his name so much?"

". . . And finished!" Professor Tzu says in an upbeat voice and clicks a last email window closed with a little flourish. She immediately turns around to face Aria with a smile. The magenta acrylic earrings hanging from her lobes sway as she leans toward Aria. "His father owns a defense-and-technology company of some sort, and there is going to be a Hane Endowed Professorship in the Georgetown Department of Government. There's quite a bit of noise about it."

"There are plenty of endowed positions. Why is this one triggering gossip?"

"I haven't had time to quite dive into it, but there are some . . . *ethical* questions about the company. A lot of its recent developments have been in the future technologies space . . . Issues wholly irrelevant to you and me."

Aria nods. Being from that sort of wealth explains his being a brat, at least.

"Did your last exams go well, Aria?"

"Yes, they did. I studied as hard as I could . . ." Aria says, willing her face not to betray her. It's the truth. No need to mention that she studied hard for other people as well.

Professor Tzu gazes up at the ceiling, leaving Aria unable to understand the meaning behind her expression. "I only wanted to check. Is everything okay on your end? At home . . . with your aunt?"

Aria freezes at the question, the sweat on her back feeling slick inside the veritable tent that is her puffer coat. She hadn't meant to open up to Professor Tzu, not so far as to tell the professor about her mom's disappearance and Aunt Thu's being sick. But after earning the first C of her life during midterms, she'd broken down within the four walls of this very room. Aria still feels guilty about it, like she was trying to emotionally extort this overworked woman who is not actually an auntie.

"Everything is great. No more hospitalizations, and the doctor says as long as she stays off her feet for a while, she'll be okay," Aria says, painting on a believable smile. She didn't need, or deserve, pity right now.

"Are you sure there isn't anything you want to tell me, Aria?" Professor Tzu's voice is soft. "I want to make sure you're getting all the support you need." The second part of the statement is hurried, and Professor Tzu's eyes are wide for a nanosecond before going back to normal.

"I'm positive. Everything is fine," Aria says. Her heart races at the line of questioning. *Does Professor Tzu know? How would she know? Crap.* For a moment, staring at Professor Tzu's concerned face, Aria almost considers coming clean entirely.

No.

Honesty is a privilege I can't afford. Literally.

She checks her phone. It's six-thirty. "Sorry, I have to go. I need to take care of Aunt Thu's evening meds."

Professor Tzu stares at Aria, her expression unreadable. She opens her mouth as if to say something but quickly purses her lips instead.

"You go on home, Aria. It's late. I don't want to keep you."

"Thanks again for letting me borrow that book, Professor," Aria says, the indescribable feeling of relief blossoming. The professor is just concerned. No need to worry. It's a false alarm.

As Aria stands to leave, Professor Tzu speaks again.

"You're not alone. If you ever need help, I'm here."

Aria nods politely and turns her back.

Professor Tzu means well, but she's wrong.

From childhood to now, Aria's been the one taking care of herself and Aunt Thu and juggling twenty different balls so one doesn't drop. Aria's always had to rely on herself. Being alone is the only way Aria knows how to do *anything*.

♊

An altar is for the dead, and Aria's been in denial of what it means to have an altar for her mom. They're using a dresser for it, one with faded cherrywood and ornate Georgian brass hardware. Aria remembers going with Aunt Thu to a garage sale in Maryland to pick it up. Nine-year-old Aria had hid in the middle of a bunch of garden gnomes while Aunt Thu haggled.

On top of the dresser sit two red-and-gold candlesticks, a plate of fruit, and the cooled bowl of wonton soup Aria placed there after heating dinner. Aunt Thu is already asleep, so Aria stands by herself, studying her mom's portrait. Her nose and the skin under her eyes sting from repeated bouts of crying and being wiped with scratchy dollar store tissues.

Xuân's eyes. Aria's eyes. They stare back at her.

The dead were honored at altars, and her aunt had quietly placed Xuân's photo here nearly five years ago. Aria knows what that means, but she allows herself the comfort of delusion. Her mom couldn't be *gone* gone. But if that was true, why has she been dragging around the police officer's voicemail all day like a shackle? If her mom is truly alive, why isn't Aria jumping at the possibility of being reunited?

It's then that Aria hears, beyond the throbbing of her own head, three sharp raps on the living room window.

When she stumbles to her feet and swipes the thin gingham curtains aside, Aria's eyes find a familiar mop of hair.

Hey, Philip mouths, his eyes darting to make sure Aunt Thu isn't around, a habit from sneaking out. Of course, that only mattered when Aunt Thu still had the energy to check on Aria. She hasn't checked in on Aria's room since Aria's junior year of high school. That thought makes Aria's heart hurt more.

Philip's thin hands hold a white cake box, and he is smiling so big, Aria wonders if he'll break his face. What a dork.

Aria creeps quietly to the side door, opening it to let him in. The rusted hinges squeak.

"I brought cake." Philip's voice is tentative after he sees Aria. His smile falters and is replaced with a look of concern. His shirt collar is smashed underneath his backpack strap, and his hair is askew.

"I told you not to."

"Yeah, I ignored you."

Aria snorts. The growing pressure in her chest wanes. She is grateful Philip never listens to her efforts to keep him at arm's length. He's unabashed in his care for her. It kind of scares her.

Wordlessly, Philip slices through the cake, careful to get one neat slice with perfectly proportioned icing. Even layers of fluffy white cake are interspersed with Chantilly cream and berries. This is the same cake they shared for the first joint birthday that Aunt Thu and Mrs. Kim held for them as children, though Philip is about a month older. Aria watches his fingers slide the piece carefully onto a chipped Corelle plate.

Philip places the cake on the altar and then lights the incense. Smoke weaves upward from the burning sticks toward Aria's popcorn-white ceiling, and the ashy scent makes Aria tear up again, or at least that's what she tells herself.

"Philip."

"Yes?"

"I received a voicemail from an officer in Minnesota. He said he has information about my mom."

"What kind of information?"

"I . . . don't know yet," Aria says pathetically. "I need to call him back."

Turning to Philip, Aria realizes he's already facing her. His hand is held out toward her with an unreadable expression.

"Then let's call him back."

The careful compartments keeping her numb fall away as she takes Philip's hand and follows him to the brown corduroy couch on the back wall of the living room.

Once he releases her hand, Philip sits quietly as Aria takes out her phone and stares at the screen in her lap. The silence of the living room is unbearable, but the high-pitched ringing sound after Aria finally hits the call button is worse. For a second, she hopes Officer Badiou, who should be off the clock, won't answer.

"Hello?" Aria manages to croak once the call's picked up. She hits the speaker button.

"Hello? Am I speaking to Thoo Nu-jin? This is Officer Badiou. Thank you for returning my call."

"It's Thu Nguyễn. And no, this is her daughter," Aria replies, the words rolling off her tongue instinctively. Aunt Thu usually put down Aria's number for anything important, a habit that became the norm once she started having trouble using her fingers. For Aria, calling herself "daughter" instead of "legally adopted niece with a missing mom" was easier, both for Aria and for the poor strangers who would feel obligated to try to comfort her.

"Is your mom available to talk?"

"May I ask what this is concerning? She's resting right now."

"It's about her sister, your aunt."

The man's words grip Aria's heart, and she feels herself breaking all over again.

"I'm sorry to be the one to tell you this, miss, but we found her body."

They found her.

Mom.

The rest of the call unfolds in an incomprehensible blur. Philip scribbles down some Minnesota address on his arm in Sharpie. Aria vaguely recalls telling Officer Badiou that she'll see him soon to verify the body's identity. After she hangs up, there's only silence.

Aria's eyes move listlessly to the old television and the broken dining chair shoved in a corner. Philip says nothing but instead hugs her.

Contrary to what Aria wants, she starts to shake. The

composure she had on the phone carefully disintegrates, and she's now sobbing.

"She's dead, Philip."

"I'm sorry."

"And I'm alive."

"I know."

"I wish I weren't."

Being alive while her mom has been dead for god knows how long . . . Aria can't explain what that fact stirs in her. She had envisioned a reunion in which her mom would be so proud of the daughter she'd become. That will never happen.

Philip says nothing again but continues to hold her, and Aria sinks into the familiar embrace of someone who understands her more than she understands herself. The inkling that has been snaking in the dark recesses of Aria's mind for forever finally shifts into an ugly truth at the forefront.

She'd let herself believe her mother was still alive, hiding out somewhere in the world, and that was the difference between herself and Philip. His mother was dead, but Aria's was not. It once meant they were different, that Aria was superior, somehow— a cruel and selfish thought that's come undone.

CHAPTER FOUR

Aria

"Cưng ơi. What's wrong? What are you thinking about?" Aunt Thu asks as she sits, leaning back into the hollowed maroon armchair, the sharp edges of her shoulders barely sinking into it. Aria's aunt looks thin and brittle, save for the swelling of her legs. Aria suppresses the feeling of pity rising in her chest, pity her aunt despises with all that is left in her wraithlike body.

Aria hardly slept after the phone call last night. Philip had offered to stay the night, but she'd declined. She needed time to process without an audience.

Maybe it's the revelation about her mom, but the apartment she and Aunt Thu have lived in for most of Aria's life appears sallower. The pale canary walls and the swirling beige carpet elicit a stronger feeling of apathy than usual. Philip said that grief sometimes works that way, makes you disassociate from reality.

Aria and Aunt Thu moved here, to Falls Church, Virginia—a Washington, DC, suburb where the Việt population is concentrated—years ago, after their basement unit in DC flooded during a severe storm. Everything was destroyed: photos, clothes, toys, and furniture. Aunt Thu managed to fill their new home over time, but everything is fading now. The only way Aunt Thu can even afford the mortgage is because she purchased their house from Mrs. Kim and Mrs. Kim's late husband for an undervalued price. As a child, Aria thought this place was grand.

Now she only sees faded walls. Faded floors. Faded sunlight streaming through faded curtains, the fabric worn so thin, Aria can count each thread separately. And Aunt Thu, a faded woman, surly and angry about her condition, matches the interior. At one point, the roles were reversed, and Aunt Thu was the one kneeling on the ground and tending to Aria's wounds. Thu used to be a vibrant woman, shining brighter than lightning zipping through the sky. She is still that woman . . . but it seems like everything around them is doing its best to stifle her.

"Nothing, Dì," Aria replies finally, wiping the Betadine soap from Aunt Thu's legs. It's a lie. Something is very wrong. She tossed and turned all night, preparing for this moment. She is going to be the one to tell Aunt Thu that her sister is confirmed dead.

The wet gauze slides easily over her aunt's bloated flesh, across the roughened brown of her kneecaps, and toward her rounded toes. This step in the care of Aunt Thu's swollen legs is easy. So is the next: an application of compounded antimicrobial powder to the skin.

Amyloidosis was the diagnosis physicians landed on after a battery of tests and hospital stays. Aria understands it only on a basic level—Aunt Thu's organs and tissues are affected by abnormal proteins. She's stabilized in the past few years with medicine for her organs, but every so often, there's a flare-up that causes this painful swelling. It took a long time for Aunt Thu to get a medical diagnosis—Aria remembers the long treks back and forth from various hospitals, where whole teams of specialists were scratching their heads. It wasn't until a stray comment from another patient, a Vietnam War vet during one of Aunt Thu's hospitalizations, that the pieces started to fall together.

In the years before, when Aunt Thu could still work and the doctors were still clueless, Aria remembers smearing Tiger Balm all over her aunt's back, then scraping her skin with an old dog tag until furious red lines appeared. Coin scraping and other Vietnamese medicine solutions were all they'd had then. Aria hated it . . . There was something counterintuitive about causing her aunt pain to make her feel better. But Aunt Thu insisted that Aria was helping unleash the body's bad energy.

It's the final stage of dressing Aunt Thu's legs that's most difficult. After an uncountable number of times, Aria still hasn't mastered the art of wrapping the dressing and the gauze elegantly. She's clumsy, her hands winding and pulling out too much gauze or pulling too tight as Aunt Thu suppresses a wince.

"Ouch! Cưng! Are you wrapping me or some bánh tét? That's fine. Leave it." Aunt Thu swats away Aria's shaking hands, and her niece nods, using snub-tipped medical shears to cut away the extra bandaging as she's supposed to. When Aria was younger, Aunt Thu would show her how to properly roll a banana leaf around pork-and-mung-bean filling to make bánh tét. Life was a little simpler back then.

When Aria glances up again, Aunt Thu is staring at her with a smile. The lines around her mouth crinkle, and her hooded eyes round slightly.

"What is it?" Aria asks.

"You are a pretty girl. A soft girl. Your grandfather would be happy."

Aria swallows, nodding and turning her attention back to the task at hand. *A soft girl.* Aria knows more about her grandfather than she does about anything else in their family's past. Grandfather wanted a soft life for his children and for his children's children. Aunt Thu never said so, but she wanted the same for Aria. It was a straightforward fantasy—a roof over their heads, jobs that didn't involve backbreaking labor, and the ability to stroll outside in the sunlight and listen to chirping birds and the wind. Technically, that's what they have. But without her mom, Aria feels empty.

Aria uses an alcohol wipe on the scissors and places everything back into its plastic tote, which she returns to the side table next to Aunt Thu. Her heart races as she watches the seconds pass by on the wall clock. What good is being soft? Soft things can't protect themselves. They get crushed by anything tougher than them. Aria braces herself and exhales.

"I have to tell you something."

"Yes?" Aunt Thu asks, leaning back in the chair and fixing Aria with her trademark stare. Aria has always been envious of her aunt. Assertive and put together. She couldn't imagine Aunt Thu ever being too afraid to say something.

"I spoke to a police officer last night."

"Why? What happened? Are you in trouble?" Aunt Thu leans forward again, her eyes widening at Aria.

"No! No. It's nothing like that."

"Don't scare me like that! Out with it, then. What was the call about?"

"It's about Mom. She's . . . They . . ."

Aria can't bring herself to finish, lowering her gaze instead. She presses her palms onto the floor, pushing as hard as she can to make the tingling in her fingers stop. It's now or never.

"Her body. They found her body," she finishes.

"Where?"

Aria is taken aback by Aunt Thu's question and quickly turns her head to meet her aunt's gaze. It's even more inscrutable than usual. For a moment, Aria second-guesses whether she even said anything.

"Minnesota. A small town south of Saint Paul . . . It's by a river."

"Ah." That's it. One syllable. Aria continues to stare at Aunt Thu, hoping for some reaction that might indicate she knows what the hell is going on. Their family has no ties to the Midwest as far as Aria knows. But she gives away nothing. Despite how much sympathy Aria has for her aunt, this non-reaction unleashes a flare of anger.

"That's it? 'Ah'? Why was she found in Minnesota?" Aria asks, letting her voice venture into whining territory.

"Who knows? It's better to put this behind us, anyway . . ." Aunt Thu's voice is hurried, and she scoots forward in the armchair to stand.

"Are you serious?" Aria raises her voice. "My mother is dead. Dead. They found her *dead* body."

"Enough!" Aunt Thu roars, and she's so loud that Aria's lips seal immediately.

Aria grits her teeth, making tenuous eye contact with Aunt Thu as she stands and grabs her cane.

"It doesn't make *sense*. They need us to go identify the body. Don't you care? Aren't you curious?"

"I am not."

There's a tightness in Aunt Thu's voice. As always, she's hiding how she truly feels. Her salt-and-pepper hair blows in the ceiling fan's current as she starts to walk back toward her bedroom. It's a sign that the conversation is over, but Aria isn't ready for it to be.

"Did you lie to me?"

Aunt Thu stops at the question, her cane digging into a squeaky spot in the floorboards. The sound is sharp for some reason, and it stings Aria's ears. But she won't be deterred.

"Dad died after I was born. Mom left for her night shift at the hospital on Capitol Hill and never returned. We have no family left. Is that the truth?"

It's a story Aria can recite by heart, a story about which she could never pry more information from her aunt despite her best efforts. They had no other family, save for some extended relatives in Vietnam. They had only each other. But bits of the story puzzle Aria. Like the sometimes-changing timeline of when her dad died. Or tidbits about their life that Aria doesn't recognize. And . . . there are the letters Aria's received. There is a truth that Aunt Thu refuses to reveal, and Aria's suddenly tired of not knowing.

"It is the only truth you need to know," Aunt Thu replies after a long silence. She walks toward her bedroom again with no intention of answering.

A sudden urge rises within Aria to grab her aunt and scream. She wants to shake Aunt Thu until some emotion, *any* emotion, spills out. Instead, like a coward, Aria whispers, "I hate you."

Aunt Thu doesn't even pause at the confession, and the bedroom door squeals as it slams behind her.

♊

Nguyễn Giang Xuân is dead. And yet there is a new letter in Aria's hands, the one Philip delivered. If not Xuân, who are the letters from?

Aria first started receiving letters when she was seven, only three years after her mother's disappearance. She knew better than to talk to strangers. She knew, in her heart, that the letters didn't make sense and that they might be dangerous. But when her aunt wasn't paying attention, small Aria always sorted through the mail herself. The first envelope was tucked between a sheet of coupons from Safeway and a note about their nonexistent car's warranty.

The letter was different from the other mail they typically received—both the envelope and letter inside were made from thick cardstock. Aria thought it might have been sent to her mistakenly. The script of her name was elegant, the letters flowing in sharp cursive. When Aria closes her eyes, she can still picture the exact weight and curvature of the handwriting. There was no return address. It was like a secret message from a different world, and, curious, she opened it.

Inside the folds of the luxurious white envelope were not just a letter but also a drawing. Disappointingly, the letter was typed, using a font-replicating script on plain printer paper, with only the greeting and Aria's name appearing handwritten. The drawing, however, was on the same dense paper as the envelope.

Aria read the letter in the glow from a flashlight under the safe haven of her blanket. The dense fleece, embroidered with a gray heron and a white tiger, would shield Aria's activities from the probing stare of her aunt if she were to ever open the door wider.

Dear Ariadne,

Do you know who you were named after?

The drawing was of the Minotaur, and the letter outlined in brief that Ariadne was the daughter of King Minos of Crete.

The princess's unrequited love for Greek hero Theseus allowed him to defeat the beast. Aria remembers tracing the lines of the Minotaur's body on the page, pretending the invisible line was the thread that Ariadne used to help Theseus navigate his way out of the labyrinth.

The letter had no signature—only a beautiful inky stamp of a begonia. She'd tucked the letter into a shoebox under her bed and told no one.

Over time, the letters continued to steadily arrive, one every year afterward. The timing was also consistent, with most letters arriving within two weeks of the day her mother disappeared (and her mother's birthday). Zeus surrounded by bolts of thunder and Artemis shooting an arrow were some of the illustrations provided. The art style was minimalist in black ink. Each letter's stamp was different, showcasing a new flower. In time, Aria became obsessed with floriography and attempted to discern some secret code from the letters. Aria did not tell her aunt. She didn't dare tell anybody. It was a secret she guarded closer to herself than her grief.

She'd been certain that the letters must have been from her mother. It was the only explanation Aria could imagine. The letters were discordant and confusing. In truth, she eventually wondered if they might simply be for someone else.

But she coddled the delusion that they were at least written by her mother. And the mentions of Ariadne had taken on gargantuan proportions in her head, supporting her theory. Her aunt had once briefly mentioned that her mother enjoyed studying Greek mythology. At some point in the past few years, the letters started making less and less sense, to the point where she started to think her mother was having a mental break, and Aria couldn't help her. The letters discussed events in Vietnam that

Aria knew only from history books or Aunt Thu's old stories. But her mom? She would know about them, meaning Xuân Nguyễn obviously had to be alive.

Aria picks at her fingernails; they are rough and uneven from the sharp edges of her teeth. The newest letter is taunting her, and Aria has half a mind to rip the whole thing in half. But something stops her.

She used to get excited every time she saw this familiar cardstock and her name in elegant script. It became a tradition to her—a thrill she stoked like a flame. As long as she had the letter, her mom was still alive. Now, with one phone call, that illusion has shattered.

The return address was always blank, but occasionally the notes were on letterhead listing random locations. Often, Aria looked up the addresses, hoping to discern some pattern from them, too.

They were locations around the East Coast and the Midwest, always something like a museum or a library. As a child, Aria thought they might be clues. She thought maybe her mother was traveling on a secret mission. When she got older, she started calling the locations to ask if a Vietnamese woman worked there. Most of the time, the staff was bewildered, but sometimes an unsuspecting stranger was nice enough to entertain Aria's theories, and they would connect her to someone. However, the woman on the other end was never Xuân.

As long as Aria could rationalize it, twist the unknown into a reality that seemed plausible, she could breathe. It's not as if Aunt Thu helped fill in any missing pieces. She never told Aria anything, and Aria never told her about the letters, so Aria invented truths where she could.

She bites her tongue, and she tastes blood.

She clutches the letter and stands.

The past is a puzzle Aria has spent her entire life trying to solve. Perhaps confessing to receiving the letters will be the key to finally unlocking the truth.

But, as she approaches her aunt's door, her pulse impossibly loud in her ears, Aria hears another sound.

Aunt Thu is sobbing, an all-consuming and monstrous weeping. It stops Aria in her tracks. Has she ever seen her aunt cry? Her hand hovers above the tarnished brass doorknob.

"Xuân ơi," her aunt wails. "Why can't I have been the one to die instead? Aria can't go, not yet. I can't let her face you alone. I need to be healthy enough to see you, too."

Aria turns her back to the bedroom door, holding the letter close to her chest.

She can't do it now, not while her aunt is so distraught. The "I hate you" line probably didn't help, either.

Once she returns to her room, Aria takes a deep breath and then tears open the letter by herself.

Dear Ariadne,

It's been a long time since we've last spoken, hasn't it? I feel a bit guilty about it, but I think it was for the best. There are only so many tales to tell, and a lifetime to tell them.

You've probably heard the tale of Pandora's box at school. Although it is my belief that our institutions do a pitiful job of truly conveying the beauty of these stories.

In the simplest terms, Pandora was created as the

*first woman and as a punishment to humans. She
was beautiful and faultless, carved by the god of fire,
Hephaestus, from clay. She received various gifts, each
one making her more clever, more charming, and more
discerning than other humans.*

*The infamous gift, the one I presume you know, is
the pithos, the jar that contained spirits that Pandora
was forbidden to release.*

*I've imagined what it must've been like for
Pandora, gazing upon this lovely and forbidden thing.
What did she think as her fingertips traced the
lines and elaborate etchings of the pithos? I know
temptation. I am sure you do, too. But it can be a
wicked thing.*

*The gods gave Pandora everything. The gods gave
her a life of beauty.*

*What enormous greed must have consumed her to
relinquish everything in exchange for the unknown?*

*Don't you think it would be better to have kept
the box closed? Would curiosity kill you?*

The stamp at the signature line is of a vibrant purple flower.
It's a begonia—the same as when Aria was seven—the ink outlining the cylindrical spiral of the rounded petals.

A begonia flower represents peace and gratitude.

Or caution.

CHAPTER FIVE

Caliste

Caliste knows three things to be true about her family. The first is that her father is not to be questioned. His infuriating authoritative streak isn't surprising, as he is an only child . . . an only son, no less. Caliste knows there was once a time when Paul was a young boy named Phúc. She wonders what Phúc was like. Was he capable of having fun? Did he cry when he got hurt? All she knows of her father are his ambition and his absence.

Caliste learned bits and pieces of how difficult her father's childhood was . . . mostly from Grandma and a cackling gaggle of great-aunts. He and his parents came to a new country from Vietnam, and he was their only hope of achieving the American dream. She's almost sympathetic to the impossible pressure he must have been under.

But Caliste is a daughter. A girl. The eldest child. First shipped off to boarding school and then welcomed back under the murmur of gossip and whispers after skipping out on graduation. The policy, as with most scandalous Việt family rumors, is to spread them on your own time. Caliste isn't ready to confront these nosy hens on her father's home turf.

Alas, today is Dylan's birthday. Dylan Hà, Caliste's two-year-old brother, is the venerated heir. And some people she'd rather avoid are going to be at the house for a big party to celebrate him.

The second truth is that there is only one living person in the entire world who can make her dad bow down: Grandma. Bà Nội. A woman as volatile as a storm with the power to sink ships. She had only one son, who also had one son. Thus, this celebration is as much about their family's legacy as it is about a toddler. Caliste already feels her stomach churning, thinking about the uncomfortable conversations she's bound to have, and she chews a piece of mint gum to calm herself. This will be the first time she's seen Grandma in years. Grandma has lived comfortably in Boston with her siblings and various nieces and nephews. Whenever she visited, it was always to see Dylan, so Caliste was able to avoid interaction.

Caliste's white BMW cruises down the long street to her family's house. Theirs and not hers—an important distinction. Paul moved to Brentwood the same summer he shipped Caliste off to Lockshire Academy. Once his second wife, Priscilla, was in the picture, she swiftly made it her home, too. A new era arose for a new family, one in which Caliste didn't have a place, as if she *ever* really did.

The third truth is that the Hà family empire does not have time for weakness. No grief. No heartache. No yearning or panic attacks. The magnificent house on the hill that Paul Hà built from nothing is a testament to his strength. And Caliste's only choice in life was to feign strength. She's trained the muscle. The farce is her armor.

The iron gates of the driveway swing open as Caliste approaches, and she allows herself to frown in peace in her car. Paul and Priscilla designed everything for this bash to their taste, which is tacky as hell.

"Jesus Christ. Is that the Arc de Triomphe?" Caliste mutters as she pulls in. The structure in question spans a story high and is made from a multitude of silver balloons arranged in the shape of the Parisian arch. If not for the sheer ridiculousness of commissioning something like this for a two-year-old's birthday party, Caliste would be impressed by the artistry. Undoubtedly, it was Priscilla's idea. Caliste knows Dylan would prefer balloons that resembled those cartoon police dogs. Or a bunch of fire trucks.

The first time Caliste ever saw this house was when she was sixteen and returning home from Lockshire. Its enormity struck her then. It resembled a multimillion-dollar house in a prestige family drama, fitted with its own fence and blossoming cherry trees. The path to the house was long and manicured to perfection.

The razor-straight lawn was beautiful, but Caliste remembered missing her old two-bedroom townhouse in Garden Grove, tucked a few blocks away from Little Saigon. It was modest then, before housing prices all skyrocketed. When Caliste closes her eyes, she can still picture the lavender walls and her mother's framed photo of Grace Kelly (the source of her chosen English name) perched on the vanity.

On that first day free of Lockshire Academy, she was greeted by her stepmother. Priscilla sat in an armchair in a corner, the chair's luxurious cream contours encasing her like a cloud. Her light chestnut hair, which usually was styled and worn down, was pulled into a bun, exposing a plump face.

Caliste, for a moment, thought Priscilla was an angel. It wasn't until Caliste's eyes fell to Priscilla's waist that she fully comprehended why her stepmother appeared so different from their most recent family video chat. She was pregnant, the rounded curve of her belly hidden under the soft, fluffy folds of a fur blanket.

Caliste stood frozen in place under the chandelier of the foyer, staring at her doting father and a smiling Priscilla. He hadn't breathed a word about this, hadn't shared even an ounce of news regarding his expanding family at any point during the one five-minute call they'd had weeks prior.

As Caliste watched her father, his face beaming in a way she hadn't seen for years, she'd realized that they didn't even know she was there. In front of her was a family, but she wasn't a part of it.

After everything—especially that hellish semester that caused her to break down crying to her father's assistant, of all people—seeing them together was a slap in the face. Even more so because Priscilla was originally meant to protect Caliste.

When Paul's work started taking him across the country, he hired one Priscilla Ly-Weber as Caliste's live-in nanny. Paul chose someone else to keep tabs on his daughter so he could focus on more important things. As was his habit, he intentionally selected someone well versed in Vietnamese expectations and who had an impressive (to him) pedigree. Priscilla, whose mother was a Vietnamese American housewife and whose father was a German American immigrant and Silicon Valley engineer, was the perfect choice.

Priscilla was nicer back then, but it wasn't long before Caliste realized she was being used by the woman. After Paul and Priscilla ran into each other at a Vietnamese charity event, Priscilla became fiancée instead of employee. Caliste pretended to be indifferent to the promotion, but she was secretly hurt at being used as a trophy wife's stepladder.

As Caliste stands in the foyer, she blinks a few times and refocuses on the chaos of a child's birthday party. The mansion is flooded with staff going about their marching orders.

"Anh, anh! No! The ice sculpture needs to go here. That's too close to the vent."

"Oh, trời ơi. Here, let me do this myself. Cô Priscilla is going to get mad at you."

"The swan cakes have arrived!"

Caliste stifles a sigh. She's barely stepped inside, and she's already tired of the spectacle. Swan cakes? Ice sculptures? It's then that she hears the cursed voice over her shoulder, ringing through the foyer and silencing the staff immediately.

"Con ơi. You're *late*," Priscilla says. Caliste turns as her stepmother descends the stairs in a pink feather-swathed dress that flutters around her. Caliste hates to admit it, but it's cute.

"I'm sorry, Mẹ." Mother. The word is metallic and rotten on Caliste's tongue, and she's still not accustomed to saying it. Priscilla is closer to Caliste's age than she is to Paul's, which makes calling her "Mom" an effort. "I was caught in some traffic on the way. You look beautiful." The former is a lie; the latter is the truth. Priscilla is beautiful, and Caliste has thought so ever since their initial meeting.

Priscilla is bright, a world's difference from the austere expression Paul often wears. The energy she brings into Paul's surly house is electric. At one point, Caliste had hoped Priscilla might love her. She'd even made herself act like a grown-up and bury the resentment and fury she carried from her own mother being declared legally dead just so that Priscilla would love her.

Of course, that wish was another unfulfilled.

Priscilla's eyes narrow, and it's clear she thinks Caliste is lying. She aims her glare straight at Caliste before glancing up and down her outfit. Caliste knows to brace herself for some back-handed comment on her weight, her face, how she's dressed, or her makeup.

"You always turn into such a mess this time of year. Please keep it together for Dylan today, all right?" The words drip with fake concern. Thank God her brother's birth date is a day *after* the date of her mom's disappearance.

Forcing a smile on her face, Caliste turns away so she can't give her stepmother the satisfaction of seeing her pain. "Is Dylan upstairs? I'm going to say hi before the party."

Priscilla's energy abruptly shifts, and Caliste catches an anxious expression on her face before it disappears.

"He's been in a mood all morning, so make sure not to agitate him. Bà Nội is with him now."

Bingo. Caliste knew something was off. Priscilla's a little mean, but Grandma is meaner.

Caliste doesn't reply before making her way up the spiral staircase, while Priscilla huffs behind her. In truth, Priscilla is merely a distraction—she's an easy target for Caliste's ire. Especially when Caliste's father is nowhere to be found. It's not like Caliste can be moody at thin air.

Paul Hà has been too busy growing his empire. First, there was the grocery store in Orange County that expanded to two more locations and then a dozen. By the time Caliste started middle school, the chain had stores on the East Coast, as well as in Vietnamese enclaves in the Midwest and the South. Restaurants came next, both fancy and fast-casual eateries. Ha Foods was a behemoth of Paul's making, and he was worshipped for it by those in the local Vietnamese community and beyond.

"Chị! Chị!" A small voice and the clatter of clumsy steps emanate from the primary bedroom, making Caliste smile. Dylan, dressed in a tiny yellow suit, scrambles down the polished parquet toward Caliste with his arms outstretched. Caliste doesn't like Priscilla, but that woman did make an adorable-ass baby.

"Em!" Caliste coos and reaches out to swoop Dylan into her arms. His dark hair is soft, the messy tufts cuddling into her cheek before he plants a wet kiss on her face.

"I'm two." Dylan's face is beaming when he says this, a little dimple on his cheek indicating a smug little smirk on his face.

"You are," Caliste says as the weight of Dylan's warmth in her arms instantly calms her and slows her restless heart. He smells like roses and baby powder.

"For once, you're dressed respectfully," a voice echoes down the hall, and Caliste bows her head immediately.

"Greetings, Bà Nội."

Caliste inhales, concentrating on not dropping Dylan as she finally looks up. Her grandmother wears a simple garnet-colored gown, its cowl neckline and a strand of pearls framing a face both fierce and elegant.

As Bà Nội approaches, Caliste suppresses the irrational thought that her grandmother can read minds (and see that her black sheep of a granddaughter puked her guts out last night from underage drinking).

"Come. Take a walk with me, con."

There is something soft about the way Grandma says this, so much so that Caliste is caught off guard. It's suspicious.

"Why, Bà Nội? The party is about to start."

"I need to talk to you about some news. It's about your mother."

Caliste's heart seizes inside her chest, and she can't stop her own outburst.

"What? What about Mom? Tell me."

The gaggle of staff milling about in the foyer below them glance up at Caliste's standoff with the senior Hà matriarch, who sighs as if she's dealing with a child's temper tantrum.

"Keep your voice down. Grace . . . your mother, she's been found."

♊

Grandma did not care for her daughter-in-law, Caliste's mother. Caliste doesn't know the whole story behind their friction. Then again, the story of the Hà family is more fable than actual history—at least, it is for Caliste. She's heard many iterations of it, some dramatic and others more somber.

It starts with Grandpa, Ông Nội, or Hà Văn Lai, who was a high-ranking officer of the South Vietnamese military. In Grandma's version of events, the family left Vietnam in 1975, with Caliste's father in tow. The family settled in Southern California with Grandpa working as a civilian for the first time in his life. After years of hard work, they sent their son to an Ivy League school, and Paul became a success. Professionally, that is.

They wanted an educated and obedient Vietnamese daughter-in-law, and Grace was far from that. She was headstrong and independent, as well as vocal about her disdain for traditional Việt gender roles. This is as much information as Caliste was ever able to glean from Paul. Periods of Paul and Grace's marriage were often glossed over with sanitized language. Caliste had always assumed the strain was due to her grandmother's disapproval.

Grace was a unique girl, she'd say.

Caliste once asked Yến, her cousin—technically, by American standards, Yến is a first cousin once removed, but all that gets simplified in Việt culture; they are simply family—about the time between her parents' marriage and her mom's disappearance. Yến had frozen, then reprimanded her for being too curious. Caliste never asked again.

Grandma stands staring out the large floor-to-ceiling windows overlooking the backyard, which houses a grotesque water feature that was installed last year. Caliste hovers in front of Grandma, equal parts astonished and terrified by the news just dropped on her.

"Your dad informed me that he received a call from a police officer in Minnesota earlier," Grandma says. Caliste stares down at her in disbelief. Bà Nội has always been tiny . . . but for some reason, her grandmother looks smaller than usual. Her white hair is cropped in a neat pixie cut, and despite the simplicity of her clothing style, she exudes a regal air, as she always has. "He'll be late to the party because he has a meeting, so he asked me to talk to you."

A million questions rattle through Caliste's brain, but Grandma's concentrated expression makes her hold the stream of consciousness inside. Caliste learned early in childhood that Grandma *hates* being interrupted.

"He thought it would be best for me to tell you that they found your mother's body there."

Body.

Body.

The word barely registers before it ignites a panicky rage inside Caliste.

"In Minnesota? Why would she be there? And what are you talking about, her body? Was she mur—" Caliste can't help herself; the series of questions erupts out of her.

"It's best we resolve this quickly." The tone Grandma uses to interrupt her reminds her of Paul: exacting and ironclad . . .

"What does that even mean?" Caliste can't keep the hard edge out of her voice. The uncomfortable truth is that she's always hated her grandmother. Their interactions have been few and far between and are usually composed of Grandma remarking on her weight (an inclination she shared with Priscilla) or the shortness of her skirts. Caliste is usually invisible, especially when Paul and Dylan are around. But now Grandma's full and undivided attention is focused squarely on Caliste.

"Tch. Your father was too soft with you. You are mentally weak, just like your mother—having fits over nothing. She is dead. It's unfortunate, but there's nothing we can do now. It's best we move on, Caliste."

Only the deep and melodic breaths of Dylan in Caliste's arms while people are preparing to celebrate him keep her from totally and absolutely losing her shit. Caliste inhales, the grip she has on her own composure slipping by the second.

Having fits over nothing? *As if finding out your mom is dead means nothing.*

"No. I refuse to believe it. She wouldn't leave us. You—"

"She died, as she should have," Grandma abruptly snaps. Both the cruelty of the statement and her attitude startle Caliste into silence. "Mothers are supposed to die before their children. I know it's upsetting that you didn't have more time with her, but you need to look toward the future instead of always wallowing in the past."

There's a hurried way in which her grandmother utters these words, like they've been long simmering inside her.

Mothers are supposed to die before their children.

"What would you know about that? Since you're so callous about death, what about me? Would you care if I died tomorrow?" Caliste asks, the viciousness she's inherited from this very woman coming to the surface.

"You . . ." Surprising Caliste, her grandmother's voice wavers, rising in anger before settling into silence. Grandma takes a shaky inhale and squares herself with Caliste, their eyes locking. "Don't ask ridiculous questions. I am saying this for your own good. My only concern is to protect my family, and that includes you. Your mother is gone. I cannot protect a corpse."

"Was Mom ever considered a part of your family?" Caliste snaps. Her jaw is painful from how hard she's clenching.

"Of course she was. Women become a part of their husband's family in marriage. But Grace . . . your mother is not here, so *I* am responsible for you, and *I* will protect us. You do not understand. You will *never* understand because you're a pretty girl raised with pretty things."

Grandma purses her lips. In this aggravating moment, something flashes across her face that catches Caliste off guard. If she isn't imagining things, it's a look of pain. Caliste jumps at the sudden noise of clicking heels. She's crying, and as she glances down, she sees small damp spots appearing on Dylan's clothes.

When she turns her head, she spots Priscilla halfway up the stairs and motions to Grandma.

Bà Nội says, "Cali. Go rest in the sitting room and calm down.

If you want to talk to the officer, I wrote down his number. For your brother, it will be best to keep this secret for now." This is a command, not a suggestion. Grandma takes Dylan from Caliste's arms, and the trio walk downstairs without her.

Finally, after the clubbing and the brand shoots and the emotionless family members, Caliste is happy to be alone.

$$\text{II}$$

Caliste has dreamed of the day they would finally locate her mother, has spent her entire childhood imagining it like a scene from a movie. In this scene, Grace returns to them, and everything goes back to the hazy time from before, when Caliste could still recall her dad's warmth. It's a moment so sweet, her teeth would hurt from the anticipation.

She never considered what it would be like if they found her mother dead. Why would anybody fantasize about a nightmare?

Officer . . . Baboo? Ballon? What-the-hell-ever his name is said that his team identified Grace from a missing persons database. Her mother's body was discovered in some partially dried-up riverbed in the middle of nowhere, yet her father can't be bothered to answer a goddamn phone call.

Grandma and Priscilla confirmed earlier that Paul is currently stuck in some meeting, which explains why he's not answering the phone. The cynical side of Caliste can't help but think there are other reasons why he doesn't want to talk about Grace, though. She wonders if he married someone so young the second time around because he knows a woman his age would never put up with rarely ever seeing him.

Paul Hà does not care that his late wife's remains have been found. Like mother, like son. He's moved on, dragging Caliste with him. There are shiny new things that demand his attention—high-rise buildings and new developments with his name on them.

Bootstrap stories don't have the space for dead wives.

Caliste inhales four counts through her nostrils and exhales eight through her mouth. She concentrates on the counting and not the anger seething underneath her skin.

They hadn't buried Mom. They'd buried air. They'd buried the past so Paul Hà could start anew. It was a forced burial, and Caliste remembered the day as if she'd lived it only yesterday. The gray sky and the 5 slick with oil and rain. The pithy little tombstone, a sad little black square underneath a canopy of old tree branches. Her holding Yến's hand and learning what the term *legally dead* meant.

On that day, she learned that humans can simply declare things even if they aren't the truth. It was this same day when she realized she hated her father like she hated his mother.

Everything was according to their father's will. Caliste's grief had been on a timeline, a corporate timetable of expectation. Mourning—socially acceptable mourning—was okay up until language classes in the evening or before piano. Priscilla monitored a petulant young Caliste as Paul went on business trips.

So, to no one's surprise, he's MIA when she learns that her mom is really gone.

Memorandum for the Record

August 27, 1975

TO: PAUL S. McCLOUD

SUBJECT: Placement of Lt. Col. Lai Van Ha, Formerly of
the Vietnamese Air Force

In our discussion, I noted that I would do my best to
assist Lt. Col. Ha in acquiring a nonmilitary job. I noted
that we would attempt to place Lt. Col. Ha with his
sisters in Boston, MA, but separation may be necessary.
Not all are as lucky as Lt. Col. Ha, and I am sure he will
be grateful.

However, we do guarantee placement of his wife,
Thanh, and young son, Phuc, together. I express my
deepest condolences to Mr. Ha on the loss of his two
eldest daughters. I was a bit surprised to learn this, as
neither of Lt. Col. Ha's daughters were mentioned in our
early correspondence.

Dr. Theodore Marrs
Special Assistant to the President
White House
1600 Pennsylvania Avenue NW
Washington, DC 20500

CHAPTER SIX

Caliste

Caliste is addicted to her phone, but these days, her habit of tapping her screen is out of control. Every time she swipes away the glossy lock-screen picture of the Tanah Lot Temple in Bali, her digital reality flashes to life with a stream of notifications.

ares_the_scholar and 809 others liked your photo

Squat With Abby started a live stream

[stunna19] replied to your story: babes ur a star

None of these messages are what Caliste is looking for: a missed call or a voicemail from Paul Hà.

Some sign that Caliste's memory of his warmth isn't fictional.

She lies on her side on the floor of Priscilla's massive closet, wrapped in a puffy white blanket, reflecting on the interactions with her grandma and stepmother. With her face smashed against a pile of pillows, Caliste shuts off her phone, tosses it onto the rounded George Nakashima coffee table, and sits up.

Caliste hasn't seen Priscilla or Grandma since the party's

official start. They're telling the guests that Caliste is sick. It's funny, realizing she needs an excuse to be absent but Dad does not. Paul Hà always has "legitimate" reasons to miss his own children's birthday parties.

A platter of cookies and two cups of tea that cooled long ago are sitting on the coffee table. Caliste is sure one of the staff put it together, but it was still a strange surprise when Priscilla carried it upstairs along with makeup wipes. It means the woman is capable of something proximal to love. Although the thought that Priscilla knew about Caliste's mother before Caliste did irritates Caliste to no end.

As for her grandma . . . Caliste doesn't quite know what to make of her reaction. Was there gentleness in some of her words, or did Caliste simply imagine it? *I am responsible for you, and I will protect us.* If not gentle, surely her words were mindful? They've certainly never had a *good* relationship.

Caliste is always *too.* Too emotional. Too flashy. Too undisciplined. Too thin. Too large. Eventually Caliste formed a skin against the jabs, and eventually she stopped seeing her grandmother altogether. The doting Dylan receives is foreign to Caliste.

Caliste's phone buzzes, pulling her thoughts away from the people downstairs.

Artemis8072: just saw your message. that's a terrible piece of news. I'm sorry.

Caliste holds in a laugh. Of course her internet friend is checking in with her before her own father.

Well, if he isn't going to acknowledge the news on his own, she'll force him to.

Stumbling to her feet, Caliste shuffles quietly toward the door.

The hum of the crowd immediately hits as the door opens, triggering a bitterness in Caliste. All the people milling below, laughing and chatting among themselves, know nothing about the conversation between Caliste and her grandmother. The sight of all these designer clothes and rich friends of her parents makes Caliste's stomach turn. There are some aunties here whose daughters used to be on the middle school debate team with Caliste, and she'd love to avoid them. Caliste mentally maps out a walking path that dodges all the worst offenders. She's strategic and almost makes it to the front door before Priscilla finds her.

"Con. Where are you going?" The question, for once, doesn't sound accusatory.

"I'm going to talk to Dad. He's not answering his phone. Have you been able to get ahold of him?" Caliste's eyes briefly scan their immediate surroundings in anticipation of Grandma swooping in to prevent her from leaving, but the woman is thankfully nowhere to be seen.

Priscilla shakes her head. Her peach-colored lips are pursed, and she opens her mouth to say something before closing her mouth.

"What?" Caliste can't hide her irritation, and for some reason, she feels a bit guilty about snapping.

"Nothing. Get Thuần to take you. You're in no state to drive, and your car's blocked in the driveway."

"Oh," Caliste says slowly. She doesn't have time to process her stepmother's second act of kindness of the day before Priscilla flicks her wrist and the driver appears like he's her loyal sidekick.

76

Ha Foods Corporate relocated last year from Pasadena to the Wilshire Grand Center in the financial district. Paul was a man obsessed when the building was announced: a glittering behemoth that was to be the tallest building west of Chicago. It didn't matter that it was a ridiculous move or highly inconvenient for nearly all his staff, commute-wise. The tower became his new house on the hill, the next signpost that meant he was further away from being that skinny seventeen-year-old busboy taking summer classes at Lowell High School.

The ride is quiet, and Thuần puts on some Việt ballads to fill the silence. Caliste stares vacantly out the tinted windows the entire time. She counts the number of blocks they pass to ease her mind, pretending each one is a domino falling toward Paul's ivory tower on the hill. She imagines his empire toppling down.

When she arrives at the Wilshire Grand Center, a fountain with shining gold stags greets Caliste as she ascends the many stairs to the office entrance. Inside the glossy lobby, where there's a row of elevator doors, Caliste talks to the woman at the front desk. She pings Ha Foods Corporate headquarters.

Soon her father's lead receptionist meets Caliste and leads them to an elevator. Caliste walks behind her into the sleek chrome interior without fanfare. Lindsay? Or is this one named Everly? Caliste lost track a while ago. She knows the secretaries are always white girls, girls with all-American looks and all-American accents.

The sleek lobby of the Ha Foods Corporate floor is dominated by an oddly shaped chrome statue—one that resembles a phallic pencil covered in confetti—at its center. About a dozen people are seated around the statue, presumably waiting to attend one of the many meetings in the endless string her father is always busy with.

"Miss Ha, your father has a brief opening before his next meeting. Someone will be out to grab you in about thirty minutes. Do you want a water or perhaps some tea?" Everlindsay says impassively.

"Have you answered any calls from the police?" Caliste asks, ignoring her question.

Everlindsay frowns and tentatively shakes her head.

"You know what? I'll take champagne. And I'm also not waiting that long. Tell him," Caliste says sharply, putting on the flat smile she is too used to flashing.

"I don't think I should . . ."

"Now. Please. Or I'll make a big ol' fuss right here."

Everlindsay shuffles off and returns with a plastic champagne flute, her hands shaking slightly as she hands the flute to Caliste. Her eyes widen as Caliste downs the contents in one gulp.

"Mr. Ha is ready for you."

"He'd better be."

She stands to follow Everlindsay.

The receptionist leads Caliste down a long and dimly lit corridor to a coveted corner office overlooking Wilshire Boulevard. Caliste's eyes scan the other offices on the way. The floor-to-ceiling glass walls and doors allow Paul Hà to surveil his tiny fiefdom whenever he needs to pee or exert his dominance.

The receptionist comes to a stop at the corner office's door, and the loud *click-clack* of Caliste's heels on the polished floor pauses. Paul's glass door is frosted, unlike the other offices—the

unique privilege of being a CEO who doesn't want to be sur-
veilled.

Caliste overhears, "Mr. Ha, your daughter is here."

Daughter. The word is strange to Caliste's ears. She wants to
double over in laughter but holds it in.

The door swings open, and Caliste walks through, the brunette receptionist next to her bowing slightly in some fusion
of Việt custom and Paul's version of corporate etiquette before
leaving.

Paul sits at a massive half-doughnut desk, his back to the
beautiful view behind him. Everything is built around this sense
of beauty and accomplishment, but it's all for show. Paul himself
doesn't know how to enjoy the fruits of his own labor.

Her father looks the same as always. Heavy hooded eyes and
strong cheeks, features that made their way into Dylan's face and
not hers. Despite being in his mid-fifties, Paul still has a full
head of hair (although it is all gray); his voluminous coif is gelled
and styled in the shape of a small helmet. The lines trailing all
areas of his face are the only indication of his age. In Caliste's
mind, he has far fewer. When *was* the last time she saw him in
the flesh?

"You are too American," Paul finally says after Caliste plops
herself down in one of the armchairs facing him. He utters the
words matter-of-factly, his hawkish eyes remaining focused on
the computer screen in front of him.

"You wanted us to be American, didn't you? Should I walk
out, come back in, and then greet my father properly? I'll even
kiss the floor."

"And too bratty."

"You sound like Bà Nội."

The longer the noise of Paul typing on his keyboard stretches, the more agitated Caliste gets.

"You didn't answer your phone," Caliste says flatly, her eyes darting from Paul's face to his typing: two single fingers pressing each key in quick and maddening succession. "And you're missing your own son's birthday party?"

"I'm busy, Cali. I was working. Grandma and Priscilla have things under control at home. I know where I am not needed. I'd only be in the way."

"So much work that you can't even call me about Mom? You asked Bà Nội to do your dirty work for you?" Caliste's voice is rising, and she doesn't want to control herself anymore. Dimly, she registers that her phone is buzzing in her pocket, but she ignores it. "Did you even talk to the police for more than thirty seconds?"

Paul sighs, finally pushing himself away from his desk to stand and walk toward Caliste.

"I talked to the police officer. There's nothing else to say." As if they orchestrated it, both Grandma's and Paul's answers sound the same. Once again, Caliste's phone vibrates, and the vibrations travel up her throat. She wants to pull it out and chuck it with full force at one of the office's glass panels.

"You and Bà Nội are the exact same. I don't even think she was a little bit sad at the news."

"Don't say that, con."

"Why not? It's true. She said mothers are supposed to die before their children. Easy to say for he—"

"Stop." Paul's voice thunders, startling Caliste into momentary silence. "Do not speak on things you know nothing about."

"Then tell me, Ba! I know nothing. *Nothing.* I'm tired of it!"

"Ah . . . your grandmother . . ."

"Spit it out."

"I had two older sisters."

The confession knocks the wind out of her. For a moment, Caliste doesn't think she heard her dad correctly.

"What?"

"I had two older sisters. They died a few years before I was born."

"I . . . Wait . . ." Caliste swallows, trying to wrap her head around this new piece of information. *Sisters.* Aunts.

Mothers are supposed to die before their children.

Caliste's fury and heartbreak absorb the new grief. Girls. Dead girls. Dead women. A dead mom. Fine. Bà Nội understands. But what about Paul?

"Do *you* care that she's dead?"

"What? Stop talking—"

"Did you care when Má disappeared? Or were you happy to be rid of her? I bet it would be a relief for you if I disappeared, too. So that you can go on living as Paul 2.0 without any connection to your past."

Caliste is tired, so unbearably tired, and she can't keep holding on to the stray hope that her dad will show her an iota of love.

"I've spent my whole life envisioning her coming back to me, to us. I've dreamed of her face too many nights to count. But you know the fucking thing, Ba? I can't even picture it clearly anymore. I have to look at a photo of her to remember. Even then, I forget. It's like I'm staring at a stranger. A ghost. And whose fault is it that I can't picture her? Yours, or Grandma's?"

Paul flinches. "I did not want her gone," Paul says, his voice barely audible. It startles Caliste. He's moved around his desk and is leaning back on it, facing her with his arms folded. Of course, his expression remains unchanged, but there is something in it that makes a part of Caliste's chest ache.

"Are you sure? Because you never bring her up!" Caliste says, gulping back another wave of tears.

"I think about losing your mother every day. I often think about how I failed her as a husband. She wanted a prince, and instead she got a pauper. The only thing I could do for her was to try to build something. To try to build this in her memory," Paul says, his right hand untucking itself and gesturing at the office around him.

He continues, "I couldn't keep her safe. What good is it to dwell on the past, Cali? She likely died years and years and years ago. She died running away from me. I knew it then, and I know it now."

"Right, because running from you is the only answer that makes any sense," Caliste says sarcastically. After a sigh, she adds, "I'm going to Minnesota, Ba. I'm going to see her, and you can't stop me." Caliste stands, avoiding her father's eyes and walking back toward the door.

"Wait."

Aware of his presence behind her, Caliste braces for his objection. Of course he would never allow her to go digging up old history.

She spins around and finds him only a step or two away, hand outstretched. "I'll arrange everything for you, okay? Let me make a few calls first. I won't stop you. I promise."

Caliste's hands pause on the sleek brass handle of the door as she considers his words, her eyes catching the thin decorative bookcase in the corner. It's filled mostly with stacks of miscellaneous business books and motivational self-help garbage. But there is a book she recognizes. The spine is as thick as a dictionary, yellowed and faded with time. A book of Greek myths. Her mother's.

"Thanks. I'll let you know how it goes, Ba."

No matter how insipid and pathetic it might be, Caliste can't let go of the hope, of the small light she desperately clings to in her heart. The hope that the Hà empire wasn't built on an empty grave and forgotten bones. The hope that perhaps something else that's buried can somehow fix their broken family.

As she closes the door behind her, Caliste's phone buzzes again. She lets out a guttural groan and pulls it out of her pocket, startling a staff member hovering outside of her dad's office. Who in the hell is being so persistent?

As Caliste scrolls, she sees a dozen new messages in the group chat with Beverly, Winslet, and Melina. Caliste frowns, wondering what could incite this much chatter. There's a thumbnail for breaking news from the *Los Angeles Times* in a message from Melina with "bev u ok?" tagged on hastily.

Rufus Ambrose, the brother of former California senator Geoffrey Ambrose, has been reported missing. Hands were sawed off and left in a gruesome scene at Malibu Beach. Investigation is ongoing.

Numb, Caliste scrolls through the article as quickly as she can. At most . . . Caliste expects to feel indifferent at the news. Or at least empathetic on Beverly's behalf. But she doesn't.

As Caliste rushes out to the elevator, she catches a glimpse of herself reflected in the building's shining interior. She doesn't recognize herself.

Three weeks ago, Rufus Ambrose's disgusting hands tried to slide up her leg.

And now they're no longer attached to his body. Uneasy, Caliste recalls telling her father's assistant so Rufus would stop being invited to company events.

For a few nauseating seconds, Caliste wonders if her father is capable of such gruesome retaliation. She laughs, the sound coming out as a cough and joining the elevator's dings.

No. Of course not. Her father? Paul Hà? Risk a *murder* scandal, of all things, to protect Caliste? He would never. The fact that she even entertained the thought makes her sick again.

CHAPTER SEVEN

The Ghoul

Usually, I wait until twilight to hunt. However, I am restless and anxious, so I wake from my slumber at dusk. I do not venture from the water, not unless there is someone for me to kill. It is unexplainable, the bloodthirst I feel. There is no logic I can sense. All I know is the instinct. Silly humans trudge past, their limbs grazing the water. As the vibrations flood through, I can taste bitterness on my tongue.

Sinners.

Humans cruel and disgusting who deserve not to live.

Every time I take a soul, I hold their mortal bodies down in the water until their struggling ceases, until their limbs begin to float and their pulse becomes nonexistent. However, there is no satisfaction when I do it, because I couldn't save all who suffered at their hands.

Something tells me that I could relegate them to my same fate and turn them into cursed dead things like me. I could escape this purgatory by switching my soul with theirs, leaving them trapped in the water. But I do not. I let their bodies go, and they drift away before useless policemen come to discover my crime.

After all this time, I've discerned there is a reason the water needs me to kill: It's begging me to hold the immoral accountable. My fate was sown into the silt. Now I know why. The smell of my long-slain body and the scent of the man who murdered me and left me trapped in this river are intertwined. It's new . . . Nothing in the water has ever held his scent.

Poking my head from the water, I can tell that this man is near, and I will find him.

This hunt is the only way I can justify my days swimming endlessly through the water, hoping for a whiff of him. Hunting like this is not part of my nature. My other victims, the others who deserve death—I find them once the fragrance of sin bleeds through the water. My fingers find their eye sockets. My throat devours their livers. I consume them, all the same.

But I've never sought them out. Cowards tend to stumble their way to me.

However, this man . . . I cannot wait any longer for fate to bring him to me.

I must find him.

I will.

My identity. My name. Where I called home before this— I've lost it all because of him. The hunger within me is stale and exhausting, and I'm unsure how much longer I can hold on to this cursed life before I let another soul take my place.

Fading light glimmers above the ripples of the water and dims. The sun is well on its path to the other side of the world.

My nails dig into the ground as I crawl through thick mud and shallow water. I do not know how long I travel while my killer's scent permeates the air.

The journey reminds me of a time in my past.

I remember walking through mud like this, the thick, sloppy gunk of the river clinging to my ankles and weaving in between my toes. Earth and flesh gloriously united as one.

My sister hated the mud.

Sister.

The word rattles my core.

Sister.

This word threatens to break me.

Before the thought has time to settle, a light flashes above. It must be artificial; its fluorescent glow stings my cold skin.

I surface, blinking. A coating of mud slips off my eyes, and I am staring at a man through the glass. In an instant, I know this is the man I've been looking for. Seeing him now, I feel my stomach drop. For a second, and only a second, I am afraid. My limbs writhe in clear water, attempting to make sense of where I am. There are smooth walls around me and a hard surface under my feet. This river has been altered and the water here is free of mud and weeds. It feels artificial. Claustrophobic. It feels like the death of something beautiful.

As I peek back up to where the man stands, I realize I can see into his house. The sight triggers a gag. *I remember this place.*

He paces in tight circles on the other side of a large window, his steps erratic and his body rocking anxiously. Suddenly, he lets out the most wretched shriek. I wish to choke him like I did the others. I have the urge to tear his tongue from his mouth and pry his fingernails from their beds. But I can't. Not until I understand what he did to me. How—why—am I like this?

The light fades, and I fall into complete darkness . . . where I am safest. So, for as long as the night protects me, I watch him.

There are a few things I observe. He is unremarkable in appearance but not demeanor. I spot a hole in a wall that I think has been recently created with his fist (he wears bandages on one hand). Broken plates are shoved into a corner of the kitchen near a trash can. It looks like pictures have been ripped from a wall, and there's a shattered window. His violence is sprinkled throughout this house like breadcrumbs.

The man must have a family based on the array of portraits I can see. He has a beautiful wife with long reddish hair and a dignified expression. However, there is also something vacant about her eyes: sky blue and unfocused, as if she is staring at a point in the distance. And her face . . . is familiar to me. The thought makes me uneasy. Her hands are on the shoulders of a child who, through a series of pictures, grows from infancy to the reedlike state of adolescence. Then I see a photo of the man when he was younger. His hair was a shimmering gold. I imagine what it would look like in the water as I strangled him. Pretty.

The rest of the house is dark and gaudy. But many windows allow me to see the full interior. Somehow I know the things he owns are expensive. I circle his home, occasionally wandering into small ponds or streams that go nowhere. I realize that this fake river must be connected to the real one, engineered by this ridiculous man to suit this ridiculous house.

Something catches my eye from the house, and I spot a large portrait hanging in what appears to be a study. It's a wedding photo, and the bride wears a lovely gown with lace trim.

Lace?

The word seizes on my tongue, burning in the hollows of my gut as it arranges itself into a solid memory.

I recall a different wedding gown. Silk faille and antique lace scattered with pearls and swirled in the shape of roses. I saw a photo of a woman in such a dress once, and I couldn't stop thinking about it for what seemed like forever.

The dress worn by the woman I remember was beautiful. I pictured its glamorous folds of fabric trailing behind her as she moved. This . . . this . . . lace. I imagined holding it in my hands, caressing the intricate threads and the spun roses, envisioning a life in which I'd own something so luxurious.

How peculiar. Who was that woman to me? When I think of her, I imagine a castle. A princess . . . A woman who lived a fairy tale. It's the story I wanted for myself.

When I blink, the portrait disappears, and I realize I am back home in the murky parts of the river where I belong. How long have I been swimming?

A sudden sensation hooks itself onto my body: sadness. The man in the house . . .

He . . . is . . . my killer. Why don't I remember his face? When I try to picture the events surrounding my murder, all I see is a gaping hole where his face should be.

♊

Aria

Philip's name flashes once more on Aria's phone screen, and she promptly tosses the T-shirt in her hand over it. Her ceiling fan whirls above her, the ancient thing rattling with a regular *click-click-click* sound, its loosened screws shaking in place. She isn't trying to avoid Philip entirely, but the hours she spent weeping in his arms are still too raw and shameful for her to confront him again so soon. Plus, she's escaping and doesn't need Aunt Thu to wake up.

A mess of clothes, books, and toiletries are strewn about Aria's bed. She'll throw them in the beat-up polka-dot rolling suitcase she purchased last spring for cross-country college visits—that was before she came to terms with the fact that a school close to home was really her only option.

She isn't usually so scatterbrained when she's packing, but her routine is seriously compromised. Aunt Thu has a habit of speaking only Vietnamese when on pain medication or recovering from anesthesia, so Aria's gotten used to hospital sleepovers.

But Aria isn't packing for a hospital visit. What is one supposed to take when traveling to the Midwest to view their mother's corpse? She extracted and replaced the same cream cardigan three times before giving up and tossing a random assortment of clothes inside the suitcase, leaving her wardrobe to the will of the universe. And, of course, she left room for the letters.

After the ice between them had thawed for a good twenty-four hours, Aunt Thu was insistent Aria needed to wait to leave. Aunt Thu wanted to be cleared to fly by her doctors first, because she wanted to go to Minnesota together. Aria promised her she wouldn't go yet and that she'd tell the police officer that they'd leave as soon as possible. But it was a lie; Aria couldn't wait. After their tense conversation, Aunt Thu seemed to have had a change of heart. She promised answers once they arrived in Minnesota, but there was no guarantee of that. So they were even, right?

Officer Badiou had wanted to ask Aunt Thu some questions about Xuân's disappearance and had told Aria there was something a bit odd about the body they found. He'd offered a conversation over the phone, but he'd also offered for them to come to Minnesota instead.

In case your mom wants to see her, you know? And you, too, of course.

Aria had yearned for that reality—for a family reunion—for so long, but the moment looming ahead isn't what she once imagined. If she thinks about that fact for too long, she'll absolutely freaking lose it, and Aria does not have time to absolutely freaking lose it.

Aria takes the T-shirt she's tossed over her phone and rolls it into a tight ball before adding it in with the others. Once again, her phone lights up with the notification of a voicemail from Philip, taunting her. She wants to tell him goodbye, or at least what's going on.

As if on cue, she hears a familiar pinging on her window. Aria holds back a reluctant smile and lets the pinging continue for a few more seconds before relieving Philip's torture.

"Hey, answer your phone, mophead," Philip says, glaring up at her from outside her window. He must have come directly from the laundromat, which is close by, the soft smell of clean linens and lavender wafting up and into Aria's nose.

Aria doesn't respond, instead rolling her eyes and backing away to give Philip space.

"It's rude to ignore me, you know." Philip huffs behind Aria, hoisting himself over the windowsill and toppling into her room. Aria pretends to be deeply invested in a pair of woolly socks she's thrown on her desk.

"You? Not people in general?"

"Yes, of course, just me. You don't have any other friends."

Aria feigns hurt. "Ouch. No need to rub it in."

A melodic sound rings in the air, and Aria sees her phone light up again.

"So your phone does work. Interesting," he says.

"I'm sorry. I've been juggling, like, a million things," Aria says, elbowing Philip.

She unearths her phone with its cracked screen, instantly frowning at an email notification and the subject line that's appeared.

Georgetown: Urgent Notification

Aria tosses everything else to the side. It's not a bill, is it? She sorted out the issue with the financial aid office, so everything should be covered now. She slides her thumb against the screen and taps on the message. Aria's eyes scan the email, and her heart stops.

December 10

To: Ariadne Nguyen

Student ID: 10999200187

Re: Notification of Georgetown University Student Code of Conduct Violation

The Office of Student Conduct has been informed of a potential violation of the Student Code of Conduct. A summary of facts has been provided below.

- Ariadne Nguyen facilitated academic dishonesty by knowingly taking an examination on behalf of another student.
- This information was verified by the student affected and by information provided by the Office of Technology Support.
- Assistant Director of Student Conduct and Student Conduct Officer Alyssa Jones was made aware of the allegations and is the assigned Student Conduct Officer for this case.

Please log into the Georgetown University Student Portal to verify receipt of this notification and schedule a disciplinary hearing. Your Student Conduct Officer will be in contact for next steps, including processes on Right of Appeal.

"What is it? Your face is scaring me, Ari," Philip asks.

"Crap. Crap, crap, crap." Her heart is racing now.

"Okay, calm down. Now you're really scaring me . . ."

She collapses on her bed, her phone falling from her hands to the floor with a soft *thunk*. The words *Office of Student Conduct* and *disciplinary hearing* burn like cursed glyphs in Aria's mind. *Of course* she got caught. This must be why Professor Tzu was asking all those vague and ominous questions yesterday.

Did she know then that Aria was a fraud? Would it have been better for Aria to confess?

"Oh, damn. Ari—" Philip starts, his eyes scanning the phone he's picked up from the floor.

"Don't say it, okay?" Aria snaps, her voice rising despite herself. "You were right. Is that what you want to hear?"

"Hey . . ." Philip's voice attempts to soothe, and he kneels until he's eye level with Aria. She avoids his gaze and wipes her sleeve against her snotty nose. This is the second time he's seen her cry in a matter of days. What kind of useless record is she trying to break?

As Aria sits up, calming herself and trying to will her tears to stop, Philip holds her hand.

Despite her very best efforts, the prospects of suspension and losing her scholarship jump to the forefront. She can't breathe, and the word *expelled* flashes in her mind's eye relentlessly.

"Shit!"

"It's going to be all right," Philip says, the curve of his bent index finger wiping her cheek.

"How do you know?"

"Because worse has definitely happened to you. No offense."

The ridiculousness (and truth) of the statement makes Aria laugh, an ugly guffaw that radiates from her chest. After she hits him, Philip chuckles.

"But seriously. One step at a time. First, tell them about going to Minnesota. You need to deal with all that. There must be someone you can contact at school for help?"

There he goes again, making way too much sense for Aria's liking.

"Maybe Professor Tzu. She's looked out for me all semester . . . I think she was actually trying to talk to me about this code of conduct thing."

Aria has worked too hard for everything to come tumbling

down on her after her first semester. It's only a disciplinary hearing. It could go multiple ways, right?

But it's not a false accusation; Aria *did* help people cheat. Does it matter if she isn't the one benefiting (academically, at least) from the cheating? A flood of scenarios play out in Aria's head, and the one she chooses to focus on is the one in which she gets to miraculously stay at Georgetown—guilty but still enrolled. Perhaps it is delusion, but Aria might need a little delusion to survive going on the trip to see her mom without having a meltdown. Now is not the time (as if there is ever a good time) to melt down.

"We'll fix it. One little letter can't break you." Philip says the words with his typical annoying calmness. However, unknowingly, he triggers something else for Aria.

"Speaking of letters . . . I . . . There's—" Her voice catches. What's she going to say? What can she possibly tell him that will make any semblance of sense?

I've been receiving weird letters, but it's okay. I thought they were from my dead mom.

A stranger has been my pen pal since I was a kid, and I haven't told anybody.

They know stuff about me, but it's all good, isn't it?

The words catch in Aria's throat as she stares at Philip's expectant expression.

Nonsense. If she shares, maybe unveiling this sad and ludicrous secret will make up for the years of smugly thinking herself better than Philip, the years of hiding the ugliness of her belief that a missing mom was superior to a dead mom.

She knows nothing can dissipate the guilt she's carried for even having such a thought, but the words fall out anyway.

"I . . . have to tell you something, and don't judge me until I'm done."

"Okay," Philip says.

She explains the letters and how they share explicit details about her namesake and her family—details she thinks only her mom would know. She speaks of how the letters stopped when she graduated high school. Stopped until now, after her mother's body was discovered in some random town. And how this letter, unlike the others, sounds threatening. After poring over them again and retracing what she thought she knew, Aria is less sure that the letters were ever from her mom. It was another one of Aria's delusions, and it took a dead body for her to fully see that.

Aria watches Philip's expression, waiting for it to reveal disappointment or exasperation.

"I know it's ridiculous. I know I should've thrown them away or reported them . . . or something. I thought . . . I thought they might be from her."

"I get it," he replies. "I would have done the same."

Aria is relieved. This secret, this dark thing that's been a source of shame and joy, now belongs to someone else.

"Do you think you can help me?"

"What do you mean?"

"The letters. I need to figure out who sent them. If they're not from my mom, then who?"

Philip's nose scrunches up as he considers Aria's question.

"Do you think the person sending these letters is dangerous, Ari?"

". . . I don't know," she answers honestly. "I used to think the letters were safe. Fun riddles . . . But now . . ." She lets the sentence die off, and Philip starts shaking his head. "Listen, I know I'm asking you for a lot, and I'm sorry. Really. Think of it like a game, you know? Like when you used to be obsessed with those true crime podcasts and you did all that internet sleuthing. Remember when your tip helped that one case in Montana?"

"That was different . . . They were strangers. Plus, I quit because I felt weird doing all that. I was fifteen with too much time on my hands . . ." Philip's voice trails off, and Aria can tell she's made him uncomfortable.

"You're right. Forget I asked. But I still want to wait until after I get back to do anything about school—"

"No . . . I will take care of it. You can count on me!" Philip says, interrupting, the cheerful tenor returning to his tone. He hits his chest with his fist, though anxiety is written on his face.

Aria knows there's something he isn't saying, but she can't take on his stress, too. "The letters are in an Adidas shoebox under my bed. Some of them . . . they don't even make sense. They talk about a house in Vietnam . . ."

A thought occurs to Aria as she wracks her mind for the details she remembers from the letters. There was a point a few years ago when the language of the letters became more fragmented and simplified before returning to a cadence she recognized. Voices can change, Aria had reasoned.

The reality is, she has no idea what her mom sounds like, written or verbal.

"Have you shown them to Aunt Thu?"

Aria shakes her head aggressively in response. "Not yet. I can't." She imagines the letters sending Aunt Thu into shock, or worse.

"Got it. I'll see what I can do."

"Thank you. Thank you so much. You're the best, you know that?"

"I know. And you're welcome. Now, let's fix this freakin' suitcase. What are you, an animal?"

Overwhelmed with relief, Aria instinctively reaches for Philip.

"Hey, Ari . . ." He's surprised by her touch, which kind of makes her sad. Aria hugs him from behind, her nose digging into the base of his neck.

"Thank you again . . . for everything. Seriously, you're a really good friend," she whispers.

Philip doesn't say anything for a minute, merely patting Aria's hand with his.

"I am. And so are you," he finally responds.

Aria breathes in deep. She's not, though. He deserves a better best friend. But only she knows it. She supposes everyone has their own delusions.

CHAPTER EIGHT

Aria

Aria picks at her lip, locating the roughened strips of chapped skin sticking out and peeling. She does it until the soft sting goes too far, until a bubble of blood follows and there is a change to her body. The pain is calming, and neither Aunt Thu nor Philip is around to yell at her about the bad habit.

Aria thought she was used to the cold, but home has nothing on Minnesota. Sure, DC gets hit with the occasional debilitating snowstorm, but it rarely drops to bone-chilling temperatures for long. The second she walks through the Minneapolis–Saint Paul International Airport doors to find the rideshare pickup spot, her face stings as if a million tiny shards are stabbing her.

The scent hovering in the air, however, is stale, a hint of late fall's wood and leaf litter lingering. She hates autumn for obvious reasons. Not only is it the time of year when everything starts to die, but it's the time when her mom's disappearance always makes her the most depressed. The only pro to the season, if she's being sentimental, is that Aunt Thu's name means "autumn."

Shuffling her feet on the sidewalk, Aria's soles make an ugly squeaking sound against the faded patches of salt. She dodges and winds through dozens of people making their way to and from the airport terminals.

She is blotting her lip with a crumpled tissue from her coat pocket right when her phone buzzes, likely indicating that her driver is here, because a black Ford SUV turns the corner. The cost of getting a ride to Les Eaux, Minnesota, is almost enough for Aria to second-guess the trip entirely. There aren't any other options, though. She isn't old enough to rent a car, she doesn't know anybody in the area, and none of the big-city shuttle services are even aware of Les Eaux. Her credit card will just have to suffer the consequences.

As the SUV parks in front of her, Aria lets out a shaky breath and taps her foot against the metal base of the light pole she's standing next to, its muted clang working overtime to ease her anxiety.

"Aria . . . Nuh-gwen? Riding to Les Eaux?" The driver rolls down his window, saying Aria's name more like it's a question. She nods with a grimace, and he gets out of the car to help her with the bag. It's been a while since she's heard that pronunciation of her last name. If Philip were here, he'd correct the guy. *It's pronounced "when."* That isn't actually correct, either, but it's closer than the driver's abomination.

Aria shakes off the smile that's formed from a memory of Philip before handing her bag to the driver. She vaguely hears Philip reprimanding her in the back of her brain, so she pauses to verify that the license plate matches what the app on her phone says.

Satisfied, Aria settles into the seat behind the driver. She taps the "share ride" button before she gets a text from Philip to do so. After Aria shares the ride information, Aunt Thu's name and contact photo appear on her phone screen for what seems like the billionth time.

"God . . . Again?"

"What was that?" her driver, allegedly named Tyler, asks.

"Oh, sorry. I'm talking to myself."

When Aria taps on the latest voicemail message Aunt Thu left, the AI transcription cobbles together a nonsense string of texts (presumably from trying to make sense of both the English and Vietnamese together). There is some text Aria *does* understand.

I forbid you. Come back home, now.

Aria turns off her phone screen and buries the device in her coat pocket. Whatever Aunt Thu has to say, Aria isn't ready to hear it.

"You're headed to Les Eaux, right? It's a long drive! Two hours."

Aria confirms Tyler has the correct information. She's also surprised to hear the city's name pronounced for the first time. *Lay Sooz*. It's decidedly un-French-sounding.

"Do you live in the area?" she asks. Usually, Aria enjoys quiet rides. But to avoid having to answer well-intentioned questions from her driver that might make her uncomfortable, she leads the conversation.

"Me? Oh yeah. Born and raised in Saint Paul!"

"Do you like it here?"

It triggers the exact reaction Aria is hoping for. Tyler tells her about a childhood in the suburbs and traveling to Spain for summers with his family. He mentions in passing something about his mom being controlling and his younger brothers being "brainwashed." Aria laughs at timed intervals to let Tyler know she's still listening. When she senses he's about to turn a question on to her, she diverts to something he said prior.

Aria wants to consume someone else's life instead of her own, like a movie or a trashy reality-television show. She wonders what life would feel like if she'd grown up like Tyler . . . an all-white American boy in an all-American middle-class suburb.

"Let me know if you want to change the music or anything. The drive to Les Eaux is boring. Why're you heading there, anyway?"

Crap. Aria missed her cue to divert Tyler, and she considers what the most effective answer to the question might be.

"I am . . . visiting a family member." It isn't technically a lie.

"Oh, really? All the way out there?" Tyler's response sounds genuinely surprised. Aria wonders how many Asian families live in the area.

"Do you know anything about the town?" Aria asks, trying to avoid a question about exactly *who* she is visiting.

"It's a weird place, for sure. The lake there is nice. Growing up, I thought it was for a bunch of rich old folks."

"Interesting . . ." Aria says. What's interesting is how Tyler says *rich*—as if snorkeling in the Mediterranean Sea, as he's done, isn't a rich-person activity. "What makes you say it's weird?"

For the first time during the car ride, Tyler is silent.

". . . Is everything okay?"

"Yeah! Sorry, my mind wandered a bit . . ." he says sheepishly as he makes a right turn. "Les Eaux . . . How do I put this? I've heard plenty of strange stories about the place is all."

"Strange stories? Care to elaborate?"

"Uh-huh. There's a camp there that some of my friends used to go to. Typical summer camp for kids, except *real* fancy. There were all these stories of drownings and ghosts . . . creepy crawlers stalking the water to grab kids like some Jason Voorhees shit." Tyler laughs.

Drownings. Aria swallows, and for a brutal nanosecond, she imagines her mom floating in the water. Before the image can fully come to life, she rolls down the window and chokes on a blast of frigid air.

"Whoa, you all right back there?"

"I'm fine. There was . . . a bug," Aria says, rolling up the window and hoping Tyler doesn't try and check her absurd lie.

"Anyways, I always thought they were just stories. But a camp counselor drowned in Lake Agatha last year." Tyler ends with another uncomfortable laugh. "Sorry! They're only stories. Well, except for the camp counselor. She did die. Ha. Not that dying is funny . . ."

"Don't worry about it," Aria says at the snafu. She relaxes into the back seat, focusing on Tyler's bobbing brown hair in front of her.

"So . . . do you have a boyfriend?"

"Oh. No," Aria says, startled. For a second, Philip's face flashes in her mind. But that's odd, because they're just friends.

"Cool, cool. Well, if you end up having some free time, my buddies and I are going to try to do a hangout soon. We could even stop by Les Eaux . . . Like I said, Lake Agatha's nice. If it were warmer, I'd take you for a swim."

"I can't swim."

"Can't swim?" Tyler sounds horrified.

"No. I also don't take baths or do boat activities. Water scares me. Also, you spent ten minutes talking about people drowning in that lake," Aria says, amused at how flustered Tyler is. She would usually say no without a second thought . . . but the attention is a welcome distraction from the god-awful purpose of this trip.

"Yeah, I know. But I mean . . . Ugh." Tyler groans before Aria interrupts.

"I'll think about it. You're a strong swimmer, right? You could save me."

Tyler visibly straightens in the seat in front of Aria. He goes on to regale Aria with a tale of losing his life vest while sailing with his dad and getting tangled in a bunch of seaweed but emerging triumphant.

Aria listens to him, hmming and aahing to hide the fact that her mind is elsewhere.

She keeps thinking about the water, what it's taken, and how she's going straight toward it.

♊

The police station is up ahead, appearing around a curve in the road. Les Eaux is a tiny town, and they've already passed the densest part of it: a main street filled with colorful shops and quaint Prairie-style homes straight out of a Hallmark movie. Aria started pretending to be asleep about thirty minutes into the two-hour drive, and Tyler obliged with his silence, then turned on some very experimental rock music.

Eventually, the SUV rolls to a stop in the police station parking lot. Aria makes a show of waking up by stretching and yawning. Sliding her phone into the water bottle holder of her backpack, Aria opens the car door.

Tyler gets out of the car to help with her luggage. He moves slowly, and it occurs to Aria that he's stalling.

"Would it be okay if I get your number?"

"Sure," Aria says, although she normally says the opposite. Tyler smiles, and his shaggy mop of brown hair bounces as he moves to haul her suitcase out.

In the face of the unknown, her *sure* is almost cathartic. She pulls her phone out of her coat to send a message through the app's messaging portal.

Your Ride with Tyler

> Hi, this is Aria. Here's my contact info.

The trunk of Tyler's car shuts, and Aria watches him pull up the handle of her suitcase.

"Thanks," Aria says, avoiding his gaze as she reaches for the handle.

"Of course. Stay safe, and I'll text ya for our swimming lessons later," Tyler says, winking at the joke, and Aria fakes a laugh.

When he shuts the driver's-side door, the force kicks up wet dirt and a splatter of snow. Aria coughs, dragging her suitcase behind her as she heads over to the police station's entrance. When Aria enters the station, the pale and otherwise uninteresting face of a young, smiling clerk appears. The woman opens her mouth as if to greet Aria, but the smile falls almost immediately.

"Miss, uh. Miss Aria Nguyen . . ." the girl stammers.

"Yes. Aren't you expecting me?" Aria asks, too tired to put on an act. "I'm here to talk to Officer Badiou about Xuân, my m— I mean my aunt."

"R-right. To see your aunt. Your cousin? Wait . . . Oh my god . . ."

"Cousin? What are you talking about?" Aria asks. She pulls back the hood of her jacket and turns away from the stammering clerk.

Then she notices what—or rather, *who*—is causing this woman to act like she's seen a ghost.

Seated on a dingy green love seat in the lobby's corner is a nondescript brunette man who Aria assumes is Officer Badiou. And seated next to him is a girl. A girl Aria recognizes instantly as an uncanny Valley girl version of herself. If Aria weren't still standing near the clerk, she'd think she was sitting next to Officer Badiou.

After several stinging seconds of silence, the man stands and finally speaks.

"You . . . do know each other, don't you? You're . . . cousins?"

"No. I don't. She's not my cousin. What the hell is going on?" Not-Aria says loudly, her eyes—Aria's eyes—staring directly at Aria.

"This makes things complicated," Officer Badiou mutters, and his clerk quips a helpful "Ya think?"

Not-Aria stands, striding toward Aria without breaking eye contact. This girl is a version of Aria, one she's pictured in her dreams, a version who exercises, who has nice skin and shiny hair. A version of Aria that must be a maladaptive daydream taunting her. But, no, this girl is very real and getting closer. Aria can't begin to comprehend how, though.

Aria can hear her own heart beating clearly, a ringing thump in her ears. Wait—is it her heart? Or this stranger's? As Aria freezes, working through the tenuous net of confusion in her mind, Not-Aria finally reaches her.

"You. You . . ." she whispers. Then Aria's look-alike hugs her, her long manicured fingernails piercing Aria's sides. Not-Aria is crying, and now so is the real Aria.

Twins. We are twins.

July 17

LES EAUX, Minn.—Authorities are investigating the drowning of 19-year-old Riley Cochran at Lake Agatha. According to the Les Eaux Police Department, Cochran left the cabin she shared with campers at Camp Griffon at 4:21 a.m. on Tuesday and failed to return.

Responding personnel immediately began a search of Lake Agatha and the nearby Les Eaux Slough, where Cochran's backpack was found and articles of clothing had washed ashore. Recovery efforts were called off late Thursday evening as a storm front moved into the area. Her death has been ruled an accidental drowning.

Cochran's death is the latest in a recent string of Lake Agatha drownings, reminiscent of the series of drownings that occurred over a decade ago. Some Les Eaux citizens are suspicious: Are the drownings truly accidental, or are they the result of something sinister? Cochran was on the women's swimming and diving roster at the University of Minnesota, fueling skepticism that her drowning was an accident.

At a town hall, Officer Gordon Badiou addressed the skepticism: "This is a moment of particular pain, and I empathize greatly with those who've been affected. However, I advise the public to avoid groundless speculation. The Cochran family deserves time to grieve quietly."

The string of drownings in Les Eaux prompted long-time town patriarch Eric Hane to address Les Eaux residents in the recent town hall via video call. He emphasized a renewed commitment to increasing the safety of the area with a $20 million gift to the Les Eaux Water and Recreation Committee.

CHAPTER NINE

Caliste

Caliste has always been sure of her place as the unwanted daughter of House Hà and its empire. It isn't an irrational thought; both her grandmother and her dad have always treated her with the same barely guarded irritation. Caliste isn't unreasonable or prone to flights of fancy. But this feeling of being an outsider . . . it was *intuition*.

That instinct is now in her arms, evidence validating the sneaking suspicion that her father has always resented her. He kept the wrong daughter. The girl before her, the one who looks identical to her, might've been a better fit. This girl—who has, until this very moment, lived an entirely different life from Caliste's—is her sister.

Her family.

And that means one of them was chosen over the other. Or perhaps this sentiment applied to them both. The thought makes Caliste's insides tangle into knots.

"So . . . you are positive you don't know each other?" the harebrained officer interrupts, and Caliste has to pry herself off the other girl to retort.

"Are we acting like two people who know each other?" she snaps, the snot and tears on her face causing her to make an ugly snorting sound. Her hands linger around the other girl's shoulders protectively. The other version of herself is rigid and robotic, but Caliste is too overcome by the thunderous heartbeat in her chest to realize she might be overstepping this stranger's boundaries.

"I've never met her. And we're not cousins. Thu Nguyễn is my aunt; I call her my mom because it's easier. She adopted me," the other girl says meekly, as if she's the one at fault.

Officer Badiou's face alights with an ambiguous expression, and he shakes his head. "No . . . you're right. I'm sorry. Gosh . . . Well. Have a seat. Do you want coffee or tea?"

Caliste imagines what kind of watered-down beverage this station might deign to call "coffee" and promptly replies, "Tea, please."

At the same moment, so does the other girl. The two glance at each other, and Caliste offers a small smile.

"Your name?"

"Aria," she says, her voice setting the hairs on Caliste's arms upright. It's Caliste's own voice but firmer, somehow. She even sounds more mature.

"That's pretty. My name is Caliste."

Aria's face screws up, and Caliste is worried she's offended the other girl already.

"Oh. I . . . Never mind," Aria says.

"What is it? Are you okay?" Caliste can't tell whether Aria is nervous or afraid.

"Let's . . . sit."

The two perch in the lobby seats where Caliste was sitting with Officer Badiou before. She and Aria answer an inane series of questions about their flights—small talk about the narrow plane seats and the stale air of the airport. Caliste asks why the station has only two people, and Officer Badiou explains that everybody else is working security for a local event. Caliste wants to be annoyed with him, but she truthfully doesn't know what sort of talk might be appropriate for the occasion. It isn't as if he's going to open with her dead mom.

Aria and Caliste sit opposite each other now, their bodies like fun-house mirrors. Caliste says nothing, unnerved by Aria's earlier reaction. It's perfectly and awkwardly silent except for the white noise of Officer Badiou and the clerk whispering loudly. The sound of Caliste's pulse fades behind the teakettle hissing awake.

"When's your birthday?" Caliste asks, breaking the silence.

"May first. What about you?"

"May second . . ." Caliste replies.

Huh.

"Ariadne is my name, by the way."

"What?" Caliste asks, startled as Aria changes topic. Her gaze breaks from the two people attempting to hide their own stares to look at Aria. The girl seems to be more at ease now, sitting up straight and leaning toward Caliste expectantly.

"My first name is actually Ariadne. I mean, it's the name I was born with. But no one calls me that. I've always gone by Aria. My aunt can't even pronounce my full name." She scoffs and starts chewing on her lip, a bad habit Caliste recognizes in herself.

Caliste opens her mouth to reply, but she hasn't formed a complete thought yet.

"My name comes from the story of the Minotaur. It's Greek. I always thought it was weird. What Việt immigrants name their kid after a Greek myth?" Aria prattles on, her nerves evident in the speed of her words.

"I . . . My—I mean, our mom named me, I think. She wanted me to be beautiful. *Caliste.* Although, in Greek myth, Zeus assaults Callisto because he's obsessed with her beauty." Caliste repeats the information like a fact from a history book. "And Ariadne means . . . ?"

" 'Holy.' It means 'holy,' " Aria replies, her eyes drifting to stare somewhere near Caliste's feet. "Did you know? Do you know . . . Crap."

Caliste stifles a laugh as Aria curses and throws her head into her hands.

"I'm sorry. I flew out at the ass crack of dawn, and I'm only vaguely sure I'm not hallucinating," Aria adds.

"I get it," Caliste says, taking her sister's hand. Her *twin's* hand. "I . . . had no clue. I don't know what's going on, but I need to ask my dad."

"Wait, your dad? He's still alive?" There is desperation in Aria's voice.

Caliste's mouth falls agape again. "Er, yeah. I . . ." She's unsure how to proceed, mostly because she still has no clue what the hell is going on.

In that moment, Aria's phone buzzes, and Caliste is silently grateful for the interruption.

The reprieve is short-lived. Aria glances down at her phone screen before quickly shutting off the display.

"Is it important?" Caliste asks.

"Not really," Aria says. "It's a party invitation."

Caliste suddenly recalls Paul's constant refrain, a phrase that's always haunted her.

You look just like her.

Up until now, Caliste always assumed he meant she looked like her mother. But did Paul mean Aria?

"Hold on a minute, sorry," Caliste blurts, standing up and dropping Aria's hand. "I need to talk to my dad."

There was a reason for Paul's peculiar mix of care and anxiety before he sent Caliste off. And that reason must've been about her potentially meeting Aria for the first time. He must've known their aunt—Thu, was it?—would be notified about Grace's body, too.

She lets the creaky door of the station swing behind her as she races over to the Mercedes-Benz SUV that Ha Foods Corporate arranged for her. The dusty kick-up from the country roads has already marred the sleek sheen of the car. She slides into the leather seat and counts to calm herself down, thinking hard about what words she'll say to her father first as she turns on the car. As the dashboard's backlight flashes, an endless thread of questions weaves through Caliste's mind.

Is Aria my twin sister?

Why were we separated?

Why did you never mention her?

Do you not care about your whole other child?

What else aren't you telling me?

Does Priscilla know? Grandma? How many people maintained the lie?

Each question prompts a new one, and the waterfall of queries makes Caliste queasy.

The SUV's Bluetooth connection rings, loud in the empty vehicle. Caliste fully expects her father not to pick up.

Guilt must have gotten to him.

"Hello? Cali? Did you land?"

". . . Yes, Ba. I left the airport already."

"Good. Good . . ." He sounds tired, and Caliste can picture him sitting at his desk, brow furrowed, a drink surreptitiously balanced on his knee.

"I have a question, Ba, and I need you to answer it honestly." The word for *father* rolls off her tongue, its weight different from ever before.

"Yes?"

"Is there something you need to tell me?"

"Hah. Don't be cryptic."

"Ba. There is a girl here."

"I . . ."

It's that single syllable, that single breathy and astounded vowel, that reveals everything to Caliste. He knew. Paul knew. He knew and was never going to tell her.

"She's there? I thought Thu was . . ."

"Thu? Her aunt? Sorry, I mean *our* aunt? Ba, what the hell?"

"Stay put. I'm coming. Christ . . . I should never have listened to her."

"What? Ba? What is going on? Who's 'her'?" Caliste yells. The defeated tone of Paul's voice is making her angry. But before she gets another word out, the line is dead.

"You have to be kidding me. Always on his terms. Always."

Without thinking, she slams her fists into the wheel, and the SUV's horn shrieks, startling her so badly that she doesn't realize Aria has left the station and is approaching her.

Caliste's face is hot, and her heart rattles in her chest. *Calm down.* When she glances out the window, something about Aria's face appearing relaxes her.

"You all right?"

"Yeah, I'm fine. My dad . . . He's coming. He wouldn't answer any questions over the phone."

"Figures. My aunt didn't pick up at all," Aria says, her voice deflated. Caliste can't read the expression she wears.

"The detective or cop, whatever—he told us we should take a break for today. He's going to review the files."

"We can't go see her now?" Caliste asks, processing each piece of information one by one. The undersides of her palms are slick with sweat, and she's concentrating hard on not letting her emotions overwhelm her.

"No . . . He claimed it's protocol, but I'm not sure. They want to get their facts straight before they have us identify her body." Aria is grimacing as she says this.

"Right," Caliste says dryly. "As if the answer to what the hell happened is hidden in some files."

Aria laughs meekly before her gaze darts around the interior of the SUV again. "Is this your car? You're not allowed to rent here, are you?"

"Oh . . . no. This isn't my car. It's, like, a company car. My dad arranged it for me."

"I see . . . Well, have you found a hotel nearby?"

"Ugh . . . yes," Caliste replies. She'd tried to find at least a three-star hotel, but the only place in town is a quaint Victorian inn right by the river.

"Would it be weird if we stayed together? Not in the same room or anything!" Aria interjects, waving her hands frantically. "I mean, it would be nice. To . . . maybe stay at the same place?"

"Yeah. It would be," Caliste replies, cracking a smile. Nothing made more sense.

Aria is her sister. She has never been more relieved to meet a stranger in her life.

♊

Aria

Aria sits in Caliste's passenger seat, acutely aware of the silence and how clean the car's interior smells. The car looks brand-new, and the soft scent of lemon and rosemary gives off the air of a very fancy spa. As Caliste drives, Aria takes the opportunity to cyberstalk her sister. One earphone in, of course, so she can still hear Caliste.

Cali Hà is pretty, fit, and perfect. She executes burpees as if training to be in some superhero movie. Her following is big but not too out of control. When she speaks to her audience, she's commanding but sweet. She's posted collaborations with Adidas and Lululemon. It surprises Aria that no one in her life has ever stumbled across Caliste's page. But Aria remembers she has a barely used account and follows exactly twelve people—Philip and a myriad of DC-area foodies. Anonymous. Invisible. Aria is a background character, and Caliste is not.

Thankfully the ride is short, so Aria doesn't stew too long in her insecurity. It takes a few turns down brick roads before the Victorian inn appears, flanked by beautiful aged hemlock trees. The place has some charm to it. The siding is a rosy mauve with ornate marigold yellow trim and an emerald front-facing gable. Aria imagines herself lounging at the base of a tree and reading a pulpy period romance, pretending to be a girl in a poufy Regency-era dress being pursued by some gentleman.

"Ick," Caliste says, cutting off the car and glancing at the inn with an ambivalent expression.

"I think it's cute," Aria says as she opens the SUV's passenger door. She's surprised to hear the subdued babble of water.

"Let me guess: You also think scraggly little dogs are cute?"

"Of course I do," Aria replies, suddenly thinking of Sir Barkley van Floof—and Philip. Shaking her head, Aria accepts her suitcase, which Caliste effortlessly dislodged from the trunk.

Once they walk up the stairs of the wraparound porch, Aria spots a heavy, engraved metal sign:

THE INN AT AGATHA CREEK
BUILT 1893 IN THE QUEEN ANNE STYLE

The aforementioned creek seems to curve around the inn's back and to the right of the porch before entering a shielded cluster of trees. The water level is low, with mud-slicked banks reaching several feet on each side of the creek. A decent number of local hikers must come by, as a well-worn dirt path follows the creek into the woods.

They enter a parlor with rosy floral wallpaper and dark wooden furniture that appear to be straight from some period drama. The floor is a faded orange tone and made from walnut wood, with an elaborate interlocking parquet pattern. Luxurious fabrics are everywhere—there's a pale blue-and-gold rug and eggshell-colored velvet curtains, and dainty layers of lace are draped over various horizontal surfaces. It's faded in a regal way—not in the way Aria and Aunt Thu's house is faded.

Quietly, Aria walks behind her sister, watching her gait and how she moves. They wait in front of a long reception. An older woman has her back turned to them as she chats on the phone. Once the woman hangs up, Caliste easily greets her. Aria studies Caliste, who's talking with her back arched and her polished almond nails tapping the handle of her luggage. The bag is a matte black and was soundless as it wheeled across the floor, a stark difference from the high-pitched squealing of Aria's.

The innkeeper is typing into her keyboard, each of her index fingers punching one key at a time. The badge hanging from her mauve cable-knit sweater reads ROSE LAWRENCE - INNKEEPER. If Aria had to suddenly conjure up a name for an old lady who owned a Victorian inn, she'd probably guess something like *Rose* or *Violet*. If Aria weren't so exhausted, she might find it funny that the old lady checking them into this inn's name is indeed Rose.

"There must be another bedroom available. It's a Wednesday, for god's sake."

Aria's coat pocket vibrates, and she swallows. *Is it Aunt Thu?* However, when she fetches her phone, the cracked screen flashes with Philip's name instead.

"Excuse me for a sec."

Caliste nods, watching as Aria walks toward a glass tulip lamp in the parlor's corner. Aria still can't get over how strange it is to be perceived by this alternate-reality version of herself.

"Hey. Philip?"

"Hi, Ari. How're you holding up?"

"It's . . . a lot. We're checking into an inn now."

"We?" Philip asks.

Aria doesn't know how to respond. It's a lot to fit into one sentence.

"I met a girl here . . . She's my twin sister. It's complicated. What's up?"

There's a heavy pause, and Philip's sharp inhale on the other end of the phone triggers a snarl of anxiety in Aria's throat. He's not pressing her for more information, which he would otherwise do *immediately*.

"What's the matter? Did something happen?" she asks.

"It's all under control."

"What's under control?!"

"I had to take Aunt Thu to the hospital again . . . She was acting pretty weird when I stopped by to help with her evening meds. It looks like another infection, but they're running additional tests. She's sleeping now."

"When did you take her?"

"I don't know . . . about three hours ago?"

"Three hours?! Why didn't you say—"

"She told me not to tell you. You're dealing with enough as it is . . ."

Philip knows only a fraction of what she's dealing with. But Aunt Thu? Aunt Thu knows. She knows the whole story. No wonder she was frantically trying to stop Aria from coming here at first.

"Okay. Yeah. Thanks for telling me. Keep me updated, okay?"

"Of course. We've been through this before. She'll be fine."

Aria nods, focusing on Philip's voice. *Fine. Fine. It has to be. It will be.*

"Did she . . . say anything about me coming out here? She called me like a dozen times when I was on the plane. I'm not surprised that literally getting sick again is the only thing that stopped her."

"No. Not to me. It's creepy. I've never seen her so quiet."

Aria thinks back to the night she overheard Aunt Thu sobbing, then shakes off the memory. Logically she knows she didn't *cause* her aunt's infection. But there's a nagging guilt Aria can't ignore.

I hate you. She'd said those words to Aunt Thu. But Aria can't afford to feel guilty.

Philip's voice drops, startling Aria.

"Hey. You'll be all right, too. Do you hear me?"

"Mmm-hmm."

"Nope, not good enough. A full sentence, please."

"I heard you. But the same goes for you. I feel like I'm asking you to do, like, twenty million things for me."

"You'll just owe me twenty million and one things."

Aria can almost hear Philip wink through his voice.

"Thank you for everything," Aria says before hanging up. When she returns to Caliste, the other girl is looking at her with an eyebrow raised.

"You okay?"

"Yes. I mean, no. Kind of. My aunt's in the hospital again. It's probably a urinary tract infection that's gotten bad, but it's happened before . . . She'll probably get antibiotics pumped into her and be sent home after a few tests." Aria feigns a carefree attitude, too afraid yet to show this girl her true self. In the dark of her mind flashes the night when Aunt Thu battled sepsis.

Caliste nods, squeezing Aria's upper arm before turning back to Rose. Finally, after clicking through what can only be a booking system from the 1990s, the woman peers at Aria and Caliste with an apologetic expression.

"I'm sorry, miss. Nearly three-quarters of our rooms are undergoing renovation, and the rest are booked. Your suite is the only room available."

"Right . . ." Caliste says, and Aria senses the disbelief in her voice. She turns suddenly toward Aria and asks, "Do you want to share a bed? It's a king."

"I don't mind," Aria responds, managing a weak smile. Panicked, she takes a subtle whiff of her underarm. God, she stinks. A shower is definitely needed before she tortures Caliste with her stench.

Soon old brass keys are in Caliste's hands and they are trudging up a creaking staircase to the guest floor. The staircase connects to a landing, where it splits into two symmetrical flights. It's the kind of staircase Aria's seen only in movies or textbooks. Her bag makes loud thudding noises as she drags it upward, cursing silently so Caliste won't notice her struggling.

"Here, let me get it."

Before Aria can protest, Caliste's taken her suitcase in her other hand and is marching up the steps with ease. Despite the thick burgundy cardigan Caliste's wearing, Aria can see the contours of Caliste's biceps and shoulders. They are muscles Aria thought were fictional until now. She glances down at her own nonexistent biceps and flexes involuntarily. When Aria catches herself, she glances up quickly to make sure Caliste didn't see.

"Do you work out a lot?" Aria asks.

"Uh-huh . . . It's kind of my job." Caliste doesn't sound even a little out of breath.

"Job? Are you a trainer?"

"Ha," Caliste barks, her voice hitching ever so slightly. The fact that she is exerting some amount of effort makes Aria feel better. "No. I'm an influencer, I guess. I do beauty and fitness stuff. I promote protein shakes and waterproof mascara. It's fun."

Aria's struck again by Caliste's openness and honesty. Every sentence is uttered without a single shred of self-deprecation.

Their suite is at the end of a hall, and Aria winces as their steps creak loudly on the polished parquet floors. She stares at the back of Caliste's shiny head and perfectly voluminous ponytail, peering over her shoulder as the keys rattle.

Like a critter skulking about in the night, the ugliness returns, and a thought is laid bare in her mind.

Once, certainly, Aria and Caliste had been the same. Equal. Given the same capacity to live similar lives. Then something or someone shifted gears, their paths diverged, and now they live two entirely different lives. Ones in which Caliste gets luxury SUVs and biceps and Aria gets a mountain of debt and a potential expulsion on her record.

In this moment, gazing at shiny hair and a life that could've been hers, Aria resents her sister without fully knowing her.

CHAPTER TEN

Aria

"You have so much crap," Aria says, slouching against the head-board and watching the contents of Caliste's overturned suitcase pile atop the ivory rug at the foot of the bedroom's sole armchair.

Aria's never stayed in a hotel suite before and is overwhelmed by how much space it has. After the door swung open, it took a second for Aria to register that she was staring at a living room and that the bedroom was behind an entirely different door across the way. Aria offered to sleep on the couch in the living room instead of in the same bed as Caliste but was quickly re-buffed. Now that they're settled, it occurs to Aria that Caliste is unfazed by their lavish lodgings.

"Yes? Your point?"

"I don't have one."

"Then zip it," Caliste replies, her long nails clicking as she does a zipping motion across her lips.

Everything's strange. Including the fact that Aria has spent the past six hours with her long-lost identical twin, not one other thing that's happened makes any sense. Aunt Thu still isn't answering the phone or returning calls despite knowing about Aria's journey to Les Eaux. Philip had texted that Aunt Thu was awake and fine when he dropped off some soup from Mrs. Kim. Even though Aria prepared and practiced a speech to ask about Caliste, she lost her nerve and told Philip not to say anything to her aunt. Aria thought she was ready for the truth, but as always, she's not sure.

Although all Aria has are guesses, Caliste must be the reason Aunt Thu was so insistent that they come here together. Would Aunt Thu have told Aria on the plane ride over that she's been lying for years? And her silence now . . . Could it mean that Aunt Thu is embarrassed or ignoring Aria altogether?

Aria suppresses a nagging feeling in her gut and focuses instead on the mess that is Caliste sorting through her things. Aria recognizes most of it as high-end skincare and luxury makeup brands (she's only recently learned that a jar of face cream can cost *more* than her senior prom dress).

"You're rich," Aria says, deciding to be up-front. Caliste isn't just anybody. She's her sister.

"I mean, yes. That's accurate," Caliste replies, not hesitating as she untangles what appears to be a wad of belts before dropping them in her lap and looking up toward Aria. "My . . . family is ridiculous, and so is my life. I'm not clueless enough not to realize that most people don't live like I do."

"So you admit that you might be a little clueless?" Aria teases, avoiding Caliste's eyes. Could she share her life, including the messy parts and the parts she's hidden from the world? Straight-A student and scammer. Would Caliste judge her?

"You're from DC, right? Do you ever go to Ha Mart?"

". . . Yes?"

125

"Hà. Caliste Hà. That's Dad's company," Caliste says flatly. When Aria looks at Caliste, she's thankfully back to organizing her things.

"Oh. So you're *rich* rich," Aria says, teasing again to hide her discomfort. Caliste's dropped the "my" while discussing her dad and family. The unspoken truth floats between them. Is Caliste's family now Aria's family? Can you be family if you don't even know each other?

"As opposed to just rich?"

"Yes, that's like a doctor's family."

"And what's more than two *rich*es? Rich enough to send a phallic rocket into the sky?"

"No, that's at least five *rich*es," Aria replies.

Caliste laughs. "Fine, I am *rich* rich. But it's not like Dad invests in tech companies and splurges on mega yachts."

"What does your family splurge on?" Aria asks, imagining what this father figure might look like. She realizes she can search on her phone and makes a mental note to do so when Caliste isn't watching.

"Dad doesn't buy much for himself. It's mostly for my stepmom and their son, Dylan. She's been on a Chanel kick lately. Oh, and trauma."

Aria snorts, and Caliste smiles.

"Now that you've learned about me, what about you? What's your latest splurge?"

"Splurge?" Aria asks, her voice attempting to mimic Caliste's coolness and nonchalance. It's a voice she's always practiced for meeting clients but never perfected. For a moment, Aria thinks she should provide a polite and decidedly *fake* answer. But looking into her sister's eyes, Aria decides she can't lie. Caliste must be as curious as Aria. What type of life has existed parallel to Caliste's for the past eighteen years?

Right. Aria is going with the honest answer.

"I guess . . . the dress I wore to graduation."

"Ooh. I love a good dress. What did it look like?" Caliste asks.

Aria leans over the side of the bed and anchors herself to a velvet pillow, clutching it to her chest. She steadies her breath as she eyes Caliste with her peripheral vision. Caliste's elbows are propped up on her knees, and she's staring intently in Aria's direction. Her interest is so forthcoming, it frightens Aria.

"We don't . . . have a ton of money. My—our—aunt is on disability and had to retire when I was in middle school." Aria glances up, but Caliste's expression is unchanging. "I saw this dress once at Bloomingdale's and became obsessed with it. I waited for it to go on sale . . . like . . . no-returns sale. Then I bought it."

"Can I see it?"

"Sure." Aria pulls up the browser on her phone and taps the bookmark she'd saved. The dress ends at the model's knees and is architectural and flouncy in design. It's a bright shade of green and very attention-grabbing—a design that's decidedly *not* in Aria's comfort zone.

"Pretty!" Caliste exclaims, taking Aria's phone and squinting at the screen. "Mac Duggal. Very nice. Do you have any pictures from graduation?"

"Uh . . ." Aria's voice falters. The only photos Aria has are blurry ones they took at home with Aunt Thu's phone. Their old Camry broke down en route to graduation, and Aria missed the entire ceremony. Thinking about it now still fills Aria with an acute sense of embarrassment.

Caliste seems to sense something is off, and she pivots. "Anyway, the green must've been gorgeous on you."

"Really? I thought it was a little . . . I don't know . . . edgy. For me, that is."

"No way!" Caliste says, nearly thrusting the phone into Aria's chest. "You must be a little edgy for you to like it so much, right?"

"Ah . . ." Aria pauses, recalling the afternoon navigating Tysons Corner Center with Philip for Mrs. Kim's birthday present.

This color would be pretty on you, Ari.

Did Aria like green, or had she only wanted Philip to see her as pretty?

"I guess," Aria says finally.

Caliste doesn't challenge her nonanswer. "Well, I'm excited to see you wear it. We can have a fancy dinner to celebrate."

"Celebrate? I already graduated."

"And I wasn't there for it. Plus, I *also* graduated. There's, like, a million joint celebrations we need to catch up on. I'm already planning your next graduation party, and you can't stop me."

Caliste's playful laugh rings between them, and Aria inhales, tempted for a nanosecond to correct her sister: *if* she graduates from college. Her mind wanders to the email from Georgetown.

She might not graduate. She might fail to make any part of her mother's and Aunt Thu's story worth the sacrifice; Aunt Thu's entire life revolves around Aria's future success. An airplane ride from Vietnam. A flooded house. A daughter/niece who can't get her life together.

"Are you okay?" Caliste asks, noticing that Aria's gone quiet. She appears concerned.

"I'm tired. Let's get ready for bed." Aria stands to turn toward the window and away from Caliste. She's about to cry, and it's far too soon to let her sister know she's a mess.

♊

There's an incessant knocking on the door. Blinking, Aria sits up.

"I said, just a minute!" Caliste yells from the bathroom before rushing out with a plush lavender robe draped around her body. Aria's still registering where she is and who she's with. As she rubs the crusted sleep from her eyes, she watches Caliste stride toward the door.

"Yes, hello?" Caliste asks after opening the door. From the bed, Aria can't see who stands in the doorway.

"I'm sorry to bother you, miss. But an officer is waiting downstairs for you." The voice belongs to the innkeeper, Rose. Her tone is more solemn than serious.

"Fine. Tell him I'll be down in a minute."

Caliste shuts the door and turns toward Aria with an eye roll.

"Oh, you're awake? You were sleeping like a log."

"I'm up . . ." Aria mumbles, finally mustering enough cognitive function to untangle her legs from the bedsheets and slide out. "Is this a fitness thing? Waking up so early?"

"It's not early. It's almost nine," Caliste says.

"That's early," Aria retorts and drags herself to the bathroom. The swirled marble counter is littered with travel-size bottles and an array of makeup tubes and brushes. "Did you bring your entire bathroom here? Jesus Christ."

"Yes, yes, mock the influencer for how much stuff she has. Very original. I'm done. I'll clear some room."

129

"I don't need any space. I'm just brushing my teeth," Aria mutters, grabbing her teal toothbrush from its place next to Caliste's pink one.

Caliste juts out her elbow, shoving everything on the countertop into an open cream-colored tote bag on the floor. Aria flinches, watching a bottle of Chanel perfume and a jar of La Mer face cream fall with a reckless *ka-thunk*. Before the moment fully registers, Caliste's already dragging the bag away, staying true to her words and clearing out. The near meekness in her movement's almost enough to distract Aria from the differences between them. Almost.

She turns to stare at her reflection instead of dwelling on the discomfort she's feeling, but what stares back at her is just as disconcerting. Aria looks like some crypt keeper from a horror movie. The space under her eyes is hollow and dark, the skin swollen and textured like that of overripe fruit.

"I have some undereye patches. But, like, only if you want some," Caliste says from behind, startling Aria. Her sister stands next to her, studying Aria in the mirror as intently as Aria's watching herself.

"Are you saying I need them?" Aria replies through a mouthful of Oral-B and toothbrush bristles.

"I mean, yeah. A little," Caliste responds easily, a fledgling smile inching onto her face.

"Hey, don't make me fight you." Aria turns to elbow Caliste, but Caliste is too fast, cackling as she darts out of the bathroom. The scent of her perfume, a soft citrus, lingers. As with their mom's plum blossom, Aria finds her sister's scent comforting.

♊

Officer Badiou is seated on a merlot-colored sofa and flipping through an old *Town & Country* magazine when Caliste and Aria finally make it to the inn's parlor. Once he sees them, he stands abruptly and offers an uncomfortable wave.

Aria didn't get a good look at him yesterday, mostly because she was so surprised by Caliste and the entire mess of the situation. Officer Badiou is middle-aged and stocky, with a brunette buzz cut, a square face, and a beard shaved close to his face. All the folds of his uniform are meticulously pressed, which is a little bit surprising considering his clumsy way of doing things. He seems like a man who commands authority (and Aria thinks, a man Aunt Thu would say is đẹp trai, though, to be fair, Aunt Thu tends to think all men in uniform are handsome).

"Good morning, ladies. Did you sleep well?"

"I suppose," Caliste says, her voice drawing out that last syllable as she crosses her arms. It's an honest but leisured answer—a sharp distinction to Officer Badiou's cheerfulness. Caliste doesn't seem the type to deal in habitual niceties.

The officer seems taken aback but quickly regains composure. "I apologize for disturbing you this morning, but I'm afraid I won't be able to talk to you about the investigation today."

"What do you mean?" Aria asks. "Isn't the whole reason we couldn't see her yesterday because you were going to get your facts straight?"

"Well. Yes. I was able to speak with your father, Paul," Officer Badiou says, addressing Caliste. However, he quickly averts eye contact and fusses with the left breast pocket of his coat. Aria admires Caliste's ability to scare grown men.

"And what did my father say?"

"He verified that you two are twins. He will be taking a red-eye flight and arriving early tomorrow morning. He asked me to wait until he arrives to take you to see your mother."

"We're here now. Don't we get to see her first?" Caliste asks, her arms folded. She may be staring up at Officer Badiou, but her glare is making this man shrivel.

"I'm very sorry, to both of you. He's next of kin and, as Xuan's spouse, the first point of contact. We can't go against his wishes."

Officer Badiou's explanation draws a sharp huff of irritation from Caliste.

"Well, do we at least get to know her official cause of death? You said she drowned?" Caliste asks.

Officer Badiou's face tenses before he nods.

"Unfortunately, yes. Xuan drowned." He pauses. "Take it easy, girls. I know this must be real hard for you. Your father will meet us at the station around eight a.m. tomorrow, so I'll see you then."

Caliste sighs. "Thanks for the update. Good luck with the investigation, or whatever."

When he leaves, Caliste turns to Aria.

"Are you okay? You sounded kind of stressed."

"I . . ." Aria considers lying. Just then, she receives a text from Tyler—an invitation. The drownings . . . Their mom. Could it all be related to Tyler's camp stories?

"I have an idea of how to kill time today," Aria says finally. She takes both Caliste's hands in hers and does her best impression of her sister.

"What?"

"We're going to put on cute outfits and go to a party."

It *is* a pretty absurd statement, all things considered, and Aria half expects Caliste to reject her at first.

"Okay," Caliste says. A bewildered expression on her face says she has no idea what's going on. Maybe it's the sleep deprivation of the past few nights, but Aria laughs. Soon Caliste joins in. The sound is odd. Is this what Aria sounds like to others?

And despite everything . . . Aria can't help but believe she's found a treasure on this cursed trip to the place where their mother died.

CHAPTER ELEVEN

Caliste

Not one single fiber in Caliste's body expected the present scenario. She sits, legs crossed, on a wooden pier overlooking an expansive lake. A few feet away, standing in dirt, is a cluster of teens she met exactly thirty minutes ago. They are crowded around a firepit, attempting in vain to keep a flame alive. It's afternoon, and while the sun is well on its way to the other side of the world, it's hidden behind a dense overhang of gray clouds. Caliste breathes out, the cold air condensing in a weak cloud in front of her. Apparently, the temperature is warmer than usual and it's "good weather" for a party. Caliste finds it hard to agree as she nestles her chilled fingers between her thighs.

Aria sits next to her, close enough for her breath to snake through the air and join Caliste's. After returning to their room at the inn and getting ready, Aria explained that her extroverted driver sent an invitation to hang out by Lake Agatha. This boy—Tyler—had spoken to Aria of death and drama, which, naturally, spiked Caliste's curiosity.

The Aria in the current moment is a new version from the one Caliste met yesterday. Her shoulder-length hair is curled (Caliste's doing) and now falls in gentle waves to her chin. In contrast to Caliste's cinnamon-red balayage highlights, Aria's hair has never been dyed, so her black hair shines with a neutral blue tint in the sun. She only accepted minimal makeup assistance from Caliste; the compromise was a silvery eye shadow and brown liner. She's beautiful. (Is it egotistical for Caliste to think that? Probably.)

But, aside from aesthetics, *this* Aria is on a mission. And the mission is to pry out as much intel about the area as possible. Aria didn't exactly provide many details, but on the car ride to Lake Agatha, she shared not being able to shake the feeling that there's something connecting the string of drownings to their mom's death.

Unexplained drownings. Apparent ghosts in the water. A mom who disappeared fourteen years ago miraculously shows up dead . . . in the hometown neither of them knew they had. Caliste may not fully understand why Aria thinks a clue is hiding in this gaggle of tipsy teenagers, but a piece—or five—is missing from this puzzle.

Caliste trains her ear to focus on the different conversations percolating around them. There's the typical fare of budding (or newly ended) romances, test-score anxieties, and meaningless gossip.

Close by, a cluster of girls lounges, wearing sweaters and woolen coats devoid of obvious branding but crystal clear in their level of careful craftmanship. They whisper, voices low but excited, among themselves.

"Wait—you're going with Lloyd to his father's birthday party in Monaco? That's huge!"

"Shh. Don't be weird about it."

"Still! Meeting the parents is major. Will his mom be there?"

"Oh no . . ." The girl speaking glances toward the still-in-progress bonfire before turning back to her friends. "Lloyd's sister was the girl who died last summer . . . His mom is *not* into going boating anytime soon." As if on cue, the guy Aria knows, Tyler, throws his hands up in the air as an argument between two other boys erupts near the fire. Caliste turns toward the noise, pretending she wasn't just eavesdropping, and watches Tyler walk to where she and Aria are sitting. He's a bit antsy, especially when addressing Aria. There's a boy-next-door charm about him, with his head of brassy curls and goofy smile. Despite the cold, he wears sandals and a corded leather shark's-tooth necklace as if he's just strolled off some tropical beach.

"Are you cold? We have some extra blankets," he says.

"We're okay. Thanks, Tyler," Aria says. "And thanks again for the invite. We'd be stuck with nothing to do otherwise."

"How do you all know each other, by the way?" Caliste asks suddenly, flicking her head toward the mingling crowd.

"I know most folks," Tyler says. "A lot are from high school. Carter . . . I've known him since we were kids. I'm surprised he's here, though."

Tyler points a finger at a lone figure in the group's center. He's kneeling and prodding the stack of smoking wood in the firepit with a metal poker, his back facing Caliste and Aria. Despite being surrounded by people, he seems to be on his own. Caliste can relate, honestly.

"Why are you surprised?"

"Well . . . he was working at Camp Griffon last summer when Riley drowned. I feel a little bad that I invited him . . . but now that the camp is on hiatus, the campground is a great location for lake activities. Although . . . there're stories of a ghost haunting the water."

Caliste continues to stare at the black wool–clothed back turned toward them. It occurs to her, after seeing Tyler's expression, that Carter is dressed like he's attending a funeral and not a lakeside bonfire. From the conversation those girls were having, Riley is the dead girl mentioned. It's no wonder those girls were sneaking glances at Carter.

"I know hanging out in the cold isn't the most exciting excursion . . . but do you want some hot chocolate?" Tyler's babbling, each word rushing out. When he finishes speaking, he jogs over to a duffel bag nestled at the base of a young oak tree and rummages through it.

Caliste takes the opportunity to scoot closer and nudge Aria, glancing at Carter and the gaggle attempting to light the fire.

"Wanna make a bet? Will they figure out how to light the damn thing before we freeze to death?" Caliste asks.

"We won't freeze to death."

"It's a joke—though probably in poor taste, with the counselor and all," Caliste replies, sticking out her tongue. "So, what's the plan? We are out in the middle of nowhere with strangers . . . why, again?"

Aria glares, but there's a small smile tugging at the corner of her lips. "We're here to hang out and maybe learn some things."

"What kind of things?"

Aria is pensive, pressing her lips together until a thin line forms. In that moment, Tyler returns with two Styrofoam cups and a cherry-red thermos covered in a variety of stickers.

"Here you go! I hope it's good. It might be bad."

"Fantastic," Caliste says, hiding the sarcasm behind a smile as she accepts a cup. "You drink it first." Her father taught her to be suspicious of everyone.

"You can't mess up hot chocolate," Aria says, clearly trying to butter Tyler up.

A sudden bout of whoops erupts, and there's a bright flare of orange in the periphery of Caliste's vision. A charred scent tinges the air, and she blinks away the sting of blowing smoke. When she looks up, Carter is walking away from the fire. Their eyes meet. His are large, dark brown, and framed by an envious fan of black lashes. Caliste's only *a little* jealous. After a second, he shifts away, muttering under his breath.

"Hey," Aria says, tapping Caliste on the top of her head.

Caliste snaps her head back and realizes Tyler is standing *much* closer to them now.

"Sorry, I wasn't listening. What's up?"

"The police officer, what was his name?" Aria asks. She raises her eyebrows slightly, signaling to Caliste to ignore the fact that she's putting on an act.

"Gordon Badiou. A French name for a French-sounding town. Why do you all pronounce it so weird, by the way?" Caliste says, turning to the enamored Tyler. He hasn't looked away from Aria.

"To be honest, I couldn't tell you. It's always been *Lay Sooz* to me. I'm sure one of our ancestors butchered it forever ago."

Caliste frowns at the *our*. Because as far as she knows, her ancestors were in Vietnam, having quite a different experience with learning French.

"I mean . . . *my* ancestors . . ." Tyler quickly corrects himself. "Anyway, Officer Badiou's been at the precinct for a while. Hey, Carter—Badiou is the one who investigated Riley's death, right?"

"Yeah. They called it off almost immediately because of the storm, though. It was supposedly a tragic drowning. They didn't find her body," Carter says, approaching their cluster. A red plastic cup has materialized in his hand. He swirls it before taking a long sip and pointedly avoids Caliste's eye. He's tall, nearly a head taller than Tyler. He has a square jawline, brown skin with red undertones that's dappled with freckles, and thick, intense eyebrows that make it seem like he's on the verge of having a very serious talk. If it weren't for present circumstances, Caliste might consider him the best candidate for a little winter romance. Unsurprisingly, with the visit to see her mother looming, she's zero percent in the mood to canoodle.

"You say 'supposedly' like you don't believe it," Caliste says. She makes a point to not take her eyes off Carter, and he coughs in response.

"She was a good swimmer. It's confusing, is all."

Carter speaks in a monotone, as if narrating. For a moment, Caliste imagines what it must've been like for him, waking up to the news that another counselor was dead.

"Where did she drown? This is a huge lake," Caliste asks. Aria elbows her *hard* in reprimand, even though *she's* the one who brought them here to be nosy.

"I can show you, if you want, Caliste," Carter says. This time, he doesn't look away from her. Hearing her name from his lips is a little startling. Aria must've told Tyler, and he must've told Carter.

She's taken aback by his offer and searches his face for a sign that he's mocking her. Caliste knows the question she asked was *supremely* bitchy. She doesn't even know why she asked it in the first place. She supposes she didn't expect him to take her bait.

"I'm mostly here to pay my respects, anyway," Carter continues, gesturing at his outfit. Caliste would normally think he's messing with her, but there's a softness in his expression that she wants to trust.

"Take me away," Caliste says, though she half regrets it. She lifts her hand and offers it to Carter. He smiles and pulls her upward.

Once upright, Carter offers his cup with his other hand. She's watched him nurse it with no adverse effects, so Caliste accepts it without a thought. She downs the remaining liquid (pure brandy, gross) and peers down at Aria, her pulse quickening at the thought of both of them being alone with these guys. Aria mouths *Go ahead* to Caliste, and she suppresses the rising anxiety in her chest.

She's being irrational. There's no such thing as ghosts. She thinks about Beverly's uncle.

There are more monsters in LA than in this sleepy town.

♊

There is something abandoned and beautiful about the area around Lake Agatha. The path Carter takes Caliste down winds along a rocky shoreline where murky green water sloshes upward, coating the stones like a painter creating shadow. It's certainly not walkable close to the water's edge, and Caliste almost appreciates the lake keeping them at a distance. A dense line of conifer trees encloses this shore of the lake. Caliste can hear her own breathing, distilled only by the sound of winter birds chirping above them.

Caliste slips on a loose stone on the walking path and soon feels a firm arm around her waist.

"Careful," Carter says. He makes sure she's steady on her feet again before letting go.

Caliste clears her throat. "So, were you born and raised here?" she asks, her hands folded behind her.

"More or less. I'm from Minneapolis. I only came down here for camp when I was a kid, and I started working there a few summers ago. I also have . . . extended family here," Carter answers in the same monotone, preventing Caliste from figuring out how he truly feels.

"I imagine running around with friends and enjoying the summer sun was fun." Caliste falls in step next to him. She knows trusting a stranger isn't the smartest thing to do, but she gets the sense he's using her as an excuse to get away from his friends and Tyler's exuberant energy, not to murder her.

"Not really my scene. I prefer enjoying nature by myself, and in the shade."

"I can tell. You're dressed like a vampire."

For the first time, Carter cracks a smile. His demeanor is a bit cold, but Caliste is 99 percent sure he's shy. It's a *little bit* endearing.

"You said you're here to pay your respects?"

"In a way . . . It's silly, I know. I didn't want to come here alone."

"So you came here with a bunch of drunk people?"

Carter laughs at Caliste's question.

". . . I get it," Caliste says.

Carter points ahead. "We're almost there . . ."

Soon she's stopping alongside Carter, who stands several feet back from Camp Griffon's dock. "So, this is where . . . ?" she asks.

"Where Riley's stuff was found. They grabbed some more of her clothes from the shore over there," Carter replies apathetically, motioning out at Lake Agatha's serene water meeting the wet edge of earth. "It was the worst moment of my life." His confession surprises Caliste, and there's a change in the inflection of his voice.

"Why would you agree to come here to revisit the worst moment of your life?"

"I don't know . . ."

When Caliste looks over, Carter is staring at his feet. A heaviness sits in the air, and Caliste is sure she's the cause. Perhaps it's the cold or the alcohol finally hitting her bloodstream, but Caliste's emboldened. She turns, her shoulder brushing Carter's, and peers into his face.

"We're here for our mom. The police found her body. She drowned, too."

"I'm sorry," Carter replies. He sounds like he means it.

"Don't be. Now we both have sad-ass stories involving the water." Caliste tries to inject some levity into her tone but fails.

A tense silence falls between them.

Carter says, "I know Riley didn't drown. Someone hurt her. And I think I know who did it."

"What, wh—?" Caliste asks. Before he can open his mouth, an eardrum-shattering scream erupts from the direction of the bonfire. Caliste recognizes it instantly.

Aria.

CHAPTER TWELVE

Aria

There is a laundry list of things that are currently important. Georgetown. Aunt Thu being in the hospital again. Aria's birth certificate (though she's never seen it and has a guess as to why), or really any document that might reveal whether she came into this world alongside Caliste. A father who is not dead and is arriving to meet her in less than twenty-four hours. The truth about what she thought was her only family.

Considering everything at once, Aria starts to feel like she's sinking. So this present moment is a reprieve from all the worries on her plate. Aria lets her fingers dip farther into the icy water of Lake Agatha, her skin turning pink and comfortably numb. She stands near a shallow part of the lake with Tyler, who is giving her a brief history lesson.

"The camp used to be *way* nicer back in the day. My dad and I would come for some events, like the boat races or summer picnics," Tyler says, leaning against an old signpost that reads NO SWIMMING AFTER SUNDOWN.

"You called it a fancy camp," Aria says, shaking the cold droplets of lake water from her fingertips and shifting to face Tyler in her squatting position. He's friendly and outgoing, typical in a way that Aria's jealous of. Life would likely be less complicated if she was a Tyler.

"Yeah, it was. Les Eaux is a funny place. Carter can tell you more since he's spent more time here. But lots of old-money folks live nearby, including the founding family's descendants . . . and the population's only, like, two thousand."

"Interesting. Who founded this place?"

"The Hanes. Oldest of old money. They've been in Les Eaux for generations."

Aria is picking at a loose thread on her coat, but the name Tyler utters stops her. Hane. *Hane.* Where has she heard that name before?

"If you see a crest shield around town, that's their family coat of arms."

This isn't necessarily a new experience for her. She knows plenty of kids at Georgetown—

Georgetown. She remembers now where she's heard that name.

"You said some members of the Hane family still live here, right?"

Tyler raises his eyebrows at Aria, and she belatedly flashes a smile to convince him she's *extremely* enthusiastic.

"Yeah, the old guy's named Eric. He used to be a big shot, but he's been sick. Folks haven't seen him in years. His son, Emory, still comes around, though. He just went off to college."

Emory Hane.

"I . . ." Aria coughs to hide how flustered she is. Emory. Is it a coincidence that the boy who threatened her on campus is from

Les Eaux? She decides moving away from the present topic will be in her best interest.

"And those ghost stories you were talking about—can you tell me one?"

"How about we keep walking, and I'll tell you on the way?" Tyler asks. He smiles, offering his hand as he stands.

Aria hesitates before nodding and taking his hand. She glances over her shoulder, back toward the fire, which is getting smaller and smaller.

"It started with the first couple of drownings here. Some folks claimed they saw a monster in the water."

"A monster? Is this a Midwestern cryptid type of thing?"

"No." Tyler chuckles. "Although we have plenty of those stories, too. They say the monster has long white fingers and a rotting body and that it grabs the person right before they drown."

"You aren't telling this in a very scary way," Aria comments. She means it as a joke, but her voice is flat. She's been so desperate to poke Tyler for information related to the Les Eaux drownings. Not that she believes in the kind of monster Tyler's describing, but what if someone was killing—drowning—unsuspecting people like her mom?

"Damn, tough crowd. Anyway, the monster disappears into the water, and then the victim's body is found floating to the shore. I hear some parents tell their kids that if they're naughty, the monster will get them."

Aria snorts, then turns her head to see how far they've walked. There's a thick cluster of dead trees blocking her line of sight to the fire and the raging party. Aria's pulse quickens as she realizes no one can see them.

"Should we head back?"

"Hey, what's the rush?" Tyler asks.

When she spins around, she's startled by how close he is.

"You're really pretty, you know that?" Tyler says, placing his hands around her waist. The stink of his breath—heavy with alcohol—hits Aria in the face. "You're way prettier than your twin. She looks so fake. Blech . . ."

Tyler spits out the *blech,* and one of his hands snakes upward to graze her cheek.

Aria steps backward to try and untangle herself from Tyler's grasp. "I'm sorry. We should go back!"

"Why are you playing this game?" Tyle says, his fingers dig into her lower back. Aria holds in a desire to cry and vomit at the same time.

"Let. Me. Go!" Aria screams and pushes Tyler with all the force she can muster. He falls backward into the water, and Aria sprints toward the firepit.

Aria breathes heavily through her mouth as she runs, her feet stumbling on the lake's uneven shore. The cold air hurts her throat. Both tears and snot stream down her face; she can't even see clearly in front of her.

"Aria!"

Aria's never been more relieved to hear a familiar voice. With her sleeve, she wipes her eyes. Then she spots Carter and Caliste in the distance, running toward her.

Aria slows, her feet sliding in mud. Caliste's panicked face chips away at the last brick holding Aria together.

"What happened?" Caliste shouts right before crashing into Aria with a hug.

Embarrassed, Aria can't stop crying in Caliste's arms.

"Where's Tyler? Was he with you?" Carter asks. His face is

slick with sweat, and he stares with a furrowed brow at the sisters' embrace.

"I . . . He . . ." Aria can't get the words out.

A ridiculous idea. Everything is my fault. It's always my fault.

"Hey . . . Did he do something to you?" Caliste asks, her voice gentle.

". . . Kinda. Yes?" Aria says.

The affirmation triggers something in Caliste, and she whirls around to face Carter.

"What kind of friends do you have? Where the hell is he?"

"I'm sorry . . . Tyler's . . ." Carter's voice trails, and he looks at Aria apologetically. "Never mind. I can go find him. You two should head home."

"You're joking. I'm going to crack that little shit's spine in half," Caliste snaps before turning back to Aria, her voice softening as she makes eye contact. "Well . . . unless you want to go home?"

Aria's voice shallows, her nerves slowly returning to normal.

"I'll be fine if you're with me."

Caliste squeezes her hand, and they start walking toward where she left Tyler.

The shore of Lake Agatha transitions into a jagged bank of irregular rocks, and the walking path veers off to the side. God . . . that jerk took her down this isolated path on purpose. The thought makes her stomach churn.

They follow the path silently, and Aria spots her and Tyler's footprints from earlier. Something's different, though. Why are there three sets of footprints now?

"God. You two walked far," Caliste says, irritated.

Aria fixates on the sharp bend ahead, where Tyler tried to kiss her. Except . . . he's nowhere to be seen. The tide, or as much of one that can exist in this lake, ripples, and water rushes toward the rocky shore, pulling with it a wet plastic sandal. Aria recognizes it.

"What is it?" Carter asks from behind them.

After a series of delicate steps to avoid tripping on the loose rocks, Aria lets go of Caliste's hand and squats, heels to butt, staring at the dark water below. It's pulsing slowly toward her.

Groups of dead reeds, their skeletons sticking out of the mud, sway in the wind. However, there's an irregular quality to how the reeds stand. Aria peers closer, careful not to slip. Then it materializes: a contorted figure knotted in wet weeds and wet fabric that coils in the water.

"Oh my god!" Caliste yells, scrambling behind Aria.

Tyler's face stares up at her through the reeds, skin pale and bloodied mouth agape.

And then the victim's body is found floating to the shore.

♊

Caliste

"Favorite color?" Caliste asks. She sits on the cold floor of the police station, and Aria sits in a plastic chair in front of her. They're in some back room to give them privacy and to make Aria more comfortable, but it's all white—white-painted brick walls and white laminate. There are no windows. It's as comforting as a hug from her father.

"Purple . . . a lighter shade. Like the color of purple irises," Aria mutters, and Caliste can barely hear her through the muffle of the blanket covering her mouth. Aria's cocooned up in a beige throw blanket that's been sitting in this station for god knows how long. The curls have fallen from Aria's hair, and the eyeliner Caliste applied earlier is smeared from tears.

"Funny. I like dark purple. Most embarrassing memory?"

"I got a secret love confession in my high school locker, then learned months later that my best friend wrote it being silly. I asked the guy I thought it was from if he knew anything about the note. When he said no, I wanted to crawl into a hole. I sometimes still see him at Georgetown."

"Ouch. You're a freshman there, right?"

Aria nods before asking, "Okay. What's *your* most embarrassing memory?"

"Mine is confidently yelling 'bonjour' at a French couple who gave me directions when I meant to say 'merci.' What about your go-to snack?"

"Shrimp chips."

"Always a classic. I'm partial to lychee gummies."

"Can I get free shrimp chips?" Aria asks.

"What?"

"You own a grocery company. So I'm asking for free shrimp chips."

Caliste laughs, half from the joke and half from the immense relief that breaks inside her. It's delivered as deadpan as possible, but Aria's finally returning to some semblance of a human being.

"Have you ever been in love?" This time, Aria asks the question.

". . . I think so," Caliste says, deciding on an earnest answer instead of the smart-ass one.

"What's it like?"

"What do you think love is like?" Caliste says, passing the question back to Aria.

"I don't know, honestly. I think love scares me," Aria replies, untucking her chin from the edge of her sweatshirt.

"What about it is scary?"

"All of it. Letting someone see all of you—the messy bits and the ugly parts. Seeing theirs in return. Promising to continue loving each other despite everything."

"I don't know. Love is nice. It shouldn't always be about those ugly parts."

"That seems awfully optimistic."

It's silent after Aria's reply. However, unlike with Beverly, the quiet doesn't fill Caliste with dread. Rather—it's peaceful, all things considered. Caliste doesn't think she's ever been called an optimist.

"We're more alike than I thought," Caliste says, and Aria takes the opportunity to gently kick her from underneath the blanket.

"Is that a compliment or an insult?"

"Obviously a compliment."

There's a soft knock on the door, and it squeals as the person on the other side opens it.

"Ladies, your dad's arrived. Do you want to go out and meet him, or would you prefer for him to come in here?" The ginger hair of their attendant flutters as she pokes her head into the room. She's a bit older than the other receptionist and apparently part of the overnight staff.

Caliste looks up at Aria, reaching to squeeze her arm and signal she's okay with whatever decision her sister makes.

"We can go to the lobby."

The woman nods, and there's a muted thump as the door slides shut again. It's been a blur of a night. After calling in to the station to report Tyler's drowning, Caliste and Aria couldn't leave Camp Griffon until nearly midnight. Carter went home after the officers wrapped up their questions, but Aria had to answer a few more questions at the station, seeing as she was the last one who saw Tyler alive. They stayed in the station overnight, and the pure adrenaline of everything that's happened must be what's keeping Caliste awake.

For a moment, Caliste had been afraid that Carter would think Aria was lying. But he didn't look at the scene with skepticism; there was only fear. He said he believed Aria and complied with the story Caliste asked him to tell.

Yes, Aria was the last to see Tyler.

No, there was nothing of note that happened. Tyler wanted to walk farther, and Aria wanted to turn around.

The minute the other kids at the party had gotten wind of the situation, they'd scattered to avoid any underage drinking charges. Thankfully, letting Carter speak to the officers when they arrived was the right decision. They'd seemed to recognize him.

Caliste shudders, thinking about the devastation on Carter's face. After sprinting to where Tyler's body lay, Carter was breathing so heavily Caliste was afraid he was about to pass out. Tyler was an asshole . . . but Carter has now witnessed two deaths at the hands of the lake. She feels sorry for him.

The list of absolutely batshit events that have transpired over the past few days gets ever longer, and now Caliste needs to brace herself to see her own father. Honestly? That's the most normal thing she's done all day.

As Caliste and Aria make their way down the hallway and back to the lobby, the rays of morning's light cascade through the slats of the blinds. Caliste's caught off guard by the fact it's already morning. It either feels like a year or twenty minutes has passed since they left the shores of Lake Agatha, and Caliste can't decide which one it is. The large double doors that lead back to the lobby appear ahead, and Caliste swallows.

What should she expect when Paul Hà finally strides through the front doors of the police station?

Relief? Comfort?

Caliste's go-to state of mind with her dad is absolute and unwavering apathy. It used to be a source of pride for her to not get riled up by Paul and his inability to give a crap about anybody but himself. But in this moment, in the town where her mother died and where she's discovered a missing—no, not missing—a stolen part of herself, the apathy gives way to an overwhelming bitterness.

The doors swing open, the mechanism that controls them emitting a high-pitched shrill. Paul's familiar face appears, impassive as ever.

Caliste tenses, and she stops alongside Aria a few feet from where he stands. He looks tired, like he also didn't sleep a wink last night. Aria's shoulders tense next to Caliste, and Caliste finds herself reaching for her hand. Caliste feels guilty . . . somewhat. At least she grew up with their father.

When Paul's face registers Aria's, there's an expression Caliste thought him incapable of.

". . . Paul Hà? I mean . . . Dad?" Aria asks the question so tentatively, it makes Caliste's heart hurt on her behalf. The heartache is quickly replaced by fury. Aria should've known. She deserved to know that her father was alive and well.

"Ariadne. Caliste. My girls." He says the names as if they're forbidden.

Something breaks inside Caliste when their dad utters those four simple words. It catches her completely off guard, and there's an instantaneous bodily reaction. Whatever she's been holding in pours out of her, and the same happens to Aria.

He rushes to embrace them both, arms wrapping awkwardly around their shoulders.

"Ba," Caliste says, her voice cracking before being muffled by the wool of her dad's coat. All their foreheads touch, and Paul's shaking arms enclose more strongly around them.

"I never thought I'd hold you both at the same time again."

The authoritative and stable voice that Caliste is used to her dad putting on is gone. The voice he uses now is indescribably soft, as if he's about to cry. This is the first time Caliste has heard her father's voice sound like this. It's both alien and eerie. But . . . she finds comfort in its vulnerability. Paul will have to answer a million questions, but she can force them out of him later. She'll let herself feel some type of way about it another time. For now . . . she needs to be hugged.

CHAPTER THIRTEEN

Caliste

Officer Badiou apparently didn't want to interrupt the impromptu sobbing session that was happening in the lobby. After Caliste and Aria both calmed down, Paul finally extracted himself to talk to the detective—alone. Watching her father walk away from her, once again, triggered the latent anger lying in wait within Caliste.

"Perfect. He gives us a big hug and explains nothing," Caliste says, using her sleeve to wipe her face. A mix of tan foundation, now tinged orange, and her eye makeup smear in ugly streaks down the cream-colored fabric.

"Well ... it's nice to know we are twins and aren't ... I don't know. In some weird alternate universe," Aria offers before blowing her nose in a gross sputter on her sleeve.

She's right. They were definitely separated. But why? Caliste glances at the closed double doors where Officer Badiou and Paul disappeared. How many more secrets are lurking in their family?

She turns on her heel to grab Aria, ready to propose going back to the inn to rest, when a familiar voice interrupts their snotty exchange.

"Con, don't wipe your nose on your clothes. It's unsightly."

Caliste whirls around. Priscilla is standing at the entrance of the police station, ensconced within a mahogany mink coat with a very spherical lime-green bundle in her arms. Her face is flushed from the cold. It takes a moment for Caliste to compute as Aria whispers, "*Who's that?*" and tugs on her sleeve.

"Mę. You're here?"

Caliste's shaky voice causes the lime-green sphere to stir, and Dylan's cherubic face pops out of the bundle.

"Chị!" he yells, causing Aria to jump.

Caliste inhales and approaches the duo with arms outstretched. She expects to simply take Dylan from her stepmother, as she is used to, but is surprised by Priscilla hugging them both tight.

"Con. I'm so sorry," Priscilla whispers, her brittle voice strange to Caliste's ears. Priscilla holds on for a moment longer, ignoring Dylan squirming in between them. She releases her grip and waves her hand at Aria.

"Oh. I should introduce myself . . ." Aria's flustered as she steps toward them.

Priscilla hugs Aria this time. Dylan complains, but once he peers up at Aria's face, he shrieks.

Caliste laughs at Dylan's confusion, which produces another unsightly bubble of snot that she wipes away with her sleeve.

"Oh my goodness. It's true. You are identical," Priscilla says, pulling away from the embrace. She lets Dylan clamber down onto the station floor and takes Aria's face in her hands.

"You didn't know?" Caliste asks, squatting down as Dylan darts toward her.

"Of course not," Priscilla replies. "God. Your father is a fool. He insisted he wanted to explain in person, as if he hasn't made you both wait long enough for the truth already."

Aria's cheeks are smashed between Priscilla's manicured hands, which are massaging them like dumpling dough.

"I'm sorry, but . . . are you Caliste's stepmom?" Aria finally speaks. She only recently found out she has a sister and a dad. Now there's a baby and a woman who Caliste's called Mom. Her brain can't process these new faces fast enough.

"Yes. I'm Priscilla, Paul's second wife." Priscilla's voice tightens, and she drops her hands with a weak smile.

"Chị, what's happening? That girl looks like you," Dylan whispers into Caliste's ear as she lifts him up to sit on her hip. That said, what he thinks is a whisper is quite loud, and both Priscilla and Aria look at them.

"She's my sister. She's your sister . . . We just . . . lost each other. Somehow." Caliste brushes back Dylan's hair, which is slick with sweat from being under his puffer coat's hood. His round, nearly black eyes widen before darting to study Aria again. Distilling the present situation into something a toddler can understand really strips everything bare; the story sounds laughable in such simple terms.

"Have you two eaten yet? I heard about the whole ordeal with the boy from town. Goodness, you poor girls . . ." Priscilla sighs and loops her arm behind Caliste. "I'll take you to get something to eat."

Caliste is too taken aback by her stepmother's gentleness to disagree, and she and Aria find themselves following Priscilla out to the parking lot like a line of baby ducks.

Is Caliste hallucinating? Priscilla has *never* been this nice to her. It's such a stark difference that Caliste can't even give Aria a proper rundown of her family and what's happening. They approach a silver Audi SUV—Dad's typical choice when using a company car—parked next to Caliste's Mercedes-Benz.

As Priscilla clicks the remote, unlocking the car doors, Caliste finally mentally adjusts to the present circumstance and blurts out a question.

"Why are you here? Our mom . . . You can't be comfortable . . ." What Caliste is *trying* to say is that coming with one's husband to identify the body of his previous wife cannot be a pleasant experience.

Priscilla turns back toward them, spinning on her heel. She swings the car keys around her index finger for a few seconds as she considers her response.

"You are a daughter who has lost a mother, as am I," Priscilla says.

"Ah . . ." Caliste is speechless. After all these years of resenting Priscilla, Caliste realizes she doesn't know much about her stepmom. She had no idea Priscilla's mom was already dead; she never thought to ask.

"If it makes you uncomfortable for me to be here, I can leave."

"No!" Caliste's mouth moves faster than her brain, and she doesn't know why she refused the offer so aggressively. "Thank you, Mẹ."

Mother. For once, the word doesn't feel like a lie.

♊

Aria

Caliste and Aria haven't quite had the time to catch up on every facet of each other's lives from the past fourteen years—the details of Caliste's relationship with her stepmother being one of them. Priscilla is put together and sharp, with medium-chestnut hair styled in a way that suggests effortlessness (but Aria knows such a look takes many hours in a salon chair). However, there's an odd dynamic at play here. Caliste is acting like the person across from her is someone she doesn't know.

They've come to a small, brightly lit diner on Main Street that, on the exterior, looks like it belongs on a '50s-era movie set. The neon sign outside says JOE JOE'S DINER. The inside is more modern than Aria expected, with hanging faux vines and a muted rustic color palette occasionally punctuated by pops of red. It's quite early in the morning, with the diner having opened only ten minutes ago.

"How many, ma'am?" a waitress asks after the glass door shuts behind them. A cherry-red apron is tied around her waist.

"Three and a high chair. Preferably a booth, please," Priscilla says, looking away from the row of barstools. "I'd like my daughters to be able to sit next to each other."

The "my daughters" surprises Aria, and she catches Caliste smiling next to her.

As they make their way to a booth, Aria immediately senses the pointed stares aimed in their direction. Their crew is especially out of place here, amid the scatter of all-white patrons. However, Priscilla doesn't carry herself any differently, unlike

Aria, who often tries to shrink as much as she can in spaces like this.

"I still can't believe it," Priscilla says, her head in her hands and her elbows on the shiny vinyl surface of the table. She slides forward a bit, her cashmere-covered arms slipping across the table until she's eye to eye with Aria. "He really was telling the truth. You two are twins."

"And Dad *just* told you?" Caliste asks. She's staring down at the laminated menu in front of her, picking at the torn plastic edge so it makes a repetitive *tch-tch-tch* noise. The vision Aria has of her sister—as an enigmatic force to be reckoned with—has all but disappeared. Here, Caliste is small, her insecurities fully exposed. It's the first time Aria has thought of her sister as a normal teenage girl.

"Yes. I swear to you, I had no idea," Priscilla says before sighing and leaning back. "I gave him an earful. What kind of husband keeps something like this from his family? But it does explain some things."

"What things?" Caliste asks.

"It's complicated."

"Then uncomplicate them."

Priscilla sighs.

Dylan thumps his legs in the gray wooden high chair. He seems to be aware of the contentious conversation between mother and sister. He reaches toward Priscilla, his small fingers opening and closing like a Venus flytrap as he speaks.

"Mommy. Be nice."

"Yeah, be nice," Caliste quips, and taps her younger brother on the nose with the tip of her index finger.

Priscilla smiles at him and takes a long few seconds to gather her thoughts.

"When your dad and I started dating . . ." Priscilla stops, pursing her lips as she considers how to phrase what is coming next. "Bà Nội told me that your mother wasn't mentally well . . . that there was a risk you'd be the same."

"I'm sorry, what?" Caliste asks, her voice rising in indignation.

"I . . . didn't know better then. I should have. Your grandma told me you needed to build resilience and not to baby you or get closer than necessary. That woman . . ." Priscilla sighs and slumps in her seat. "Every time she thought I stepped out of line with you, she'd let me have it. But I am the adult here . . . and the way I treated you was my choice. I'm sorry."

"Could you repeat that? I'd love to have it recorded for future reference," Caliste says.

Priscilla's somber face finally breaks into a laugh.

"There's no good reason to have separated you," Priscilla says, sobering up. Her impeccably shaped almond nails rap on the plastic.

The diner's door opens, the sharp jingle of bells ringing in the air. When Aria looks up, Paul Hà has appeared. His is a face she recognizes in herself, weary and hollow from fatigue. She inhales to steady herself. Every moment, from the horrible outing to Lake Agatha until now, has felt like a terrible dream. Seeing Paul in this moment is like ice water to her face.

This is the father Aria spent her whole life thinking was dead.

Caliste

Priscilla scoots in to allow Paul to sit. In a move that startles Caliste, she reaches across the table and grabs Caliste's hands in hers. Her fingers and palm are soft, and she presses with a comforting firmness.

It's okay, Priscilla mouths, and her eyes are glassy. Why is *she* about to cry?

Caliste stays silently seated at the table, aware of this being a unification of father and daughter. Caliste is not the daughter she's thinking of, though. The part of her that wants to confront her father recedes behind the part that wants to give Aria the moment she deserves.

"I'm sorry to keep you waiting," Paul says, sitting down with a sigh. He slips off his herringbone wool coat and reaches over to give Priscilla's hand, which is currently holding Caliste's, a squeeze.

Caliste is amused that Priscilla glares at him in return.

"Did you finish your talk with the officers?" Caliste interrupts as Paul starts to glance at the menu.

"... Yes, I did."

"And?"

There's a long and painful stretch of seconds before Paul responds.

"My girls. I'm so sorry."

"Are we getting an explanation, Ba?" Caliste asks.

"It's . . . going to be a long explanation. But I will tell you everything," Paul says, and shifts his gaze to Aria. "You look well . . . Ariadne."

"Aria. I go by Aria."

"Ariadne *is* a bit of a mouthful. Your mother," Paul says,

gesturing between the two of them, "loved this old book of Greek stories a friend gave to her. She named you two. Everyone in the family asked why we'd pick such complicated names to pronounce."

"Why didn't you give us Vietnamese names?" Aria asks.

"My Vietnamese name was Phúc. You can guess what they called me when I was growing up in this country. Giving you Western names was my only criterion, and your mother loved your names so much. I couldn't say no to her."

"Are you going to tell us what happened, or are you going to keep reminiscing?" Caliste asks.

At first she wanted to remain quiet so Aria could take the lead. But now she can't help it. The lie. This all-consuming lie hangs between them. She never really understood her dad. She understands him even less now.

The waitress descends upon their table to take their orders, and Paul sighs with visible relief. Perfect timing for him.

"I'd like a coffee. No cream, but a bit of sugar," Paul says. He usually orders his coffee completely black.

Priscilla orders the same, in addition to a two-egg breakfast plate with pancakes and bacon she plans to share with Dylan.

"Can I have a coffee with cream and sugar, the Tex-Mex omelet, a side of French toast, and some fruit?" Caliste says. Now that the fog of last night's events is slowly lifting, the hunger is kicking in, and she's starving.

"Oh yes! Please add a side of fruit to my order, too," Priscilla pipes up as Dylan makes a face.

"What do you want?" Caliste asks, nudging her sister.

"Maybe the same? Except no French toast, please."

The waitress jots everything down and darts off before

returning to bring them all their coffee with a tray of packaged sweeteners and a small jug of cream.

Paul sighs, placing the cup of coffee on the table after taking a sip.

"We lived here. All of us. Your mom. Me. Eventually, Thu joined to help us. We were in over our heads with you both."

Aria nods. Caliste leans over and places her arm around Aria's shoulders. This is their story . . . but why does Caliste feel like she needs to protect Aria from something?

"Your mother . . . On the night she disappeared, Thu and I looked everywhere." Paul pauses, taking a glance around the diner and lowering his voice. "The police weren't a big help . . ." he says quietly. "She was a missing person for a bit, and then they claimed she must have run away."

Aria speaks for the first time. "Why would they think that?"

"We fought . . . that last day. We had a disagreement. One of the neighbors overheard. Then your mom drove away and never returned."

"Did they suspect you did something to her?" Caliste asks.

Aria gasps, and Priscilla coughs after taking a sip of water. Caliste ignores the sting of the reactions. She knows what it means to ask this question. But she wants to hurt her dad. And . . . it *is* a rational question.

Paul, to his credit, takes it in stride. "Yes. They questioned me and Thu. But they ultimately concluded that your mother left. We waited for as long as we could manage. But no one ever found our car . . . or her. It was awful for you two as well. The crying. Calling for her every night. At some points, you were inconsolable. We kept telling you she'd come back."

Caliste's heart pinches. He's right . . . At least, she thinks so. But something triggers a dream . . . or is it a memory?

In whatever it is, Caliste can't breathe. The wailing is constant, like waves crashing against the tide. Over and over again, she is crying and heaving, trying to fuel her next scream. Next to her . . . she hears the same powerful sobbing. Wave after wave.

Twin tides rushing toward the same shore.

"It wasn't a dream," she whispers.

"What was that?"

Her father, Aria, and Priscilla peer at Caliste before she realizes she's spoken out loud.

"Never mind. What happened after that? How did we get separated?"

Paul stares at Caliste, and the eye contact is so intentional, it makes her uncomfortable.

"Marrying your mother made things difficult for me. I was estranged from my family because of it. We had very little money."

Caliste frowns. She knew Bà Nội and her mom had a fraught relationship, but why would that have anything to do with being separated from her twin?

"At the time, I couldn't afford to take care of you both by myself. And Thu and I . . . simply butted heads."

"What about Aunt Thu?" Aria asks. "What did she want?"

"She wanted to keep you two together, and she was willing to take you both."

Caliste badly wants to blurt out that Aunt Thu should've done so, but she keeps her mouth shut for Aria's sake. Caliste's dad doesn't deserve her kindness, but Aria does.

"Did Bà Nội know about us?" Caliste asks.

". . . No. She didn't. We were estranged by the time you were both born. One day I was her estranged son, and the next I arrived on her doorstep with a daughter. This sounds awful, but once your mother was out of the picture, accepting me back was a nonissue." Paul pauses, as if he's contemplating his next words. "I honestly think they were relieved she was gone."

"Jesus Christ," Caliste mutters. She always suspected as much . . . but to hear the cruelty aloud stuns her.

"It's terrible, I know."

"Then why did you do it? If Aunt Thu was willing to take us both, what was the point of separating us?" It's Aria asking this time. She speaks with a level tone, and Caliste can't get a read on her.

Paul fixes them both with a clouded expression.

"It . . . seemed like the best idea to keep you both safe. You both would get the undivided attention of one guardian. I always planned . . . We always planned to tell you one day."

"When? What day, Ba? Was it ever going to be the right time?" Caliste asks.

"You can hate me if you want. I don't know if we made the right decision. But you're both here now, and safe. That is what's important."

Caliste wants to laugh, but Aria's next question stops her.

"Safe from what?"

CHAPTER FOURTEEN

The Ghoul

The powers of this perverse form are still somewhat of a mystery to me. As easily as water flows, so does this body. When I find myself at the lake, I stare up at a boy's back. He's thin, the bony edges of his shoulder blades visible through the wet contours of his jacket. And from his form wafts the familiar horrific scent of sin. He's touched someone he shouldn't have—and it is not the first time, either.

When I kill the boy, it's thoughtless. His body falls into the water with satisfying violence, his limbs thrashing against the brute force of my own pulling him into the sediment. Unlike all the other times . . . killing him does not fill me with satisfaction. This emptiness won't be satiated by anyone but the man from the window.

My memories swell like the tide, in sync with the moon, and threaten to crush me under the weight of their surge. I was always one with the water—and I remember a little more of who I am now. How long have I been traversing the water in a fog? My limbs and mind are renewed. Is it because of my body's return to the river? I leave the latest sinner behind, and I recall the time when I left my home.

My family was from Cà Mau, at the southern tip of the nation, where the wet season far outlasts the dry season. However, by the time I had a sense of being a human in this world, we'd long left Cà Mau and moved up north, along the delta. Now that I think about it, I only saw the ocean in Sóc Trăng with my grandparents. Sweat-soaked clothes and salt-soaked nostrils—these were the sensations of my girlhood.

My sister's name was Giang Thu, and I was named Giang Xuân. Our names flowed from the same source: *giang.*

Thu and autumn.

Xuân and spring.

We were the river and the seasons.

Our father was a fisherman, and at the end of long trips he'd return home with a small satchel of shrimp that we'd grill over charcoal and eat whole. The shells, pliant and thin, wedged their way in between my teeth, and I'd have to pick them out. Father saved the fish heads for my sister. Once, he tried to hide one in a roll of lettuce to feed me, but I caught on too quickly.

Thu was ten years older than me, and before my death, my darkest secret was that I enjoyed watching her fear. It was the only time she felt like my equal. Thu would whimper in the dark when the planes rumbled on the airfield, and we'd sleep clustered together under the covers. When I couldn't sleep, she'd tell me stories of standing on the tip of father's boat and soaring through the mangrove forests. The last time I saw her cry was when she saw the photographs of trees decimated by US military planes spraying Agent Orange. Her girlhood was *destroyed.*

When Ba received the news that we would go to America, he bought us candy bars from the shop, a whole one each. My sister pretended she was too old to be excited by candy, but she ate the entire thing in three bites. Meanwhile, I cherished the treat. I remember peeling back the wrapper and snapping off one fingertip-size piece before bundling it up and hiding it.

I tried to extend joy for as long as possible, whereas Thu thought it was fleeting and behaved as if someone would soon take it away. I suppose that's how she might've felt when I disappeared, when I was stolen by that man in the window.

The chocolate was a distraction meant to divert our attention so we wouldn't focus on reality. Cà Mau was one of many strongholds for the Việt Cộng, and as we traveled, the American search-and-destroy campaign rained on the South.

After eating our chocolate, my sister and I sat on empty stools off to the side of a woman who sold trứng vịt lộn from her cart. We shared three eggs, slurping down the lime, salt, and pepper mixed with the yolk and feathers. I was in the middle of a bite when I started crying.

"Chị, I don't want to go," I blurted between mouthfuls of egg and streaming tears.

I found out later that she was also scared of leaving home. But Thu hid it from me well. From there . . . what I can remember becomes hazy once more. There is a blank space in my memory of our time after we arrived in America.

One—I breathe in, and there is muggy air and the song of my sister's voice.

Two—I breathe out, and there is a sheet of snow from horizon to horizon. The tree limbs are bare, and my skin numbs from the cold. My sister commented that all the trees looked dead. She said this country was full of dead things.

Did she know then that I would become one of them?

When Father was filling out the paperwork, he asked me if I wanted an American name. I chose Grace. Thu refused.

When I was still a teenager, Father died. He was working on a construction site in downtown Saint Paul when a pillar fell on him and a few others. Thu refused to tell me for a full week how he died, afraid that the truth would also crush me.

Thus, my mind invented a myriad of scenarios that killed him and could kill me. Ba's death triggered in me an unrelenting fear—a panic that would rear its head at the most inopportune moments. Ba's death and my undoing are one and the same.

I recall a small settlement that helped sustain us for several years afterward. My sister started working with Ba after we arrived in the U.S. and held a smattering of different jobs. When she started caring for me, she switched to being a nail technician. Because she could sit down, it was better for her body, and she'd occasionally paint my nails when the mood suited her. Thu was uptight and strict, and I thought her too rigid. I know now I was naive and foolish.

When I met Him, Thu warned me.

An ambitious man who is weak cannot protect you. He will only invite those who wish him harm.

Who is he?

Who is he?

This man. His name.

That is where my story stops, and my mind fails me once more. I let out a growl, the water vibrating from my annoyance.

A catfish rushes away in the river's flow, and I settle against the bed of sediment and think.

My jaw gnashes in on itself, and I let myself drift into the darkness.

I do not know if I dream anymore. The kaleidoscope of images arranging itself in my head runs on a loop. I try to hold on to the memory of two small hands, not knowing who they belong to, and weep for the things I've lost.

Aria

Aria's learned a few things from this strained meal with Paul. Dad? Ba? She's not quite ready for those last two yet. It's more comfortable to regard him as Caliste's dad for now. Strange how easy it is to consider the missing space between Caliste and Aria as *Mother*. But a father who purposefully kept himself away? Who lived an entire life without Aria in it? That Aria regards like an abstraction, a theory from a textbook. She understands him as someone else's father, but as her own? She can't.

After the initial explanation of what transpired and their food arrived, Dylan started to fuss, so Priscilla took him out to the car to put him down for a nap. However, Aria is certain she also strategically left her and Caliste alone with Paul.

When Aria glances at her sister, Caliste is polishing off the final bite of her omelet, leaving behind an almost-empty plate. Aria only managed to eat half of hers, an inconsistent wave of nausea suppressing her appetite. The influx of information hasn't helped her nerves.

From what he's said, Paul lived in Minnesota after his family immigrated from Saigon. He grew up near Aunt Thu and Xuân's family in the Saint Paul area. Xuân's Western name was Grace. These facts are now burned into Aria's mind. They are disparate pieces of information she's comfortable slotting away. What they mean together is a whole different story. There is also another family, a whole side of Paul's family in Boston and California, that she's learning about. She grew up believing Aunt Thu was the only relative she had.

"How many sisters do you ha—" Aria begins, but she is interrupted by a loud yell and a man rushing toward their table. The memory of Tyler haunts Aria, and she tenses in fight-or-flight mode before Paul suddenly speaks.

"Eric?"

That name . . . Wasn't the head of the Hane family Tyler mentioned named Eric? Aria shakes off the sensation of Tyler's hands on her, and she suppresses the thought. It's a common name. There are plenty of old men named Eric.

Paul stands and quickly slides out of the booth to greet the man who's come to their table. Their father does not appear happy to see him.

He's nearly half a foot taller than Paul and appears a bit older . . . or at least . . . weaker. His figure is hunched as he clasps Paul's hands excitedly. Aria notices one of his hands is bandaged, and there's an unsteady quality to the way the man moves.

"Paul, my friend. It's been too long!" Eric smiles and glances down at the table. His eyes shift erratically from Aria and Caliste, and he drops Paul's hand forcefully.

". . . Grace? My love?" Eric takes a slow step toward the table, but Paul intervenes, his face tense at the greeting.

"I thought you knew, Eric. She's been missing. Grace is dead."

There is a pause, and Eric clears his throat.

"I . . . forgot. Forgive me. These are the girls all grown up, huh? Ariadne and Caliste? They look so much like her that I was mistaken for a moment."

So it's true. They once existed together, and this man must've known them then. Their twinship wasn't a secret to everybody in this world.

"Yes, she goes by Aria now . . ."

"Gosh, I heard the news and knew you'd come to town. I meant to reach out, but I got busy with some company meetings. You know how it is!"

Paul frowns at the statement, and his hands waver as if ready to catch Eric if he falls.

"Yes, of course. It's fine. We just finished eating. I'd love to catch up, but we have to leave."

Aria doesn't know her father at all, but she knows he's lying.

When she glances at Caliste for a sense of why Paul seems so on edge, her sister shrugs, jaw clenched as she watches Paul and Eric's interaction.

"Oh, what a pity. Don't worry about me, though. My son, Emory, is joining me here soon!"

Aria's coffee cup freezes, the now-lukewarm ceramic pressed to her lips at the name.

Emory. Emory Hane. The boy at Georgetown. This *is* the Eric that Tyler was talking about.

Enjoy your time here while it lasts.

As the memory of bumping into Emory at Georgetown begins to replay, his frosty voice trickles through the parts of Aria's mind that had momentarily forgotten what he sounded like. Did he know something about her family? Did the entire town? The thought makes Aria nauseous. Now that she knows their families are tied to Les Eaux, she wonders: What did he mean?

Aria registers the diner door's bell jingling again but doesn't look up until she hears a familiar voice.

"Mr. Ha. It's a surprise to see you here. I've heard so much about you."

In the flesh, only a few feet away, is the boy Aria last saw in DC. The world is small, smaller than Aria thought when she was younger. But this . . . this is strange. Back on campus, Emory spoke like he knew who she was . . . and from this interaction, Aria can guess how.

Next to her, Caliste tenses. Aria glances at her sister, careful not to invite scrutiny from their new guests. Her lips are thin, and she stares at Emory in disbelief.

Emory strides toward them, his dark blond hair pushed back in the same way Aria remembers.

"Emory? My god, I haven't seen you since you were a boy." Paul smiles weakly, and he pats Emory on the back. Next to the Hanes, Paul looks small.

"It's been quite a while, hasn't it, Mr. Ha? I'm so sorry about the discovery," Emory says. How he phrases it—*the discovery*—feels wrong. *Discovery* doesn't come close to describing the horror of what happened to their mom.

Paul nods, a grim expression on his face. "Thank you, Emory. It's . . . been difficult for our family." It's a vague statement, and Aria is curious how much Eric and Emory know about the Hàs and the Nguyễns. Do they know about the separation? Or do they think Paul, Aria, and Caliste have lived as one happy family for all this time? An endless string of questions burns on the tip of her tongue.

"How do you know each other?" Caliste asks abruptly, her voice hard. Paul glances at her with an expression that borders on reproach.

"It's a pleasure to meet you. Although we did meet as children. I suppose you don't remember. My name is Emory," he says with a smile. He reaches out his hand to Caliste, and she ignores it. Aria is quietly grateful that it seems like she and Caliste both get the same bad vibe from him.

"You've never told them, Paul?" Eric laughs, and his face lights up. "We were childhood friends. My father helped Paul's family come to the States. We were close before things fell apart so dreadfully. Isn't it astounding? You are here *because* of us."

"Shall I call you Ba, too?" Caliste asks.

"Ah," Aria says at the same time, only able to muster a syllable. Another detail all the adults magically forgot to disclose. Another link to their past that was wholly unknown to them.

"My father's investment paid off, didn't it? I've heard your company is doing well. You've expanded into Europe recently, haven't you?" Eric asks.

Paul frowns, and so does Caliste.

"My dad expanded into Europe years ago . . ." Caliste whispers. Aria watches Emory and his father and is surprised when Emory makes direct eye contact with her.

"You'll have to forgive my father. His . . . memory is not what it used to be," Emory says with a smile. It makes Aria shudder.

"Anyway, if you're in town for long, I'd love to have you over for dinner," says Eric. "It will be nice to have us all together again."

"That would be nice, but I don't think it'll work," Paul replies.

The way Eric said *us,* as if they're one big happy family—it causes a rising panic in Aria's chest. If this is their shared history, why on earth was Emory so hostile? Judging from Paul's stiff answer, Aria can't help but think Eric's friendly exchange is a farce. Something must have happened for Paul to be acting this way. Even an estranged daughter can sense the chilliness.

"Anyway, it really is a pity. I know Grace was unhappy, but I never thought . . ." Eric says, his voice trailing.

"What? What is he talking about?" Aria asks.

"It's nothing. We'll talk about it lat—"

But Paul doesn't get to finish what he's saying.

"We heard your mother killed herself à la Virginia Woolf. That must be upsetting for you all. I'm sorry," Emory said.

He is staring squarely at Aria. Her stomach drops, ushering in a fresh wave of nausea.

Emory doesn't seem the least bit sorry to be telling them this.

♊

Caliste

After the discovery of two dead bodies, Caliste was sure nothing else could possibly be more upsetting. She was wrong.

"What the hell did you say?"

Emory—or whatever his name is—and his *most gracious* dispensing of news is the last rush of fire that thaws whatever funk Caliste's been stuck in since earlier this morning. And . . . there's something strange about the way he speaks. It's as if Caliste's heard his voice before. But unless he sounds the same as when he was a child, there's no way she could remember his voice.

"Cali. Be nice. I told you we'd talk about it later." Paul is back to wearing an expression Caliste recognizes, the one she pictures when asked to conjure an image of her dad. It's the one he wore when he'd tell her to stop crying when she was a kid.

"Okay, then let's make later happen *now*." Caliste needles Aria with her elbow and stands. Aria scrambles quickly, following Caliste's lead and exiting the booth.

"Con . . ." Paul says, but Caliste knows it's only a half-hearted protest. Her father's care is superficial—all lip service, zero action. It's why she can do whatever the hell she wants as long as she doesn't publicly embarrass him.

She doesn't feel bad for making a beeline for the door, squeezing between Emory and his father to do so. As her shoulder brushes past Emory, she hears him say something behind her.

"It's been nice meeting you."

It takes everything not to deck him then and there. Boys like Emory—arrogant and haughty—were a dime a dozen at Lockshire.

Once she's outside, Caliste is shaking as she walks, and the bristle of tears threatens to spill over. Caliste purses her lips and blinks hard.

"Hey, are you okay?" Aria is running after her.

"Sorry . . . I'm still kind of shaken from this morning." Not a lie. But also not the truth.

"Did you know about what he said—about how Mom died?" Aria asks as she catches up.

"No. It sounds like Dad did, though. Which of course he did."

The unease in Caliste's stomach from Emory's voice is triggered again at Aria's revelation. Soon the diner door opens once more, and Paul appears. Caliste is already tired of looking at his face. Funny how she was almost grateful to see it earlier.

"It's cold. We should get into the car," Paul says, his voice tight.

Caliste nods wordlessly and walks back toward the SUV. She makes note of the car that's now parked next to theirs: a sleek black Bentley with a Georgetown bumper sticker on the back. Tacky. Aria tenses as they walk past it.

Their car is silent except for the sound of the engine and Dylan's soft snores. Priscilla quietly asks if they're okay when they're seated, and Caliste offers an aggravated nod.

"What's with Eric?" Caliste asks.

"What do you mean?"

"He mistook us for Mom and called her 'my love.' That's objectively weird."

"It's just a habit of his," Paul says with a sigh. He turns to look at them in the back seat. "There's a folder in the pocket of my seat, Cali. It's for you . . . you and Aria."

Caliste leans forward, taking out a red folder flush with paper. Her father's answer isn't satisfying, but her curiosity gets the better of her.

"What is it?" Aria asks.

"They are the things we kept from you . . . our documents. Our story. Everything is in there."

Caliste swallows, flipping open the folder. Aria inches closer, the stale smell of the bonfire's smoke on her clothes wafting. The first things they see are two birth certificates, each carefully placed in plastic sheeting.

Ariadne Ha born May 1 at 11:57 p.m.
Caliste Ha born May 2 at 12:01 a.m.

"We weren't born on the same day," Caliste says. She thought one of them might have the incorrect birthday when she asked Aria before.

"Grace Nguyễn," Aria says. It's a statement, not a question. "She was prescribed this?"

Aria hands a paper to Caliste, a somber expression on her face. It's a faded prescription sheet, the doctor's winding hand slithering down the bottom edge of the paper labeled with their mother's name. Caliste recognizes the script. Sertraline, an introductory script that Caliste learned was prescribed for an assortment of mental issues from depression to panic disorders and PTSD. Caliste's psychiatrist prescribed it to her last year, but Caliste ended up having nightmares and drenching her sheets in sweat night after night. Caliste had needed her dad to sign off on getting the medication filled, and she was surprised he didn't say a thing to her about it. Was it because Paul had already been through this with their mom?

She swallows. The panic. The sense of dread that engulfs her at the drop of a hat over the most basic of things. Caliste thinks back to her argument with Grandma before she left California. Bà Nội said she was mentally weak and vulnerable, just like her mother. She even referred to her "fits." Is this what she meant? Daughter-in-law and granddaughter both plagued by panic attacks and mental health demons? The thought fills Caliste's mouth with a bittersweet taste.

Caliste nods, and Aria squeezes her in a sideways hug.

Returning her attention to the remaining papers, Caliste

shrugs off the discomfort and spots what appears to be the edge of a stack of photos. The top photo in the stack is a picture of her father pushing a double stroller in front of a car. It's an old-school white Oldsmobile sedan with a square front and a cracked windshield. Behind that photograph is another ripped in half. In it, Caliste is standing proudly between Paul's legs (for some reason, she holds a praying mantis). She knows it's her because she recognizes the gingham romper from her other childhood photos. They appear to be standing in a restaurant; a backdrop of large round tables and chairs is slightly unfocused in the background.

"Oh my god," Aria says, her head pressing against Caliste's as she peers at the torn photo in Caliste's hand. "The other half of the photo. I know where it is. It's hanging up where my aunt used to work . . ."

Caliste makes eye contact with Aria. This photo . . . it's proof of the childhood they'd lost. She almost can't believe it.

"We should go see her," Paul finally says. He glances up and meets Caliste's gaze. His fingers are tapping on the steering wheel to a specific rhythm, and Caliste realizes what song it is.

The tune catches in Caliste's throat . . . a murmured lullaby she faintly remembers from her dreams, a song she believed was sung by her mother.

I will see you again in my sleep, my sweet child . . . my baby.

They were going to see her again.

CHAPTER FIFTEEN

Caliste

There are no words—not in the English language she knows nor in the Vietnamese she doesn't—to describe the density of the emotion ensconcing them now. Caliste can feel her pulse in her eyeballs and her heart in her feet.

In the next room is their mother's body. She wants to puke.

Aria's arm is snaked around hers. The lobby of Riverside Funeral Home, disturbingly, is designed with the same aesthetic as the inn's parlor. Before coming here, Paul checked Priscilla and Dylan into their hotel room and gave Caliste and Aria a break to shower and rest after the ordeal of the previous night. Their rooms were only a few doors down from each other. It was odd, considering how Rose had kept insisting rooms weren't available, but Caliste decided not to press. If anyone can overcome an impossible scenario, it's Paul.

Paul didn't tell them anything else about the investigation, except for the conclusion that their mother died by suicide. He said it with so little inflection, Caliste almost thought he was referring to someone else entirely. The rational side of her brain might venture that he was being the adult for his children, but the rational side of her brain had fed her lies before. And to be honest, she didn't want to waste any more time attempting to understand her father. He never tried to understand her.

He's sitting diagonally from them, flipping through an issue of *People* magazine from three years ago. He pauses after turning another page.

"There is something I didn't tell you."

"God, Ba. What is it now?" Caliste says. The past twenty-four hours have provided both too much information *and* an infuriating lack of information.

"The officers said it's likely your mother died recently."

"Recently?" Aria is asking, but the surprise is both of theirs.

"What do you mean? You mean she's been alive all this time?" Caliste's voice catches at the question. *No . . . It . . . There's no way.*

"Mr. Ha? We're ready for you," the mortuary director says, appearing from behind a fake rosebush and approaching. Caliste stands with Aria and paints on a half-hearted smile.

The man looks as old as time, and Caliste suppresses the bitter thought that he's still alive, but her mother is not. Why do some get to live forever while the tethers of others' lives are cut short?

"Here are her possessions," the man says, holding a plastic bag out to Paul.

"Possessions?"

"It's the clothes she was wearing. We've laundered them for you as well."

He takes the bag. "I see. Thank you."

The director stands patiently, wearing an appropriately

neutral yet empathetic expression on his face. Caliste wonders if that's part of the training for this field of work.

Paul pulls a red sweater from the bag, and seeing this sign of their mother in the flesh triggers a rush of melancholy. Her dad doesn't say anything, but his thumb traces gently over the fabric. The cardigan has a line of pearl buttons; one is missing from the very end, though there's a bit of trailing thread.

"Are you ready, Mr. Ha?"

Paul nods. Wordlessly, they follow behind the mortuary director, passing by picturesque paintings of flower fields and windmills. Every door they pass is large, a carved wooden behemoth that's shut like a vault. Eventually, they arrive at the fifth door, and the man stops.

"You may enter. As requested, we've covered her up. But because of the upcoming cremation and out-of-state transport, we didn't fix her up or anything." The old man is apologetic, but this only confuses Caliste more. Fix *what* up? As dark and painful as it sounds, she expected only pieces of her mother to be left, but knowing she died recently changes everything. How long does it take for a body to decompose?

When the door creaks open, she closes her eyes instinctively, reaching for Aria's arm and gripping it tightly.

"What in the world?" Paul's voice is a whisper.

"Oh my god." Aria's voice is barely audible next to Caliste.

When Caliste peels open her own eyes, first glancing at the ugly swirling brown carpet and then at the metal table holding their mother, she sees herself.

"Mom? She . . ."

On the table, swathed in a plain white linen blanket and with her head resting on a stack of pillows, is a woman who, as forewarned, looks like she just died. Her long black hair is tucked under the white blanket.

"I don't understand," Paul says, his face pale.

After a few painful seconds, her father approaches their mother's side.

"I. She . . . erm. God. You haven't changed." He is weeping, and it's only the second time Caliste has seen her father cry.

♊

Aria

Aria prepared herself for this moment, tried to steady her nerves and brace herself for the wave of emotion that might come crashing to shore once she laid eyes on her mother again. But . . . it doesn't come. Instead, all she feels is the heaviness of something wedged in her throat. The sensation is off-putting.

Silently, she grips Caliste, standing behind Paul. She glances sideways at Caliste to see how she's doing and notices that she's equally non-emotive. Aria can tell Caliste is watching Paul; her eyes are tracing his bobbing head and the way his hands move to clutch the linen blanket covering their mom.

Aria inhales before taking a step forward. Caliste follows suit.

Their mother's face.

Grace. Xuân. A woman of two names with two daughters and no soul . . . not anymore. She strikes Aria as someone who can't be much older than forty. Smooth skin. Sleek black hair—not peppered by white strands like her husband's. And . . . she is whole. This is not the body of someone who disappeared and died over a decade ago. Even if she did die recently, why hasn't she aged? Asian genes aren't *that* strong.

There are *some* signs that paint the picture of an unwelcome death. There are bits of bruising scattered over her skin that Paul touches with shaking fingers—bruises the funeral director explains are injuries from struggling in the river, perhaps from grabbing on to logs or stones to keep from drowning. Their mom's skin is sunken and thin, and her face appears gaunt.

"Ba . . ." Caliste lets go of Aria's hand and moves to stand next to her father. Tentatively, she reaches to touch him, but her hand stops an inch shy of his shaking shoulder.

Aria walks toward their mother's feet, resting her hand on the spot where her ankles are covered.

"Are we sure it's her?" Aria asks. The question levitates, unwelcome, among them. The Xuân here is the same Xuân in the picture on the altar at her home. The same woman seen hanging on the wall of Mrs. Kim's laundromat, Aria hiding behind her legs in the photo. But that's impossible.

"It is. It's her. I don't . . . I don't doubt it." Paul straightens. He seems to have regained his composure, resealing the cracks in his armor.

"This makes no sense."

"Cali . . ."

"No. I'm serious. So, what? She disappeared fourteen years ago . . . then magically reappears in the town we used to live in and drowns herself? It's—" Caliste's voice breaks with a visceral anger. "Something happened to her. Someone *did* something to her, Ba. I'm sure of it."

"And how are you so sure?" Paul raises his voice, startling them both. Aria steps back, and Caliste flinches but remains rooted to her spot.

"Look at her! She hasn't aged."

"Let it go!" His voice thunders in the small room, and Aria is acutely aware of her heartbeat thumping uncontrollably in her chest. Aria realizes tears are dropping from her face onto the linen blanket.

"You. You are the reason she's gone. Not me. Not Aria. She left *you*."

Paul releases a slow breath, and Aria feels like it rattles the entire room.

"You're right."

"What?" Caliste says, stunned.

Paul faces them now and lowers his voice.

"You're right, but I need you both to stay quiet. There is something strange going on. Please, I beg you to let it go. I'll figure it out."

"Ba, you can't be serious!" Caliste protests.

"I'll arrange for her body to be shipped to California so we can get our own autopsy."

He squeezes her shoulder. Caliste swallows back her retort and nods.

"What do you think happened?" Aria asks.

"I don't know. But you both need to return to the inn now. I think it's best we all leave Les Eaux as soon as we can."

"What? No!" Caliste says, triggering Paul to place his finger on his lips—a sign to keep her voice down.

"I truly have no idea what's going on, but you have to trust me. I haven't earned it. Still, go back to your room. Avoid the Hane family. Pretend you are suspicious of nothing."

Avoid the Hane family.

"Wait, do you think they are involved?" Aria asks, considering Tyler's words. If the Hane family has been here for generations . . . then their influence must weave more deeply than Aria can imagine. What could their mother have done to deserve the Hanes' ire?

"You're right. You haven't earned it," Caliste says. Paul doesn't respond. Instead, he pats them both and walks to the room's exit.

"I will let you two have some time alone with her. My decision is final."

Aria puts her arms around Caliste, squeezing her eyes shut and letting her tears fall while she trembles with rage or fear or both.

The heartache of fourteen years, of missing her mom and wishing her into existence, of imagining Xuân traveling the world, comes crashing down. Like a wave beating the shore . . .

It isn't fair she's not around anymore.

It's not.

It's not.

And there is no closure here. Only the opening of Pandora's box as their mother's body lies, ageless, on a metal table.

♊

Aria was afraid of the dark for a long time. Until the age of thirteen, she had a night-light in an outlet near her bedside table. Aunt Thu picked it up from the Salvation Army, a yellowed bulb behind a shield. It was some Arthurian design with a knight holding a sword. Confusingly, there were also two flowers on it.

Whenever the light was on, her room glowed, the two stained

glass flowers illuminating the opposite wall with a faint amber glow. It reminded Aria of the color of her eyelids when she closed her eyes against the sun. It was warm, like the imaginary friend who kept her company when Aunt Thu was at work.

The same feeling of warmth appears now as she and Caliste cry in each other's arms. Aria understands now that it wasn't an imaginary friend but Caliste she was conjuring.

She doesn't know how long they hold each other, but eventually the full-body sobs stop and the strained grip they each have on the other loosens.

"I have to pee," Caliste suddenly whispers, her voice tickling Aria's ear.

Aria laughs, a wet and snotty sound that makes Caliste laugh, too.

"I think the bathroom's right outside. I'll stay here . . ." Aria says, releasing Caliste and turning her gaze downward at her mother's blank face. It's unsettling, seeing her still body. She's like a wax figure and not a woman.

"God. I hope Dad isn't out there," Caliste says, wiping her nose with her sleeve before heading out.

The door shuts, and Aria is alone with her mother. The tears are gone, but the heaviness, that unwieldy and sinking dread, is securely inside her.

Aria reaches forward, afraid, before grazing the bottom edge of her mother's face. The feel of her skin is cool and pliable, and it shocks Aria. It's not like she's ever handled a dead body before . . . but the way her mom's flesh feels is *wrong*.

"This is the first time I've touched you in fourteen years . . ."

Her hand is ready to retract, but Aria pauses, frowning as she studies her mom more closely. There seems to be a second layer underneath the blanket, a sheet pulled tight and tucked around her neck and shoulders. It seems like it'd be uncomfortable.

It's silly, but it's a small act in this grand, terrible scheme. Aria has practice from helping Aunt Thu get comfortable during her hospital stays. A heated blanket or two and a pillow under the backs of her knees. She thinks about how uncomfortable death must have been for her mother, and Aria feels useless all over again.

"Your sister . . . Aunt Thu . . . I do this for her, too . . ." Aria's voice catches as she speaks to her mother. Gently, Aria loosens the fabric that's tight around Xuân's neck.

There's a bruise.

"What are you doing?" Caliste's voice might as well be a firework going off. Aria jumps backward, stifling a yelp.

"Jesus Christ, you scared the crap out of me."

"Well?" Caliste isn't suspicious, but her eyes are wide with expectation.

"The sheet seemed so tight. I . . . You should see for yourself."

"Oookay," Caliste says, walking behind Aria. Her reaction is immediate.

"Oh my god. Who did that?"

The acute sadness is replaced with newfound anger.

Aria moves to the opposite side of the table to inspect her mother. Like on the right side, there's a bruise on the left side of Grace's neck, too. "It looks like someone strangled her, right?" Aria says, suppressing another wave of nausea. The bruises on their mother's neck are clear in the fluorescent light of the funeral home. Aria is *this* close to vomiting.

"I need to get my dad," Caliste says, moving suddenly toward the door. Right then, a loud knock echoes, and the two freeze.

"Visiting hours are over. We'll be closing soon." The mortuary director's voice comes from the other side of the door. Before, he sounded unimpressionable and wheezy, and now he unsettles Aria. The investigation was one thing . . . but the mortician's passing mention of bruising didn't do justice to whatever *this* was. If she did simply die by suicide, why were there so many marks? She makes eye contact with her sister.

"Ah. Okay, we'll be right out. Saying our goodbyes!" Caliste yells, and darts back to Aria and their mother. Out of the black leather handbag slung over her shoulder Caliste pulls her phone and furiously taps the screen.

"What do we do?" Aria asks.

"My dad isn't answering his phone. Jesus." Caliste holds the phone to her ear, and Aria can hear the repeating ring emitting faintly.

Aria swallows, shaking off the disgust at what she's about to do. Aria's hand trembles as she takes her phone out of her pocket and aims the lens at the bruises on her mom's neck.

"What are you doing?"

"I'm taking a picture."

"Quick."

Once Aria pockets her phone, Caliste reaches forward, tucks the sheet back around their mother's neck, and smooths the blanket back into place.

"Ladies!"

"Oh shi—" Caliste yells, and the door opens.

The mortuary director is smiling, but his knuckles are white as he grips the door handle. "It's time to go. I'm very sorry for your loss."

♊

Caliste

Caliste often wondered about the ways in which she and her mom might be similar. Was it only appearance her father was always commenting on? Was her mom afraid of heights, too? Maybe Grace also didn't like cilantro—a sin for a Vietnamese girl. Did they laugh in the same manner, throwing their heads back and baring their teeth like a hyena? (Art had made that animal comparison. Caliste liked it better than what Dylan used: a donkey.)

Of all the commonalities Caliste imagined, she never thought a panic disorder would be one of them.

Caliste's first panic attack was in the bathroom stall at Lockshire, staring straight into a bloodied porcelain hell. It made sense then . . . the other times, not so much. Afterward, she had them at random intervals. She could feel completely at peace lying on her dorm bed at Lockshire and watching a true crime documentary. Then her heart would start beating erratically, and a rapidly rising sense of doom would come out of nowhere. The worst was the sweating . . . She would be drenched in the span of a few minutes and often completely soaked through her pajamas. Other panic attacks were much more ill-timed, like the morning she had to take the SAT. She barely made it in time.

Apparently, their mother felt the same level of anxiety after her father died, with it escalating after getting pregnant. A knot forms in Caliste's throat as she imagines how lonely and terrifying motherhood without parents or in-laws must have felt for Grace.

How fast was her mother's heart beating before it stopped forever?

Aria shifts next to her, pulling the quilt as she rolls over on her side and leaving part of Caliste's ankles exposed. Aria must be tired, because gentle snores emanate from her side of the bed in semiregular intervals. It's cute. Like a sleeping squirrel or hamster.

Caliste stares wide-eyed at the vaulted ceiling and the scattering of streetlight peeking through the room's blinds. She's glad Aria's finally getting some rest. She can't believe this trip started and ended with two different dead bodies. After returning to the inn, Paul told them to sleep and retired to his room with Priscilla. He wanted Caliste to return home with him.

She's pretty sure that's a mistake. Mom couldn't have died from a simple drowning. Her father has his own plan to solve the mystery surrounding the state of his late wife's body, but Caliste can't shake the feeling that it's the wrong move.

The mortuary director, the markings on Grace's neck, and the impossible state of her body. Caliste has no idea where any of it might lead, but she knows the answers are here, in Les Eaux. They can't leave. Not yet. And the Hanes . . . Paul didn't react to the diner run-in with the Hanes in a way that makes sense to Caliste. At this point, she knows only that the Hanes helped her family leave Vietnam in 1975 and that there was some business investment from their former patriarch in the early days of Paul's company, but that's it. From the outside looking in, the Hanes seem like a nice, nondescript white family who are old friends.

But Paul did not seem like he was reuniting with a friend earlier. And that *punk* Emory. Something about that kid makes Caliste's skin crawl.

Caliste sighs, muting the sound so she doesn't wake up Aria. Turning onto her side, she shuffles under her pillow for her phone. When she taps the sleeping screen, she's taken aback by an absolute barrage of notifications. A link to a news article in her friends' group chat stands out.

Bella Vera Beauty Faces $3 Million Lawsuit After Product Line Causes Chemical Burns

That's the tip of the iceberg. Caliste's public accounts are also getting flooded with notifications. *What the hell?*

Caliste swings her legs over the side of the bed to sneak away without disturbing Aria. She steps slowly toward her coat and purse slung over the armchair, careful not to knock anything over in the dark.

She'd *told* Beverly about some of the Reddit posts she found before they signed the contract with Bella Vera, but Bev was insistent the commenters were just typical disgruntled consumers. It didn't help that the CEO is a friend of her mom's.

The door to their room squeaks slightly, and Caliste walks out to an expectantly quiet hallway. There isn't anyone at the front desk so late at night, so she's thankful to be alone in the parlor to figure out what the hell is happening. Caliste settles into a red velvet armchair and runs through her notifications as quickly as she can. Honestly? A social media scandal feels puny compared to what's happening here, but this much attention means Caliste can't possibly ignore it.

Bella Vera Beauty Faces $3 Million Lawsuit After Product Line Causes Chemical Burns

LOS ANGELES (*Los Angeles Times*)—Menlo Park–based beauty company Bella Vera has been implicated in a class action lawsuit alleging chemical burns, use of carcinogenic compounds, and false advertising around the promotion of a "natural" product line. Known for beauty products targeting the fitness industry and athletes, Bella Vera's impacted products include their line of aerosol deodorants, antimicrobial facial sprays, and hair care line. The company issued a voluntary recall as soon as news of the lawsuit dropped.

COMMENTS

> Hugposse: oh god, I've been using the face spray like religiously for the last month???
>
> ailabout1: came here after watching Beverly Ambrose's live. This is so heartbreaking!!
>
> sheepand88: lol the CEO always gave me bad vibes

Caliste frowns, flicking her finger to scan more comments posted under the article. A recurring theme is Beverly, and every time her name pops up, the sinking sensation in Caliste's stomach gets heavier. She returns to her home screen, and there's a red alert on her chat room conversation with Art.

Artemis8072: hey have you seen this? It looks like Bev sold you out.

His message makes no sense to Caliste, because there's nothing to sell out. She already told Bev and the girls she would be out of town because of a family emergency. Shaking her head, Caliste taps on the screen-recorded video of Beverly's live stream and thinks Art must be overreacting.

Beverly's uncharacteristically naked face appears on-screen. Caliste can tell there's a light, dewy layer of foundation, eyebrows brushed with gel, and Beverly's favorite brunette mascara that softens her eyes. Her hair is tied back, and she's donned a cozy cream sweatshirt, the sleeves slightly too long as she fusses with them off camera. This curated "natural" and unkempt look is one Caliste knows. The voice telling her Art is overreacting starts to fade.

"Hey, guys. Sorry it's been so long... There's been a lot going on." Beverly dabs her eyes lightly with the tips of her fingers and inhales sharply. What a goddamn actress.

Beverly looks emotional, but nothing is tipping off Caliste yet. She touches the screen to fast-forward to the time stamp Art provided from the ten-minute video. Now Beverly is full-on sobbing.

"I don't know how to say this, but, like . . . a good friend of mine, a *best* friend . . . gave me advice on something, and I shouldn't have taken it. I can't say much yet, but... *ugh*." Beverly's voice is hoarse, and she sniffles between sobs.

"I'm not one to say 'I told you so,' but . . . I don't know. I'm going to be in big trouble, and it's only because I trusted her so much, you know? It was her birthday when we got the proposal in spring, and I didn't want to push back too much."

Beverly pauses to dab a pink wad of tissue to her face, fanning herself to dry her tears. It is a quintessential Bev performance.

"She even got this *amazing* opportunity recently. I support my girls, you know? But if I'd known this earlier, things would've been different."

This is about the Adidas campaign. This is Caliste's punishment for her F-you moment.

"I feel so bad for everybody I hurt. If I'd only trusted my gut . . . Thank you all so much for your support. It means so much. Once my attorney gives me the all clear, I can talk about it in more detail . . ."

This is where Beverly's voice breaks completely, and the live stream comments are filled with strangers comforting her. When Caliste scrolls through them all, she suddenly understands what Art meant.

Comments

> eldmedia111: wait who is it?
> rtdaypass: look at the other comments. Only cal has a birthday in spring
> Manatea_love: haven't they been friends since they were freshman in hs???? First her uncle and now this?
> Poor bev

The time stamp on the video says 6:21 p.m., which means this live stream was yesterday. The news article dropped at midnight. Caliste recalls Beverly's sickly sweet warning when they last saw each other in person.

I made you, Cal. Don't forget that.

Caliste lets out a mangled laugh. Of course the universe won't give her a nanosecond to breathe.

CHAPTER SIXTEEN

Aria

When Aria wakes up, Caliste is gone. It's pathetic, but sleeping alone already feels weird without Caliste there. She pulls herself out of bed and spends the stretch of silence brushing her teeth, washing her face with Caliste's fancy cleanser, and becoming more or less human. It's been a whirlwind . . . and there's still one person Aria wants to hear from. Aunt Thu. Just a few days ago, Aria was receiving back-to-back calls from her. Now . . . silence.

She's in the hospital, which should be a valid excuse. But Aria is annoyed if she thinks too long about it. Too little time has passed between them, but mountains have moved . . . Aria's father is not dead. She lived another life that Aunt Thu never breathed a word of.

Why? *Why?* Aria can't conjure up one good reason, and this alone makes her want to go back to sleep.

"God, my hair is a mess," Aria says, using damp hands to try to press down her flyaway strands. She learned to cut her hair herself, which results in a relatively average shoulder-length haircut that looks better from some angles than others. Unlike Caliste . . . whose red highlights appear freshly done and immaculately styled when she wakes up every morning. (She explained this was because of some treatment—Aria doesn't remember its name.) Standing alone in the bathroom, Aria's confronted again by the stark difference in their lives, and she hasn't figured out how to feel about it.

Having someone else—someone to consider family, no less— is enough to buoy Aria so she can look past the crashing waves in front of her. But in the silence of this hotel room . . . all she can hear are her thoughts.

Did Paul Hà not want *her*? Given the choice between the two of them, what was it about Aria that he didn't think worth keeping? Could he just tell that little Aria would grow up to be a cheater, someone who sold her moral integrity for money?

Three sharp knocks hit their door, interrupting Aria's contemplation, as well as her attempt at making herself appear less like an ungroomed ferret. She slaps her cheeks and takes a deep breath. Today is going to be the day they find answers.

"Just a second!" Aria yells, jogging from the bathroom to the suite's sitting area.

When she opens the door, Aria is surprised to see Priscilla with Dylan in her arms. She's also able to make out disruptive background noise from elsewhere in the inn: Paul and Caliste arguing.

"Good morning, Aria. Con, tell your sister good morning," Priscilla says, and shifts her torso so that Dylan is closer to Aria.

"Hi," Dylan says simply, retreating into his mother's arms as far back as he can go. He resembles Priscilla, who has a narrow face with round brown eyes and strong features. His hair is a few shades darker than her chestnut brown, reminding Aria of coffee beans.

Priscilla makes a disapproving noise at him, but Aria shakes her hands apologetically.

"It's okay! He's still getting used to having a brand-new sister."

"Your sister is being too nice," Priscilla says as Dylan continues to stare at Aria suspiciously from the safety of her arms. "Anyway . . . I don't suppose you mind helping me mediate a little bit?"

Aria can't make out what's being said, but both Paul's and Caliste's voices continue getting louder.

"Sure . . ."

As Aria approaches the parlor, the argument between the two becomes clearer.

"Cali, you should let me help you. You're a child, for goodness' sake."

"A child? I'm sorry, I've been doing just fine without you up until this point."

"'Fine'? Who paid for your high-rise apartment for the first five months? Whose lawyers review your contracts for you?"

"Please. We all know those are pity gifts to make up for the fact you're an absentee father," Caliste says with a hiss just as Aria finally arrives through the arched doorway. Poor Rose is busy dusting a fake plant behind the counter. Her inn has become a war zone.

"What is happening?" Aria asks tentatively. She walks toward Caliste, who is standing with her arms crossed and looking pointedly out the window and not at Paul.

"It's nothing," Caliste replies.

"Nothing? Please. Your manager already called me. Three

different brands have dropped you, and I wouldn't be surprised if more are on the way."

"And I'll figure out how to fix it myself," Caliste says in reply. Despite her toughened exterior, her eyes are glassy.

There's a tense silence between all parties in the room, and with perfect timing, Aria's phone buzzes in her pocket. Philip's contact photo—a picture of him holding two mooncakes over his eyes like glasses—appears on her screen.

"I think it's Aunt Thu," Aria says, which elicits a reaction from both Caliste and her father. She gives her sister a small nod and walks to the corner of the lobby to take the video call.

"Hey, Ari. I'm with Aunt Thu. We're back at home." Philip's voice releases a knot in Aria's chest, and she smiles. It looks like he's gotten a haircut; the formerly loose strands are cut close to his head above his ears. The collar of his shirt is frayed, and Aria can tell from the lime-green hue that it's the fundraising shirt from sophomore homecoming. His face is familiar yet different enough from when they last saw each other that Aria does a double take.

"Nice haircut."

Philip rubs the top of his head. "Thanks."

"No, thank *you* for taking care of her. Seriously. I . . . I don't know what I'd do without you."

Philip returns the smile. "Whenever you need me, I'll be there. You know that."

Aria nods. "How is she?" she asks.

"The infection is under control, and they gave us antibiotics for her to take."

"And emotionally?"

"Not great. Not like we talk much, but I think she's nervous.

She's barely eaten." Philip's voice is calm and even-tempered. It's the voice he uses when he's trying to mirror Aria and keep her calm. "She's in the living room. I'll give her the phone."

"Thanks."

It seems the Hà Cold War is put on hold as Aria waves over Paul and Caliste. She settles into the center of a decadent orange sofa alongside a bookshelf-lined wall and thinks about what she might say to her aunt first.

"Are you ready?" Philip asks right as Paul and Caliste sit down on either side of her.

Aria nods.

"Okay, I'm passing the phone to her now."

Finally.

♊

Caliste

"Con hả?" The voice is low and raspy, but somehow it reminds Caliste of a song—the kind of rhythmic folk music Priscilla sometimes listened to. Caliste waits to see her aunt for the first time. The woman is leaning back, a fuzzy blue quilt pulled up to her chin. Her left eyeball is ever so slightly obscured by the camera angle. In this woman's face lives Caliste's mother, and Aria, for that matter. None of the great-aunts on Dad's side bear much resemblance to Caliste.

Out of the corner of her eye, Caliste spots Priscilla talking with Rose before slipping something into her hand. A tip. Soon Rose exits the parlor, and they are left alone. Her father is leaning away from the camera, his arms crossed and jaw clenched. A slick of sweat slides down his forehead. Their verbal sparring match wouldn't cause Paul to lose his cool. It seems chatting with Aunt Thu might be another story.

"Yes, it's me. Are you okay?" Aria asks.

Aunt Thu purses her lips and waves her hand as if she's dismissing Aria's concern.

"I'm fine. The doctors are too strict."

"If you say that again, I'm going to cancel your subscription to the Việt TV channels. Stop being so stubborn," Aria says crossly.

"I'll live. After all, I can just go to your room and watch the DVDs you collect instead. Are you still watching those sappy dramas filled with pretty boys?"

It's a little amusing, seeing Aria argue with her aunt like an equally curmudgeonly old lady.

Through the screen, Caliste's eyes lock on to Aunt Thu's, and her new aunt draws in a sharp breath.

"Wow."

That's the only word uttered, and Caliste bows her head awkwardly and says hello.

"Hello, Chị," Paul says. His eyes dart across the screen, and there's an agitated quality to his movement.

"It's been a long time, Paul," Aunt Thu replies. She doesn't look too happy to see their father, either.

"Ah . . . it has. I've heard from Aria that your health's been poor?"

"My health is fine."

The answer is terse and the vocal equivalent of a baseball bat covered in spikes. Seeing someone who outwardly dislikes Paul fills Caliste with a little satisfaction.

"I suppose you two must have questions," Aunt Thu says after several seconds of silence.

Aria's arm tenses as she holds up the phone, and Caliste places a hand on her shoulder. She knows this anger. It was hers just the other day. It's still hers. But now they've switched places. It is Aria's time to be angry, and Caliste's time to mourn.

"Will you tell us everything?" Aria asks.

"I will. I will try . . . of course. I don't know what Paul's told you already." Aunt Thu is tired, but she also sounds relieved, as if the rope tethering her to this weight has finally been severed.

"I gave them the basics, but it's probably best for them to hear it in your words, too."

"Then I'll start from the time your father has no idea about. You can't understand our choice, and I wouldn't expect you to. Your mother . . . Xuân . . . She spent much of her life unhappy, and I know this fact preceded her birth."

"'Preceded'?" Aria asks, her free hand tapping her knee anxiously.

"To give birth during war is a violence I wouldn't wish on my worst enemy. It was a terrible night. And your grandmother, Ba Ngoại, died shortly after Xuân was born. It was a fact Xuân obsessed over, searching through medical books she barely understood to find clues as to why our mother died. A clue to see if she would meet the same fate when she became pregnant with you."

Caliste listens, laying her head on her sister's shoulder as Aunt Thu recalls the past. It's bittersweet—a story both comforting and somber. This isn't the way Caliste wanted to know her mom, but something is better than nothing.

"Our father was a countryman and skilled in fishing. Both your mother and I were born in Cà Mau but left after the bombing started. Eventually we made it to Saigon. An old friend owed Dad a favor, so we managed to leave."

Caliste nods at the information. Her dad also left in the '70s. Two disparate families who departed the same year only to unite in an entirely different country. Both likely seeking the so-called American dream.

Aunt Thu explains that while their father worked at construction sites, Aunt Thu was responsible for taking care of Xuân, who took on the English name Grace because she aspired to be like some actress turned princess.

"Ba was always exhausted after work, and I took us to school. We kept our heads down and tried to stay out of the way. It was not . . . easy . . ."

Caliste glances at her sister. The expression on Aria's face is written in a language in which Caliste isn't fluent yet.

"Can I ask a sensitive question?" Caliste says, her pulse thumping in anticipation.

"What is it?"

"We found a prescription in the documents my dad saved."

"Ah." Aunt Thu's face twists, her thin lips quivering. Caliste is afraid she's made a mistake, but Aria squeezes her arm with encouragement.

"I know now that your mother struggled her entire life, but I was too proud and too narrow-minded to understand back then. It became much worse when our father died, and it spiraled out of control once she became pregnant."

Aunt Thu stares at Paul when she gets to this part of the story.

Her words are steeped in equal parts anger and grief . . . but Caliste senses that most of it is inward facing. The expression Aunt Thu wears is one of immense guilt.

"Sometimes she would start crying uncontrollably, and I'd have to fill a bag with ice and glide it over her back for her to calm down. That's the only thing I agreed with Paul about . . . Xuân told me not to come to Les Eaux, but I started living with them a few weeks before you both were born. I told her I needed to take a break from the nail salon I was working at in Saint Paul because the skin on my fingers started reacting badly."

Caliste nods, processing the information.

"Why did you separate us? Why did you lie?" Aria asks. Unlike Caliste, she says this without any outward signs of anger at her aunt.

"I'm surprised your father hasn't already explained this."

"I want to hear it from you," Aria replies.

Instead of answering, Aunt Thu looks toward Paul, who's said nothing this entire time.

"It was to keep you both safe," Paul says.

"That doesn't make sense," Aria says. Her voice is shaking.

Aunt Thu replies, "I know it doesn't. It was an impossible decision, but we made it. I lied to you because I couldn't bear to tell you the truth. We are villains. We are liars. Be angry at me all you want. We kept you safe. And tonight, all of you will finally leave that wretched place."

"Leave?" Aria says, raising an eyebrow.

"I have a board meeting to attend in LA," Paul says, "and I already booked your flights."

"No, we are staying here," Caliste says, whirling around to face her father. Of course he has a meeting. There's always a goddamn meeting.

"I already told you, there is no point in you both staying here. We will send your mother's body to—"

"This morning you wouldn't take no for an answer, and now, here we are again. For someone who screwed up his family so much, you sure do like making decisions for us."

Caliste stands, unable to hold in her anger any longer.

"I'm sorry, Aunt Thu. We're not leaving. It was good to meet you." Caliste bows and rushes out before her dad can stop her. As she heads for the front door, she hears the next bit of conversation.

"Aria. Do not defy me. You will come home. Today."

Aunt Thu and Paul may act like sworn enemies, but to Caliste, they seem like two sides of the same damn coin.

"Why? We're eighteen. It's not like you can make us do *anything* anymore," Aria retorts.

"You both need to listen to us," Paul starts to interject, which makes Caliste laugh from across the room.

"I'm being serious," Paul's voice thunders, low and dogmatic. Aria freezes, and Caliste stops laughing in shock at his outburst.

"Paul, they don't need to know . . ."

"Know what?" Aria asks.

"We are not telling you without reason. I . . ." Paul casts a wary glance at the screen and Aunt Thu's face. "I fought with your mother before she left. Before she went missing. Do you know what about?"

"Well, obviously not," Caliste says.

"She told me that Eric, my oldest friend, tried to hurt her. That he tried to hurt *you*."

"And what? You think he'd try and hurt us now?"

"No! I admired him deeply. He and his family are the reason I have my life today. And now he has dementia," Paul says, causing Aunt Thu to narrow her eyes. "The man he is now and the man he was . . ."

"He *was* a man of perfectly sound mind when he tried to harm Xuân and your daughters," Aunt Thu says. "You never change. Do you feel bad for him, Paul? He was and still is a snake, even as his mind fades. The bottom of his boot stays clean because of you and your weak tongue."

Paul exhales, Aunt Thu's retort prompting several seconds of tense silence before he speaks again. Even with Bà Nội, Caliste has never witnessed Paul take such a verbal lashing. "Regardless, I think it's better if you both leave as soon as you can. If you stay, I can't protect you."

"Let me ask you this, Ba. Did you even try to protect Mom?"

"I didn't believe Eric would do that," Paul murmurs, his voice heavy with shame at the confession.

"Do you think she was telling the truth now?" Caliste asks, holding her father's gaze.

"She *was* telling the truth," Aunt Thu interrupts. She waits a few moments, but Paul declines to reply. "I was angry at your father, but . . . neither of us could afford to keep you both. Staying together also wasn't an option. At the time it seemed like the best solution. She was gone. We couldn't ask her any questions."

Caliste didn't think she could hate her dad more, but here he is, ushering in a new era of resentment. Caliste pictures what her mom's face might have been like when her own husband didn't believe her about being *assaulted* by another man. Caliste remembers the look on Eric's face when he mistook her for Grace, and it gives her chills all over again.

Now they will find out what happened the night Grace disappeared. They have to.

♊

Dear Sister,

When Mother was pregnant . . . do you think she felt joy? Or was she frightened? I have no reason to complain. I have a house and a husband. There is nothing for me to be afraid of. Well . . . except for the fact I'm too old and the doctors tell me I'm high risk. But that seems trivial. Mother had a real reason to be afraid.

Me? I'm simply a coward.

I have nightmares every night. Remember when I would get night terrors, and you had to wake me up because I was screaming? Ba said I sounded like an animal getting dragged through the night. You know what I see when I sleep? My baby severed from me. I see a child floating away to an island I can't reach, no matter how fast I swim. Eventually I give in to the waves, and all I see is darkness. You'd call it a silly dream.

When Ba died, you became my parent. You must have been afraid.

Phúc is nice to me, contrary to how you thought he'd behave. He does work a lot. But he takes care of me. All day I'm sick, and I can't keep anything down, not even porridge. He stops by Banh Mi Number 8 on his way home and brings me a bowl of pork vermicelli. Every day. It's the only meal I can keep down nowadays.

You are right about one thing, though . . .

Phúc's job doesn't make sense. He went to a good school. There's no reason for him to be suffering in the position he works while I'm waitressing at the restaurant. I know Ba would tell me to be grateful, but it's odd. Phúc's last job let him go because of performance, but you know how he is. I can't imagine him not working harder than the rest.

I'm including some candies Eric brought back from France. His father is sick with cancer. It's quite sad . . . I don't believe the prognosis is very good.

His wife is pregnant, too! I believe she just passed her first trimester. I want to talk to her about it . . . but I think you're right about that as well.

She won't ever see us as friends. I think she found out about Eric's crush on me. I told her that was years ago and meant nothing, but I don't think she appreciated that.

I hope work is treating you well. I'm sending some hand salve the woman at the shop gave me. I think it will help your eczema.

I love you. I swear, I'm all right. The incident at my job was minor. I must just be very tired. Phúc couldn't leave work, so Eric picked me up. He suggested a doctor for me to talk to, so I'm sure it will all come to pass. I'm fine, really.

Love,
Xuân

CHAPTER SEVENTEEN

Caliste

The only car ride Caliste remembers with her dad is from when he took her to Monterey Bay Aquarium. Caliste can't recall why her father took her that time instead of pawning the birthday activity off on someone else. But he'd played his favorite songs—the ones he always changed when someone who wasn't Vietnamese visited the house. They were a mix of German disco and old Vietnamese artists. Sometimes her dad sang along, and Caliste would tell him he couldn't carry a tune.

Her dad had watched her through the rearview mirror. Hanging from the mirror were a jade Buddha and a red tassel; both had swayed to the beat of the music. In that moment, she could *almost* forget that Mom wasn't there.

Almost.

It's been twenty minutes since she left the inn to get some air, and now she's driving alone in the eerie town where her parents lived. Caliste never expected a phone call to emotionally destroy her like this, but this trip has been full of surprises. She's preparing to make a U-turn on an empty road and return to Aria and her dad when the SUV rocks abruptly. Caliste's body lurches forward as the car connects with something.

"Crap!"

When she gets out of the car to inspect, the left front wheel is blown out. Tattered pieces of rubber trail in the gravel on the side of the road. *Great. Perfect. This is the cherry on top of a fantastic day.*

Caliste kicks the tire for good measure and screams into the air. When she turns around to look toward Les Eaux proper, a black car is speeding toward her. She's ready to wave them down, but her hand stops in midair. She recognizes this car.

Caliste forces herself to take deep breaths as the Bentley slows to a stop next to her and the face she prayed not to see appears above the rolled-down tinted window.

"Are you in trouble, Caliste?" Emory says, cocking his head.

Caliste's heart leaps into her throat.

"It's nice to see you again. Although it's too bad it isn't under better circumstances."

Keep calm. There's no reason to freak out. Caliste channels the persona she uses on camera or at parties where everybody is clamoring for her father's attention. It isn't the time to let paranoia overwhelm her . . . yet.

"My tire blew out. I must've hit something," Caliste replies, offering a slight smile. Emory turns off his engine and opens the car door. He steps out—he's clad in a long, black, woolen Burberry trench and slacks—and passes by wordlessly in front of Caliste. The toes of his immaculately polished Chelsea boots kick up dust as he crouches to survey the tire.

"I imagine this is a rental?" Emory says, standing forward and dusting his hands off on the thighs of his slacks.

"It's a car my dad arranged, but there's probably a spare in—"

Emory doesn't wait for her to finish before walking toward the SUV's trunk. There is an uncanny efficiency in how he moves. In another circumstance, Caliste would be grateful.

Soon he's unearthed the spare tire hidden in the bottom compartment of the trunk. Caliste moves to help him, but he rebuffs her as soon as her hands touch the wheel.

"I've got this."

Caliste bites back a mean retort. She doesn't need his help. She doesn't want to owe this snot anything.

"I can do it myself, you know."

"I'm sure you can. But it's cold, and you should sit in my car."

"I'm not cold."

"Really? Because your fingers are turning purple."

Caliste looks down, realizing she's already tucked her hands back into the depths of her sleeves. When she flexes her fingers, she realizes Emory's right. Her face is numb, too.

The absolute last thing on earth she wants to do is get in his car, but this might be an opportunity to figure out exactly what this guy's deal is.

"Okay. Yell if you need anything."

Emory says nothing in return.

Caliste turns toward his Bentley and opens the passenger's side door to settle into the seat. The car is as streamlined as Emory. Everything is a sleek black, with only the orange contrast stitching serving as any pop of color. There isn't a single speck of dirt. Caliste imagines this is the kind of car the guy from *American Psycho*, a film her father has rewatched in their theater room, might drive.

The car's key fob is sitting in the cup holder next to a single unopened bottle of Evian. There isn't any music playing, either.

"What a freak," Caliste mutters as her curiosity gets the better of her.

Glove compartment: nothing except for the car's manual.

Middle console: perfectly aligned miniature packets of tissue papers and a USB cord, neatly coiled.

Compartment above the dashboard: a pair of black Tom Ford sunglasses with gold detailing.

Caliste glances up through the tint of the window to spy on Emory. He's still kneeling beside her car. She can't quite discern his progress, which means she doesn't know how much longer she can snoop. Her hand slips, grazing something in the side compartment of the passenger-side door. It's a necklace entangled with . . . something else.

She can feel her heartbeat in her fingers, and she pulls out a knotted mess. It takes her a second to register what exactly she's looking at.

A shark's tooth on a leather cord.

Tyler. Caliste swallows, a million thoughts racing through her mind at once.

It's a coincidence that they own the same necklace, right? There's no way it's Tyler's.

Maybe there's a weird tradition with Minnesota boys and shark's-tooth necklaces?

Caliste slips the necklace in her pocket and jumps when the driver's-side door opens.

"Hey!"

"Did I startle you?" Emory asks dryly from the driver's seat. His gaze lingers on Caliste's hand shoved deep into her pocket but says nothing about it.

I need to get out of here. Based on what she's seen so far, Emory has everything. A spotless family legacy. Old-money wealth. What could he possibly gain from Tyler dying?

"Th-thanks. Aria is waiting for me," Caliste stammers as Emory shuts the door. The realization sinks slowly into place just before the latch triggers. "Did you just lock me in here with you?"

Emory grins. "Don't fret too much. I only did it because I knew you'd run away."

"Yeah, that makes it better." Caliste glares and reaches for the passenger-side door to confirm Emory isn't full of crap. The handle moves but the door doesn't open, and the child lock's engaged.

"My father keeps pestering me about inviting you to our house."

"We're busy," Caliste retorts.

"I thought you'd say that," Emory says, throwing one of his hands in the air with an exaggerated flourish before he starts the Bentley's engine. It roars to life, and Caliste's entire back is damp with sweat now.

"My dad is flying out tomorrow morning. He doesn't have time."

"I'm not asking your father. I'm asking you."

"We have plans tomorrow. I'm not lying about them," Caliste says. It is the truth. Their plan is to go to the library and comb through the town archives after Paul leaves.

"We can do it the day after."

Caliste breathes in to steady herself. *Emory really doesn't like no, does he?*

"Unlock the door."

"Since I did you a favor, you'll have to come over for dinner."

Emory stares at her, his left hand on the wheel and the most insufferable smirk on his face.

"Or what? Unlock this door!"

Calmly, he drops his voice and replies, "You don't really want me to answer that."

Caliste doesn't want to give in, but the voice in her head that's terrified to call his bluff drowns out every other thought.

"Fine. We'll come to dinner."

The car's locks click.

"Perfect."

♊

Aria

"Are you sure you don't want any more than that?" Paul asks from a few feet behind her. Aria is walking down a narrow brick alley, a shopping bag with two pairs of gloves hanging from her arm. The historic part of Les Eaux is blocked off for a Christmas market, and colorful stalls line the road along with a glittering array of lights. After stopping by a woman selling various hand-made knitwear, Aria picked up two pairs of gloves, one lavender and one emerald green. The green pair is for Caliste.

Aria shakes her head and continues wandering and pausing at the various stalls that catch her attention. There's a table of hand-painted nutcrackers and glass jewelry. Whenever Aria sees something pretty, she thinks of her sister.

After Caliste stormed out of the inn, Aria was left to wrap up the phone call by herself. Aunt Thu spent a good five minutes reprimanding Aria for being stubborn, but ultimately both she and Paul lost that fight. It was easy to leverage guilt in the moment. How could they enforce parental authority when they had just confessed to lying to both Caliste and Aria for over a decade?

Paul called Aunt Thu on his phone to chat privately, and Aria escaped to Priscilla's room. Dylan is now accepting Aria watching him play, but participation is still off the table. According to Paul, his business meeting was successfully rescheduled. She assumed Aunt Thu was to thank for that change of heart. Regardless, he is staying in Les Eaux another day. After Dylan fell asleep, Priscilla instructed Paul to take Aria to "play outside."

Now, as they walk down Les Eaux's eclectic main street lined with brick row houses adorned in bright red Christmas decorations and ribbon-entwined evergreens, Paul occasionally mentions a memory pertaining to a passing point of interest (for example, the pharmacy where he used to pick up packs of licorice for their mother).

They stroll by a restaurant named Harrod's Eatery, which is as quintessentially all-American as Aria can imagine. It's filled with cowhide, exposed wood, and a lot of romanticized rockabilly decor—complete with a vintage record player in the corner and a giant portrait of Elvis Presley visible from the street.

"We went here many times as a family," Paul says as Aria stops to look through the window of the restaurant.

Family.

"We should come here with Caliste later."

Paul smiles, his face reflected in the glass. It's a rueful expression.

"I'm sorry about Caliste. She gets like this sometimes. She'll return after she blows off some steam," Paul says.

"Do you think she has a temper?"

Paul laughs at the question. "Cali does, but she gets it from me. And your mother, for that matter. Your sister was quite angry when she received her rejection from Dartmouth. Although she pretended not to be."

"Oh, she applied to colleges?" Aria asks. "I figured that was optional for influencers." That said, everything Caliste has said since their meeting has pointed toward her not being in school.

"She did. I believe she was choosing between USC and Berkeley before she decided not to go to college altogether," Paul says with a sigh.

Aria thinks her sister doesn't quite have the right idea about her dad . . . Paul is clearly very attentive or at least monitors the environment around her. Even now, his mind seems to be wherever Caliste is. It bothers Aria . . . a little.

"Why this restaurant?" Aria asks.

"Ah . . . yes. I suppose I should explain. When we moved to Les Eaux, both your mom and I worked here for a bit. She was much better than I was and much more charming. People gave her more tips."

"Here?" Aria asks, confused. She doesn't exactly understand the trajectory of Paul Hà from immigrant kid to millionaire, but she does know he attended Dartmouth and graduated at the top of his class. Unless, of course, the internet was lying.

Paul seems to understand the deeper meaning of her question.

"I had a hard time finding work after I graduated. We came back to Les Eaux because it was easier."

Saint Paul is a city with a huge Vietnamese community. Paul's family lives in Boston and California. How could Les Eaux be easier?

"Was it because of Eric Hane?" Aria asks finally.

Paul tenses. "Yes. Eric's father was the reason my family came to the United States. My father was in the military and became acquainted with Eric's father during a company visit to the Tân Sơn Nhứt air base. They helped us a great deal. I thought he might be able to help us out again."

"A company visit? What does that even mean?" Aria asks.

"The Hanes' company was a contractor for the U.S. military. Eric's father had joined a group of civil engineers."

"Eric said his father invested in your business?"

"That was true in the early days, but we no longer have any sort of business relationship."

"Didn't it worry you? You had all this history with him, and then your wife told you he tried to harm her."

"I'll never know what truly happened. Back when I struggled to find work, Eric offered us a place to stay, free of charge, and jobs working for his friends. We'd all been friends for years. Especially after your mother became pregnant, it was simply the most logical option. He helped us then, so I can never resent him for that."

"Even if he put his hands on your wife?" Aria asks, turning to face him. She and Philip aren't a couple, but she knows he'd deck another guy for hurting her.

". . . I could be angry at him. I could storm his house and ask for the truth, but what would that do when his mind is suffering?"

Aria doesn't say anything, especially since she believes his line of thinking is cowardly. Eric didn't always have dementia, and Paul never confronted him.

"Was your work why our grandmother hated Mom so much?"

The second bomb of a question. Caliste had been sparse in her explanation, but it was a common-enough story for Aria to wrap her head around. Just like in the dramas she read, the mother-in-law and daughter-in-law did not get along.

"My mother certainly was displeased about my work. But she was also displeased with your mom."

"Why?"

"In simple terms, your mom didn't have the pedigree my mother valued. Neither Grace, Thu, nor your grandfather were highly educated. On top of that, she . . ."

"She was diagnosed with panic disorder . . . and probably had some other, undiagnosed issues," Aria says plainly, finishing the sentence that Paul is ready to let falter.

"To my mother, it was a weakness she couldn't understand. It was an illness that meant Xuân would always be a terrible mother. It was a test of strength of will, and your mother lost."

Aria is silent at the confession. How lonely must her mother have been, struggling with no help?

"So, do you believe the officers?"

"What?" Paul asks. He's startled, and his eyes glance around to see if anyone is within eavesdropping distance. "I don't . . ."

"They say she died by suicide. Do you believe it?"

"No, I do not," Paul says, his voice dropping dramatically in volume. "But please, this isn't the place to discuss that."

Aria senses that she's pushed her luck. Paul's jaw is clenched, and his hooded eyes look intensely at his estranged daughter.

"There is something else I wanted to talk to you about," Paul says, jerking his head to the side to indicate they should continue walking. Aria follows as Paul guides them under a line of trees. "Georgetown. I heard about your disciplinary hearing."

"H-how?" Aria asks, panicked. Not even Aunt Thu or Caliste know at this point.

"Don't look so alarmed. Your friend told me."

"Friend? Who? . . . Philip?" Aria asks. When would he have had time to even do that?

"Yes. He ended the call on Aunt Thu's behalf and took a few minutes to explain to me what happened."

"I can't believe he would do that." Aria sees red. *How could he?*

"He's a good boy, and a good friend. I'm glad he told me. Aria . . . I haven't acted as your father, so I won't lecture you now. But I can help you. That's the least I can do."

"No," Aria says, resolute. She's ashamed, embarrassed, and angry. God . . . she's angry. "I will fix it myself."

"How? You're a smart girl, and you have so much potential. There's no reason for you to risk expulsion over something like this."

"Something like this? You mean breaking my morals so we aren't in debt? If you had come down from your tower to help Aunt Thu with her medical bills, I wouldn't be here. You don't get to save me now."

"I tried. I did— I know you don't have any reason to believe me, but I sent checks to your aunt. She always sent them back."

This revelation doesn't strike the chord Paul hopes.

"Thanks, Father. I really appreciate it, but again, I will fix this myself. You can go back to ignoring me."

Paul opens his mouth to say something, but whatever he's about to say, he seems to decide against it.

"Are you sure about staying here? Our flight leaves tomorrow afternoon, and I can still book flights for you and Cali. Wouldn't it be nice to spend time together?"

Caliste. The girl living a life that in theory was also Aria's.

"Why did you pick Caliste?"

Paul stops in his tracks and faces Aria. Clouds drift by, blocking out the sun and casting Paul's face in a soft shadow.

"I didn't choose Cali over you, Aria."

"No? That's what it feels like."

"We tried to let you choose . . . truly. I don't know—" Paul sighs. "I'm sorry."

Aria laughs, and she doesn't care how cruel that might be. *Sorry. Sorry. Sorry.* That's all she's heard for the past few days, and she's tired of it.

CHAPTER EIGHTEEN

Caliste

Caliste woke up to another barrage of messages on her phone and a note slipped under their door.

> There's been an emergency. Something came up with your grandmother. Don't worry, she's fine. I won't make you come back with me. Be good. Take care. Don't stay here too long, and remember what I said.

She recognizes Paul's handwriting immediately. In follow-up messages from Priscilla, Caliste learned that her father, with Priscilla and Dylan in tow, grabbed the first plane back to California from Saint Paul's airport this morning.

He told them to stay away from the Hane family, with a half-hearted acknowledgment of something possibly transpiring between Eric and their mom. As much as Caliste hates it, going directly to the Hanes is the only solution she can think of to find out the truth.

Since I did you a favor, you'll have to come over for dinner.

In roughly twenty-four hours, she will have to see Emory and Eric Hane's faces again. Their weird savior complex made Caliste's skin crawl.

"Hey, you missed the turn," Aria says from the passenger's side, and Caliste snaps back to the present.

"Crap. You're right."

"Usually am," Aria says, making Caliste laugh.

Today they're poking around the Les Eaux Public Library. The SUV's wheels make a heaving and grinding noise as they make their way from the main road to the library's parking lot. Caliste turns off the car and grabs her backpack from the back seat before following Aria toward the library's elaborate gilded double doors.

"Jesus Christ," Caliste says, half to herself and half to Aria, as they walk to the entrance. The exterior is like something from a child's imagination, where one might get tortured with the acquisition of knowledge. It's made completely of old stone. Dried ivy snakes up and through each of the crevices, with each edge jutting in unexplainable shapes. It appears to be very, *very* old.

"Edgar Allan Poe would love it here . . ." Aria says, her eyes scanning the outdoor area. Clusters of evergreens are shielded by a wrought-iron fence. Time has clearly had its way; each barbed spike of the fence is painted with dark orange rust.

"Whatever . . . Let's get in and out of this creepy-ass place as fast as possible," Caliste mutters, and her sister's soft chuckle is carried away by the wind.

She follows behind Aria, noting the absolute stillness around them. Isn't it almost Christmas? Caliste imagined small towns would be . . . livelier. Like a Hallmark movie. Then again, she's never hung out at a library.

"Decor's pretty normal," Aria says as the entrance doors close behind them. The pale beige wallpaper and ugly gray-and-black carpet under their feet do seem similar to the sterile environment at the police station.

There's a woman with graying hair and a festive green sweater-vest minding the front desk. As they approach, she peeks up from the book in her hand. For whatever reason, the slight hint of holiday festivities makes Caliste feel a *little* better and not like she's walking into some haunted house.

"How may I help you?"

Caliste's palms are sweaty as she thinks of what to say to not invite suspicion. If the Hane family founded this town, then their influence very well may have survived the centuries.

"We're interested in historical archives of the local newspaper," Aria says first, and her tone is saccharine, full of respect, with an almost exaggerated sense of civility. Aria wants this woman to trust them.

"Of course. We have some of the newer newspapers—up through the past three years, at least—on the shelves in the back left corner. Anything older will be digitized. That's all searchable on any of our computers."

"Is there a guest log-in we can use?"

"Of course! Here, I'll write it down for you, Aria." The woman smiles, and Aria returns it easily.

Once they escape earshot, Aria pulls down the scarf cocooning her neck and whispers to Caliste, "She used my name. I never said it, did I?"

"I mean, it's a small town, and we gotta be the only Asian identical twins in, like, a three-hundred-mile radius."

"True. So, we play it cool. We're two patrons using public informational services, as is our right . . ."

"Yes, and you saying that out loud absolutely makes us sound normal and not at all suspicious," Caliste says.

"As if you can lecture me, Miss I'm Wearing All Black Like I'm Double-Oh-Seven."

Caliste rolls her eyes and digs her all-black elbow into Aria's side, forcing her off-balance. She ignores her sister's glare as they arrive at a set of computers next to the physical copies of the newspaper.

"Game plan is to find everything related to the drownings, yes?" Caliste asks as Aria slips her coat over the back of one of the library's oak chairs.

"Right. Mom, Tyler . . . and Riley. But when I was talking to Tyler, he made it seem like there were more," Aria says with a nod. "And maybe we should . . ."

Aria leans in closer to Caliste and reaches out to tuck a piece of hair behind her ear. "Also see if Emory connects to any of the drownings?" she whispers.

Caliste nods as Aria continues to pretend to fix her hair. When she steps back, the front desk worker seems to have migrated to the shelf of World War II history books within their line of sight.

They decide to split tasks by time, with Caliste tackling the year their mom disappeared and anything else that might be related to drownings in that general time period.

As expected, the library's system is as old as dirt and as slow as a snail. The cursor's spinning wheel takes what feels like an eternity to stop before the next page loads.

Grace Nguyen. The name in print on the screen isn't unexpected, but it still stuns Caliste. The truth has been available in these archives all this time.

When Caliste scrolls down the page, there's an odd message that she almost misses.

PER A PRIVACY REQUEST, THIS ARTICLE IS NOT INDEXED FOR PUBLIC AVAILABILITY.

She's tried researching her mother's disappearance before, of course. But she found nothing outside what her father had already told her.

Why is this article hidden from public availability? Did her dad put in a request to the library?

Caliste concentrates on the content of the article. It outlines their mother's missing persons case and the Hane family's close relationship with the Hà family. There is a hazy photo of Eric Hane, young and uncannily like his son in appearance. They even have the same arrogant smirk.

Eric is quoted in the article discussing how sad Grace's disappearance is. He asks the public for any information related to the case. There is explicit reference to how polite the Hane family is, and Caliste can't help feeling bitter at the characterization. Polite boys do not act the way Emory acted.

The image they use of Xuân is another surprise. Caliste's never seen it before. Her hair flows wildly behind her, and she smiles in front of a house. The sweater she's wearing has rounded pearl buttons and is the same sweater the funeral home gave them.

"She's beautiful . . ." Caliste breathes, not realizing she's speaking aloud.

Soon Aria is hovering over her shoulder, and her arms are wrapped around Caliste.

"She is..." Aria says. "That's the outfit she was wearing in that photo of us... the one my aunt tore in half."

"Whenever I get to visit you, I'll have to make a copy of it," Caliste says as she leans back into Aria's hug and stares at the grainy image of the newspaper. "No wonder my dad complained about how alike we are..." She holds on to Aria like something precious. "I see it here especially."

"Her hair is always in braids in our photos at home. I've never seen it loose like this..."

"What's the matter?" Caliste asks, turning toward Aria's face after clocking a hint of a question in Aria's voice.

"She's the same. What we saw at the funeral home and here..."

"I know." Caliste swallows. The impossible factor at hand. She tells herself it's a grainy photo originally printed on newspaper and scanned God knows how long afterward. It's not possible that their mother's body was frozen in time, right? And yet the woman they saw at the morgue couldn't have been much older than forty.

As if on cue, both their phones buzz. Aria fetches hers from her pocket while Caliste has to riffle through her bag. Caliste frowns as she reads the text message from Paul.

> There's been a mistake. They cremated your mother despite my request.

"What?" Aria says, the shock audible in her voice.

Caliste swallows and avoids making eye contact with the library worker, who is still hovering. She reads the message twice more to confirm she isn't hallucinating. *Mistake.* That's impossible. The funeral home *mistakenly* cremated a body that was supposed to be shipped for autopsy?

"Let's wrap this up as quickly as we can," Caliste says, and Aria nods numbly. Another puzzle piece, but they have no idea what the full image is supposed to be.

♊

There have been nine drownings since their mother disappeared, with the most recently discovered three being Riley, Tyler, and Xuân herself.

Two of the nine included individuals who had active criminal cases—one involved a sexual assault and the other involved the death of two children. Caliste thinks back to Tyler the Groper. Is it a coincidence?

Caliste stands, stretching upward like a cat to relieve the tension that's built up in her neck and traps.

Aria is still intensely focused on the recent newspapers, so Caliste decides to dig into the Hanes. She walks casually around the shelves, hoping her "browsing" is convincing enough. The librarian lost interest a while ago and returned to the front desk, but Caliste still feels uncomfortable.

"Come on. For such an egotistical family, there must be something . . ." she mutters under her breath as she crouches in front of a bookshelf in the Local History section. Most of it is Minnesota state history, but there is a tiny section devoted to Les Eaux specifically. Indie-published thrillers by a local author named S. E. Henkins. Books of photos of fish. An entire collection of sightings of a rare owl during Christmas 1989.

A name catches Caliste's eye, and she holds her breath.

"Hane Pacific . . . Pacific?" Caliste says quizzically, picking up the clothbound book. When she flips it open, a black-and-white portrait of a man's face she doesn't recognize appears. A big mustache and square jowls—he reminds her of a caricature of a circus ringmaster.

She reads on.

Everton "Ed" Hane. A Les Eaux native who left on scholarship to attend Stanford and built an impressive transportation firm on the West Coast. He returned with his son, Eric Hane, and wife to Les Eaux.

Eric. There is an image of him as a child, and Caliste drags her finger against the date. No . . . That can't be right. The Eric they met was old but not ancient.

"Eric Hane the First . . . and—ahh! Eric Hane the Second . . ." Caliste says to herself. There's a family tree a few pages later. Emory's father must be Eric Junior.

The book goes into detail about Hane Pacific's boom in the 1960s and '70s. Caliste freezes once she passes through pages of preserved contracts. Southeast Asia. Vietnam.

The tome has no title nor author, and Caliste isn't sure it's even a real book. Regardless, it is in pristine condition. Each page is crisp, as if no one has checked it out in some time.

There's a myriad of articles written about and by the Hanes. The more Caliste reads the headlines, the queasier she becomes.

Hane Family Helps Redevelop Main Street
Eric Hane Donates Funds to Rebuild Church After Fire Damage
Courthouse Ceremony Honors the Hane Family

Eric Hane Commits $150K Toward Refugee Resettlement Efforts

The family's hand seems to have touched everything in town. The book is full of not only accolades and admiration but some personal news, too. Some have been reformatted from the newspaper, and others are direct scans of newspaper clippings. Surprisingly, not all of it is fluff news. She spots a short article about environmental activists and Eric making some sort of alteration to the flow of water around the Hane estate. There's also an article about Emory's parents getting divorced several years ago and the acquisition of an up-and-coming tech company based in Silicon Valley. A well-formatted section outlines a record of Emory's college acceptances to almost all Ivy Leagues, making Caliste roll her eyes. How is *that* worthy of being printed in the local newspaper?

She smirks, scanning the article further and wondering what poor sap at the paper was tasked with writing this kiss-ass information. However, the smirk quickly falls as Caliste reaches the article's end and finds a short interview with Emory himself.

"I'm carefully weighing my choice between Georgetown, Berkeley, and the University of Southern California. The West Coast might be a good change of pace . . ."

USC, Berkeley, and Georgetown. The schools that Aria and Caliste were respectively considering.

"No way." Caliste shakes her head.

She scours other documents and finds records dating back to the war and an article about the acquisition Hane Pacific made almost fifteen years ago.

Military Prime Contract File

REPORTING DEPARTMENT: Air Force
MULTI-YEAR PROCUREMENT
SOUTHEAST ASIA: VIETNAM, LAOS, CAMBODIA
CLAIMANT PROGRAM: Airframes & Related
Assemblies & Spares
COORDINATED PROCUREMENT: Other
CONTRACT PLACEMENT: Foreign Military Sales
CONTRACTOR NAME: HANE PACIFIC CORP
DATES OF ACTION: February 1968 / November
1970 / July 1972
NOTE: Per a request of donors, any
additional records related to contracts
from 1955 to 1975 have been archived with
the Ford Presidential Library and Museum.
The Les Eaux Public Library will no longer
retain these records.

♊

HANE PACIFIC TO ACQUIRE TNS TECHNOLOGIES, EXPANDING INTO BIOTECH

Hane Pacific's final bid to acquire TNS Technologies has been approved. Predominantly known for aerospace and military contracting, Hane Pacific continues to pursue a multidecade strategy of expansion, with biotech as the next frontier. Originally, Hane Pacific invested in TNS Technologies as a fledgling start-up, which was perceived as a risky endeavor by then acting chief executive officer Eric Hane Jr.

TNS Technologies, based in Palo Alto, California, specializes in cryotechnology for the primary use of research and transport. Just last month, TNS Technologies announced five new active contracts with several major hospital systems in the United States, as well as commercial and government labs.

At a public briefing for the acquisition, Eric Hane noted the company's commitment to improving health outcomes for the American public and reiterated Hane Pacific's mission of social responsibility: "The aims of Hane Pacific, to contribute meaningfully to public good and protect the American public, remain steadfast. We can all do good—together."

CHAPTER NINETEEN

Aria

"Now that you've told me, the Hane influence is really obvious," Aria remarks as they drive down the picturesque main street back to the inn. At stoplights, where Aria can read the placards on some of the buildings, she identifies at least three that directly thank the Hane family for their contribution. There's a sign pointing toward the Hane Arboretum near the courthouse, and another that supposedly signifies the previous site of the previous Hane Gallery of Art before it relocated to Minneapolis.

"It's creepy," Caliste says.

"Is your family's name on anything?" Aria asks, and Caliste returns the question with a laugh.

"I mean . . . the company name is everywhere. But no, there is no Hà Auditorium, if that's what you're asking."

"You never know what the threshold for 'name on thing' is."

"Well, Dad would *love* to see his name on more stuff."

Caliste's music choice, an album by a SoCal indie pop artist, hums in the background. It's somewhat peaceful, sitting in a car like this. She isn't alone on a busy bus but with her sister. In an alternate universe, Aria imagines this is what a typical car ride would've been like if they'd attended school together. She could tease Caliste about her music choice, and they could joke about street names that also serve as innuendos. The thought leaves a bittersweet taste in Aria's mouth. Would she have enjoyed going to high school with Caliste? The prettier, shinier, muscly-er twin to whom she'd likely be compared? Or might she have been just as pretty and shiny had she been raised by someone who cared about appearances?

"What are you thinking about?" Caliste asks at the next stoplight.

"Nothing."

"You're lying."

Aria grits her teeth. Is she so easy to read?

"Why'd you become an influencer?" Aria asks instead of admitting to her daydreams about how different life could've been. "Your—*our* dad said you got into Berkeley and USC. Why didn't you go?"

"Your answer is in the question. I wanted to piss off my dad."

"Did it work?"

"Obviously not. He paid for my high-rise apartment without batting an eyelash so that I could pursue influencing," Caliste says, her voice huffing.

"That doesn't sound like a problem to me," Aria replies.

"No. You're right, I guess. I may quit, though."

"Wait. Why?"

Caliste rolls her eyes. "Don't act like you didn't hear that I'm embroiled in some controversy right now." She slams on the steering wheel and accidentally hits the horn, startling an elderly man walking his Scottish terrier on the sidewalk.

"I have no clue what you're talking about. I'm not online that much."

Caliste side-eyes her. "Must be nice."

"I guess it's not as glamorous as it sounds, then," Aria follows up.

"There are some downsides, but I like making videos and choosing the composition of the brand photos I have to post. Do you like Georgetown?"

Aria gulps at the question.

"No. Not really."

"Then why did you go?"

"For my aunt," Aria says honestly. Her mind wanders to Paul's offer to help her fix her own scandal. Aria would be lying if she didn't admit it was tempting. But what would she be asking Paul to save in the first place? Her spot in an uppity school? Her nonexistent reputation?

No matter what the future holds, in this moment with Caliste, Aria *is* happy, and she'll do anything to protect their still-fragile bond.

$$\text{♊}$$

As the two ascend the stairs to their suite, light seeps from underneath their door. Wordlessly, Caliste and Aria stop and make eye contact.

"What the hell? Is someone in there?" Caliste whispers.

Aria musters up the courage to go ahead of her sister. She opens the door, ready to swing on the intruder, until she registers the person standing in their suite's living room.

"Ph-Philip?" Aria stammers.

"You know our burglar?" Caliste asks. Her arms are raised, ready to aim her purse squarely at Philip's astounded face.

"Jesus Christ . . ." Instead of fear, Aria senses wonder in his voice. She doesn't quite remember him sounding like this, not since they were children and the Presidents' Day blizzard dropped over a foot of snow in their front yards.

Aria remembers she should be angry at him for telling Paul about her disciplinary hearing, but seeing him in the flesh thaws the rage instantly. She's never been more grateful for his presence.

Meanwhile, Philip is pointedly staring, mouth agape and with uncensored concentration, at Caliste. Aria's stomach sinks a little.

"Yes, I know him. This is Philip, my best friend. Philip . . . this is Caliste. She's . . . well . . ." Aria's voice trails at the very obvious connection between her and her sister.

"Right, the guy on the phone," Caliste says. Her voice is calmer now, and she's lowered her hands, so her purse is no longer in projectile formation. "How the hell did you get into our room? Did Rose let you in?"

"No. I was going to wait outside your door, but you left it open," Philip says directly to Caliste, a slight panic in his voice once he realizes the implications of a strange boy appearing in their room. For a second, Aria fights off a smile. Of course he'd waltz in if he thought it was only Aria's room.

He walks toward her, wearing his half smile. Philip is moving like a scared cat, ready to run if Caliste so much as twitches.

"I was going to yell at you about it, actually."

Once he's close, he taps Aria on the forehead. Hard.

"Ouch! What the hell is that for?"

"For leaving your door unlocked! I know this is a small town and all, but you shouldn't be so relaxed about stuff like this."

"I . . ." Aria pauses, glancing at Caliste, who's inched closer to her side.

"We definitely did *not* leave the door unlocked," Caliste says a half beat before Aria can ask her.

"No, you definitely did."

Aria scans the room quickly, but nothing's out of place. She shakes her head.

"I had the key last. I probably forgot," she says, hoping the admission will calm Caliste down. She doesn't want her to bite off Philip's head. The day's been long enough.

"I . . . I mean . . ." Caliste starts to lose her edge. "If you're sure. Whatever."

"You two really are twins . . . huh?" Philip says.

"Well, duh. I thought you were bizarrely good at recognizing patterns?" Aria says. Out of the corner of her eye, she sees Caliste's posture relax at the playful banter.

"Anyway, why are you here?" Caliste asks, eyebrow quirked.

"Your dad and Aunt Thu asked me to come. He's worried about you two being alone here, right?" Philip handles the word *dad* carefully, and Aria ignores his pointed glance.

"Yes, but I didn't think that meant sending *you*," Aria says, rolling her shoulders back and letting out an inelegant sigh. "Don't you have work?"

"Nah. I rescheduled all my dog walks, and Jared took over some of my hours for dry cleaning. No biggie!" Philip shrugs. He's brought his backpack and one larger bag. The worn navy duffel is placed right next to Aria's open suitcase.

She is embarrassed by how relieved she feels staring at his goofy face. After seeing their mom; meeting her dad for the first . . . well, not the first time, but again; and walking the town in Caliste's glittering, self-assured shadow, Philip feels like a piece of home. And as much as she hates to admit it, she needs a piece of home.

"Oh, hey!" Philip exclaims, startled as Aria pulls him into a tight hug. She buries her face into his chest. Warmth envelops her, as does the soft soapy scent she's used to.

"Thank you for coming," she whispers before letting go.

"You're welcome," Philip says, staggering back. He seems surprised by the sudden display of affection. Now that Aria's processing what she did, she's blushing.

Caliste's eyebrow is raised, but she doesn't comment. Instead, she asks a very logical question: "Where do you plan to sleep? Our room?"

"Um, I was going to get my own room, but it's a wee bit expensive." Philip sounds embarrassed. Aria got only a brief glance at the rates listed online, but she knows that's likely true.

"I can vouch for him," Aria says, making eye contact with Caliste, whose expression is decidedly suspicious. "He is pretty broke."

"I'm going to ignore that jab. I asked if the inn has those little cot beds. The innkeeper said they do. But only if it's okay for me to stay in here!" Philip is quick to jump in with the last part. It dawns on Aria that he's trying to soften Caliste.

"I'm okay with it if you are." Both Aria and Caliste utter the phrase at the same time, and there is an awkward silence for a few seconds.

"Freaky," Philip says.

Caliste sighs, but she's smiling now. "I'll go ring the front

236

desk. Aria—you shower. Boy—get your dirty socks off my yoga mat, thank you very much."

♊

"What was your GPA?"

"Three point nine eight."

"Not bad. Criminal record?"

"None. What is this? Am I being investigated?"

"No questions yet. What's Aria's favorite snack?"

"Shrimp chips."

"Okay. What about her favorite movie?"

"*Kung Fu Panda Two.*"

"Really?"

"Hey!" Aria says, interrupting the rapid game of twenty questions between her sister and Philip.

They've settled around the fireplace in their suite, the gentle flames swirling and casting the room in a warm glow. Caliste is sitting nearest to the fireplace, wearing plush pink slippers. A fuzzy throw pillow shields her shoulders like some royal robe. Pointedly, her right hand is lingering a few inches shy of a brass poker.

Philip is sitting on the cot that was rolled into their suite, its metal frame and thin mattress buckling ever so slightly from his weight. When he jolts upward, the cot squeaks and startles Aria.

"I almost forgot!" Philip exclaims and moves toward his backpack that's sitting on the floor. He rummages through it before taking out a beat-up orange folder. Aria recognizes it as the one he used for SAT prep.

"The photo!" Aria says as Philip carefully takes out a torn photo from the folder. It's the picture that was hanging in the laundromat, the other half of the photo Paul gave them earlier.

"This is so weird . . ." Caliste's voice trails as she moves next to Aria. "We look the same . . ."

"Well, we should," Aria says.

"Thanks, smart-ass. Where's my dad's photo?"

"It's on the bed. Philip, can you grab it?"

Once he returns, Caliste takes the other half of the photo and puts them together. The tear splits the photo perfectly in two. On one side is their mom, with Aria hiding behind her pants, and a petite Asian woman Caliste doesn't recognize. On the other, a beaming Caliste stands between Paul's legs. Caliste is holding a praying mantis, which appears to be the reason Aria is scared. They are in matching outfits: gingham rompers with ruffles on the sleeves.

"Did you have to ask Mrs. Kim?" Aria asks Philip. She sniffles, blinking away the slight tears that developed after looking at the completed photo.

"Is this Mrs. Kim?" Caliste interrupts, pointing at the other woman in the photograph.

"Yeah. I also asked her what she knew," Philip replies.

Aria nods, handing the photos back to Caliste, who brings them closer to her face to scrutinize.

"I guess this was when you were, like, two? You visited my aunt's restaurant and met her for the first time there. She thought you both were so cute that she asked for the photo."

"Did she know we got separated?"

"Yes. When Aunt Thu reached out to her, my aunt helped her get a job locally. She never asked, but I think she guessed something awful went down. My aunt also kept the secret from you, Aria. I'm sorry," Philip says.

"Nothing surprises me anymore." Aria yawns but quickly moves to fan it away. She's not ready for bed yet. It feels like a slumber party . . . one she and Caliste *would* have had together had they not been separated. She can't help but imagine the Aria that would exist if she'd been in Caliste's shoes. Would she be less of a mess?

"It's way past your bedtime. Even on nights when you're doing someone else's homework," Philip teases. He falters as Aria glares at him. The tiredness is now completely gone from her body.

"Other people's homework?" Caliste asks, an eyebrow raised in Aria's direction. She gingerly places the photos back down on top of Philip's orange folder and focuses her gaze on Aria.

Aria doesn't make eye contact, turning her burning face away from the fire.

"It's . . . a side gig. Sometimes kids pay me, and I write their papers. Stuff like that. It's not a big deal—"

" 'Not a big deal'? Are you joking?" Caliste's voice rises. Whatever playful cadence she had with Philip is gone now.

"Whatever. Chill," Aria snaps back, turning to Caliste. "What's done is done. Are you actually going to lecture me right now?"

Caliste holds her gaze for a second longer before sighing.

"You must be joking. I can't believe you would do something like that."

"What?" Aria says, indignation rising in her chest. Maybe it's because she's *that* tired, but she feels angry at Caliste. Another first in their relationship.

"It's such a huge risk. And for what? To help some rich kids who don't care about you?"

"Rich kids like you?" Aria asks. Caliste's mouth snaps shut at the retort.

"Hey. Let's . . ." Philip tries to intercept, and Aria glares at him in warning.

"Fine. You're right. I'm just some rich girl who posts pictures of her abs on the internet. Ignore me." There's something hard in the way Caliste says this. Aria feels guilty for throwing Caliste's own drama back in her face.

"I'm going to bed," Caliste says, her voice flat. She rolls from being cross-legged to standing up without using her hands.

Aria wants to apologize or say something to dissipate the tension in the air. But she doesn't. Caliste walks away from their seats in the living room and lets the bedroom door slam behind her.

"Crap. Why did I do that?" Aria says under her breath before groaning.

"You're tired. And have been through a lot," Philip says, scratching behind his ear and hopping off the cot. The metal squeaks, free from his weight, and the mattress bounces back to a somewhat parallel position.

Philip moves, dropping to his knees and sliding in close to Aria. "And? So has she. But I'm the one being a jerk, not her."

"You're allowed to be a jerk. You're too nice, so you're going to apologize tomorrow anyway."

Philip bumps his shoulder into Aria's, forcing her to flash him the smallest smile.

"Aunt Thu was doing okay when I left, by the way. My aunt's taking care of her, so you don't have anything to worry about."

"Mrs. Kim? Jeez. They must be about to strangle each other by now."

"They'll survive. I'm more worried about you."

Aria pulls her leg as close to her body as she can manage.

"Philip . . ." she whispers.

"Yeah?"

"I have a family. I had a family . . . It's . . ."

For the first time during this whirlwind week, Aria confronts the meaning of having a sister. It's soul-mending and soul-breaking at the same time. At once she's full and completely empty. She has a sister, and she was left by their father. Both realities live inside Aria.

"Hey." Philip turns toward Aria and wraps her pathetic little fetal form in a hug.

"Aunt Thu . . . she and my dad apparently decided it would be easier to split us up. They . . . let us choose who to go with. Like we were choosing toys. Or a channel to watch on the television. Not who we would stay with for the rest of our lives. And neither of them said a word for fourteen years. How *wild* is that? I had a whole family, and Aunt Thu . . ." Aria's voice falters before she can finish the sentence. She wants to say:

lied.

deceived me.

tricked me.

made me believe she was all I had.

But she can't quite speak her resentment aloud.

In another world, Aunt Thu would have been all alone. A dead sister, dead parents, and no other family to speak of. Aria wanted to blame Aunt Thu for being so selfish and shielding her from the truth. But Aria understands somehow. She understands somewhat that if their dad had taken both her and Caliste, Aunt Thu would have no one to chide, no one to change her dressings, no one to split a grilled pork bánh mì with at night (Aunt Thu always complained that the pork bánh mì they got from the bakery in Eden Center were too large).

"It's okay. Let it out." Philip's arms are still wrapped around her, and Aria can't stop shaking. She stifles her cries so they don't disturb Caliste, snot and tears bubbling up inelegantly onto the cotton knit of Philip's T-shirt.

"I'm mad at her. But I'm mad at myself, too. God . . . and that punk Tyler? He . . ."

"Who is Tyler?"

"The kid who invited us to that party. The kid who died. He tried to kiss me, and I . . ." Aria's voice breaks before she can finish the sentence, recalling her pure panic and disgust at the lake. "If only I weren't like this . . ."

"Stop," Philip says. "Nothing that's happened is your fault."

She's mad at Aunt Thu for lying. But she's madder at herself for squandering away all her aunt's sacrifices. How much did she give up for Aria to have a shot at Georgetown? And now Aria has screwed it all up.

Philip kisses her forehead, which only makes her cry harder.

He doesn't leave her side, not even when she begins to snore on his shoulder.

♊

Caliste

Pretending to be asleep, Caliste counts the contours of the various antiques around their bedroom as Aria cries quietly on the other side of the door. She so badly wants to burst out and ask what's wrong, but she has a feeling that would be absolutely the worst thing to do.

Caliste doesn't share well, or at least, that's what one of her elementary school teachers noted in her class evaluation. What was hers was hers.

It wasn't until Caliste got older that she rationalized this. She shares her dad with his company. Her grandmother adores Dylan and not her. She eventually shared her nanny, Priscilla, with Paul. She has nothing to herself. Now . . . she has a sister. Aria. Her twin. The only person genetically identical to her. They were meant to share the world before it was taken away from them, or they from it.

Caliste wants to bask in this new reality, a discovery that changes everything. But when Philip's face appeared on the other side of their suite door, the change in Aria was palpable. She immediately relaxed. She was at ease.

And that is annoying as *hell* for Caliste.

Maybe that's why Caliste pissed Aria off. She still thinks she's right . . . but does she have the right to share opinions like this? Aria's right, too. She's lived an entirely different life . . . one that Caliste can never understand. While Caliste was jetting off to Bali and being emo about her dad, Aria didn't even know her dad and struggled.

"Is she sleeping out in the living room with him?" Caliste asks the air, allowing the annoyance to come to the surface without an audience to judge her.

Restless, she stands up and steps carefully toward the bathroom to avoid triggering the squeaky floorboard and alerting Aria and Philip to the fact that she is awake. The bathroom's light flips on, flickering before it settles.

"God. I need sleep."

Caliste runs her hands down her face and stares at her

reflection in the mirror. She hasn't had eye bags this bad since the all-nighter after senior prom.

She shuffles through her pile of beauty items on the left side of the counter until her fingers brush a tube of eye serum. Running the cold metal of the applicator under her eyes, Caliste thinks back to what Philip said.

You left it open.

Aria lied earlier. She isn't the one who had the keys last; it was Caliste.

And Caliste fucking *swears* she locked the door.

"I'm losing it," Caliste huffs.

When she moves to place the tube back among her beauty stockpile, she notes something is off.

The space next to her eye serum is empty.

She owns a bottle of Chanel Chance Eau de Parfum.

Her perfume is missing.

CHAPTER TWENTY

Caliste

"Are you going to eat that?" Philip asks, pointing his fork at the last sausage on Caliste's plate. Caliste raises her eyes to scan Joe Joe's Diner. It's far busier than when they were here with Paul before. In a way, the clamor of families and children running amok provides a nice reprieve. It's unlikely anyone will hear them over this noise.

"No . . ."

"All righty then," Philip replies before swiftly spearing the piece of meat and shoving it into his mouth.

"Philip!" Aria reprimands, but it's too late.

"I didn't eat *your* sausage. Calm down."

Caliste doesn't have the energy to react to the squabble, although she thinks it's cute. Aria being the cute one. She can take or leave Philip.

At some point, Aria and Philip ended their little nighttime chitchat, and Aria stumbled into bed at whatever ungodly hour it was. Caliste, for her part, couldn't stop thinking about that goddamn bottle of perfume. When it was reasonable to expect Aria to be awake, she'd asked her.

No. Aria hadn't seen her perfume.

The question of where it went gnaws at Caliste. But she can't tell Aria about her suspicions . . . not until she has proof.

"Okay, so . . . it's time to share my findings," Philip says.

"Your findings?" Caliste asks, her mind finally breaking from the perfume bottle's spell.

"Aria asked me to research the letters she's been receiving," Philip says quietly, leaning close to them across the table.

"Oh." The letters. The creepy-ass correspondence Aria's apparently been receiving her whole life. "What makes you so good at stuff like this, anyway?"

"For one, the bizarrely-good-at-recognizing-patterns bit," Philip quips. Aria smiles as he repeats her exact phrasing from last night. "I used to be into true crime before it made me feel gross. You know, the human theater of it all."

"All right, Sherlock. Take us away," Caliste says.

"Well . . . Aria, you received twelve total over time. The earliest was a year after your mom disappeared, and the latest one you received was, like, three weeks ago, right?"

"Right," Aria affirms with a hint of apprehension coloring her voice.

"They're written by two different people."

"What?" Both Aria and Caliste blurt out the question at the same moment.

"It's hard to explain. Basically, you can kind of tell a difference in cadence. Rhythm. You know how you like that god-awful literary writer from Michigan, Aria?"

"Low blow."

"I'm being serious. You could tell that dude's writing style from a mile away, right?"

"Sure."

"Well, these letters also have their own distinct writing styles. The first and the last letters are definitely written by two different people."

Philip taps his knuckle on the edge of his ceramic plate, which is full of maple syrup, before turning to shuffle through the backpack he's brought. He slides out two photocopied letters, both the penmanship and the original paper's texture showing through in the printed ink. He's highlighted and annotated all over both pieces of paper.

Leaning in, Caliste peers at the lines Philip is pointing to. The colors correspond to words or stretches of sentences he's identified.

"The vocabulary is different. It's subtle, but the way each speaker words things is distinct. Kind of like Ernest Hemingway versus, I don't know . . . a writer who is not Ernest Hemingway."

"That's a deeply unhelpful comparison," Caliste says. "Do you think they did that on purpose?"

"Maybe. But there are some other weird things, too. Did you ever notice any changes, Aria? Even something as minute as how they used punctuation?"

Aria is wringing her hands under the table so Philip won't notice.

Caliste reaches and squeezes Aria's left hand.

". . . I thought I was maybe imagining things, but . . ."

"Yes?" Philip asks. Gone is the slightly excited edge to his voice. He brought himself back down, immediately faced with Aria's trepidation.

"The letters became more distant. The tone . . . I felt like they were mad at me or something when before they were gentle. I don't know . . . like how I imagined a parent would talk to their kid? God, it sounds ridiculous."

"I mean. All this is ridiculous, to be fair," Caliste says. But she is worried. If there are multiple letter writers, were multiple people responsible for their mom's death? Were multiple people taunting one of her daughters?

Philip points to sections highlighted in pink. "One obvious example is here."

> Do you have any ambitions to travel, Ariadne?
> Washington National is quite close to you . . .

"The airport?" Caliste asks.

"It's minor, but the first weird inconsistency I noticed since we live in the DC area. The airport was called Washington National Airport until 1998, when it was renamed Reagan National."

"So? It's just an airport name," Caliste asks.

"Ah . . ." There's an odd cadence to how Aria exclaims this. "People around our age just call it DCA or Reagan National . . ."

"But people who lived there or knew it from before call it Washington National. The letters switch. I definitely think they were written by two people, and specifically two people from entirely different generations. And the switch happens around here . . ."

Philip pulls out another letter. This one was sent five years ago.

If this was the time before—the normal times, when Caliste was not someone trying to solve a life-and-death mystery—she would've called Philip's guess a flimsy stab in the dark.

But this is not the time before, and something strikes Caliste about the letter's date. It's the anniversary of Emory's parents' divorce.

At the phrase "different generations," only two faces claw their way into her mind's eye.

"Did you find anything else? Anything more concrete?" Caliste asks, her voice wavering with anticipation. She scoots close to Philip and the letters, following his fingers as he outlines his notes on the pages. Aria tenses next to her.

"I searched and tried to see if anything exists online that matches these letters. You know, weird turns of phrase or the writing style."

"And?" Aria asks, wearing a pensive expression as she stares at the papers.

Philip pauses, and there's a second when Caliste catches his eyes flickering to Aria. He wants to lie.

"Yes . . . actually. An op-ed posted in a high school newspaper."

Philip takes out another paper deep in the stack of letters. It's a printout from a website. Advertisements and the URL bar border the text.

www.brixleyhampton.edu/chronicle/opinions/06728

The Brixley-Hampton Chronicle

The Case Against Affirmative Action— the Devaluation of Merit

By Emory Hane

After scanning the article, which is filled with a dense and tedious accusation of schools being filled with allegedly underperforming students, Caliste feels vindicated. She feels sick.

"And I found this . . ." Philip says. His voice softens as he lays a final piece of paper between them. It's a scanned copy of a handwritten letter. The contents appear innocuous and seem to be Eric Hane writing well wishes to the citizens of Les Eaux for the Christmas holidays. (Caliste can't quite wrap her head around the fact that Eric is important enough for his holiday letter to be included in the local newspaper.) In it is a list of congratulations for some Les Eaux–born citizens and their accomplishments.

Congratulations to Jonathan Ariat for his debut performance with the New York City Ballet!

Quietly, Philip slides one of the envelopes containing Aria's letters across the table.

Jonathan Ariat
Ariadne Nguyen

In many of the letters, only Aria's full name is handwritten. The script is the same.

"What does this mean?" Aria asks, her voice shaking.

"It means that our dear friend Emory and his dad are the ones who have been writing you letters," Caliste says.

"Aren't you going to dinner at their house tonight? Do you think that's wise given all this?" Philip asks.

"Probably not," Caliste says. She's not sure if she's being sarcastic or sincere.

"I'm sorry, but what are you trying to figure out by going there?" Philip asks.

His concern is palpable, and Aria can't blame him. The smart decision would be to heed Paul's warning and respect Aunt Thu's authority. But there are too many coincidences and missing pieces of information between the two families to let this go.

"That family killed our mom or played a role in Mom dying. We've been waiting for her for *so* long. I can't walk away after seeing those bruises on her neck. Someone took her from us and is now paying off the police department to say she unalived herself."

She and Aria lock eyes, and Aria nods.

"If there are answers to find, they're in that house," Aria says, exhaling sharply.

Today might be the longest day of them all.

♊︎

There's too much tied to the Hanes . . .

One: the Hane family's influence is somehow woven all throughout Les Eaux, the town where their family lived, and the town where their mother died.

Two: there were many details that Paul kept Caliste in the dark about, including the Hanes sponsoring of Paul's family, their investment in Paul's first business, and the apparent long-standing history between Paul and Eric.

Three: Tyler died within walking distance of Aria and Caliste, and his necklace was in Emory's car.

Four: Emory is enrolled at Georgetown, where Aria just so happens to go to school, and he also coincidentally was considering Berkeley and USC, two schools Caliste had applied to.

"Remember to text me the second—" Philip starts to say, but Aria cuts him off.

"We know. Nothing bad will happen if you're here . . ." From the back seat, Caliste spots Aria reaching toward Philip and placing her hand on his forearm. Since Philip's arrival, the two of them have been dancing around their obvious feelings for each other.

The SUV rattles down a single-lane road leading into woods. It's dark now, and the beams of the car waver as they get closer to the Hane estate, which is located on the outskirts of town and farther south along the river. The address Emory provided didn't even show up on Caliste's maps application like a normal address would. All it picked up on was the forest. If she didn't know better, she'd think he was pranking them.

Caliste counts the trees they pass and reaches fifty before a sign with the house number etched in gold appears. There's a dip in the road, where they drive over a short wooden bridge, and Caliste realizes they've crossed a creek. It's uncannily straight and flows directly in the direction of the house.

Once he drops them off, Philip is going to wait at the nearest cross street to be their getaway driver. Aria will distract while Caliste does her best to snoop. It's reckless . . . and there's plenty of room for mistakes. But there must be something in the home that explains what actually happened to their mom.

The house that emerges after a final bend in the road is like nothing Caliste could've imagined. Aria gasps in the passenger seat as the behemoth gray stone mansion gets bigger before them. The Hane estate makes the inn look puny. There's even an iron cross woven with dried climbing ivy on the peak of the home.

A central tower is the building's focal point, with sharply arching ebony windows along each of the tower's five visible sides. Perfectly trimmed hedges are thinned from the cold weather and speckled with snow. There's a balcony on the upper level looking out at them. A porch on the ground floor has the same ornate walnut banisters. Each post is topped with a metal figure of a bird that Caliste can't identify.

It's beautiful, Gothic, and terrifying.

The engine quiets, and Caliste takes another second to gather herself before opening the door. As she exits, she catches Philip walking from the driver's side to get Aria's door.

"Be careful, Ari. Please?" he says after helping her out of the car.

"We will," Aria replies. The glass-paneled black front door swings open, the light inside scattering over the porch. Seeing Eric Hane approach, Philip returns to the car and waves before he leaves.

"Girls! Welcome! Is your friend not coming in?" Eric asks, hobbling down the steps of his porch with his arm pointed in the direction of their departing SUV.

"Ah . . . No. He has some work to do," Aria says, her arms folded close to her body as she leans away from Eric's touch. *Who said our driver was our friend?*

"Oh, that's a pity. Is he Korean?"

Caliste is taken aback by the question, but Aria isn't.

"He was born here, but yes. He lives near me in Virginia. He's a family friend."

"I'm usually right about this sort of thing!" Eric enthuses, as if he's playing a game of guessing weights at a carnival. "There is quite a large Korean population in Virginia, along with the Vietnamese population. Did you know that you can track the flow of immigrants if you look at enrollment in DC-area schools? It's quite fascinating!"

Fascinating. Aria smiles politely while Caliste rolls her eyes. Eric doesn't seem to notice.

"Thank you for inviting us. I'm sorry my father couldn't make it," Caliste says.

"It's perfectly fine! Paul was always too busy for me," Eric says. There's an attempt at lightheartedness. But underneath his jovial tone lurks something Caliste is well equipped in spotting: jealousy.

"What's that noise?" Aria asks, and Caliste registers the faint sound of trickling water.

"We are near a little creek. It's very nice. I also built this artificial moat around the house. Isn't it splendid?"

"Yes . . . it is . . ." Caliste replies.

When they enter the foyer, the house's immense yet suffocating presence only gets stronger. The walls are a deep mossy green, and all the wood surfaces are as dark as the night outside.

"Your house is lovely. I assume it hasn't lost its character?"

"Good God, no! An old Minnesota senator built this back in the day. He replicated all the Gothic houses in Washington. My father bought it when I was young. History must not be forgotten, wouldn't you agree?"

"You are very right," Caliste says, taking off her coat to hand over to Eric. Aria follows suit, her eyes darting around.

"We've done some maintenance, of course. My ex-wife hated this house . . . but it's a beauty to me. Why would I touch it?"

Caliste nods.

Eric's architectural lecture fills the silence. Caliste follows behind him, only half paying attention to his effusive tour. Contrary to Eric's claim that he hasn't touched the house, there's a spot in the wall that's been filled with plaster, the white contrasting sharply with the green paint. In the corner is a window that's been taped over with plastic, and Caliste wonders how much maintenance an old house like this needs. Out of the corner of her eye, she spots a frame she can't make out. When she moves closer, she realizes it's a floating glass frame ensconcing a single pearl button. A familiar face in the picture frame next to it stops her.

"Is that . . . my father?"

"Oh yes!" Eric says brightly.

It's a large print of Dartmouth's male tennis team. The boys are dressed in crisp white polo shirts and shorts, and their hands hold rackets over the front of the net. In the center is Paul Hà . . . decades younger . . . and the only non-white face among them.

"Your dad was very talented! Did he ever tell you?"

"No, he never mentioned playing tennis," Caliste mutters. Aria carefully looks at the photo. Caliste can sense how tense her sister is even inches away.

"I could never keep up with him!" Eric exclaims, but once again, it makes Caliste feel more anxious than proud. "Anyway, Emory and Carter are helping set the table. There are plenty of appetizers. I hope you girls came with empty stomachs!"

"I—I . . ." Caliste stutters, certain she's heard wrong. "I wasn't aware you had another guest."

"Carter is a good boy, my older brother's son. A bright young man! I hope you don't mind that I invited him."

Aria squeezes Caliste's hand. They've entered this house outnumbered.

CHAPTER TWENTY-ONE

Caliste

When Caliste and Aria walk into the lavish dining room of Casa de Hane, Carter appears equally surprised to see them. Thankfully, Emory is nowhere in sight.

"C-Caliste? Aria?" Carter stammers, putting a small silver dish onto the place setting closest to him. He's wearing something much less somber than his lakeside outfit, when they first met: an emerald cable-knit sweater and tan herringbone pants.

"Hi, Carter. How . . . have you been?" Caliste asks, strolling toward the elongated black walnut table and ostentatious decor. The lakeside bonfire is such a blur, and Caliste only remembers a hurried goodbye before she and Aria returned to the police station. Aside from coordinating their stories, she and Carter never finished their conversation from the pier and certainly didn't exchange numbers. Although that was only a few days ago, it already feels like a different era.

"I've been better. But okay. And you, Aria?"

Carter walks toward them, his brow creasing as he eyes Aria with concern. Caliste wants to believe Carter is a good guy. She recalls her father's recent confession. His wife had told him that Eric assaulted her, and Paul chose not to believe her. But Carter, even after seeing his friend's literal corpse, hadn't breathed a word of disbelief toward Aria.

Thinking about what Tyler could've done resurrects Caliste's anger.

"I'm better, I think," Aria says with a small nod and a smile. "I cried it off. No biggie!"

Caliste hates the fact that Aria is trying to laugh it off.

"We had no idea that your extended family in the area is Emory," Caliste says, lowering her voice in case that devil is lurking somewhere like a rat.

"Yes. He's my cousin. It's more legal than biological, but yes. Eric's brother is . . . was . . . my stepdad."

"Ah . . ." Caliste says. Having Carter here could very well mess up their already fragile plan to snoop around the Hane mansion.

"Uncle Eric told me an old friend was coming. Grace?"

Caliste casts a sidelong glance at Aria before explaining the present situation to Carter.

"I see. That would make sense. He's been . . . rather lucid lately, but he occasionally slips into the past."

"Not to pry, but how long has his dementia been progressing?" Aria asks.

"Pretty sure it's been for the past several years. He's undergoing some experimental treatment, which I think has slowed symptoms of the disease," Carter replies with a hint of apprehension. "Why?"

"I'm curious is all," Aria replies, offering a half smile.

Caliste brings her fingers to her lips, picking at the dry flakes of peeling skin. How the hell are they going to pull this off with multiple sets of eyes on them?

"Where's Emory?" Caliste asks, painting on a bright smile in case either Emory or his father decide to walk in at that moment.

"Emory went to his room to grab something. He'll be back soon."

Caliste studies Carter's body language when he answers her. He's antsy, his eyes darting around to avoid making eye contact and his hands fidgeting with his pockets. Carter is so tense she's sure he might make a run for it at any moment.

"Are you scared of him? Your cousin?"

"Wh-what?" Carter stammers, the anxiety evident on his face.

"I'm only teasing you," Caliste says. She's not. "And where is Emory's room? Will it take long for him to get down here?"

She does her best to convey the necessity of this information through a very intense stare aimed at Carter. His dark eyes squint for a moment before nodding.

"Second floor, past the portrait of his great-grandmother."

Thank you, Caliste mouths, which is right on time, because she spots the devil over Carter's shoulder.

"Ladies, it's lovely to see you," Emory says, emerging from the doorway that leads back to the foyer. "And what a coincidence. I suppose great minds think alike?"

Caliste glances down at her outfit and back to Emory. Her teal jumpsuit is the exact same shade as Emory's sport coat. She plasters on a smile and pretends she's pleased and not royally creeped out.

♊

Dinner starts off smoothly, mostly because Eric is quite happy to yap away at his captive audience of teenagers. If Caliste weren't aware of this man quite possibly being the reason their mom went missing, she might feel a little more sympathy for him.

Carter was being generous with his characterization. Eric talks in a near-constant stream of consciousness, which regularly loops from past to present. He addresses both Caliste and Aria as "Grace" before being politely corrected (and politely apologizes afterward). Emory seems well versed in communicating with his father in this state. Carter, on the other hand, looks like he's having dinner in a den with hyenas. Caliste thought she and Aria were on edge, but Carter is as rigid as a brick in his seat.

"By the way, Carter, are you still seeing that lovely little ginger girl?" Eric asks, leaning forward in his seat in anticipation. "What was her name? Riley?"

Caliste coughs on her mouthful of salad at the same time Aria chokes on her water. *Riley.* The girl who drowned?

Carter's utensils make a shrill dinging noise as he puts them down and considers how to answer Eric.

"No, not anymore, Uncle Eric."

"That's a pity. She's quite intelligent, and her family has always been our good friends. I'd hoped she might be interested in my Emory, but I suppose we can't all have what we want," Eric says with a delighted chuckle.

I know Riley didn't drown. Someone hurt her. And I think I know who did it.

That is what Carter confessed at Lake Agatha. When Caliste

glances at him, he's staring down at his plate with an ambiguous expression. Riley wasn't just a fellow camp counselor. Riley and Carter were dating.

"I'm sorry. Something must have upset my stomach. Where's the bathroom?" Caliste asks, standing and flashing a weak smile toward the elder Hane.

"Of course! The closest one is right up the stairs."

"Thank you! Please, continue without me."

Caliste breathes deep. If she doesn't take the plunge now, she's going to lose her nerve. This is her only chance.

♊

Aria

Aria wishes she was braver. She stares down at her plate and moves the roasted vegetables to and fro. Caliste is brave. That's why she mustered the strength to bolt headfirst into the metaphorical mouth of a serpent. Meanwhile, Aria is here, staring at the Hane patriarch and doing nothing but sweating.

After a long discussion of his time at Dartmouth (Eric wanted to study classics but ultimately studied philosophy instead), Eric launches into an impassioned monologue about his youth with Paul. From Eric's portrayal, he and Paul were the best of friends. But the stories he tells all have the same quality to them: Eric is the star, and Paul is on the periphery.

"It's quite interesting, Ariadne . . ." Eric says, finally breaking through Aria's ruminations. She looks up, and he's staring at her with an expression she can't quite place. He's dropped his fork, and his hands are folded, settled on the table, as if he's preparing to give another lecture. Meanwhile, Emory's arms are crossed, and he's leaned back as far as the dining chairs will allow him. If Aria focuses too much, she can literally feel the disdain in his gaze as it locks on her. She noticed it before but thought she was being sensitive. He looks at Caliste like he wants her intimately, and he looks at Aria like he wants to see her destroyed.

"What's interesting?" Aria asks, choosing to force her gaze onto Eric.

"You and Emory are in the same year at Georgetown, no? It's interesting you haven't met before your coming to Les Eaux."

Emory speaks up. "Oh, we've met." There's an edge to his voice now that Caliste is gone.

"Really? I don't remember," Aria lies, shifting in her seat and bringing herself to meet Emory's eye. The dim light from the chandeliers and candlelight makes his irritated expression flicker.

"It was in passing. An insignificant moment," Emory replies with a smile. He emphasizes the word *insignificant* ever so slightly, with a dip on the first syllable that digs into Aria like a hook.

Aria tries to stay calm. If she squirms and gives him the satisfaction of a struggle, she knows it will only pull her closer into whatever twisted little game he's playing.

"Carter. Where are you attending school again?" Eric asks.

"I took a year off," Carter replies. His tone, patient and slow, suggests he's answered this question many times for his uncle. "I'm not sure where I want to go."

Aria pokes at the peas on her plate, wondering if the reason for his gap year is related to Riley's drowning.

"Ahhh. I hope you reconsider. Just like your mom, Ariadne. She was too smart not to go to school. And quite beautiful. I hope my saying so doesn't make you uncomfortable."

It does. Aria counts her breaths, listening to Eric's words and scrambling for another topic that might get Eric talking nonstop again.

"When Paul walked in with her . . . phew. She blew my socks off," Eric continues.

Aria feigns a smile but internally grimaces. *Is his dementia revealing his innermost thoughts?*

"We were all quite close, you know. What happened . . . everything that happened . . . It is my biggest regret. She was a very unhappy woman . . ."

"What about Mother?" Emory suddenly asks.

These words alone trigger something, and Eric's face dramatically shifts. "You always do this. That's neither here nor there."

"I don't think Mom appreciated it. The Ha woman is dead, and you continue talking about how beautiful she was."

Carter tenses in his seat while Emory swirls his drink like a cartoon villain.

"Dead? What do you mean?" Eric frowns, and the way his face contorts frightens Aria. It's as if a switch has been flipped. "Don't you dare lie to me, boy." Eric's voice rises erratically, and he starts rocking in his seat, each movement getting increasingly agitated. He grips his armrests, and his rolled-up sleeves reveal bruising on the wrists.

Before Aria can register the detail and the rage, Emory stands.

"My father needs to rest. I'll be taking him upstairs . . ."

Aria panics. "I can help! It's the least I can do." Jumping to her feet, Aria attempts to slide out from between her chair and the table, but somehow Emory is already at her side.

"Please. Aria." Emory is smiling, his hair and the shadow

shielding parts of his face as he peers down at Aria. "You're our guest. I wouldn't dare ask you to step away from dinner."

His hands are firm on her shoulders, and Aria is momentarily taken aback by his boldness. While Eric shakes his head, Emory digs his fingers into the flesh right behind her neck, and the pressure is sharp enough to make Aria yelp. Easily, like he's manhandling a marionette and not her body, Emory forces her back into her seat.

"I'll be right back. Continue chatting without me. The cook should be bringing out dessert soon. The crème brûlée is divine," Emory says cheerfully. Before turning on his heels, he winks at Aria.

He escorts his father, who is putting up a weak fight, upstairs. Aria winces, realizing that Emory is using the same force on Eric that he used on her. Carter is staring down at his plate again. Why is he even here if he clearly dislikes his cousin so much?

Once Emory and Eric are gone, Aria lets her smile fall and sends a frantic text message to Caliste and Philip.

> Eric and Emory are going upstairs now. Be careful.

The pressure from Emory's fingertips still burns on Aria's skin. No, he's not just a creep who likes to intimidate.

He might be more dangerous than they thought.

Caliste

Caliste silently thanks Carter for the straightforward instructions to Emory's room. The stairwell from the foyer is all dark wood carved with intricate brutalist patterns. It fits in with the house's overall vibe while also contrasting starkly against the other Victorian updates. It's not a long walk, but Caliste could spend hours studying everything in the hallway.

There's minimal light; a flower-shaped chandelier illuminates the area at the top of the stairs, and gold-and-crystal sconces line the hallway, bathing it in a soft gold light. There's a continuous stream of art on the walls, mostly still lifes and re-creations of religious Italian renaissance paintings. All the decor choices in the house are decadent and excessive, and together they overwhelm Caliste.

Just as Carter advised, there is a massive portrait right before Emory's room. The portrait is at least four feet tall, and the frame is brushed silver and brass. Caliste doesn't have time to stare *too* long, but something about the woman in the painting catches her attention. Emory's great-grandmother sits in a cream armchair with legs crossed and back pin straight. Caliste can see Emory's face in hers: the same deep golden hair, emotionless blue eyes, and thin lips curving into a smile that appears as mostly a smirk. Underneath the grand portrait is another placard, this time reading ARTEMIS HANE.

"That name . . ." Caliste mutters to herself. Now that she's thinking about it, *her* Art hasn't sent a message since the lake incident. Although her Art might be busy, considering the upcoming holidays. *That must be it. It's only a coincidence . . .*

"Whatever, I don't have time for this." Caliste turns away from the portrait and heads toward Emory's room.

She isn't sure what she's expecting, but Emory is a goddamn stereotype of a self-important teenage boy who thinks himself an intellectual. There's a beautiful walnut grandfather clock in the corner and a gold enamel globe next to a curtain enclosed window. Accolades and awards line the walls, breaking up the hunter-green wallpaper with an eerie exactness.

Valedictorian. Varsity tennis. Photos from prom and homecoming. Emory's date has the same terrifying blank expression as Emory. And both his dates were Asian girls. Caliste shudders.

She steps softly, willing her muscles to remember ballet lessons from a decade ago, trying to avoid making any of the floorboards creak. Caliste doesn't know how long she has.

The room is dark. It doesn't look like the room of a teenage boy who lived like a *normal* teenage boy. Caliste half hoped to find a poster of some busty woman plastered over his bed, but there's only an oil painting. In it, an eagle appears to be eating from the torso of a contorted nude man. It's graphic, and Caliste grimaces at the vivid red stains of blood in the painting. A placard underneath the painting reads PROMETHEUS BOUND (RUBENS).

"Jesus Christ . . ." Caliste mutters, making her way past the perfectly made and utilitarian black king-size bed and toward an imposing walnut desk. It appears as one solid hunk of wood, the marbling of the wood grain barely perceptible through the almost-black stain.

The only item that suggests a teenage boy lives here is a sleek black gaming computer on Emory's desk with two enormous monitors. It surprises Caliste. Emory strikes her as someone who would mock video games as an intellectually inferior hobby. Her mind flashes to *her* Art once more before she forces the thought away. *No. They can't be the same person. That's impossible. Right?*

She turns her attention to the other items on his desk, which are meticulously arranged, and tries to commit them to memory. A brass cup full of pens is three inches away from a childhood photo of Emory holding a dead rabbit (gross). Before she goes snooping, she needs to make sure nothing is left out of place if touched. The last thing Caliste needs is for Emory to know she was here. Against her attempts to calm herself, Caliste can already feel a slick of sweat developing on the palms of her hands.

After another second of scanning the desk, something shines, catching light peeking through the shadows. It takes her a moment to register what it is. Lurking behind a figurine of a rabbit is a glass bottle. It's perfume.

Her perfume.

Caliste's hand shakes as she reaches for it, and she uses her other hand to brace her wrist so she doesn't bang the glass bottle of Chanel against the wood. Caliste might be able to convince herself it was some mad coincidence, but she knows this bottle is hers. There's a teardrop of pink nail polish on the cap, right where it meets the bottle—the same exact shade of pink that's on her nails now. It's the perfume bottle that went missing the night Philip arrived. The night their room was unlocked.

"I knew you took it, you creepy little shit," she says, the words hissing between her teeth.

When she focuses, she realizes she can faintly smell the slight notes of citron and jasmine in the air.

"Focus. You're here for a reason," Caliste says, setting the bottle aside and suppressing the disgust rising in her chest. She needs to pick her battles, and there is a much more pressing one to conquer today.

She pries open the middle drawer of the desk, scanning quickly for anything suspicious. Everything in the drawer matches the exterior and is organized with alarming precision. There are old papers, each one emblazoned with a bright red $A+$. Of course he'd save them. There are some receipts from luxury hotels in Europe and a stack of theater tickets tied with a ribbon.

There's a pile of ID cards spanning from middle school IDs to government licenses. Emory's face somehow looks the same in all of them—which is annoying. However, when Caliste moves them aside, she sees something familiar.

"What the hell?" Caliste exclaims as she picks up *her* ID card. It's her fake one . . . and it appears to be the one she lost the night that Beverly's uncle Rufus tried to feel her up. What the hell is it doing in Emory's possession? *How* the hell is it here?

Stifling her anxiety, Caliste moves through the stacks quickly, shuffling them back in place. There must be something that explains what role the Hanes played in her mother's death.

Pages sticking out of a book catch her eye, and Caliste freezes as she recognizes the cover. It's the book of Greek myths that was in her dad's office . . . the very same one her mom treasured. She picks up the book and quickly scans the papers tucked between its pages. They are copies of invoices with staggering dollar amounts: A large order of art from a studio in Lower Manhattan. Multiple sheets of flight information to the Hane Pacific headquarters in El Segundo, California. And a recent invoice . . . from the Inn at Agatha Creek.

Date of Issue: December 12
Billed to: Emory Artemis Hane
Invoice Number: 0214

Account Due: $20,000
Description: 10 rooms at a discounted rate
for the week of December 13 through 19

"He booked all those rooms?" Caliste says in disbelief. She thought it was odd how Rose claimed all the rooms were booked, but they'd seen only a handful of other guests at any given time. And December 12 is the day they were informed their mother's body was found.

A photograph falls out from the pages and immediately draws Caliste's attention. In it, she sees herself.

"Oh my god . . ."

Caliste voice falters as she continues to stare at the picture. The print is old and weathered and feels like it might crumble between her fingertips. She's not quite correct. The photo isn't of her. It's of her mother.

Xuân stands in front of an old-looking blue house with a basket slung over her left shoulder, but because she's too small, its bottom is resting on the ground. Next to her must be Aunt Thu. She stands a few feet taller than Xuân but wears an expression ten times more intimidating. They're young. A flowering plum blossom tree frames the photo. Some of its petals have fallen to the earth, blanketing the smooth dirt underneath Aunt Thu's and Xuân's sandals. A creek, its water reflecting the light, flows at the edge of the photo.

Caliste turns over the photo. Written in an elegant script she doesn't recognize are the words *The house in Cà Mau*. Why does Emory, of all people, have this photo?

The invoice. Her ID and perfume. This photo.

Before she has time to romanticize this new find, Caliste

slips the photo carefully into the front pocket of her jumpsuit. Her skin is burning, and the fabric of her clothing is sticking to her sweaty skin. There's more paper tucked between the book's pages. Her hands pause on the book and its contents, considering how best to take it with her. Should she hide it and then ask Carter to bring it to her?

Caliste stands, shuts the wood drawer of the desk with a quiet hiss, and takes a nanosecond to calm her nerves. She slips her phone out from her pocket and realizes she's missed several texts from Aria. Caliste swears at the last one.

Eric and Emory are going upstairs now. Be careful.

"Time to get out of here," she mutters. It's then that a sharp click echoes in Emory's bedroom. The sound of his bedroom door locking.

When she turns around, Emory is standing with the door shut behind him. There isn't anger or accusation on his smug face, but rather amusement.

"My, my. What a pretty little mouse I've discovered sneaking around my room."

His voice, as serene as the surface of a still lake, makes Caliste's blood run cold.

CHAPTER TWENTY-TWO

Caliste

Caliste runs through about twelve different scenarios in her head. She hides the book behind her back, which is clearly a futile effort, but she can't think to do anything else.

Emory doesn't say anything, and in the stretch of silence between them, the grandfather clock in the corner of the room starts to ring. Six chimes evenly spaced but unevenly shrill.

The truth Caliste wanted to deny is laid bare between them. She knows that sound. She's heard it many times from the speaker on her computer and phone.

Emory Artemis Hane.

"You say odd things when discovering someone snooping around your room," she says, not allowing the stress to register on her face.

"I expected it, you know. You aren't exactly the most strategic girl." Again, there it is: a slight tenor of amusement in Emory's voice. He steps toward her, and Caliste presses her lips together, bracing herself for what comes next.

"Why do you have my perfume?" She grabs the bottle from the desk and holds it up, eyes locked on Emory's. Against her better efforts, the bottle shakes slightly right before Emory takes it from her.

"This? Yours?" he asks, his slender fingers wrapping themselves around the bottle's neck like he's grasping a knife hilt and not a bottle of Chanel.

"Don't act dense, Emory. You're the one who broke into our room." Caliste's heart is rattling, but it's too late to turn back. It's full steam ahead into Emory's trap.

"At the inn?" Emory answers with another question, and he steps closer than Caliste would like. He's a head taller than her, and she's slid back against his bookshelf to keep him in full view. Her own perfume, the sparkling scent of citrus and teak, pushes into her nose.

"You're wearing it now, aren't you?"

"Of course. It's a pleasant scent. Bright. Although . . . unpredictable. It starts out sharp and fades to something very minimal. Nonexistent . . . even," Emory continues, his voice dropping, and he places the bottle with a clang on the shelf next to Caliste's head. She jumps, and Emory smiles.

"So what? You caught me in your room. Are you going to answer me, or are you going to play games instead? Do something that makes sense for once."

"You're so interesting."

Caliste stares, forcing her breath to steady. She's as far back as she can go; the hard edge of the bookshelf is digging uncomfortably into her shoulder blades. Emory's face is inches away, and he's studying her like a bug under a microscope.

"That inn is a historic building. I remember every time I visited, Rose would give me candy."

"Is there a purpose for telling me this?"

Emory ignores her, instead reaching for something behind Caliste's head. She flinches, every cell in her body screaming at her to bolt. Something tickles behind her ear, and she realizes he is toying with a strand of her hair.

Caliste swallows, fixing as ferocious a glare as she can manage at Emory. His eyes don't waver, and as she stares at them up close, she's suddenly aware of how much they look like the sea. A dark, humorless blue sea.

"There was always a sweet little treat for me when I got to the inn. I was simply picking one up the last time I visited."

Caliste wants to punch him right in his smug face. She imagines what his face would look like on the floor, swollen and bloody instead of so sickeningly pompous and near hers.

"So you admit it? What were you searching for in our room?"

"You first." The smile falls from his face, and he peers even closer at Caliste. So close, she can see his eyelashes flutter.

"Art, stop this."

Finally, Emory reacts, his face tensing at the name. It fills Caliste with a little self-satisfaction.

"It took you long enough."

"So why befriend me online? A forum for video games does not seem like it would be one of your typical haunts. Did you hate my mom? Did you hate our family? Why? What did we ever do to you? Luring me in under a fake name . . . Sending creepy letters to Aria. Why?" Caliste snaps. She blurts out the questions with as much force as she can muster. It works, and Emory backs away in surprise. She takes the opportunity to duck and run past him.

Caliste thinks she's going to make it—the door to Emory's

272

room is just a few feet away—before she feels a tug and a forceful arm snaking its way around her waist. *Crap.*

"Don't fucking touch me!" she yells. "I know what you did to Tyler." His arms are gripping her tightly. Her back is pressed against his torso, and Emory's hands have locked together across her waist, pinning her to the book held to her chest.

"Tyler? That flea? I didn't do anything to him. But I did find him floating in the water during your little party."

Lies, she thinks. How long had Emory been watching them? Caliste's forearms tingle with the force of Emory holding her in place.

"I'll let you go. And you can even keep that book of letters you've stolen from me. They're a nice read. Your mother and my father were quite the writers," Emory whispers.

"And? The catch?" Caliste stops herself from finishing with *you creep.*

"You read them. Right here and right now."

Caliste grinds her teeth, trying to figure out what his angle is. He's not even acting like he has something to hide.

After what seems like an eternity, she simply nods.

"Good," Emory says, not yet releasing his locked arms. Caliste thinks she's been duped before sensing his mouth and nose pressing to the top of her head with a sharp inhale.

"What are you doing?" Caliste demands, trying to shrink as much as she possibly can.

A kiss and an inhale. That's the Vietnamese way to kiss. How and why does he know that? As soon as the thought crosses her mind, Emory spins Caliste around to face him. He doesn't look it, but he's alarmingly strong.

"You are beautiful. But you know that, don't you?" Emory is

whispering, and there's a disgusting softness in his words. Caliste stares at him, at his half-shut eyes and parted lips. He is so close, she can count the freckles on his cheeks and feel his breath on her upper lip.

"Let me go," she says, forcing herself to maintain eye contact even though all she wants to do is look down. She's about to stomp on his foot when he finally relents.

"My father and I . . . I believe we are more alike than I care to admit," Emory says.

Emory takes the book from Caliste. "Freakin' pervert," she mutters. Emory stays calm, leaning back against his desk and handing her the book.

Caliste opens the book to the back, where there's a small folder. The contents are organized, like everything else here. A neat stack of letters is divided into small sections with neon sticky notes. She realizes they are arranged in chronological order.

> Dear Eric,
>   Thank you for the book! It's so pretty. I don't think I've ever owned something like this. Do you have favorite stories? I don't know why . . . but I like the ones about Ariadne and Callisto. It's unfair . . . Their stories are so unjust, it makes me angry on their behalf.
>   Oh no, maybe Thu is right. I do only like stories that make me angry.
>   Is your wife well? I pray for the safe delivery of your son. I still think you made a mistake. Why tell her about your crush on me? Women don't like that. And we know it was all a joke. Both you and Paul have the

worst timing. No wonder you have always been such good friends.

We find out the gender next week. I'm so excited!

Sincerely,
Grace

♊

Dear Eric,

We're going to have two girls! Paul is so happy.

Can you do me a favor? Convince him to mend things with his mom. She may not like me, but I know she wants to hear about her grandchildren. Knowing her, she might be disappointed neither are boys, but still. He hasn't told her anything. (He won't listen to me, but he might listen to you.)

I want to name them after the stories . . . Do you think it's too much? Ariadne and Callisto . . . I know I complained about their stories being unjust, but that is what I like about them. Despite everything . . . I want my children to maintain their dignity. Their beauty. Their honesty.

Thu calls me a romantic. I understand why now.

Sincerely,
Grace

♊

Eric,

   Can you be honest with me? Paul is so exhausted at work. I don't think he's ever been meant for a service career. I don't know what happened at the company, but can you find a way for Paul to get a job again? He's too full of pride to ask, but it's where he should be. He's smart, and I worry he's going to just exhaust himself here at the restaurant.

   Also, Paul said you were going to visit your family in DC? Tell us when; we are trying to plan a trip, too. Thu has a friend there, and we want to see the capital. It will be fun for our families to go together!

Sincerely,
Grace

♊

Eric,

   I am so tired every day. I'm losing my mind. I can't talk to Paul or Thu about it; they'll worry too much. The girls. My beautiful girls. They cry nonstop, and I am only one woman. If I asked Thu for help, I know she'd drop everything to come here. But I can't do that.

Does your wife feel the same way? Every day feels like I am drowning.

Every night I dream of the vilest scenes. My children are dead in them.

Sometimes I am dead.

Is this normal?

I have no one to ask . . .

Paul doesn't want me taking medicine, but it might be for the best. Will you take me to the doctor whenever you have free time?

Thank you,
Grace

♊

Eric . . .

I don't know what to say.

I am grateful.

And of course, I love you.

But let's chat in person. It's only fair.

Sincerely,
Grace

As Caliste flips through the pages, a chill climbs up her spine. Those three words.

I love you.

It's written in her mother's handwriting and looks almost foreign on the page. Caliste frowns, trying to piece together what she's gleaned from the letters.

"My mom's first language was Vietnamese . . . She was being nice . . ."

"Spare me," Emory finally snaps. His steps are unexpected and aggressive, and Caliste drops the papers as she flinches away from him.

He grabs her chin, his thin fingers sinking hard into her skin until it hurts.

"Stop it, assho—" Before Caliste gets the words out, Emory drags her face close to his, and she bites her tongue at the force. She tastes blood.

"Now do you know why I hate your family so much? Your mother? My mother was devastated when she found out about my dad's infatuation with your mom. After the divorce, she jetted off to Europe with a new boy toy."

Caliste swallows, trying to remain calm and not set Emory off any further.

"My father was ignorant even before he started losing his fucking mind. He was obsessed with Grace. After she was gone, he became obsessed with Aria. He would've gone after you, too, if not for your dad watching you like a hawk."

The letters suggest something that Caliste refuses to believe is true. But a sliver of doubt writhes into her mind from an unwelcome place.

She does not know her mother, the person.

She only knows her mother, the memory.

Her mother, the memory, would never, could never, have an affair with a married man.

But her mother, the person?

"I lost everything because of your family," Emory says, and he immediately starts laughing again, a barbed and wretched sound that echoes loudly in her ears.

"Everything? That's rich coming from you. What have you lost? This giant house? Your spot at Georgetown?"

His voice softens, making Caliste's stomach turn.

"We are the same. Aren't we? You have your pretty apartment and pretty friends and pretty face . . ." Emory says this as his eyes flicker up and down Caliste's face. "But you're lonely, too."

"You don't know what you're talking about," Caliste snaps.

"Mmm, pretty sure I do. Either way, none of these letters will tell you what you want to know. Your mom and what happened to her. How she ended up dead at the bottom of the river, where she belongs."

Caliste bites down so hard, she starts to shake.

"And what about your friend Beverly and her foul, perverted uncle? You told me about them. You confided in me."

"You tricked me."

"Did I? But wasn't Art your friend? A confidant. Not like Beverly. You trusted me. What's different now, Caliste?"

"Screw you."

"If I can have you . . ." His eyes flicker to her lips. "I'll tell you the truth about your mother, and I can make all your problems disappear like *that*," Emory whispers.

The thought of Emory touching her makes every inch of Caliste's skin crawl.

"In your dreams."

"If only your mother had the same amount of self-respect . . ."

Emory's hands squeeze her throat on the word *respect*, and tears involuntarily pool at the edges of Caliste's eyes.

"Let. Go!" Caliste yells and pushes him with all the strength her photo shoot–trained muscles can muster.

He stumbles back. Caliste swiftly moves forward to knee Emory in the crotch, and his yelp pierces her ears. He swears, and she scrambles away, grabbing the folder and the papers before darting to Emory's door. There's no plan, but Caliste needs to get out of here. Out of this house. With its darkened memories. Away from the smell of her own perfume wafting off Emory's skin.

CHAPTER TWENTY-THREE

Aria

Caliste is asleep on Aria's lap, her breathing uneven and her eyelids fluttering. She must be in REM sleep. Aria grimaces, imagining what her sister is dreaming of. She hopes it's peaceful. She hopes her sister is dreaming of a warm house and the scent of food wafting in the air. Not the hell that's been the past week.

They're back at the inn after leaving the Hanes' place. Aria had heard Caliste clamber down the stairs, breathless. She and Carter had exchanged a flurry of words before he'd assured them that he'd deal with Emory.

"Here, she can take this," Philip says now, holding out the pistachio-colored quilt from his cot.

Aria takes it, trying her best not to disturb Caliste as she lays the blanket over her sister.

"What are you thinking about?" Philip asks, his voice low as he settles on the floor in front of the couch.

"Honestly? Everything and nothing."

"That sounds normal."

Aria laughs.

"Do you know what happened between Caliste and Emory?"

Aria doesn't. When they got into the car, she immediately knew something had, though. Caliste was in tears, and her body wouldn't stop shaking. Making sure Caliste was okay was the most important thing. Eventually, on the ride back, she'd calmed in Aria's arms. Aria recalls Caliste's reaction to their mother's prescription and the revelation of them both having panic attacks. Aria had wanted to ask about them, but she felt like she didn't deserve to know. Would it be considered prying? Aria feels helpless. She hates not being able to do anything for her sister.

Emory only exacerbated things.

"I want to punt that kid into the river."

"I'll do it," Philip says in response, and Aria suppresses a laugh.

Still, the vibration of it disturbs Caliste, and she stirs, suddenly shuffling her body away from Aria and settling her head onto the couch cushion.

Aria quietly moves off the couch and stretches, her strained joints popping at the shift.

After she stands, she watches Philip adjust the couch cushions around Caliste, as well as the blanket.

"Damn. I guess that's the fitness model life. She looks pretty even after crying."

It's an innocuous statement. Caliste came out of the Hanes' house a mess, and Philip's taking care of her because he's a good guy. But an ugly feeling rears itself in Aria's chest, and she walks to the window to hide her face.

"Hey, Ari. Are you okay?"

"I'm fine."

"Are you jealous?" Philip's voice grows louder, and Aria realizes he's standing behind her now.

"I'm not a jealous person," Aria says, leaning closer to the window and away from Philip so he can't see her face. He's watched her skin change over the years, watched it grow mottled from sunlight and acne, and watched it stretch out. He's witnessed the smile lines deepen and her eyebrows change from bushy to tweezed. Philip's witnessed her face in too many iterations.

She also knows his face and can tell that, despite his cheerful veneer, he's just as stressed as her and her sister. His under eyes are puffy, and he fidgets when overwhelmed. Aria knows that when he dodges questions about college, he doesn't want to be honest about his fears (namely that he'll have to leave Mrs. Kim by herself, and something catastrophic will happen like it did with his mom). They know each other as well as they know themselves, and that's enough to stir the complicated mess of emotions within Aria.

"No, you're right. You aren't," Philip says simply. Her breath steams up the window glass, burying his reflection behind a thin sheen of mist. He touches her hair, and she flinches. "Then why are you acting like this?"

"What do you mean, 'like this'?" Aria asks, turning abruptly to face him. Philip's nose is inches from her eyebrows, and he's smiling.

"Like someone took something that belongs to you," Philip says, and he pushes back a strand of her hair. He is so close that Aria can see the dapple of freckles on the bridge of his nose. She can see the slight shadow in the cupid's bow of his lip as it curves. She sees the twitch of his eyebrows once he notices her eyes scanning his face. Her heart feels palpably loud, as if it's ramming itself into her chest and rattling her ribs like a trapped bird in a cage.

Aria is embarrassed and terrified of this moment, but she also wants to be closer to him. For a nanosecond, she contemplates how the top curve of his mouth might feel, and before she realizes it, her left hand's reaching up, and her index finger is tracing it.

"Careful," Philip says, and the snapping edge of his voice startles her. He grabs her hand and pulls it back, and the callused edges of his fingertips burn on Aria's. Philip is looking down at her more intently than he ever has. Or at least, more intently than Aria's ever noticed. His thumb traces the line where her palm ends and her fingers begin. Slowly, his fingers intertwine with hers, and his eyes flicker to her lips.

When a summer storm downed the tree in her backyard a few years ago, Philip was there to cover her ears. Aria remembers feeling his pulse cocooning her own hammering heartbeat. She feels the same way now.

When Philip leans down, pulling their intertwined hands to his chest, Aria contemplates how a kiss between them would feel. She wonders how much the bright and warm smell of Philip would envelop her. And she sees the version of Philip that's changed from being her friend to . . .

Caliste stirs on the couch behind Philip, and Aria's brought back to reality. Her sister is suffering, and she's trying to kiss a boy? What's wrong with her?

Aria pulls back. She lets the softness and the fantasy flutter away and diverts her eyes from Philip so she can't be swindled by his understanding and gentle eyes.

Aria decides to walk as quickly and quietly to the doorway as possible, and Philip's hushed voice echoes behind her. "I'm sor— Aria, wait!"

She makes her escape through the hall, down the stairs, and out of the inn, grateful that she doesn't yet hear his footsteps following her. In the faint light outside, she can see a storm's rolling clouds overwhelming the sky. The cool air coats Aria's body, tempering how hot her skin feels.

Once she's stopped, Aria's feet are sinking into the soft, muddy layers of the creek's edge. Philip is off-limits. Shaking her head, Aria banishes the moment from her mind, forcing it to settle underneath all the other memories of Philip. Memories of running around the laundromat. Memories of visiting his mom's grave. Memories of going to prom as friends and ignoring the girls who asked him to dance all night. He is her *only* friend.

And she can't lose him.

"Aria! Jesus. It's freezing. What are you thinking?"

When Aria turns toward the voice, she spots Philip jogging toward her with the inn's door swinging shut in the background. His hoodie is haphazardly thrown on, and he holds his own puffer jacket out toward Aria as he approaches.

"Go back inside. I'm fine."

"It's cold. And I'm sorry. We can go back inside together."

"There's nothing to be sorry about. Nothing happened," Aria says. If she repeats it enough, it will be true.

"Aria. Are you joking?" Despite the question, Philip is exasperated. "You! Christ, Aria!"

When she glances up, Philip's thrown his hands into the air and is walking down the muddy stretch along the river. Just when she thinks she's avoided confronting their tenuous relationship, confronting the thread tying them, and confronting the painful pang of her own heart, Philip abruptly turns, his face in his hands.

"Aria, I love you."

"I know. I love you, too," Aria says. They say this to each other all the time.

"No, not like that. Like, I'm in love with you."

"Why?" Aria asks. "There isn't a good reason for you to be in love with me. I'm not nice to you, and I take you for granted all the time. I don't understand."

"Don't say that."

"Why?" she asks again.

He sighs. "Because you make me laugh. Because you know when to push me and when to leave me alone. You work *really* hard, and you do your best not to burden anyone else."

"That's not true. I burden you all the time." Aria doesn't mean it as a joke, but Philip laughs.

"Then let me hold on to your burdens, Aria. I have them, too. I love you, and I mean it."

"You can't . . ." Aria stammers. Her voice rises, and tears are threatening to spill over. She takes a step toward him, but before Aria can see Philip's face rise from behind his hands, the worn soles of her Converse slide on the muddy rocks.

"Aria!" Philip yells, lunging at her, but he's a second too late. A rush of icy water surrounds Aria's toes, and her arms flail in anticipation of the fall.

Please, please, please. Aria begs whatever pathetic gods might be watching over her to protect her before she hits the hard edge of stone and water.

"Crap! Ow," she yells, the curses coming out sputtery and muted as she contends with the constant sprinkle of rain. Aria's left hand finds a smooth edge of rock, then immediately plunges into the water, too. A sharp pain radiates in her wrist, dulled only by the frigid temperature.

Philip is at her side now, his right hand pressing into her back and his face creased with worry. "Are you okay? I'm sorry!"

Aria almost laughs, but the pain is too overwhelming.

"My wrist. Crap, it hurts . . ." Aria allows her voice to veer into a whine.

Philip's left hand is holding on to her wrist. His thumb is tracing the blue lines of her veins, sliding softly against her damp skin. There's a slight pressure, not enough to hurt, but enough for Aria to know he's holding something back.

"Let's get this taken care of." His voice is so quiet that Aria can barely hear him after the wind carries most of it away. She wishes he would yell or throw a fit like other boys his age. He knows, must know, she's avoiding his confession. Aria wants him to do *anything* that would confirm doing so is the right choice. But Philip never gives her the satisfaction. Steadfast and good.

Good.

Aria doesn't deserve good. Not when she lies and cheats and pushes him away. He's so close, she can see the strands of his hair wavering slightly in the breeze and the others stuck to his wet forehead. Philip is so close, but Aria feels miles away.

"I'm going to help you up, okay? Tell me when you get your footing."

Philip's expression returns to normal, as if nothing's happened. She nods, leaning into his torso as his arm supports her from behind. Her left foot finds ground first, and she allows Philip's strength to pull her out of the water.

"You really are a klutz supreme—" Philip starts to say with

a chuckle, but an explosion of water erupts between them, and Aria is falling again.

Philip screams; then his voice is cut off by the sound of violent gurgling. Aria barely registers what's happening before the water settles. Then she's sitting in the water again, alone.

"Philip! Philip!" Aria screams, launching herself to where she can see his neon yellow hoodie floating above the water.

Someone . . . or something, is dragging him away. Aria keeps screaming as she stumbles. In a splatter of mud and gritty water, and with Philip's muted voice yelling her name, Aria can barely make out what's happening in the dark. Whatever is dragging him is . . . a mottled mess of rotting plants, mud, and flesh. It's a thing from nightmares, loose pieces of gray skin dripping from exposed bone.

Aria's fingers grab on to the edge of Philip's sleeve, tightening as the force attempts to wretch him out of her grasp.

There're stories of a ghost haunting the water.

Aria grits her teeth, pulling with all her might. Philip's contorted face emerges, hacking, from the water.

"Leave. Him. Alone," Aria yells. Suddenly, the force dragging Philip down lets go, and Aria falls back, her hands clutching Philip's arm with as much strength as she can muster.

In the instant before the creature disappears into the water, the scent of plum blossoms overwhelms Aria's nostrils, and it's a sucker punch to her gut.

This thing, whatever it is . . . has eyes that lock onto hers for a moment.

As Philip coughs in Aria's arms, she opens her mouth to say something, but the creature is gone.

♊

THE GHOUL

The last time a man touched me was the last time I was alive. Rain was pouring, much as it is now, and I was at the river's edge, snarling up at his pathetic face as a boot slammed into my stomach.

"I'm sorry. I really am . . . I love you, you know? If only you'd followed your heart, too, you could've been safe. I wouldn't have to do this . . ."

Love. *Love?* The cursed word coated my mouth with astringent rage. This fool. This wretch. But when his boot repeatedly slammed into my body and I saw stars—before everything went black, his hands around my neck, and a knot of fabric damp with grit shoved into my mouth—I didn't think of men. I thought of you.

When my mind faded and I was reborn as *this*, all I could remember were the men and the rage.

It isn't until your face appears before me now, drenched and wearing a panicked expression, that I remember love.

Desperate, I rise from the silt, a cloud of mineral matter and parasites float around me, and I swim toward you. I almost forget myself and my place in the depths. You look as if you're crying.

I recall pulling off your dirty clothes and bathing your small form, wiping your tears and shielding your face with my body. As quickly as the memory comes, it slips out of my grasp, and shame replaces fleeting joy.

You are scared, and I soon see why. There is a
boy.
Boy?

Man.

My teeth gnash, bones crack, and I imagine his slender limbs crushed under rock.

And he is chasing you to the river like the man who chased me.

As he races toward you, I muster all the strength I have to grab him. His thin legs are like reeds in my grip.

As he struggles against me, I sink, allowing my shame to pull me like an anchor. I'm a monstrosity, and all I have is this distorted vengeance. I wanted to protect you, but I can't even do that. It is then that I see you.

You.

My daughter.

One of two.

You utter words that I cannot hear, but I can see your face. I can understand its contours, no longer small but stretched thin. As if you've suffered. As if

I

have made you

suffer.

You are afraid of me. Not of him.

The realization punctures the last hole in my gut, and I let go.

This boy struggles back to his feet, and he is holding your hands as I sink even lower in the dark. He is protecting you.

Your protector.

There was someone who promised to protect me, too. But he failed. My fingers grasp at the water, entwining themselves with knotted clusters of dead grass that have sunk down to the riverbed. I recall his hair. There was so much of it, dense and coarse under my fingertips. His hair started to gray over time from the stress.

I focus, trying to conjure an image of my family. There are no faces, but I see you. There are two of you, my lovely daughters. We dressed you in matching outfits, and you both hated it. For the longest time, I didn't think you'd ever come. I waited decades to become your mother.

My husband would try and hold your arms as you wriggled out of our grasp and ran through the living room in only your diapers. You both laughed, and the sound was like a symphony in our small home.

Don't you think our children would be prettier? the man who killed me once asked.

That should have been my first clue to distance us, but I was naive and still believed that wretched man was our friend. I excused it as a terrible joke.

Then, one night, while my husband worked late and my sister was too sick to travel to us, I asked him to watch over you both. While I finished the laundry, he was supposed to bathe you and put you to bed.

I remember folding your matching outfits, freshly fetched from the drying machine, the warmth still radiating on my fingertips. In that moment, your crying rose above the clamor of the washing machine. When I rushed upstairs, you both were in the bathtub, and the water was nearly to your necks. I will never forget your panic, your small faces contorted in terror, and your wrists and legs entangled in the bath sponge's netting.

He claimed it was an unfortunate accident. But after this betrayal, after what he did to my precious daughters, I dug.

I found threads linking him to our past and present. He was the reason my husband could never find work. He was the reason our housing applications were rejected. Leaving this house—his house—was the only option for our family.

I told him he was no longer welcome in our home. I hoped to resolve the issue without bothering my husband.

It is then that I felt his hands around my throat.

It is then that he claimed to love me. Trying to eliminate my family were his acts of love.

Love?

I also thought my husband loved me. But when I told him, he told me to stop making up stories. I am brought back to the night of shattered glass and his face contorted with concern.

You haven't been taking your medicine. Are you sure? You must have imagined it. Eric would never do that.

Eric. My killer.

I hope my girls will never know the rage I felt in that moment. I knew my mind then. I knew what happened to me.

But now it's too late.

I'm floating back toward the surface. My husband's exact face eludes me, and I struggle to find its shape in my memory. You are gone now, my child, though your fear lingers.

Of me.

Of your own mother.

My daughter.

Daughter.

This is not how I want you to remember me.

CHAPTER TWENTY-FOUR

Aria

Philip's favorite color is red, and for some reason, it's the color Aria blurted out when the nurse asked her what color she wanted her cast to be. She hates red. It's too loud. It proclaims importance. Too cliché. But now she has a red arm, and as she sits alone in the waiting room of the hospital, Aria is forced to stare at the giant red cast and try to not lose her mind.

"Hey, water?" Caliste asks, approaching Aria with a bottle of Dasani and a pack of Skittles.

Aria nods, takes the offered bottle, and then realizes she can't open it.

"Oh, crap, hold on!" Caliste scrambles into the seat next to her, taking the bottle out of Aria's limp grasp and prying the top off. It splatters a little water on the both of them, and Aria can't help but laugh.

"Sorry," Caliste says a little meekly, and places the bottle in Aria's hand. She doesn't let go until she sees Aria's fingers close around it.

"I'm the one who should be sorry. You should be resting."

"Shut up," Caliste replies. "I don't want to hear that."

The water is disgusting and metallic, but Aria welcomes the cool sensation bringing her back to reality.

After a panicked scramble back to their room at the inn, Aria woke up Caliste, who then drove at a very illegal speed to get her and Philip to the nearest hospital, which was located a town away.

It wasn't until they arrived that Aria had noticed her sister was wearing a leather boot and a sneaker and was clearly in her bathrobe.

The ER had been full of drunk college kids, and it took both Aria and Philip hours to see anyone. Aria had only been released just now, after enduring X-rays and a gauntlet of medical professionals fondling her wrist and asking her if it hurt (it very much did). Currently the waiting room is nearly empty, with only a handful of people left. There's still one college-age girl asleep in her chair, who earlier was tearfully asking someone over the phone if they loved her. A middle-aged white man waits near the vending machines, cradling his knee with a pack of ice. And there's a young family in the back corner for whom Aria feels bad. The mother, a young Black woman with long braids, holds a gently snoring toddler who was fussing for quite a long time earlier.

"Can you finally tell me what the hell happened?"

Aria takes a deep breath. She's contemplated all the ways she could phrase this so it won't sound completely made up. Turns out, there aren't many options.

"I saw Mom."

Caliste, who is in the middle of tearing open the packet of

Skittles, freezes. "What are you talking about? Do you have a fever?"

Aria shakes off Caliste's attempts to touch her forehead. "No! I'm fine. It's just . . . in the river. Whatever . . . attacked Philip. It . . . She . . . looked like Mom."

There is an insufferable stretch of silence before Caliste speaks again.

"Are you sure?" she asks. She's solemn, the half-opened bag of Skittles and her hands resting in her lap.

"I swear to you, it was her. I know it. I know how it sounds, but—"

"I believe you."

"What?"

"I believe you. If I can believe that her body's been frozen in time, then I can believe you also saw her in the river."

Aria swallows back a wave of tears and offers her twin a weak smile.

Caliste reaches out and holds her hand. "Philip apparently needs to wait for more tests and a rabies shot before they'll let him out," Caliste says.

At first, Aria thought she was too tired or too hopped up on adrenaline to think straight. But the image came to her so clearly when she was drifting off while waiting for her X-rays.

Her mom's face—or a version of it—was in the water . . . on that *ghoul*. The smell of plum blossoms still lingers in Aria's nostrils.

Crap. She's crying. Aria takes a wad of tissues and blows her nose without saying anything.

A ghoul? A ghost? And if so, not just any ghost. Her mom.

"Do you know why she would attack Philip?" Caliste asks.

Aria remembers long, bloody scrapes up the entirety of Philip's shins. Puncture wounds were around his knees. His pants were ripped to absolute shreds.

Her mind wasn't yet ready to try putting those two things together ... the fact that Aria saw her mom's face in the water and the fact that Philip was truly, and viciously, attacked.

"I don't know," Aria says, slumping at how pathetic the answer sounds.

Caliste squeezes Aria's hand again, and there's a stretch of uneasy silence before her sister speaks again.

"So ... you know how Mom and I both have ..."

Aria glances up to meet Caliste's gaze, but her sister is looking down this time. The hand holding Aria's in comfort is shaking.

"Do you mean ... the diagnosis?" Aria asks.

"Yes. The panic disorder. I'm sorry I didn't tell you first."

"You don't have to apologize. We would have gotten there eventually."

"They're so embarrassing. I get really sweaty, and my heart feels like it's going to fall out of my butt," Caliste says with a laugh. She's downplaying it.

"If it does, I promise to catch it," Aria says.

Caliste snorts at Aria's reply, and there's another stretch of silence. With her free hand, Caliste is wiping her fingertips against her eyelids and blinking away tears.

"I wanted to ask ... Are you okay? You seemed to know what her prescription was for."

Are you okay?

It's a loaded question. In this moment of vulnerability, Aria wants to be honest. She saw Sertraline on a Google search of

"How to treat depression" after another search of "Am I depressed?" She wants to share the truth with her sister, but she can't.

"Guests for Philip Kim, please come to the patient area."

"Let's talk about it later," Aria says, standing with the water bottle.

Caliste moves to stand, her arm outstretched, but sits back down. "Actually, you go in alone."

"What? You aren't coming?"

"I'm going to go put your stuff in the car. I'll be back." Caliste swings a plastic bag filled with Aria's wet clothes over her shoulder and waves Aria off before she can ask anything else. Once Caliste's back is turned, she slumps and Aria hears a sigh.

"All right . . ."

Aria stands and checks her reflection in the shiny door that leads to the back of the ER. What the nurse gave her to replace her wet clothes amounts to oversize hospital pajamas. She looks like a toddler.

The receptionist buzzes Aria in, the sliding door opening with a slow squeak. After getting directions from a nurse, Aria passes by a partitioned stall that she had waited behind earlier. Philip is all the way in the back corner, in an individual patient room behind glass walls. When the doors open, Aria finds that he's asleep on the bed.

Aria walks slowly to the left side of the bed, opposite the doctor's chair. Philip's stuff—torn clothes and a wallet—is in a clear plastic bag hanging on the wall. The sight of the bloodstained pants triggers a slight gag. Aria watches Philip breathe, his chest rising and falling softly. It's then that his eyebrow twitches, and she realizes he's not asleep.

"Hey. Smart-ass. I know you're awake."

Philip groans and opens one eye to look at Aria.

"You could be nicer to me, you know."

"I could," Aria says, letting her teasing hide the magnitude of her relief. But it's bittersweet. There is only one reason that Philip is lying in this hospital bed all bandaged up.

Her. It's her fault.

"Does it hurt?" Aria asks, letting her fingers graze the blanket covering Philip's leg.

He coughs, the tips of his ears turning pink. "It hurt like a mofo when they were treating me, but it's fine now. I got my rabies shot and a dose of some immunity goop. I'm supposed to get more shots, though . . ."

Aria presses her lips tight, absorbing the information. A rabies shot. That . . . would be the appropriate response to getting attacked by some unknown wild animal. Except the unrelenting and slithery weight in Aria's stomach knows her mom did this.

"Did you see anything in the water?" Aria asks.

For a moment, Philip's smile falls.

"Did you see what I saw?" Aria asks again. She forces herself to hold Philip's gaze. The otherworldly. Only one other person on this planet would entertain these thoughts from Aria.

"I don't know. I . . ." His voice falters, and he holds out his hand. Aria takes it.

"It is absolutely wild. Bonkers. It makes no sense. But . . ."

"But?"

"A woman. For a moment, I saw a woman."

Aria inhales a shaky breath to steady herself. Her hand feels cold against Philip's palm. "What did she look like?"

"You. She looked like you."

"I'm sorry, Philip. I'm *so* sorry."

"Oi. Stop it," Philip says, his voice stern. Aria leans into his chest, her knees buckling slightly and digging into the hard metal side of the bed. Philip's arms envelop her wordlessly, and his chin rests on her scalp.

"I'm fine. You're fine."

Aria inhales, the sterile scent of clean hospital sheets mixing with Philip's.

If her mother's restless spirit is haunting the waters of Les Eaux, Aria is anything but fine.

♊

Caliste

Caliste is pretty sure she's living some weird preteen boy's fever dream and not her real life. Caliste's body is at its breaking point. She sits outside in the driver's seat of their car, taking a minute for some quiet. Caliste also wanted to give the lovebirds time to themselves.

Throttling Emory in the balls and sprinting out of the Hanes' mansion feels like it happened years ago at this point. Underneath the stress, anger, and fear simmers something else. Or rather, someone else. *Art.* A friend. A confidant. A liar. Is it possible to mourn a friendship that was never a friendship in the first place? Caliste thinks back to the way Emory held her face, and she nearly gags. *Now is not the time to recall his disgusting face.*

Leaning back in the seat to stretch, Caliste digs her hands into the pockets of her coat.

"What's this?" she says to herself as her fingers touch something. When Caliste pulls out the offending item, she realizes it's some sort of tiny square tag. It's plastic, but it feels like it's for something electronic. An initial coldness runs through her body, and Caliste shakes her head.

No, this must be a security tag she's never noticed before. But as a precaution, she rolls down the window to chuck it outside.

Right as the window rolls back up, Caliste's phone starts ringing. Caliste failed to tell Aria about the number of notifications on her phone—all from their dad. She wants to talk to him, too... but what if he confirms what Emory told her? What Emory said... it can't be right. She refuses to believe it. Sleep helped her brain put things together in a way she can make sense of.

Caliste's eye flicker to the dashboard and the time glowing at her in the dark. It's 4:14 a.m. in Minnesota, which means it's 2:14 a.m. in California. He's still awake? Why?

"Hello? Con?" Her dad sounds relieved once she answers his call.

"Hi, Ba."

"I called you many times, but you didn't answer."

"I'm sorry... Is there an emergency?"

Paul is silent for a long stretch of seconds, and Caliste almost believes the line's dropped.

"Do you remember what I told you before I left?"

"Of course I do," Caliste says. How can she not?

"I've been trying to find out what I can from here. The funeral home claimed to have received new instructions to cremate your mother."

"Instructions? From who?"

"From you."

"That's a lie! How would that even work? Aren't you next of kin?"

"I know you didn't do it. I'm next of kin, but as her adult child, you can also make that decision. What they have on record is that you requested the cremation. It was sent through email. There is a form with your signature, and I compared it with your passport. The signature is the same."

"I . . ."

Caliste racks her brain. Then it dawns on her. Emory has a fake ID of hers, and it includes her actual handwriting.

"Why . . . why would someone do that?"

"Well. We can no longer get an autopsy." And that was that.

"How's Bà Nội? You left so suddenly. Is she okay?"

"Your grandmother is fine. Something just frightened her. You don't have to worry."

"Ba!" Caliste says, her frustration boiling over. "Now's not the time to keep more secrets."

"You're right," Paul says with a sigh. "Someone slipped a threatening note under her door. I thought it might be a practical joke, but when the building staff reviewed the CCTV, we were able to identify the person responsible."

"And? Who were they?"

"A man wearing a Hane Pacific factory uniform. He must be an employee from the California location."

Caliste doesn't have the best relationship with her grandmother, but the idea that Bà Nội might be the newest addition to Emory's toxic web makes Caliste's stomach churn.

"I don't know what's going on . . . if Eric is behind this or not. It doesn't matter. I just want you and Aria home safe. Are you going to leave?"

Caliste pauses, and for the first time since this entire ordeal started, she's not sure. She's sick of Emory and sick of the Hane family. Is the truth worth finding out anymore?

"I'll talk to Aria."

"Thank you, Cali."

Something about the relief in Paul's voice is comforting for her. But Caliste doesn't have the luxury of being nostalgic right now.

"Ba. Emory told me something, and I want to confirm it with you."

"Yes?"

"He said that Mom was having an affair with Eric. Is that true?"

"What?" Her father's shouting nearly bursts a hole in her eardrum. He must be in his study, which is farthest from Dylan's room and his shared room with Priscilla. "No. That's not even remotely true. How dare he insin—"

"Okay, Ba. I believe you. That's all I wanted to know," Caliste says calmly. That seems to do the trick, and her dad stops mid-sentence.

"I'm sorry."

"Me too. And I'll come home soon. I promise."

♊

Philip snores, fast asleep. His bandaged body is lying on the cot in the suite's living room. The hospital kept him for several hours, and he's been asleep since they returned to their suite late in the morning. Caliste sits slouched on the sofa, watching as her sister attempts to heat up water in a kettle for ramen they bought from a convenience store. Collectively, they all decided that they didn't have the energy to figure out alternative dinner plans after eating hospital vending machine snacks for lunch. The rapidly accumulating snow also wasn't incentivizing them to leave the inn.

Caliste watches Aria's slow movements, careful to avoid making too much noise and waking Philip. She focuses on her sister's body language as a kind of meditation—Caliste's mind is all over the place. What now? Should she listen to her dad and just go home? When she shifts her attention to the window overlooking the street, the snow flutters with increasing intensity. There's already a thick bank of snow sticking to the window's frame.

There's a loud clang, and when Caliste looks back at Aria, steam is rapidly swirling around her face. She hits the exhaust fan above the kitchenette stove, and it whirs on with a wheeze right before there's complete darkness.

"Crap!" Aria yells.

"Ugh, the power's out. Hold on, Ari!"

"Wha—" Philip's garbled voice wheezes in the dark.

Caliste reaches through the dark as she makes her way to the living room wall closest to the bedrooms. There should be flashlights on a shelf there, if she's remembering correctly.

"Caliste! Where are you?"

"Wait a sec!"

Caliste hunches over in the dark and uses her phone's flashlight to make out what's what. There are books of sewing patterns and travel guides. Little ceramic knickknacks and crocheted flowers.

"Wait . . . What the hell is this?"

Tucked right next to the flashlights is a small teddy bear. In the daytime, it appeared innocuous. But now its eyes reflect the bright light from Caliste's phone. Caliste can clearly see a camera lens in the left eye.

"Caliste, is that—"

Aria's voice is cut off with a loud bang.

Caliste can hear her own brain too acutely and too sharply. She hears her own blood pulsing through her veins. In the dark, the SOS symbol flashes on her phone's screen.

No signal.

Then a strange scent fills the air, and Caliste screams.

CHAPTER TWENTY-FIVE

Caliste

Caliste's lids are heavy, and the more she tries to pry them open, the more she feels like the task is impossible. She takes a few moments to put together what's transpired—or what she *thinks* transpired. After being in the living room earlier, she remembers a burning in her throat and nostrils before passing out. One moment, she was scrambling to find flashlights, and the next she's here. Now, where exactly *is* here?

Wherever Caliste is, it's almost completely dark. Caliste can only vaguely make out the contours of a square room. Her arms and legs are secured with zip ties. The tight plastic digs into her wrists and ankles painfully, securing her to a metal chair.

As her eyes slowly adjust, she sees a door a few feet away. The gap underneath glows. Caliste clenches the muscles around her mouth, willing herself to fight through the waning effects of whatever drug flooded their suite earlier. With tremendous effort, she's finally able to part her lips. The saliva is gummy in her mouth. It's like she's swallowed glue.

"Aria?" Caliste croaks into the darkness. Unsurprisingly, she hears nothing except for her own voice echoing faintly back to her. Then, after a few seconds, Caliste makes out a scraping sound. A chair leg?

"Aria? Aria!" She lets her voice climb just the tiniest bit louder. Maybe it's being in complete freaking darkness, but she's never been more aware of her body—her skin and the cool damp air (*Are we underground?*), her heart thumping erratically in her chest, and even shifts in the barely existent shadows.

"Caliste . . ."

There. It's Aria's voice, so muted that Caliste second-guesses it for a second.

"Aria! Where are you?"

"Here, I'm . . . here." It's so faint.

"Hey! Stay awake," Caliste says into the dark. All those Pilates lessons and hours at the gym *can't* just be for aesthetics. Bracing her core and pressing her toes downward as much as she can, Caliste scoots in the direction of Aria's voice. One, two. One, two.

The shrill screech of metal against concrete echoes around Caliste. Each unbearable *eeek eeek eeek* across the floor makes her heart race faster and faster.

"I'm here. Caliste?"

"Yeah, I'm coming to you. Don't move!" Caliste says with relief. *Good . . . this loud-ass chair is helping Aria wake up.*

After what feels like an insufferable stretch of seconds, Caliste makes out the dark silhouette of Aria, who's also tied to a chair, against the room's back wall.

"Thank God!" Aria says, and Caliste finally scoots close enough to see the outline of her sister's face.

"Crap. Where are we?"

"I don't know, but it's musty as hell. A basement?" Aria says, squirming in her seat.

Caliste's eyes are mostly adjusted to the dark, and she makes out tall empty wooden shelves flanking them.

"It looks like a cellar or something?" Aria says.

"What's going on—"

"Shh," Aria hisses.

Aria's shadow shifts with the light source emanating from underneath the door. *Someone's here.*

Should they pretend to be passed out still? Or is this person someone who can help them? Should they scream? About a trillion thoughts race through Caliste's mind in the nanoseconds that pass.

Then there's the sound of the door opening, and light erupts around them. Caliste shuts her eyes, squeezing so tight, her heartbeat gets louder. *Crap.*

"Caliste?"

Caliste blinks. If she understands her positioning correctly, her back is to the door. The sharp fluorescent lights buzzing overhead hurt her eyes. Aria's eyes are wide and staring at the person behind Caliste.

"Carter?" Aria gasps.

"Crap. Hold on," Carter says.

Suddenly something cold presses against Caliste's wrist, and she feels the warmth of Carter's hand on hers.

"Try not to move. I'm cutting the zip ties, and this knife is sharp."

"Never thought the phrase 'this knife is sharp' would be music to my ears," Caliste says after the second zip tie snaps and her hands are finally free.

She rubs the raw indents on her skin; there are clean lines of red from the zip ties. The valleys that have formed from them are perfectly and eerily straight.

Soon her legs are free, too, and Caliste looks up, watching as Carter takes the same knife to Aria. When she scans the room, she realizes it's a massive underground bunker of some sort. There are a handful of vehicles down here. A vintage cherry-red Pontiac Firebird. Two vintage Ferraris Caliste can't identify.

And a beat-up white Oldsmobile with a crack in the windshield. It's the car from the photos. The car Mom was driving the night she disappeared.

Caliste swallows hard, struggling to untangle the myriad of thoughts racing in her mind. This . . . *must* be Emory's doing.

"Where are we? How did you find us?" Aria asks as Carter cuts through the zip ties around her ankles.

"I was outside the inn when I saw Emory's car leaving. I followed him, but . . ."

"But what?" Caliste asks. "Listen, I'm going to need you to explain what the hell is happening *way* faster." Carter is a Hane. Is he really on their side?

Carter turns, pausing to stare at Caliste as he flicks the blade of the Swiss Army knife back into its sheath. His dark eyes are more prominent than usual, the hollows under his eyes purple and puffy. There's a slick of sweat on his skin, and there's something notably fraught about his expression. Caliste wants to trust him. But what if that's another mistake?

"We're back in the Hane mansion," Carter says, sliding his hands into the pockets of his navy trench coat with a pitiful shrug.

"Did he see you? Is Emory here?" Aria asks. She looks exhausted but okay overall, which is a major relief.

"No. I waited for a while before I drove up to the manor. His car is gone. I think you're safe. We need to go."

"No. Not yet," Caliste says.

Out of the corner of her eye, Caliste sees Aria turn toward her. "What the heck are you talking about?"

"You happen to know where we are. You happen to have a knife on you that can cut us loose," Caliste continues. She ignores Aria's gaze, which is boring into her. "How do we know you're helping us get out of here and not leading us straight to him? Are you in on his twisted little game? Are all your stories about being scared of Emory even true?"

Caliste's voice teeters on the edge of cracking. She's so damn angry and so damn tired of being played. Her father, most of the family . . . her friends. Emory. She's been surrounded by liars this entire time, and there's no compelling proof that Carter isn't also one of them.

"You don't have to believe me. But would you prefer to be zip-tied to those chairs?"

Caliste wishes she had a retort for Carter that made sense, but she doesn't. Even if he is leading them straight to Emory, having her arms and legs unbound *is* the better option.

"Fine," Caliste says, relenting, and stands to walk toward the open door.

However, she moves too quickly, and her vision flashes a hazy black as blood rushes to her head.

"Hey, steady," Carter says, his hands grabbing her by the shoulders.

Instinctively, Caliste wants to wriggle away, but she doesn't have complete control of her body. After a second, her vision clears, and she feels normal again.

"Don't trust me. It's fine. I wouldn't, either. But let's get you both as far away from this mansion as possible."

"Yes, let's go now!" Aria snaps. Caliste doesn't think Aria's been this assertive the entire time they've been together.

Carter steps in front of them, reaching an arm out like a weird (and probably not-that-effective) shield.

"I have to warn you: This basement is overwhelming."

Carter shuts off the lights, and the door of the garage closes behind them with a whining creak. Caliste's eyes take a second to adjust, but everything is bathed in a dim blue light. They are standing at the end of a large oblong room built with the same concrete flooring and colorless walls as the garage. At the far side of the room is a short flight of stairs leading to the most intense door Caliste's ever laid eyes on. It's all metal, completely smooth without a single handle, and flanked by what appear to be large claw-shaped latches. *What in the holy hell is this place?*

"Carter . . . what are those?"

Along the length of the room is a series of towering metallic columns. Each one is rounded at the top and connects to an overwhelming network of pipes and a maze of mechanical parts that Caliste doesn't understand.

She walks closely behind Carter as they trek forward. There's some sort of gauge on the front of each column along with an etching: the Hane Pacific Corporation's logo and the letters TTNS. In the center of each monstrous column is a small viewing window to an inner chamber. The windows are glowing blue and are clearly labeled with electronic placards cycling a series of text. *No . . . that can't be right. She must be dreaming.*

"Caliste, don't get too close," Aria warns.

Another step.

One more to see.

Through the faint glowing window, Caliste sees Beverly's missing uncle, standing vertically with his body strapped to a metal backing and suspended in a clear liquid. His skin is mottled with patches of dry blood and bruised skin. His eyelids are closed, but one socket is concave, with a long gash running from temple to lip. It's as if his eye has been hollowed out.

The placard's electronic text rolls, and Caliste wants to puke.

`Rufus Ambrose. Status: Suspended after already deceased.`

"Hello, love. Do you like your gift?" That voice. *His* voice. Caliste's gaze snaps to the top of the stairs. The imposing metal door is now open, and the face she dreads calmly, impossibly, stares back at her.

Emory.

♊

Aria

"What the hell. What the hell. What the hell? Did you do this? Why?!" Caliste is screaming and trying to wrestle out of Carter's grasp as he holds her back. "Rufus? You killed him. Why?"

Aria glances, despite wishing very much not to, at the chamber holding Rufus's body. His face is so swollen, she can hardly believe that's the same man from the news articles Caliste showed her. Aria edges ever so slightly closer to peer into the window. She regrets it. Bandages are tightly wrapped around the places where Rufus's hands should be. Her eyes go back up to Emory before she fully registers what she's seen.

The article from the news said only sawed-off hands were found on Rufus's boat. Aria shudders.

"I really hate people who touch things that belong to me," Emory says. He's standing at the top of a short set of concrete stairs at the end of the room—in front of the door that's presumably their only way out of here.

"I don't belong to you," Caliste says. Her voice is breaking and labored as she continues to struggle against Carter, who's still holding her back.

"And you! I knew you were a liar. What the *hell* is going on?" Caliste asks, whirling around to face Carter instead.

Carter's voice is meek. "I . . . I'm not . . . Emory, *you* lied. You said you'd let them leave." There's a desperation in Carter's voice, and despite the absolutely *screwed-up* situation at hand, Aria feels a pang of empathy for the guy. This family *must* be cursed.

"That's neither here nor there," Emory says with a smile. He walks down the stairs and toward them, hands in the pockets of his slacks like he's taking a leisurely stroll through a park. His face is as serene as a still lake, which is somehow *worse* than being full of malice. The hairs on Aria's arm stand up, and she moves closer to Caliste.

"I'm not sure if Carter gave you a tour, but I'm happy to oblige," Emory says. He stops right at the metallic chamber two units away from Rufus. He taps thin fingers on the metal, the sound tinny as it echoes around them. "Hane Pacific started investing in Tithonus when I was a child and eventually acquired them when I was in high school. However, I can't take credit for all this . . ."

Tithonus. Aria wracks her brain for the tidbits of mythology she can still remember from those wretched letters and her Greek Mythology 101 class this semester. *Tithonus.* Tithonus was the man who became immortal. Suddenly, the secretive purpose of the company becomes apparent to Aria.

"Are these cryogenic chambers?"

"Bingo, Aria. My dad set all this up. Can you imagine my surprise when I wandered down here at eight years old and discovered a veritable lab from the future lurking in our basement?"

Emory starts walking toward them again, and all three slink backward in reaction—Carter dragging Caliste with him. His arms loop around her shoulders, and her fists are held behind him, the whites of her knuckles visible from how hard she's clenching. For a second, Aria second-guesses whether Carter is truly protecting Caliste or keeping her contained.

"I learned he was planning on obtaining some perverse form of immortality. After genetic testing revealed he had the gene for early onset of dementia, he thought he could eventually be preserved here until a cure was found. That, of course, could only happen if he didn't ruin my life. He thinks I'd resurrect him?" Emory snorts.

As Aria takes one more step back, her right shoulder rams into another metal chamber. When she makes eye contact with the window into the vessel, she's relieved that the chamber is empty. However, the electronic placard is still flashing, and it's as if someone's dunked her entire body in cold water.

Xuân Grace Nguyễn

Even more clicks into place. The unfathomable state of Xuân's body, unchanged from the day she disappeared . . . down to the clothes she was wearing. Her body . . . was here. This entire time. Fourteen years . . . and she was frozen in stasis like some science experiment in the Hanes' basement.

"Imagine me as a child discovering a dead woman . . . not only that, but my father's dead mistress. I'm sure he had a terrible yet romantic plan for them to become immortal lovers." Emory emphasizes each syllable.

"She was not his mistress. Your dad was obsessed with her, and all she wanted to do was get away," Caliste snaps.

"Semantics. The net effect is the same . . . He was so singularly obsessed that he abandoned my mother. He abandoned me; so did she. But you know . . ." Emory's voice trails, and he stops again. "I should thank him. Because of him, I now have what I desire most."

"What do you mean?" Caliste asks, her voice a furious whisper.

"How else would I get you out of the swampland that is LA?"

"Screw you."

Emory laughs. "If you haven't figured it out yet, I released Grace into the river. The officers had no idea what I was up to because I paid them to look away. And now you are here, within my grasp. All I had to do was send one measly employee to tease your grandmother, who you didn't even like, and your meddlesome father left immediately. Every road that led you here is one I paved."

Emory speaks as if he sees neither Aria's mother nor her twin as women, as people, as human beings. They are pawns in a revenge game. Nothing has ever filled Aria with so much vitriol.

Emory taps another chamber, his fingers moving as if he's touching something precious.

"Carter, do you recognize this lovely shade of copper?"

Carter tenses before letting go of Caliste. He sidesteps in front of her, walking in the direction of the chamber Emory is gesturing toward. Aria can't see clearly, but Carter seems to freeze once he's near enough.

"Riley? What the hell? We held a memorial for her!"

Both Carter's voice and body are shaking. His words are barely a whisper but filled with fury.

Emory says with a smile, "Cousin, you buried her belongings. Besides, finders keepers. She made a mistake when she rejected me for you. Now she's mine, my trophy. And I'm pleased to say there are two more prepared. I did hope I'd never need them, though," Emory says before fixing his gaze squarely at Caliste and Aria. The serene expression is gone, and what's left is unhinged joy.

Emory's eyes dart, and Carter backs up, his arms held in front of him defensively. He has size on Emory, but Aria's not sure he can get them all out of here. Suddenly, Carter whirls around and darts forward, shoving Caliste toward Aria. They both fall backward, colliding against the empty cryochamber with a clamoring bang. Aria's cast-encased arm stings, and she yelps.

Carter spins, rushing at Emory, and Aria holds her breath, watching for the opening that might allow them to run. Caliste is shaking, and Aria grabs on to her sister with as much strength as she can possibly manage with her good arm.

"You piece of shit. Riley . . . Human lives aren't your playthings," Carter yells, his voice muffled as he and Emory fall to the ground.

"Go! Go!" Aria screams, pushing Caliste. They spring toward the open door.

This house. The water. This town. All of it is cursed. Aria prays between painful breaths, her bare feet slamming against the floor. She suppresses the image of her and Caliste frozen in those chambers.

Whoever's listening, save us.

Please.

CHAPTER TWENTY-SIX

The Ghoul

After so many years circling these doomed waters, I thought it was my fate to roam. I thought vengeance might sustain me. And for a time, it did. My fingers soaked in blood and the sensation of evil bodies turning into empty shells—I believed their deaths were my *happiness*.

I thought Eric took my humanity from me.

But it's still mine, curled up in the space where my heart once beat. Like a dormant seed . . . I feel it blossom, and I feel it ache. I can still save myself . . . and I can still save *them*.

The snow squall, as suddenly as it emerged, fades. I sit, head buried so I don't give my presence away and watch the house for signs of movement. The inches of snow settle against the house's eaves and buttresses, but there is no other movement. There's one single dim light glowing faintly from the room closest to the patio and the fake cluster of water-falls . . . This is where I lost the scent. And while I can't see them, I know they must be here—my daughters are hidden from me. If only I had my proper body . . . and not this vessel bound to the water.

Live. Live. Live. I repeat the invocation, and I remember using the same words when my sister and I prayed for safety after Ba's passing. *We want to live.*

Then a shrill scream leaves the house, its vibrations tickling a specific memory in my mind. *My girls.* I surge out of the water to track where the vibrations are coming from and focus my eyes. The back door slams open, and two silhouettes careen toward the water so quickly, I can barely make out their shapes. Ariadne and Caliste. They're safe.

I scramble through the water to keep pace with them, and suddenly Ariadne slips. Her bare foot catches on a protruding tree root, and she slides into a mix of mud and snow.

"Aria!" Caliste yells, catching up to her and leaning down. Her breathing is tortured, and each breath out produces an uneven cloud of condensation. "Can you walk?"

"Ow. Crap!" Aria yells, and my heart twinges in response. "My ankle . . . What is wrong with me?"

"It's fine. Calm down—don't make your arm worse, too."

Behind them, a light flickers, and *that man's face* emerges, moving toward them from the same door they exited. My jaw gnashes in on itself, ready to tear his throat from his body, but I pause . . .

Eric can barely keep himself upright. He walks unsteadily, and the man I see in my mind's eye . . . the one whose hands closed around my throat . . . is gone. Instead, this shell remains. He is both the same man and not. For a fleeting moment, my heart hurts.

"Grace? Grace?" Eric asks. He extends his arm, which holds a flashlight. When he calls that name, the anger I've held within flares.

"I . . ." Caliste starts to speak but pauses. She stares down at her sister in her arms, and something inaudible is communicated between them.

"Yes . . . it's . . . Grace," Aria says, pushing up against her sister to prop herself upright.

"Oh my goodness. Are you hurt?"

"A little," Aria says, her voice shaky but polite.

She tugs on Caliste's sleeve, who whips her head around. The shadows hide her face, but as I desperately gaze upon her, our eyes meet. They widen ever so slightly, but this time I do not sense fear. "Stop!" Aria says suddenly, and Eric halts.

"Your son, Emory, is trying to hurt me. Don't tell him you've seen us. Please—let me leave."

Aria's pleading voice causes Eric's demeanor to shift.

No. Not again. Never again.

"Leave? Grace . . . you are still trying to leave?" His voice rises, and the girls shrink away from him. "Why?"

He slumps, and his hand wielding the flashlight falls to his side.

"I took this from you. Do you remember, Grace? Please, let me return it," Eric pleads, and when he opens his palm, a single pearl button rolls in the dip of his hand. It's then that he rushes forward, and I react.

I scramble up from the water, nothing else in my field of vision except this cursed man's face.

"What?" Caliste whispers as my soaked torso surges out from the water and toward them.

I stagger up the slick earth. Eric's eyes widen, and he stumbles, slipping onto his back. My jaw unhinges, and I can feel my skin aflame in the beam of his flashlight, melting as I reach for his throat.

His pathetic eyes are wide and white with fear.

Eric's pale skin is wrinkled, and the folds of his neck form a perfect divot. For my fingers. To puncture a hole and fill him with maggots. They squirm under my skin, as hungry as I am. His boot kicks, slamming my hand into the mud, and he laughs, a grotesque and jagged sound. His laugh is a barbed rake dragging through me with such violence that the sensation cracks a hole in me.

I enclose my hands around his throat, like he did mine, and I press until his windpipe collapses under my fingertips. He thrashes, and instead of comfort, my heart splits, and I finally remember.

When I am cut open, I hear your wails.

My girls . . . my daughters. In your small faces, I see my mother's joy and a home to which I'll never return.

I am in pain, and I am in bliss.

Aria's featherlight hair is damp and lies like a small bird's nest on her head. I laugh when my husband makes the observation. Caliste, who comes merely a few minutes later, is silent before her cries pierce the delivery room.

In the fleeting moments after you enter this world, I am afraid for you. Afraid of a world that will hurt you. Afraid you'll live a girlhood like mine.

I wish, as the nurses take you away to clean, that you will never be obedient; that you both, like a storm's torrent, will fight and rage against any who try to harm you. I named you after mythical stories as a daily reminder to live out different ones. Ariadne, who never got the chance to rage against injustice. Caliste, killed because of the distorted love of a man.

Scream. Scream. Scream.

Aria

In one moment, Eric Hane stands a few feet away with the same terrifying expression on his face as his son ... and the next, he is thrashing in the creek that snakes behind their house. In those seconds, despite logic and any other explanation that might make sense, Aria knows that their mom is drowning Eric.

"What the hell?" Caliste screams. Her hands quake as they hold on to Aria's shoulders. After a silent and painful few seconds, Eric Hane's body stills. The flashlight, now submerged, flickers and then dies with him.

The monster ... the ghoul ... the ghost? She appears like a tangle of white skin and sunken flesh convulsing in the water. She is spectral and formless. Her figure coalesces and suddenly ... there's a face.

"Aria!" Caliste says, startled, as Aria starts to stand.

"It's fine ..."

Aria winces as she forces weight on her sprained ankle, the numbness of the snow on her bare feet and the rush of adrenaline muting the pain a bit. Caliste braces her left side, and they stagger over to the creek's edge.

Her own face—Caliste's face—stares back at them ... and while this body bears no resemblance to the woman in the photo at Mrs. Kim's laundromat, Aria knows it's their mother. A smell wafts around ... and it knocks the air out of Aria's lungs. Plum blossom and lemongrass, a scent that wraps Aria in a cocoon with Caliste. Aria is safe.

"M-Mom? What happen—" Caliste asks, stuttering, before a crash sounds behind them.

Crap.

"Run!" Aria says, readying herself to push Caliste away. As

quickly as she arrived, their mother vanishes in a splatter of water and weeds.

"What are you talking about?" Caliste says, her voice a sharp whisper as they crouch and watch the back door of the Hane estate.

"I said run! I'll distract him."

"Are you out of your mind?"

"You—"

"My. I didn't think you had it in you . . . I'm impressed, ladies." It's too late. Emerging from the house is Emory, his gait uneven and labored. He's injured. Carter doesn't follow behind.

"Philip's called the police. Someone's coming," Aria yells, her voice hoarse as she puts full force into convincing him of the lie.

"That's a very poor lie. I have all your phones," Emory says, letting out a cruel laugh. "You should be thankful, however. I left your little boyfriend to fend for himself in that inn. Quite a lightweight, that one. He didn't even stir."

Aria tenses as he gets closer, but his path diverges, and he instead approaches Eric's mauled and very dead body.

"It's a pity . . . I wanted to do this myself," Emory says, his voice bored.

He presses the toe of his Oxford shoe to Eric's chin. Then . . . he pulls his foot back and slams it down. The crack of bone is repulsive, and both Aria and Caliste turn their heads away from the spectacle. When they look back at Emory, he is twisting his heel deep into the muddied water.

"You're being quite demure for the girls who killed my father. What do you think Officer Badiou will see when he arrives?"

"Where is Carter?" Caliste asks suddenly.

"I hate when you say his name. He's alive . . . if that's what you want to know."

"What did you do to him?"

Emory laughs.

"I didn't do anything to *him*. His little girlfriend had the audacity to reject me, and I simply taught her a lesson. He did happen to be there, though, so perhaps that's why he's still angry with me.

"It was such a good plan. He couldn't say anything about it. Who do you think the police would believe? Me or him?"

Caliste clenches her jaw.

"It's been useful to hold that over his head. He helped me, you know. Carter planted a tracker on you for me."

A tracker? Was it the security tag she found in her coat pocket? She wants to be angry at Carter . . . but he *did* come to their rescue.

Emory walks closer to them, the dim moonlight illuminating his miserable face. He is just a stone's throw away when he stops.

"What do you want from us?" Aria asks, tightening her grip on Caliste's arm. One of them has to get out of here. The cold and pain from her arm and ankle are starting to affect her, and Aria feels her vision get hazy. No, she needs to hold on to save Caliste.

"I just want to make amends."

"That's a bunch of bullshit, you entitled son of a bitch."

Emory laughs at Caliste's insult and takes another step.

"If you become mine, I'll make all this go away."

"What do you mean?" Caliste asks. She tightens her grip on Aria, whose eyes say that she's prepared to launch herself at Emory any second.

"Your dad. Your stepmother. The family you hate and your friends who don't deserve you. I can make them all go away."

It starts snowing again, thick white flakes floating down and landing on Emory's hair and bloodstained clothes. This deluded Prince Charming is smiling as he speaks, reaching out a hand to Caliste. Aria wants to spit at him, but her grip on Caliste is weakening, and she's falling. Fast. She almost thinks what Caliste says next is her imagination playing tricks on her.

"I'm sorry," Caliste whispers, and she pushes Aria down hard, her foot digging into Aria's bad ankle as she stands. Aria watches, pain, cold, and disbelief clouding her vision.

♊

Caliste

Caliste knows Aria is in pain, and she hates that's she's the cause of it. But there's no choice, not anymore. In just a few days, Caliste has come to know Aria more than she knows herself. And she knows, without a doubt, that Aria is preparing to sacrifice herself so Caliste can get away. A reckless and terrible plan.

Instead . . . Caliste is going to do it first. She just needs to get Emory out of here. Caliste silently prays to whatever deity is watching over this absurd life of theirs . . . *Please, let this not be a losing gamble.*

Caliste takes a deep breath, steeling herself as she reaches out to Emory's extended hand. Out of the corner of her periphery, Aria slumps weakly to the ground, and her voice fades.

I'm sorry.

When Caliste's fingers connect with Emory's, she suppresses a nauseating wave of disgust. Emory's fingers are clammy, and the smile on his face is equal parts deranged and delighted.

"We've been close for a long time."

"I suppose we have," Caliste says. She tries not to break Emory's gaze, but it's difficult. Art . . . their online "friendship." Everything, from the first message in her inbox, was an orchestrated deception.

"Which means I also know when you're lying to me."

"No, I'm not. I—"

Emory twists her wrist, and a radiating pain erupts up her arm. Caliste's legs buckle, and she falls to her knees, legs bashing against the sharp edge of an exposed tree root.

No. Caliste bites her lip until it bleeds. She needs to keep it together for Aria's sake . . . and her own.

Emory's face hovers above her as he forces Caliste to her knees. After he kneels down so he's eye to eye with her, his hands finally let go and circle around her throat instead. He's staring at her lips again. Caliste wants to hack a wad of spit at his miserable face.

"I don't know why you have to look at me so hatefully. You think you have everything figured out, but here's one more fact: Everything that's yours, Caliste, is actually mine. Your family exists because of mine. Your beginning is our beginning. Aria's appointment with Georgetown. Your success and your father's wealth. All of it is because of me. Will be because of me. You. Should. Be. More. Grateful."

Each word is punctuated with stifling indignation, and after every pause, he squeezes tighter. Emory's leaning in again, and the scent of her own damn perfume is suffocating.

"If you know what's best for you . . ." Emory pushes onto her, and she struggles, yelping. Caliste feels his tongue on her face, and she gnashes her teeth, hoping that a potential bite will serve as a deterrent.

Then water rushes around them, and all she can hear is Emory screaming.

There's a splatter of mud and gritty water, and Caliste can barely make out what's happening. Mom the ghoul—with her mottled mess of rotting plants, mud, and flesh—is back, and she's moving with demonic speed. Her pallid limbs stretch in front of Caliste like a shield and pull Emory into the river.

All you do is . . .

take

bleed

conquer

Part melody and fury. The voice that rings through the air is as indistinct as it is perfect.

"What the hell is this?" Emory yells, staggering backward in the water. He scrambles, the smug smile on his face replaced with fear. His limbs flail, and Caliste spots flashes of ashen limbs reaching out toward him.

You think you were our beginning . . . but I will be your end.

The ghoul's limbs distend, snaking around Emory's body with ease despite his thrashing. Mud and icy water rupture, and Emory's wails weaken, their shrill notes interjected with wet hacking and the sound of cracking bones.

"You b—"

There is silence, and the flurry of snow stops. Emory lies lifeless at Caliste's feet, and the pallid tangle of skin and weeds retracts into the water. In the instant before the ghoul disappears entirely, the scent of plum blossoms blankets them, and it's a sucker punch to her gut.

Mom. She put an end to this nightmare.

CHAPTER TWENTY-SEVEN

Aria

Five months later . . .

"Why are you staring at me like that?" Philip asks, his spoonful of sweet tofu hovering a few inches away from his face. They're standing under the shade of a vendor's cart off the side of some clothing shop, and every so often, Aria catches a girl staring at him.

At one point, it would have been impossible to imagine standing in Vietnam with Philip and enjoying a date without feeling like she was going to break out in hives. It feels like both an eternity and no time at all.

"You're too handsome."

"Wh-what?" Philip stammers, and the tips of his ears turn red.

Aria smiles, saying nothing and instead grabbing Philip by the wrist, leaning toward him, and eating off his spoon.

"Hey! You cheat!"

"You snooze, you lose, my friend." Aria laughs, turning back down the main path of the street to continue walking back to their hotel.

Aria's grateful that Philip humored her and agreed to traverse some of the nearby quieter areas of Cà Mau. The noise and the constant bustle of activity used to be calming for her, but nowadays, it's often overwhelming. Especially now . . . with the task of spreading their mom's ashes at hand . . . Aria just needs some quiet.

It took a while for the Hane saga to resolve itself. Carter's ended up being the chief testimony that revealed (almost) everything to the public. He was badly beaten but alive. Eric's death was pinned on Emory, and the multiple dead bodies found in the Hane basement were irrefutable.

When Aria thinks about it, she is still astounded by everything that's happened in the span of a handful of months. Last December, the Hane family's hellish reign ended. The mystery around their mother was solved. All of it was over.

Her hearing with Georgetown ended in a censure letter and a permanent notation on her transcript instead of suspension (much due to Professor Tzu advocating on her behalf), but Aria still decided to take a leave of absence. She helped Philip out at the laundromat and took a writing class at Northern Virginia Community College's Annandale campus. Aria worked some weekend shifts at the cat café on M Street, scooping litter boxes and drafting in between. She spent time in silence and in grief and got used to the sound of her own thoughts.

Aria does feel relieved, but she honestly also felt great sadness for the longest time. Having Caliste around helped . . . especially when they were hiding out in her apartment to avoid the media frenzy. The headlines were sickening.

Serial Killer Nepo Baby or Tortured Young Man?

A Billion-Dollar Inheritance and a Broken Family:

The Face of Emory Hane

Violence or a Cry for Help? How We Are Failing Our Boys

Emory's face was blasted all over the news and every media website known to man. A narrative started to emerge in some publications, and Aria eventually had to mute news notifications out of self-preservation.

Philip asked her to be his girlfriend after everything calmed down, and she said yes. With everything that happened, Philip's father finally reached out to him. For her part, Aria lent Philip a listening ear and stole a few kisses as he grappled with the decision to meet with his own estranged father for the first time in years. Paul convinced a begrudging Aunt Thu to let him help; he moved her and Aria into a luxury senior condo closer to the hospital with facilitated caretakers, and he also paid off the outstanding medical bills. Aria's lived five lifetimes in the past five months, and the moment she's enjoying now is a hard-earned peace. But it's peace nonetheless.

A sound, loud as a bell, catches her attention, and Aria walks quickly toward the noise. Her linen shirt flutters slightly as she walks.

"You trying to leave me behind?" Philip's feet patter after her, and Aria turns right as he slips his hand into hers.

"Hey—you already finished your tofu?"

"If I didn't eat it fast, I couldn't hold your hand like this." Philip smiles, and Aria purposefully looks away.

She's still embarrassed by how free Philip is with the PDA. Philip's agreed to move at a slow pace. Aria still hasn't said "I love you" in that way, although Philip says it often. On special occasions, when they're out and about, she'll refer to him as *boyfriend*. His company feels so natural, she sometimes forgets anything's changed. That is, until he does something heart-stopping like this.

They walk, hands entwined, toward the noise, and after they pass a couple of shop fronts, the source reveals itself: a row of wind chimes hanging off a traditional house.

"It looks like a ceramics shop."

The wind chimes make a pleasant range of sounds—some glassy and others a bit deeper, like metal being hit. A swirl of royal blue and red catches her eye, and Aria pulls them toward a small chime right next to the shop's entrance.

"Oh. Ducks," she says, reaching out to cup the hanging duck with her free fingers. The ceramic is detailed, with gold on the duck's beak and outlining its feathers. He has a dramatic plume and lines drawn like makeup.

"It's a Mandarin duck," Philip says, bringing up his index finger and tapping the duck's head. "This one is a female." His finger moves leftward, pointing to another figure hanging off the wind chime. It's like the one Aria's touching, but it lacks the bright plume and distinct markings.

"Boo. Why do the girls have to be boring?"

"I don't think she's boring. She's cute," Philip says. He's presumably talking about the duck, but he's staring at Aria.

His hair is shading his face, but his eyes are clear as day. Aria wonders how long they've looked at her like this . . . watching her intently with interest and care. Months? Years? And why did it take her so long to notice?

"Do you want to buy it?"

Aria feels like a cat jumping backward at the voice—it belongs to a woman who appears from the entrance of the shop.

"We only have one left. Mandarin ducks are very good luck for couples!" Her eyes go back and forth between Aria and Philip, and Aria suppresses the instinct to run away.

"They represent marriage and fidelity, right?" Philip asks. Aria can sense his teasing.

"Yes! They are a very good gift for weddings. But not only for weddings!" the woman adds suddenly, and Aria realizes she's making a face.

"They're very beautiful. Did you make them?" Philip asks, diverting the conversation and pointing to another wind chime by the window.

The shopkeeper nods, explaining the process to craft each of the wind chimes. Aria is only half paying attention and realizes she's still thinking about weddings and those damn ducks.

"Okay, I'll buy it," Philip says, and the shopkeeper beams as she rushes to grab a bag.

"Why? You don't need a wind chime," Aria says.

"I think it'll make a nice wedding gift," he replies, waggling his eyebrows at Aria.

He's always surprising her, and Aria figures it's her time to return the favor. She stands on her tiptoes (which are slightly numb from the mild frostbite she acquired when she was barefoot in the freezing water outside the Hane manor). When she kisses Philip, his lips are soft, and his hands find their way to her waist. They've kissed plenty of times before, but today is different.

"I love you. I am in love with you," she says through parted lips before pulling away from him.

Except Philip doesn't let her. His arms wrap around her again, but this time, there's something more desperate about how he grips her. It's tender, his hands settling into the low of her back. His fingers press firmly, as if gripping something that might fall out of his grasp at any moment.

"You can't say something like that and expect to escape so easily," Philip teases.

"Philip, people are watching . . ." Aria whispers, painfully aware of how much attention they must be getting.

"I wouldn't know. I just see us," Philip replies in a voice so low only Aria can hear. Her skin grows warm, and Philip smiles, pressing his nose to her forehead before tracing it upward to her hair and kissing her softly.

When he pulls back, his hands on her waist loosen. He doesn't let go as he gets the final word.

"I love you, too."

Aria's heart surges. She's overwhelmed. Euphoric.

For the moment, surrounded by the melody of the wind chimes, instead of every other worst-case scenario her mind can conjure up, she lets herself imagine what a lifetime with Philip would be like.

And it's perfect.

♊

Caliste

Dylan is sleeping in Caliste's arms, his hair buried in her shoulder and his drool pooling on the inner part of her sleeve. She's surprised he did so well on the flights from LAX to Hong Kong and then Vietnam. Priscilla didn't even have to whip out his favorite penguin toy.

Caliste walks, continuing her gentle rocking for Dylan but also taking time to enjoy this sacred place. The house they lived in before they had to leave . . . Aunt Thu. Mom. It's quiet in the yard, with the throngs of greenery and the sounds of the stream babbling.

"I'm fine!" Aunt Thu huffs, and Caliste turns to see Ba and Aunt Thu walking toward her, Aunt Thu swatting away Paul's outstretched arm. The move to the senior living facility seems to have gone well— Aunt Thu moves a bit more quickly with her cane, and she consistently has energy to berate Paul. According to Aria, she was being a better sport about accepting help and taking the new medicine for her mobility. Aria said that she was also motivated by the desire to travel to Minnesota and spit on Eric's grave.

"Con. There you are!" Aunt Thu says. Once she reaches Caliste, she links her free arm with hers.

"You'll take Cali's arm but not mine?" Ba asks with a scowl on his face.

"Yes," Aunt Thu replies without skipping a beat.

Caliste smiles at her dad and lets herself get steered by Aunt Thu toward the water. It's been . . . difficult. She hasn't spent meaningful time with him for the past year. After severing ties with both Beverly and any remaining Beverly-facilitated or affiliated contracts, Caliste spent most of her time either jetting off to visit Aria or being a homebody and filming workout videos in her overpriced apartment. It was cathartic in a way, producing content that she wasn't trying to make money off.

But all that time alone was also difficult. Caliste was trying to figure out the person she wanted to be.

In some ways, it made Caliste sympathetic to her father. The truth has been a lot to accept. Regardless . . . Paul had the power to stop all this from happening by listening to his wife. He could have abandoned the Hane family's conditional assistance and taken the danger Eric posed more seriously. Maybe something bad would have still happened . . . but at least they would be together. And . . . their mom might still be alive.

It haunts Caliste, but she knows it haunts him more.

"We're lucky it's not too hot today. There's no rain, either," her dad remarks. He stands next to her in front of the plum blossom tree as Aunt Thu lets go to fuss over the garden. Apparently, their childhood home was kept in the extended family and is now owned by one of Aunt Thu's distant cousins. The blooms have only started to burst from the tree's tips, small clusters of pink emerging in little capsules. It's bittersweet.

"Did you ever visit? When Mom was still alive?" Caliste asks.

"No, though we could have after things opened back up in the nineties. There just was never time. She never returned here—not until now."

There is a pain in her father's voice that nearly breaks Caliste. Their mom left Vietnam as a child only to come home as ash.

"Anything you do, whatever path you take, your mom—she would be happy. I will be, too." His voice is awkward and staggered as he speaks, and Caliste smiles to herself. He must have practiced.

"I understand, Ba."

"Good."

A gust of wind blows Dylan's hair, flopping it to the side. When Caliste looks up, Aria and Philip are walking toward them, with Priscilla and Bà Nội following behind.

Aria squeezes Caliste's shoulder and stops to kiss Dylan on the head once she's close enough. Being together feels natural now, as if they hadn't lived an entire lifetime unknown to the other.

In her grandma's arms is a royal-blue urn painted with apricot-and-gold flowers. Aria and Caliste chose it together.

"My two pretty girls," her grandmother says, smiling at them both. Caliste and Bà Nội lock eyes for a moment, and her grandmother's expression is uncharacteristically soft. Perhaps the most startling event in the past few months was when their grandmother sat both Aria and Caliste down and *apologized*.

I thought your mother was weak because of her sadness. But the truth is, I am sad, too.

It was an apology over a decade too late . . . but Caliste thought it was still better than never. And, oddly enough, the words were a comfort to her, too.

"Ái da," Aunt Thu mutters. Her cane has been left to lean against the tree, and her hunched figure is fussing over the flower bed. "I told my cousins to plant this earlier. It's so small! Tsk . . ."

There is a small frangipani bush, barely a foot tall, at the base of the plum blossom tree. There aren't any flowers yet, but Caliste still thinks this is the perfect site for their mother's final resting place. A stream flows just a few feet away, and Caliste pictures a version of her mother in girlhood, splashing in the water instead of being trapped by it.

Aunt Thu fusses around the soil at the bush's base before placing her hands on her knees to stand. Soon, all of them stand in a semicircle, with Aria at Caliste's side. Aria squeezes Caliste's hand, and tears spill over immediately.

It's time. Finally.

Fourteen long years.

Their mother can rest.

After the silence, Aunt Thu opens the top of the urn, assisted by Philip. They scatter the ashes over the soil, the developing flowers, and the water. Paul leans down to help, and before long, Caliste can no longer tell where the ashes begin and the earth ends.

"Welcome home," Paul says, leaning down to pat the earth. He's crying, and Caliste is, too.

Caliste turns to hold Aria tight, their fingers digging painfully into each other's sides. There are the sound of the wind rustling through the plum blossom tree's branches, tears, and the scent of the juvenile plum blossoms lingering.

♊

THE GHOUL

Do you remember when I told you I was pregnant? It was a situation so ridiculous, so comical, and so unlike you, that the image is burned into my memory, like a childhood fairy tale from Ba. You were angry at me, sister. This is when Phúc and I had nothing, and you told me I was foolish to bring life into such tenuous circumstances.

In that moment, the Thu that took care of me, the Thu who cleaned up after me, the Thu I was so used to, became someone new to me. Now I know that I became something new to you, too. A marvelous and terrifying new beast. I was embarking on the path that killed our mother. It was a path you could not tread for me.

I also know you were just afraid of losing me. Now, in your palm, you hold bits of me. I feel your pulse, a rhythm that lulled me to sleep under the cover of thick plum-blossom-scented blankets.

You return me as ash to the waters of our home. I am reborn.

What bad luck we must have, sister. I possessed a soul that was cursed to rot in the water, and you possessed a body cursed by the rot of war.

We were the river, the air, and the seasons.

Do you remember that it was you who first told me the story of Ma Da? Of the vengeful spirits who drowned? I couldn't conceptualize vengeance then, couldn't understand what type of wicked rage would tie a soul to this earth, fated to drown others before they could move on. But perhaps the rage was embedded in us in the first place.

But I no longer feel rage.

I feel love.

That boy . . . his violence . . . violence passed on by his father. If I had taken his soul, then his violence would have continued. I cannot stop it all, but I can stop them.

I wanted vengeance.

But I also want peace.

There is a song that I've always yearned to hear again. A joyful melody of my girls, my home, and my ancestors, and I hear it at this moment. I lie in the bottom of the riverbed and close my eyes to sleep. I feel everything. Mud. Silt. Memory.

Us.

AUTHOR'S NOTE

In November 1990, my family left Vietnam and flew to Thailand and San Francisco before ultimately scattering throughout the United States. In November 2021, I lost my mother suddenly. My career as a writer and the themes I explore in my stories are intimately tied with the grief of losing her.

For me, the heart of *Twin Tides* is its exploration of intergenerational grief (and intergenerational love). My mother lost her parents while she was in the United States and they were back home in Vietnam. The last time my mother saw her own mother was before she immigrated. In many bittersweet ways, losing my mother brought me closer to her.

My family raised me in Des Moines, Iowa, but I left to attend college in Southern California and eventually settled for most of my young adulthood in the Washington, DC, metropolitan area (locations that are featured in *Twin Tides*). When I received the message that I needed to return home as soon as possible because of my mother's health, I was only a three-hour flight away. My mother, however, was almost nine thousand miles from her hometown when my grandmother died. She was unable to return for the funeral. Finding out this news from a distance is heartbreaking. I can never truly understand my mother's grief, but I often recognize her heartache and rage within me.

To live as a member of the Việt diaspora is also to live within a web spun from a history of violence. This is something I've grappled with my entire life, and I will likely continue to do so. *Twin Tides* explores this legacy, through both the violence of the war and the violence enacted on Xuân and her daughters. My family is one of many diasporic Vietnamese families, each with a unique and complex immigrant story. It was important to me to render the Hà and Nguyễn families' joys and pains on the page without positioning this text as any sort of authoritative take on the refugee experience.

The fictional historical documents in *Twin Tides* were modeled on sources provided in the Gerald R. Ford Museum's Core Collections on the Vietnam War; more specifically, the documents provided in the "Indochina Refugees—Interagency Task Force (2)" of the Theodore C. Marrs Files portion of the collection. There are many military documents in the collection as well, now public after being declassified. The history of wealth built on the violence of war is woven through *Twin Tides*.

The bits and pieces readers get of Aunt Thu's and Xuan's childhoods in Vietnam are based on the real events of Operation Ranch Hand, which resulted in 11 million gallons of Agent Orange being sprayed in Vietnam.[1] The herbicides destroyed many of the mangrove forests on Vietnam's southernmost tip, where their hometown of Cà Mau is located. In addition to the massive

---

1 Institute of Medicine (US) Committee to Review the Health Effects in Vietnam Veterans of Exposure to Herbicides. *Veterans and Agent Orange: Health Effects of Herbicides Used in Vietnam.* Washington (DC): National Academies Press (US); 1994. 3, The U.S. Military and the Herbicide Program in Vietnam. https://www.ncbi.nlm.nih.gov/books/NBK236347/

environmental impact, the lingering health effects can still be seen today.

Another aspect of history highlighted in the novel is the migration of Vietnamese immigrants to the American Midwest. In my hometown of Des Moines, I lived in a community of Việt, Lao, Hmong, and Cambodian families. It wasn't until I left that I realized this does not necessarily match how others perceive the Midwest.

Many people I've met in my life are surprised to learn that there are vibrant Asian communities in areas they believe to be homogeneously white. Les Eaux (pronounced *lay sooz*) is a reference to Des Moines. Both are cities with French names that are pronounced very differently with an American accent (Des Moines is pronounced *day moyne*). The fictional town of Les Eaux is a combination of Des Moines and the Twin Cities metropolitan area in Minnesota. One of the largest Southeast Asian populations in the United States calls the Minneapolis–Saint Paul area home. *Twin Tides* is intentionally set in Minnesota and is a nod to the many immigrant and refugee communities across the Midwest.

Ultimately, I set out to write a book about two girls grappling with grief and loss caused by their forced separation and supplemented by a chilling mystery. While this is categorized as a young adult thriller, at its core, *Twin Tides* is a ghost story, and ghost stories are almost always told with an eye toward the past. The tides, too, are a continuous affirmation of the past and our histories.

ACKNOWLEDGMENTS

It took many villages to create this book, and I am immensely grateful to everybody whose hard work, support, and love helped bring it to life.

To the reader: You made it to the end! I am grateful to you for reading my words. That, in itself, is a privilege.

I have so much gratitude to my editor, Bria Ragin. Thank you for seeing the spark in *Twin Tides* even before I had a book to show you. I am so thankful for your work, both helping me in conceiving this story and in making sure my vision was always center stage.

To my agent, Katelyn Detweiler, I couldn't dream of a better partner to shepherd the beginning of my writing career. You saw value in my words and have been an indispensable advocate every step of the way.

Twin Tides would not exist without Random House Children's Books and the many people who touched this book through its many lives, including Wendy Loggia, vice president and publisher, Delacorte Press; Mallory Loehr, president, Random House Children's Books; Trisha Previte, cover designer; Reiko Murakami, jacket artist; Ken Crossland, interior designer; Tracy Heydweiller, production manager; Tamar Schwartz, managing editor; Kayla Overbey, copy editor; Kiffin Steurer, proofreader; Stephania Villar, marketer; Rachel Jensen, publicist; and Lara Ameen, Authenticity Reader. I am filled with gratitude for your hard work and care.

Thank you to my Avengers of Colour 2021 mentee cohort, and to my mentor June Hur. Your community and advice early on in my author career have been indispensable. I am cheering for all of you and am so blessed to have a shelf just for our stories. I workshopped early versions of *Twin Tides* with Pingmei Lan's "Pacing, Structure and Timelines" Winter 2024 group and am so grateful for your help. I also want to thank the many Discord communities who have made writing feel like home, including việt viết, the AAPI Writing Community, Submission Slog Comrades, Let's Get Published, and 2025 Debuts. In addition, I'd like to credit Maya for coming up with the name for the fictional town Les Eaux.

For my WriteGirl community and Round Table Mentor community: Thank you for being the tide that lifts all boats. Thank you to Echo: Writing with you and hearing your words is a privilege. Thank you to Frances: I am so excited for your stories to make their way into the world, and I am so blessed to have had your trust as a mentor.

Many friends read my work through the messy first drafts to the polished pages, or shared the burden of my publishing struggles, and I couldn't have done this without you: 'Dolapo, Haarika, Manuela, John U., Amanda K., Amanda B. & Matt, Leslie, Julie, Savini, Lucia, David, Eunice and Tom, Juan and Carolina, UVA friends, and many others. (If I have forgotten you, I owe you a boba!)

Many cheers to DC Dinner Club—thank you for your

friendship. I cannot imagine how my twenties would have looked without you all. I am so proud of every single one of you, and your friendships have made me a better human being (as well as a better cook).

Although my time with you all was short, I am grateful to Women Writing for (a) Change, Bloomington, for being such a supportive, talented, and uplifting community.

To my 2024 Ossabaw Island Retreat cohort, the island donkeys, and my faculty leader, Tom Franklin—thank you so much for both a creatively energizing time and a time filled with care, humor, and levity (mostly Lois).

To my 2024 Roots. Wounds. Words. Autumn Writers' Retreat: Mountain crew, we are bonded for life. I am so blessed to have heard your stories and felt your light. There are no words that can give justice to that transformative experience (although perhaps *gravity flushes* and *we are evacuating* come close).

I would not be here without my middle school teachers Holly and Rebecca. I am a writer because of you both. I hope you know that. Your support when I was twelve years old altered the course of my life in the best possible way.

To my high school English and creative writing teachers, Diane, Jean, and Sherry—this book wouldn't exist without me having been assigned *The Brothers Karamazov* and experiencing your joy, humor, and creativity in class.

Donna, Regina, Paul, Leila, and Martha—when I was an uncertain college kid from Iowa, your encouragement and mentorship was truly transformative.

Seirra, Iesha, Qiu, Piper—I love you all. Thank you for being my life partners.

Thank you to Tempura and Panko for your snuggles and occasional chaos.

To my family: Thank you for shaping the person I've become.

Hieu and Thao: You supported me from diapers to walking across a graduation stage. I forgive you for hiding the Easter eggs in places I can't reach and making me cry by leaving for college.

Ba: Con thương Ba nhiều lắm. Cảm ơn Ba đã nuôi dạy con bằng tình yêu thương.

Mommy Lexington: I love you. I see you. I am so grateful to you. Thank you for your sacrifices and endless love.

Uncle Rocky: I wouldn't be who I am today without you in my life. I'm sorry you won't get to hold this book, but maybe it's for the best, because you would have talked everybody's ears off about it.

Vú: Con nhớ Vú nhiều hơn Vú có thể biết. Con thương Vú lắm.

And to Joe, whose gentleness and unyielding care made this book possible. I'm uncertain of how many universes exist or how many exist where you and I stare at the same sky. Perhaps there are some where we've found each other and others yet in which we are sworn mortal enemies. I know very little, but I know that this universe, if it is indeed the only one where I have you, must be the best one.

ABOUT THE AUTHOR

Hien Nguyen is a speculative fiction writer who hails from the Midwest. By day she is a social science researcher, and by night she writes about Vietnamese ghosts, monsters, and mythology. She is interested in the uplifting and haunting forms of human connection, and how writing speculative fiction can lay those bare. *Twin Tides* is her debut novel.

authorhien.com